THE POSTSCRIPT MURDERS

FINALIST FOR THE CWA GOLD DAGGER AWARD

A MOST ANTICIPATED TITLE OF 2021
FROM *CRIMEREADS* AND *THE BUZZ MAGAZINES*

A BEST BOOK OF MARCH FROM
THE *NEW YORK POST* AND *POPSUGAR*

"This droll romp is a latter-day Miss Marple."
— *Washington Post*

"A macabre ode to the mystery genre."
— *Pop Sugar*

"A cleverly constructed story with complex, memorable characters . . . A cozy bibliophile's delight of a mystery that turns writerly research and acknowledgments into fodder for pivotal plot points, offers a tongue-in-cheek peek at the publishing business and pays tribute to friendships that transform into chosen families."
— *BookPage*

"A light-hearted, life-affirming celebration of crime fiction and the colorful characters that create it . . . Such witty and charming entertainment."
— *The Times*

"Delightful . . . Told with Griffiths's characteristic charm and gentleness."
— *Daily Mail*

"Another irresistible thriller . . . Bibliophile genre fans will enjoy the insider's look at publishing and relish the intoxicating, often intoxicated, milieu of the festival. All readers will devour the cleverly constructed story, replete with Griffiths's trademark engaging prose, well-placed humor, and always-endearing characters."
— *Booklist,* starred review

The Postscript Murders

Also by Elly Griffiths

The
Postscript
Murders

ELLY Griffiths

Mariner Books

Boston   New York

For Rebecca Carter

THE POSTSCRIPT MURDERS. Copyright © 2020 by Elly Griffiths. All rights reserved. Printed in the United States of America. No part of this book may be used or reproduced in any manner whatsoever without written permission except in the case of brief quotations embodied in critical articles and reviews. For information, address HarperCollins Publishers, 195 Broadway, New York, NY 10007.

  HarperCollins books may be purchased for educational, business, or sales promotional use. For information, please email the Special Markets Department at SPsales@harpercollins.com.

Originally published in Great Britain in 2020 by Quercus.
First Mariner Books paperback published 2022
First Mariner Books hardcover published 2021

Designed by Greta D. Sibley

Library of Congress Cataloging-in-Publication Data has been applied for.
ISBN 978-0-358-69522-6

22 23 24 25 26 LSC 10 9 8 7 6 5 4 3 2 1

'Jove and my stars be praised. Here is yet a postscript.'

William Shakespeare, *Twelfth Night*

'Do you feel an uncomfortable heat at the pit of your stomach, sir? And a nasty thumping at the top of your head? . . . I call it the detective-fever.'

Wilkie Collins, *The Moonstone*

Prologue

The two men have been standing there for eighteen minutes. Peggy has been timing them on her stopwatch. They parked on the seafront just in front of Benedict's café. A white Ford Fiesta. Annoyingly she can't see the registration but, if she uses her binoculars, she can see a dent on the nearside door. If they have hired the car, the company will have taken a note of this. Peggy makes a note too, getting out her Investigation Book which is cunningly disguised as *A Seaside Lady's Diary*, complete with saccharine watercolours of shells and fishing boats.

There are several reasons why Peggy finds the men suspicious. They look out of place in Shoreham-by-Sea, for one thing. Sometimes, just for fun and to keep her observational powers honed, Peggy makes an inventory of people who have walked past her window.

Monday September 3rd 2018 10am–11am

7 x pensioners: 2 couples, 3 singles

1 x man on roller skates, 30s (too old)

4 x singles with dogs: 2 x collie crosses, 1 x pug, 1 x doodle

(NB: people always remember dogs)

Woman, 30s, smartly-dressed, talking on phone

Man, sixties, carrying black bin-liner, probably homeless

4 x cyclists

2 x male joggers: one fit-looking, one looking on verge of collapse

1 x unicyclist (probably from Brighton)

The men outside her window do not fit this pattern. They are not cycling, jogging or accompanied by dogs. They are not pensioners. They are probably mid to late thirties, with short hair, wearing jeans and short jackets, one blue, one grey. What would young people call them? Bomber jackets? An ill-starred name if she ever heard one. The men look similar because of the way they're dressed but Peggy doesn't think that they are related. One is much darker-skinned than the other and built differently, compact rather than wiry. She doesn't think they're lovers either. They don't touch or look at each other. They aren't laughing or arguing – the two best ways to spot if people are a couple. They're just standing there, maybe waiting for something. Occasionally, The One In The Blue Jacket looks up at the flats but Peggy keeps back behind her curtains; she's very good at disappearing into the background. All old people are.

At first she wondered if the bomber jackets had driven over especially for Benedict's coffee, which is excellent, but the men don't move towards the Shack. There's an alertness about them that Peggy finds most troubling of all, and they both have their backs to the sea. Who comes to Shoreham beach and doesn't even glance at the shimmering water, looking at its very best today, dotted with sailing boats and accessorised with seagulls? But the crop-haired duo are facing the road and Seaview Court, the block of retirement flats where Peggy is currently lurking in a bay window. There's no doubt about it. The men are waiting for something. But what?

At 11.05 precisely Blue Jacket takes out his phone and speaks to someone. Grey Jacket looks at his watch which is a chunky thing, visible through her binoculars even at a hundred yards away. The two men confer and get back into their car. The Fiesta pulls out into the road and Peggy leans forward to get the registration number.

GY something. Is that a one or a seven? She needs to go to the opticians and get her prescription changed. Then the car stops just outside her window. Peggy leans back into her curtains which are loosely woven cotton. So loose that she can see through the weave. It's a little blurry but she thinks that one of the men is leaning out of the window taking photographs. Of Seaview Court. The Fiesta revs up and it's gone.

11.07

Chapter 1

Natalka: the linking words

She knows immediately that something is wrong. It's not anything tangible, the post is neatly stacked on the half-moon table, the flat is silent apart from the sound of seagulls mugging someone outside, the art-nouveau clock ticks serenely, set in its stainless steel sunset. But somehow Natalka knows. It's as if the molecules have rearranged themselves.

'Mrs Smith?'

She tries the Christian name too, although Mrs Smith is not one of the cosy ones.

'Peggy?'

No answer. Natalka pushes open the sitting room door. The air hums with something like electricity, as if a device has been left on, but Natalka knows that Mrs Smith turns the radio on for *The Archers* at two and then off again at fifteen minutes past. She can't stand the *Afternoon Drama*. 'Full of self-obsessed people talking about their lives. That or time travel.' It's now six o'clock. Time for the evening call, to help clients get ready for bed. It's insultingly

4

early for bed, of course, but Natalka has five other clients to see so what can she do?

She enters the room. Mrs Smith is sitting in her armchair by the bay window. She likes to look out to sea and even has a pair of binoculars to spot rare birds with or, Natalka suspects, spy on passing ships. But she's not looking at anything today. Mrs Smith is dead. Natalka knows that even before she checks the pulse and notes the half-open mouth and misted eyes. She touches the old lady's skin. Cool but not cold. Natalka makes the sign of the cross in the air.

'Rest in peace,' she mutters as she dials the number for Care4You.

'Patricia Creeve.' The boss is in. Miracle.

'Mrs Smith is dead.' Natalka doesn't believe in wasting words.

'Are you sure?' Nor does Patricia.

'No heartbeat.' In moments of crisis, Natalka often forgets prepositions and connectives. All the linking words.

'I'll come over,' says Patricia. 'God rest her soul.'

It's an afterthought but Natalka doesn't think any the worse of her boss for it. It's going to be a long night.

Natalka sits on the sofa to wait for Patricia. She would never just sit down in a client's house, unless they specifically wanted a chat and Peggy wasn't exactly the chatty sort. She was always polite but she knew that Natalka had a job to do and a limited time in which to do it. Now it feels odd to be sitting doing nothing, facing the silent figure in the chair which is angled to look out over the sea. Natalka gets up and walks to the window. There's the wide blue sea with white-tipped waves and seagulls circling in the paler blue above. It's a picture postcard view, if you don't look to the right and see the power station and the sinister trawlers with Russian names. Suddenly Natalka realises that she has her back to a corpse. She also has the strangest feeling that she's being watched. She spins round but Peggy hasn't moved. Of course she hasn't, Natalka tells herself. Peggy is dead. She's not about to start dancing a mazurka. One floor below, Natalka hears a door open and shut. Then there are heavy footsteps on the stairs and Patricia is in the room. Natalka had left the apartment door on the latch.

Natalka gestures towards the chair and Patricia comes over. She takes Peggy's hand with professional detachment but her eyes look sad.

'She's passed away,' she says.

Passed away. It's an English phrase that Natalka has never really understood. It sounds ethereal, ephemeral, something half seen and then forgotten. Clouds pass over the sky. But death is for ever.

'Did you call an ambulance?' says Patricia.

'No,' says Natalka. 'I mean, I could see she was dead. What do you think it was? Heart attack?'

'Probably. How old was Peggy?'

'Ninety,' says Natalka. 'She was very proud of it. We had a little party for her at Benedict's café.'

'She was good for her age,' says Patricia.

'There are pills by her chair,' says Natalka. 'Perhaps she forgot to take them.'

'Perhaps, but probably she just passed away in her sleep. It's a good way to go,' Patricia adds, patting Natalka's shoulder kindly.

'I know,' says Natalka.

'I'll call the undertaker,' says Patricia. 'They'll send a private ambulance.'

She has the undertaker on speed dial. Of course she does. While

Patricia talks on her phone, Natalka approaches the body – Peggy – again. It's only about fifteen minutes, but she's changed. She's no longer Peggy; it's as if there's now a wonderfully lifelike statue of an old woman in the chair. Her skin has a waxen quality to it and the hands, clasped in Peggy's lap, look like they've been drawn by an artist. Who was it who drew praying hands? Dürer? Natalia is relieved that Patricia has closed Peggy's eyes.

'Rest in peace,' she says again.

'You should go home, Natalka,' says Patricia. 'This must have been a horrible shock for you. Take tomorrow morning off too.'

This is quite a concession. There are never enough carers at Care4You and Natalka is usually being asked to do extra shifts. The thought of a lie-in is intoxicating.

'Have you told Peggy's family?' she says. 'I think there was a son.'

'I'll look.' Patricia is consulting Peggy's file, which she's taken from the half-moon table. The clients all have them, carers have to write in the dates and times of every visit: *Toileted, gave meds, all well.*

'Here it is,' says Patricia. 'Next of kin: son, Nigel Smith. There's a mobile phone number too.'

While Patricia telephones, Natalka turns back to Peggy. She looks at peace, that's what Patricia will say to Nigel. Passed away peacefully. There's a book open on the arm of Peggy's chair. *High-Rise Murder* by Dex Challoner. Peggy's binoculars are on the table beside her. There's also a pen, completed crossword and a pill dispenser, the sort that has the days of the week on it. There's something else too, a piece of paper just poking out from under the crossword. Natalka slides it out. It's a business card, very official, with black, curly writing.

Mrs M. Smith, it says. *Murder Consultant.*

Chapter 2

Harbinder: Panda Pop

DS Harbinder Kaur is working late. She doesn't mind particularly. If she goes home, her mother will only start talking to her about internet dating ('It's the latest thing. There's even a special Sikh What's Up Group') and her dad will rant about politics. At least here it's quiet. No Neil, DS Neil Winston, her partner – or 'work husband' as he sometimes cringe-makingly calls himself – brushing imaginary crumbs off his desk and doing those irritating bicep curls, as if every second not spent in the gym is time wasted. No Donna, her boss, DI Donna Brice, bringing in her weekly shop and complaining about the price of Pringles. Empty, the CID room feels orderly and manageable. Harbinder completes her last batch of filing and mentally awards herself a gold star. 'Best Gay Sikh Detective in West Sussex', first out of a field of, well, one. Still, a gold star is a gold star. What should she do now? Wash out the coffee cups? Water the drooping spider plants? Phone Clare and catch up with the latest straight gossip? Go on Twitter and become disgusted with the world? Play a round or two of Panda Pop? Surely this last is the best use of her time. She actually gets out her phone and is about to click on the game when the intercom buzzes.

'There's a woman down here for you. Says she's got something to report.'

'Really?' This sounds potentially interesting. 'I'll come down.'

The woman waiting in reception, surrounded by old copies of *Police Monthly*, is not what Harbinder is expecting. She's young, for one thing, with blonde hair pulled back into a ponytail. And, when she speaks, it's obvious that English is not her first language. She's very fluent but she has a light, intriguing, accent. Young, foreign women do not often come into the police station at Shore-ham-by-Sea.

'I'm Natalka Kolisnyk,' says the woman. 'I'm not sure if it is right to come here.'

'Come into my office,' says Harbinder. 'And we can talk about it.'

Harbinder takes Natalka into Donna's office. She regrets saying it was hers when she sees how untidy it is. Also, Donna has got one of those awful cutesy calendars with babies in flowerpots. Natalka sits in the visitor's chair and tells Harbinder that she's twenty-seven and works as a carer for a company called Care4You in Shoreham. 'Zero hours,' she says with a grimace, 'no benefits, no travel allowance.' Harbinder nods. Shoreham is full of elderly people, many of whom need care in their homes. It's no surprise that those who provide the care are poorly treated and paid the minimum. Natalka, though, doesn't look as if she's on the breadline. She's dressed simply in jeans and a white T-shirt but her trainers are expensive Allbirds. Harbinder always notices shoes.

'I have a client at Seaview Court called Mrs Smith,' says Natalka, looking around the room with undisguised interest. Harbinder hopes she doesn't notice the flowerpot babies. She knows Seaview Court, it's sheltered housing, right on the seafront overlooking the beach.

'She was called Peggy,' says Natalka. 'Peggy Smith. She died two days ago. It was very sad but not a surprise. She was ninety. It could have happened any time. But today I helped clear up her flat. Her son is coming tomorrow and he wants everything in boxes. He wants to sell quickly. He's that type.'

Harbinder nods again. She knows that type too.

'The son, Nigel, asked me to start with the books. Mrs Smith had many, many books. All about murder.'

'Crime novels?'

'Yes. You know, man kills woman. Or woman kills man. Sometimes it's that way round. Not so often, though.' She smiles, revealing excellent teeth, white and even. 'And the detective solves it on the last page.'

'Yeah that's how it works in real life too,' says Harbinder. 'Always.'

'Well, I started putting the books in boxes. Then I got bored and started to read bits of them. Then I noticed something.'

'What?' says Harbinder. Natalka is obviously trying to string the story out but Harbinder is in a tolerant mood.

'They are all written to her. Mrs Smith.'

'Written by her?'

'No.' Natalka clicks her fingers, trying to come up with the word. 'They are written *to* her. To Mrs Smith, without whom . . . et cetera, et cetera.'

'Dedicated to her?'

'Yes! Dedicated to her. All these murder books are dedicated to her. Isn't that strange?'

'I suppose so. Are they written by different people?'

'Yes, lots of different people. But lots by Dex Challoner. He's famous. I googled him.'

Harbinder has heard of Dex Challoner. He's a local author and his books are piled high at every bookshop in the country. They seem to feature a private investigator called Tod France who doesn't look like any PI Harbinder has ever met.

'And they're all dedicated to this Mrs Smith?'

'Some are. Some just mention her in the back pages, you know.'

'The acknowledgements?'

'Yes. Thanks to Mum and Dad. Thanks to my publishers. And thanks to Mrs Smith.'

'I wonder why.'

'I know why,' says Natalka, with the air of one putting down a winning hand. 'Mrs Smith is a murder consultant. I found this. It was on the table next to her chair. The chair she died in,' she adds, with what seems like unnecessary relish.

Natalka puts a small white card in front of Harbinder. Sure enough, in small Gothic print it says, *Mrs M. Smith. Murder Consultant.*

'Murder consultant?' says Harbinder. 'What does that mean?'

'I don't know,' says Natalka. 'But it's suspicious, isn't it? A woman dies and then it turns out that she's a murder consultant.'

'We need to find out what it means before we decide if it's suspicious,' says Harbinder. 'And why does it say M. Smith? I thought you said her name was Peggy.'

'Peggy is sometimes short for Margaret,' says Natalka. 'English names are odd like that.'

'I am English,' says Harbinder. She's not going to let Natalka assume otherwise, just because she's not white.

'I'm Ukrainian,' says Natalka. 'We have lots of strange names too.'

Harbinder thinks of Ukraine and a series of ominous images scrolls through her head: Chernobyl, the Crimea, Ukrainian airline crash. She wonders whether Natalka will prove similarly bad news.

'How did Peggy Smith die?' she says.

'Heart attack,' says Natalka. 'That's what the doctor said. I was the one who found her. She was just sitting in her chair by the window.'

'So no sign of anything suspicious?'

'I didn't think so at the time. Nor did my boss. But now I'm wondering. I mean, how do you know what's suspicious and what isn't?'

'That's a good question,' says Harbinder.

She thinks about this conversation on the drive home. On the face of it, a ninety-year-old woman dying in her chair does not seem particularly suspicious. But maybe the mysterious Natalka (mysteriously attractive Natalka) is right. Maybe they should look below the surface of things. It does seem odd that an elderly lady should be mentioned in so many books. And 'murder consultant' does have a very sinister ring to it. Harbinder tells her phone to ring Clare. She's still old enough to get a buzz out of hands-free stuff. Her nieces and nephews take it all for granted.

'Hi, Harbinder.' Clare's voice – confident, slightly impatient – fills the car. 'What's up?'

'Have you ever had a book dedicated to you?'

'What?'

'You read a lot. You teach creative writing. Has anyone ever dedicated a book to you? For Clare, without whom this book would have been finished in half the time.'

Clare laughs. 'No, I've never had a book dedicated to me.'

'Not even Henry's?' Clare's boyfriend is a Cambridge academic.

'I might get a mention in the acknowledgements of the new one, I suppose.'

'Would you think it was odd if someone, quite an ordinary person, had lots of books dedicated to them and was mentioned in lots of acknowledgements?'

'Unless they were a copy editor, yes.'

'What does a copy editor do?'

'Are you thinking of going into publishing? A copy editor checks a manuscript for mistakes, names changing, timelines going wrong, that sort of thing. Then a proofreader checks it again. Except they don't seem to use proofreaders as much as they used to.'

Could Peggy Smith have been a proofreader? It's possible, she supposes. It sounds like the sort of job a retired person might do. But the card hadn't said 'proofreader'. It had said 'murder consultant'.

'What's all this about?' says Clare. 'Are you going to come over? I've made pasta. There's loads left.'

'Sounds tempting,' says Harbinder, 'but I should be getting home. See you soon. Love to Georgie and Herbert.'

It's nearly ten o'clock by the time that Harbinder parks in the underground garage near her parents' house. She still thinks of it like that although she lives there too. Sometimes she says to herself, in suitably shocked tones: 'Harbinder Kaur was thirty-six years old, unmarried, and still lived with her parents.' If she read that in a book, she'd lose all sympathy with the character. Mind you, Harbinder doesn't read that sort of book. But, apart from a brief period when she'd shared a flat with other police cadets, she has lived in the flat above the shop all her life. In some ways, it suits her very well. Harbinder actually enjoys her parents' company and it's nice having someone to cook for you and generally look after you. But there are other drawbacks. Her parents don't know she's gay, for one thing.

She hopes that the house is quiet. The shop shuts at nine-thirty, her mother will probably be dozing in front of the TV, having left Harbinder something delicious warming in the oven. Her father will be getting outraged about the evening news and Starsky, their dozy German shepherd, will be nagging for his last walk. But, as she climbs the stairs, she can hear voices talking in Punjabi. Oh no, her parents must have friends round. How did two such sociable people produce a daughter who prefers Panda Pop to humanity?

'Here she is,' says Harbinder's mother, Bibi, as if Harbinder is the final act in a variety show. 'Here's Harbinder at last.'

The two women at the table look as if they were expecting a more exciting special guest. Harbinder recognises them vaguely from one of her infrequent visits to the gurdwara.

'How are you, Harbinder?' says one of them. Amrit? Amarit? 'Still with the police?'

No, Harbinder wants to say, I'm carrying these handcuffs for a bet. 'Yes,' she says, in English. 'I'm still with the police.'

'Harbinder's a detective sergeant,' says Harbinder's father, Deepak. 'She works very hard.' Deepak is standing in the doorway with Starsky and looks a bit as if he wants his kitchen back.

'Have you got a boyfriend?' says the other woman. Honestly, what is it with old people? Why do they feel that they can ask questions like this?

'I'm waiting for Mr Right,' says Harbinder, between gritted teeth.

'How old are you now?' says Amrit beadily. 'Thirty-eight? Thirty-nine?'

'I'm forty-six,' says Harbinder, adding ten years to her real age. 'I look good on it, don't I?'

'She's only thirtyish,' says Bibi hastily. 'Are you hungry, Harbi? I've kept some food for you.'

Harbinder would love to storm upstairs and go straight to bed but she is very hungry and her mother has cooked butter chicken. Harbinder sits down at the table.

'Shall I drive you home?' Deepak suggests to his visitors, who are both staring at Harbinder, as if expecting her to do a magic trick.

The women get to their feet, rather reluctantly. Suddenly, Harbinder realises that she can make use of the old crones.

'Do either of you know Seaview Court?' she asks.

'Oh yes,' says Amrit. 'The place on the seafront. Baljeet Singh lived there. Until he died.'

'And there was another lady there who lived to be a hundred,' says her friend. 'She got a telegram from the Queen.'

All the old aunties love the Queen. They think she's very Indian.

'It's sheltered accommodation, isn't it?' says Harbinder.

'Yes, but the warden doesn't live in. They just say that to make you pay more.'

'So it isn't very secure?'

'Oh no,' says the other woman. 'There's a passcode but people are going in and out all the time. Carers, you know. Anyone could get in. I'd never let my mother live somewhere like that.'

Her *mother*? How old must this woman be?

'Why do you want to know?' says Deepak, gathering up his car keys.

'No reason really,' says Harbinder. She goes back to her buttered chicken and, thank goodness, the two guests take the hint and leave. Harbinder doesn't know why her dad is giving them a lift. Surely they could both fly home on their broomsticks.

Chapter 3

Benedict: mindful cappuccino

Benedict Cole smiles as he tries to froth milk mindfully. I'm really very lucky, he tells himself. I have my own café on the seafront, I meet different people every day, my view is uninterrupted sea and sky. And it's satisfying to make drinks that people enjoy. He makes his own brownies and biscuits too. He's really very blessed.

'Are you going to be all day with that cappuccino, mate?'

Benedict keeps smiling but it's hard to love people sometimes, especially when they're wearing a striped shirt with the collar turned up and a flat cap, despite being under seventy-five. This man is actually nearer his own age, thirty-two, and, despite the 'mate', the voice is jarringly posh.

'Nearly done,' says Benedict.

'I haven't got all day,' says Striped Shirt, though it's hard to see what could be so urgent, in Shoreham on a Wednesday morning. And, actually, striped shirts are rare in Shoreham, it's much more working class and less pretentious than Brighton. Maybe Stripy

Shirt is an estate agent selling seafront apartments to people who haven't registered this fact yet.

Benedict puts the cappuccino on the ledge. It's a mindful work of art, creamy but still strong, a delicate leaf etched into the foam.

'Would you like a brownie with that?' he asks.

'No thanks,' says Striped Shirt. He waves a card. 'Contactless?'

Benedict proffers the machine but, inside, he thinks that 'contactless' sums up his life nowadays; or sums up society, if he wants to keep his gloom on a loftier plane. In the monastery physical contact had not been encouraged (for obvious reasons) but even during silent times there had been more actual communication than Benedict sometimes encounters in a week in the Outside World. And then there was the mass, the bread and wine, the body and the blood. Catholicism is very corporeal, when you come to think of it, which Benedict does, rather too often.

'Penny for them?'

Benedict brightens immediately because here is one of his favourite customers, someone not *contactless*, someone with whom you can have a proper conversation. Edwin really is over seventy-five but he'd never dream of wearing a flat cap. He wears a panama in the summer and a trilby in the winter, and sometimes, on really cold days, a deerstalker with furry earflaps.

'Edwin!' says Benedict. 'Great to see you. I missed you yesterday.'

He doesn't like to make his customers feel guilty if they miss a day but he really does notice if one of his regulars isn't there. He worries about it in case something is amiss.

'Actually,' says Edwin, taking off his hat (a mid-season fedora today). 'I've had some bad news.'

'Oh no,' says Benedict. He sees that Edwin really does look upset, his eyes are bloodshot and his hands shaking. Has a family member died? Does Edwin even have any family left?

'It's Peggy,' says Edwin. 'She's dead.'

There's always a lull around now and, with no customers in sight, Benedict and Edwin sit at the picnic table beside the Coffee Shack. The beach is almost empty too, miles of speckled shingle interspersed with clumps of sea kale. It's September and the children have just gone back to school, which is a shame, because the sea looks perfect for swimming, blue-green topped with tiny waves. It's had the summer's heat on it too.

Benedict makes Edwin eat a brownie, 'good for shock', and for a moment they sit in silence. Benedict is comfortable with silence – the monastery again – but he's anxious to know what happened.

'How did she die?'

'It was very sudden. Her heart, they said. I saw Natalka yesterday. She was sorting out Peggy's books.'

'She did love her books. Dear Peggy.'

'She did. I'll miss our booky chats. I'll miss everything about her, really. She was the only good thing about that place.'

Edwin also lives in Seaview Court. It's pleasant enough and it does, as the name suggests, have a spectacular sea view, but Edwin, who moved from an elegant Regency terrace in Brighton, loathes the place. Peggy had liked it though. 'Where would you get a view like that?' she often said. 'Not the Hamptons, not Amalfi, not even Lake Baikal.' Peggy often came up with these obscure places. How did she know them? It's too late to ask her now.

'When's her funeral?' asks Benedict. He'll go, of course. He's been going to a few funerals recently. They are usually held on Fridays in his parish church and Benedict goes along if he thinks that, otherwise, there won't be enough mourners. His friend Francis, Father Francis now, says it's in danger of becoming his hobby.

'Natalka didn't know. I don't think Peggy had any faith. I hope it won't be at that horrid crematorium.' Edwin is a Catholic, another thing he and Benedict have in common.

'Did Peggy have any family?'

'One son: Nigel. They weren't close. Peggy once described him to me as a *kulak*. I had to look it up. It's Russian. Means a prosperous peasant, class enemies who sided with the land owners. Typical Peggy.'

Benedict knows about death. I am the resurrection and the life, says the Lord. He knows the service from his seminary days, and from his recent bout of funeral-attending. But he thinks that Edwin, at eighty, must know death better than he does. The Grim Reaper is, if not around the corner, then definitely making calls in the area.

'You were a good friend to Peggy,' says Benedict.

'Thank you,' says Edwin, sounding rather tearful. 'I hope so. She was certainly a good friend to me. You don't make new friends at my age.'

'It's difficult at any age,' says Benedict.

Benedict grew up in Arundel, a scenic market town on the River Arun, complete with castle and cathedral. The youngest of three children, he attended a private Catholic school where he was usually known as 'Hugo's brother'. The only truly memorable thing that he ever did was to announce, aged eighteen, that he wanted to become a priest. His parents, who were Catholic in the stubborn way some old recusant English families are, sticking to their faith all through the Reformation, never expected any of their children to take it this far. They clearly found it embarrassing and rather self-indulgent, in the same way that you don't expect your gymnastics-loving daughter to join a circus. 'I thought only Irish people became priests,' his mother said once. But the truth is that even the Irish don't become priests any more. Benedict's private Catholic school had used to turn out two or three a year but he had been the first for almost a decade. Even his teachers found it embarrassing. And then to become a monk! It wasn't even as if he was a hard-working parish priest, living in the community and trundling about giving communion to the housebound. 'What are you going to do all day?' His mother again. 'Lock yourself away and *chant*?'

But Benedict had loved the chanting and he'd loved the monastery too. If he tells people that he used to be a monk – and it's not something that comes up in conversation that often – he knows that they assume he left because he lost his faith. In fact, his faith is as alive and as terrifying as ever. He left because he fell out of love with God and realised that he wanted ordinary, mortal love. In fact, he wanted to get married. It's funny, the seminary went on so much about denying the sins of the flesh, of sacrificing the chance of marriage and having children; they gave the impression that, in the Outside World, these joys were just there for the taking. It never occurred to Benedict that he would find himself, after two years, living alone in a bedsit, having not had a date, or even anything approaching one, since he'd left St Bede's. 'Go online,' his sister tells him but it's not meant to be like that. You're meant to meet someone while you're walking by the sea, or taking your books back to the library. A gorgeous woman, perhaps slightly quirky, a bit dishevelled, will turn up at the Shack and they'll have a cute conversation about vanilla latte and, before long, they'll be going to art films at the cinema and laughing as they run along the beach in the rain. He doesn't want to give up his dream of Quirky Girl even though he's never seen anyone remotely like her in Shoreham. The only young woman he knows is Natalka.

Natalka appears at midday, still wearing her blue overalls, which she manages to make look almost stylish. Benedict knows Natalka quite well, they see each other most days, and he would definitely call her a friend but, at the same time, he doesn't know much about her. She's from Ukraine, she went to university in Bournemouth and she works as a carer. He imagines himself saying this to his mother, who often asks if he's met 'someone'. His mother would roll her eyes at the 'carer'; she wants him to meet a lawyer or an accountant, or a primary school teacher, which she would consider a very suitable job for a woman. Benedict doesn't think there's anything wrong with being a carer – the monastery had been all about the corporeal acts of mercy, after all – but he does think it's a strange career choice for Natalka. Lots of carers choose the work because the hours are supposedly flexible and because they have young children or elderly parents to look after but, as far as he knows, Natalka has no family ties. 'With her looks,' Edwin had said once, 'she could be an actress or a model.' Benedict had thought this depressingly sexist but, deep down, he had agreed.

'Coffee?' he says now.

'Cappuccino please. With an extra shot.'

'I remember.'

Benedict takes even more care than usual with Natalka's coffee and, on sudden impulse, decorates it with a heart.

Natalka drinks the coffee without noticing the decoration. 'Did you hear about Peggy?' she says.

'Yes. Edwin told me this morning. He's very upset.'

'Poor Edwin. I think she was his only real friend. We'll have to look after him.'

There are no other customers so Benedict joins Natalka at the picnic table. 'We will look after Edwin,' he says. 'I'll invite him to go to church with me.'

'Steady on,' says Natalka. 'Don't go mad.' Steady on. Her English is really very good, even when she's using it to mock him.

'You know,' says Natalka, 'I was the one who found Peggy.'

'I didn't know. That must have been awful for you.'

'Yes. It was a shock.' There's a pause and then she says, 'At first I thought it was sad but just one of those things, you know? Peggy had angina, she used to take pills for it. They were by her chair when she died. But then I started to think that things weren't right.'

'Weren't right?'

'No. I'd seen Peggy only that morning and she'd seemed in good health. She used to swim and go for walks. She never used the lift at the flats.'

'She was ninety though.'

'Do you think ninety-year-olds can't be murdered?'

'Murdered?' The word comes out far too loud. From the roof of the shack, the seagull is laughing at him.

'I don't know,' says Natalka. 'But, when I was clearing away her books, I found this.' She puts a business card in front of him.

'"Mrs M. Smith,"' he reads, '"murder consultant." Murder consultant? What does that mean?'

'I went to the police yesterday evening,' says Natalka, as if this is an everyday occurrence. 'I spoke to a very nice woman detective sergeant. She agreed that it was suspicious.'

'She did?'

'Well, she didn't say as much but I could tell that she agreed with me. I said that she should come to Peggy's funeral, see what she can find out. The son must be the first suspect, after all.'

'The son? Nigel? The *kulak*?'

'That's the one. He's an oaf. I know the sort. He wanted all of Peggy's books put away. Now I know why.'

'Why?' asks Benedict. Is this a dream? he asks himself. But he never has dreams this interesting.

'Peggy had a lot of crime books.'

'I know.' This was something he and Peggy had in common. They spent many happy hours at the picnic table discussing Agatha Christie, Ruth Rendell and Peggy's favourite, an out-of-print golden-age writer called Sheila Atkins.

'I don't mean just *reading* them.' Natalka's voice is dismissive. 'Peggy was actually mentioned in the books. In the, what are they called? Acknowledgements. For Peggy, with thanks. One even says "thanks for the murders".'

'Thanks for the murders?'

'Yes. And now she's been murdered.'

Benedict once went on a roller coaster at Thorpe Park. As soon as he was strapped in his seat, he realised that the ride was a very bad idea. But it was too late, the car had plunged downwards, unstoppable and terrifying. He has the same feeling now.

'We don't know that . . .' he begins.

'There is something suspicious,' says Natalka, standing up. 'And we need to investigate. We were her friends. Who else is there?'

'The police?'

'I've told the police,' says Natalka patiently. 'But now it's up to us. We must watch everyone at the funeral.'

'Why?'

'Because the murderer always attends the funeral. Honestly, Benny, don't you know anything?'

Chapter 4

Edwin: Preview Court

Edwin walks slowly back to Seaview Court. In his head, he sometimes calls it Preview Court, which would be worrying if he ever said it aloud. He doesn't want people to think that he can't remember the name of his own place of residence. The trouble is, so much of his life now goes on in his head that he's sometimes not sure what's real and what isn't. It's like a tree falling in the forest. Is a word spoken if no one hears it? And why Preview, for heaven's sake? Is it a buried cultural reference to the old Morecambe and Wise sketch with the conductor André Previn, hilariously misnamed by Eric Morecambe? Or is it an acknowledgement of the inescapable truth that this sheltered apartment is, in fact, a preview of death?

Andrew Preview. The right notes in the wrong order. Edwin used to work at the BBC, in the days of bow ties and long lunches. He started as a researcher on a quiz show whose rules he never quite mastered, then he had a spell as a presenter on Radio 3, indulging his love of classical music. Eventually he ended up producing religious programmes and a tasteful documentary or two. Halcyon days. Edwin had many friends, even a discreet love affair or two. Homosexuality was still illegal when Edwin was a young man but the BBC had seemed like a safe haven, or almost-safe; there had been a few nasty incidents in Shepherd's Bush late at night but Edwin had lived a charmed life. He thinks of his lovers now: Jeremy, Nicky and François. Nicky and François both died of AIDS in the eighties and Jeremy, improbably, was now a married man, a father and grandfather. They'd lost touch years ago. Sometimes Edwin feels like the last man standing. With Peggy gone, he's the only sentient being left in Preview Court.

He climbs the stairs to his second-floor flat. He and Peggy had made it a point of honour never to use the lift. Of course, Peggy had been ninety, a good ten years older than Edwin, and, once you're over eighty, every year matters. It's funny, though. Edwin had always expected that he would die first. Women live longer, everyone knows that, and Peggy was such a tough old soul. A heart attack, that's what Natalka said, but Peggy had never exhibited any symptoms of a bad heart, no unhealthy pallor, no shortness of breath. Hence the stairs, hence the seafront walk every day. She'd even been a swimmer until very recently. It had been Surfers Against Sewage that had put her off, not fear of rough seas.

Edwin turns the corridor leading to his flat, number twenty-three, and to Peggy's, number twenty-one, which is diagonally opposite. His is slightly bigger but she had the sea view. He's surprised to see Peggy's door open and hear voices inside. Should he go in and see what's happening? But he doesn't want to assume the age-old role of the nosy neighbour. Nosy *old* neighbour, even worse. As he dithers, a man and a woman come out of the apartment. Edwin recognises the man as Peggy's son Nigel. The woman must be his wife.

Nigel recognises Edwin but obviously can't come up with the name. He's a large man, red faced and choleric-looking. It's hard to believe that he's related to Peggy, so neat and trim in her reefer coat and colourful berets.

'It's Edwin, isn't it?' says the woman. 'Peggy's friend.' She's better than Nigel deserves, slim and elegant in a white shirt, jeans and loafers.

Edwin hears himself declaring, stiffly, that he was, indeed, Peggy's friend.

'I'm Sally,' says the woman, 'Peggy's daughter-in-law. I know how fond she was of you.'

Suddenly, to his horror, Edwin feels tears starting in his eyes. He gets out his handkerchief, muttering about hay fever.

'The funeral's next Wednesday,' says Sally. 'At the crematorium. I hope you can come.'

'I'll try to make it,' says Edwin, although his Wonders of Italy calendar is entirely blank for next week, and all the weeks after it.

'Been tidying up the flat,' says Nigel, as he jiggles his keys about. 'I asked the carer, that Russian girl, to box everything up but she's only done half of it.'

'Natalka?' says Edwin. 'She's Ukrainian, I believe.' It's not much of a retort but it's the best he can do.

'We want to put it on the market immediately,' says Nigel, ignoring this. 'There's always a market for sheltered accommodation.'

'And such a lovely view,' says Sally.

'Yes. Peggy loved looking at the sea,' says Edwin.

'I know she did,' Sally makes a gesture of patting his arm without actually touching him. 'I've left some things aside for you. I'm sure you'd like a keepsake of some sort.'

'That's very kind.'

'I'm getting rid of all the books,' says Nigel. 'Why did she read all those crime novels? I mean, she was a clever woman.'

'Don't clever people read crime novels?' asks Edwin, making a list of murder mysteries in his head, starting with *Macbeth* and including Dickens, Dostoevsky, Charlotte Brontë and Wilkie Collins. He's a particular fan of *The Moonstone* by Wilkie Collins.

Nigel doesn't answer. 'See you next week,' he says. 'We'll have the reception here afterwards.'

'Goodbye, Edwin,' says Sally, with another of those air pats.

Edwin watches them go, thinking: idiot, boor, *kulak*. Then wondering: why is Nigel so keen to get rid of the books?

Chapter 5

Harbinder: woodland animals

'Murder consultant?' says Neil. 'What does that even mean?'

Harbinder counts to five. Her new tactic with Neil is to imagine him as a woodland creature, sly, slightly stupid but ultimately lovable.

'I don't know,' she says, 'but I'd like to find out.'

'Why?' Nibble, nibble, washes whiskers.

'A woman is dead and it turns out she's a murder consultant. Aren't you even the slightest bit curious?'

'The police don't pay us to be curious.' Examines nut, twitches tail.

'They don't pay us much at all.'

Harbinder and Neil are on surveillance, which means that they're sitting outside a gasworks getting on each other's nerves. It's not really CID work but Shoreham power station is officially classed as a terrorist target so it requires plain-clothes officers. Today they are in the car park, facing a chain-link fence and brick outbuildings. From the other side there's actually a spectacular view across the harbour but neither of them is in the mood for the joys of nature. Harbinder is dying for some chips but Neil is phobic about people eating in his car.

'Anyway, I thought I'd go along to Peggy Smith's funeral,' says Harbinder, scrolling idly through her phone. 'See what I can find out.'

'Do you really think there's something suspicious about her death?'

'It's unlikely, I know. Her doctor didn't think so. He put heart attack as the cause of death.'

'Nothing to justify a post-mortem then?'

'No. And apparently the son was very keen to get her buried – or rather cremated – as soon as possible. But the carer was worried enough to come to the police.'

'Does this carer think the old lady was murdered?'

'She thinks there was something odd about her death. Apparently Mrs Smith had talked about someone watching her. The carer – Natalka – had put it down to paranoia, maybe even the start of Alzheimer's, but then she found Mrs Smith dead, sitting in her chair within easy reach of her pills.'

'Why would anyone kill her? Was she rich?'

'I don't think so. Sheltered housing probably used up all her money. It would be good to check her bank accounts though. See if there's any unusual activity. She's got a son but it sounds like he's pretty well-off already. No motive there.'

'Then why are you going to the funeral?'

'I don't know. Just to get a feel of things. See if anyone's acting suspiciously.'

'Does Donna know?'

'Yes,' lies Harbinder, clicking onto Panda Pop.

'I won't tell her,' says Neil.

Sometimes he's not as stupid as he seems.

Harbinder isn't sure if Mrs Smith's funeral is uniquely grim or if Christian funerals are always like this. She's never been to one before although she has sat through a couple of weddings. In fact, she's only been to one funeral ever, not a bad score for someone of thirty-six. That had been the full funeral rites, the antam sanskaar, with prayers in the gurdwara afterwards. For Sikhs, death is the start of a new life and mourning is dignified and restrained – no eulogies, no wailing, no beating of chests – but there had definitely been a subdued grandeur to the occasion. Harbinder remembers flowers, chrysanthemums, and an open casket. She hadn't gone too close. Whose funeral was it? Some 'Auntie' or 'Uncle', probably not a blood relation. Her father told her that, in India, the body would have been cremated on an open pyre but, thank God, in England they had to make do with a crematorium and the oldest family member pressing the button to close the curtains.

This is a crematorium too, lots of wood panelling and muted colours, beige and lilac, some vague non-denominational patterns on the stained-glass windows. The congregation is muted too, unlike at a Sikh gathering, and Harbinder has trouble working out which dark-suited man is Mrs Smith's son. There's a smartly-dressed man near the front. Could that be him? No, he looks a bit too urbane. She spots a ruddy man, slightly too large for his black suit – that's probably him. Yes, the celebrant, a woman (vicar? minister?), is consulting him with tilted head and concerned expression. That must be Nigel's wife with him, black dress and pearls like a cut-price Audrey Hepburn. Harbinder spots Natalka easily, her blonde hair piled on top of her head, wearing slim black trousers and a white shirt. She's in a row of women, presumably all carers. Otherwise, there are a few people sitting alone, as if they need a pew to themselves. There's one odd couple, though, a man in glasses and a much older man wearing a pink bow tie that seems defiant somehow. The younger man turns, scanning the room, and smiles when his eyes meet Harbinder's. Harbinder would never smile at a stranger. Maybe she's too suspicious. That's what ten years of policing does for you. She doesn't smile back.

The service is mercifully short. The coffin is brought in by the undertaker's men, polished pine with one wreath of red roses on the top. Then the woman minister, who introduces herself 'The Rev. Jenny Piper', makes some vague remarks about celebrating Peggy's life. Next there's a reading, the son declaring that 'the greatest of these is love' in a voice that is almost entirely devoid of feeling, and a few short remarks from the Rev. Jenny about the deceased. Harbinder listens to these with interest. She learns that Peggy Smith was born in Cromer, on the Norfolk coast. She went to boarding school and the entire school was evacuated to Dorset during the war. After school Peggy passed the civil service exam and moved to London where she met her husband Peter Smith, who had been in the navy. 'Domestic bliss followed,' says Jenny, reading from the script, which Harbinder takes to mean that Peggy had to give up work. The couple had one son, Nigel, and lived in West London until Peter's death in 1992. Peggy then moved south, first to Brighton and then to Shoreham. Peggy loved the sea and was, until recent years, a keen swimmer. She did *The Times* crossword every day and was a voracious reader. She 'didn't suffer fools gladly' (dutiful laugh) but had a few very good friends, including, in her last years, her neighbour Edwin. At this the man in glasses pats Pink Bow Tie on the shoulder. Jenny also thanks Patricia Creeve and everyone at the agency for looking after Peggy so well. Harbinder feels that Natalka should have got a namecheck but maybe Patricia is the boss. Then there's the Lord's Prayer and a few remarks addressed exclusively to God and Jenny announces that the family is inviting everyone back to Peggy's apartment in Seaview Court to 'raise a glass to her'. Finally, Jenny presses the button, the lilac curtains close and classical music fills the room. Harbinder doesn't know anything about opera but the programme says the aria is called '*E lucevan le stelle*' and it certainly seems to elevate the service to something grander and more tragic.

When the music dies away, Harbinder finds herself walking down the aisle next to Natalka.

'Hallo,' says Natalka. 'It was good of you to come.'

'I wanted to,' says Harbinder.

'We must speak privately,' says Natalka. 'I have news.' Perhaps it's the accent but everything Natalka says sounds as though it comes from a spy film.

Seaview Court is a short drive from the crematorium but finding a parking place is another matter. All the streets are called things like Waterside, Riverside and Ropetackle and they are all residents' parking only. Eventually, Harbinder finds a space on a bumpy piece of road under some trees and makes her way to the flats. They are quite attractive, modern with glass balconies on the sea-facing side and surrounded by an attempt at landscaped gardens, buffeted by the sea winds which have bent all the shrubs into a crouching position. Harbinder presses the intercom but there's no answer. Surely she's not that late? Has everyone gone home already? She's just about to give up when the door opens and someone comes out. It's the well-dressed man from church. Close up, his suit looks even more expensive and he's wearing black, highly polished shoes.

'Going in?' he asks.

'Yes. I had trouble finding somewhere to park.'

'Nightmare,' says the man, 'not as bad as Brighton though.'

That seems to exhaust the subject. The man holds the door open as Harbinder goes past, then he turns to leave. She thanks him and starts up the stairs.

The door to Peggy's apartment is open. There seems to be quite a party roar coming from inside but, when Harbinder enters the sitting room, she sees that there are only about eight people in there. It's just that it's a small space. Nice, though. Harbinder's parents' house suffers from the fact that neither of them ever throw anything away so, with the notable exception of Harbinder's bedroom, it is full of tiny tables, cabinets containing china and myriad pictures of forgotten Indian relatives. Peggy's taste is cleaner and less sentimental: wood floors, a few framed pictures and lots of bookshelves. All empty now.

Harbinder sees the son standing on his own with his hands behind his back, a stag at bay window. His wife is being much more sociable, chatting with the Rev. Jenny and two women who look like carers. Natalka is in a huddle with Glasses Man and Bow Tie Man. Harbinder is about to join them when Daughter-in-Law spots her and hurries over.

'Welcome! How nice of you to come. I'm Sally. Nigel's wife.'

'I'm Harbinder Kaur. I was a friend of Peggy's.'

Harbinder is aware that she's an unlikely friend for a ninety-year-old white woman. Out of habit, she clocks the fact that she is the only person of colour at the funeral. She has prepared a story about her mum living at Seaview Court but this is easy to disprove unless she kills off the poor old dear, which seems unnecessarily cruel.

But Sally does not ask. 'Peggy had lots of friends,' she says, head on one side. Harbinder takes this to mean 'even black people'.

'She was a lovely person,' Harbinder says.

'*Wasn't* she?' Sally almost touches her arm then seems to think better of it. 'Let me introduce you to Patricia and Maria. Patricia runs Care4You and Maria was one of Peggy's regular carers. Jenny you know from the service.'

Harbinder doesn't feel that she knows Jenny at all; she also wonders if the cleric expected some sort of title before her name. She's looking a bit steely. Patricia is a tall, rangy woman who looks as if she'd be more at home in a tracksuit than a black dress. Maria is small and pretty. Her accent sounds Eastern European – maybe she's Ukrainian, like Natalka. Harbinder is aware that Natalka is watching them from the other side of the room.

'Dex Challoner was here,' says Sally. 'The writer, you know. So nice of him to come.'

'I've read all his books,' says Jenny. 'I love a good murder.'

'Was he the man in the sharp suit?' says Harbinder. 'I saw him as I was coming in.'

'Yes,' says Sally. 'Such a charmer.'

'His mother used to live at Seaview,' says Patricia. 'She was one of our clients.'

'I looked after her,' says Maria. 'She was a character.'

Harbinder is mildly interested that Dex Challoner seems to have used her alibi, of having a mother living at Seaview Court. Of course, it's the truth in his case.

'Can I offer you anything, Harbinder?' says Sally. 'Tea? Coffee?'

Harbinder notes that there are opened bottles of wine on a side table – and Jenny is holding a brimming glass – but Sally has obviously made the cultural assumption that she is teetotal. On the other hand, she did get her name right.

'I'm fine,' she says. 'Just wanted to pay my respects.'

'We'll miss Peggy,' says Patricia. 'She was a one-off.'

'She always asked about my family,' says Maria. 'She knew such a lot about Poland. Unlike most British people,' she adds darkly.

'I know,' says Sally. 'Nigel studied modern history at Cambridge but I'm frightfully ignorant.'

Harbinder's friend Clare says that people who went to Cambridge always mention it in the first ten minutes of conversation. Sally is true to this rule, even if only vicariously.

'Did Peggy go to university?' says Harbinder. 'She never told me.' This is true, because Harbinder never met her.

'No,' says Sally. 'She was born in 1929 and not many women went then. She was really clever though. She read so many books.' She gestures at the empty shelves.

'Where *are* the books?' asks Patricia.

At this moment, Nigel appears, a bottle in each hand. 'Who's for a top-up?'

Harbinder is about to ask for a glass of red when a voice in her ear says, 'Time to go.'

Harbinder turns to see Natalka, Glasses and Pink Bow Tie looking at her expectantly. 'Summit meeting,' explains Natalka. 'The Coffee Shack. Five minutes.'

★

It's about ten minutes before she can escape but, after saying all the right things to Sally and Nigel, Harbinder heads down to the beach. The Shack, Natalka said, and there's only one place it can be. A wooden hut on the coast road, right on the beach itself. It's directly in front of the flats and must, Harbinder thinks, have been directly in Peggy Smith's eyeline as she looked down from her window.

The Shack turns out to belong to Glasses, whose name is Benedict. Pink Bow Tie is, as she suspected, Peggy's friend Edwin. They sit at a picnic table and drink excellent coffee and watch as the seagulls swoop low over the waves. It's five o'clock and the seafront is quiet, just a few dog-walkers enjoying the last of the sun.

'Harbinder is a detective,' says Natalka. 'She's going to help us find out who murdered Peggy.'

'We've no evidence that she was murdered,' says Harbinder. 'That's quite an assumption.' She senses that it's important to remind Natalka of little things like this.

'No evidence?' says Natalka. She's sitting on the picnic table and smoking a cigarette, making a half-hearted effort to blow the smoke away from them. Benedict flaps his hands apologetically but Harbinder has to admit that Natalka makes smoking seem cool, like the girls behind the gymnasium, all those years ago at Talgarth High. 'Tell her, Edwin,' says Natalka.

'Sally said that I could have a memento,' says Edwin. He has a nice voice, thinks Harbinder, posh without sounding patronising. 'She'd kindly selected a few things for me, an ornament or two, a photograph of Peggy on Brighton Pier. But I thought I'd take one of her books. We always talked about books, Peggy and me. Besides, I was slightly annoyed that Nigel had already boxed them up, as though they were just *objects* to be thrown away. So I opened one of the boxes and took out this.'

Edwin is carrying something that's a cross between a briefcase and a manbag. From its leather depths he produces a hardback. The cover shows a grainy shot of a tower block with the name Dex Challoner in gold foil across a stormy sky. The title is in smaller type below. *High Rise Murder: A Tod France Mystery.*

'I'm not a Challoner fan,' says Edwin. 'But Peggy liked his books. This is the latest, an advance copy. '

'It was the book Peggy was reading when she died,' says Natalka. 'It was open on the table beside her.'

'Yes,' says Edwin. 'You told me. That's partly why I chose it. I thought it would bring me closer to Peggy somehow. Anyway, when I opened it, this fell out.'

It's a plain postcard and on it are the words: *We are coming for you.*

Chapter 6

Natalka: PS: for PS

It's all very well sitting around drinking coffee, thinks Natalka, but we need some action. She'd thought that the detective, Harbinder, would provide some momentum but she seems as cautious as Benedict. *That's quite an assumption.* Natalka likes Harbinder though. There's something watchful and ironical about her, as if she thinks before speaking, something Natalka admires in others but can rarely manage to achieve herself.

'Where are you from?' Natalka had asked that first evening, when they were sitting in that untidy office with the weird baby calendar.

'Sussex,' Harbinder had answered. But then, relenting a little, she'd said that her parents had been born in India. 'I'm a second-generation immigrant,' she said, 'the sort that's meant to be mad keen to assimilate.'

'And are you?' asked Natalka, 'mad keen?'

Harbinder shrugged. 'Not really. I do get a bit fed up with people telling me to go back home when I only live in Shoreham though.'

Natalka came to England in 2013 to study Business Studies at

Bournemouth University. While she was still getting her head round statistics and British sexual mores (the latter much harder to understand) war broke out in her home region of Donbass. Her brother Dmytro joined the Ukrainian Army fighting the so-called separatists. Despite an official ceasefire in 2014, the fighting continued with one Ukrainian solder being killed every three days. Natalka hasn't heard from Dmytro since a text in 2015 wishing her a happy birthday. The official story, as far as there is one, is that Dmytro is missing in action. Natalka has managed to track down some of his comrades, all of whom believe that he's dead. Natalka's mother refuses to accept this and spends all her time and dwindling resources on searching for her son.

Natalka's father left the family home when she was twelve and, for all she knows, might as well be dead. Natalka veers between grieving for her brother and a stubborn conviction that Dmytro is still out there somewhere. She misses her mother but nothing will make her go back to a war-ravaged country. After university, Natalka solved the visa issue by marrying another student and swiftly divorcing him. Now she works as a carer by day and, at night, buys and sells bitcoin. Most of what she earns goes in a fund named, in a moment of mordant humour, Motherland.

She's not looking for a mother figure, she tells people, because she has a perfectly good one waiting for her at home. Her father is another story. But she likes some of the old people she visits, their fortitude and understatement. 'I'm a little wobbly on my pins', when they need a Zimmer frame to get across the room. 'The old ticker's a bit dodgy', when they practically go into cardiac arrest after climbing the stairs. In contrast, Natalka's own generation seems whiny and self-obsessed. All those pictures of their lunch on Instagram, all those selfies at weird angles with eyebrows raised and lips pursed, all those status updates #whothehellcares. Natalka has learned the value of keeping a low profile, which is why she doesn't have Facebook or Twitter. The old people understand this. Mrs Smith once told her that she made a point of never giving strangers her real name.

'Is Peggy Smith your real name?' Natalka had asked her.

'Who would make up a name like Smith?' Peggy had replied. Which wasn't exactly an answer.

But now she wants to *do* something, not just sit looking out to sea and theorising about the note in the book. She waits until Harbinder goes back to work and Edwin slopes off to feel sad on his own. Then she gets to work on Benedict. He's a born rule-keeper but he's also a great conspiracy theorist and is always ready to believe that 'they' are somehow out to get him. That comes of being a Catholic. And an ex-monk. Natalka couldn't quite believe it when she found out about Benedict's past. On one hand, it explained a lot (his dress sense, for one), but on the other, it's hard to believe that anyone still does that, shut themselves into monasteries and pray to an invisible being. Natalka's family are Orthodox Christians but she left all that behind her when she caught the plane for Heathrow.

'Come on, Benny. Something's going on. They're keeping something from us.'

'Who?' says Benedict, looking troubled. 'Who's keeping something from us?'

'Nigel Smith, for one. Why was he so keen to clear Peggy's books away? Did he know that there was a note in one of them? *We are coming for you*. You can't say that's not suspicious.'

'Peggy never said anything to me about a note,' says Benedict.

'Something's going on,' repeats Natalka. 'Why was Dex Chal-loner at the funeral? Was it to watch us? And why did he leave so early?'

'Maybe he just wanted to pay his respects.'

'Maybe. And maybe he knew that there was a message in one of his books. Maybe the message was from him. We need to get into Peggy's flat and look through her belongings before Nigel sells them.'

'How could we get in?' asks Benedict. Natalka knows that she's got him now. He's talking practicalities instead of ethical concerns.

'I've got a key,' she says. She doesn't think it's worth adding that she'd had it copied before giving the original back to Patricia.

'Shall we wait until it's dark?' he says.

'No. That would look too suspicious. It's nearly six o'clock. If we go now, we'll just look like any other carers doing the bedtime call. Seaview Court is swarming with them.'

'OK.' Benedict squares his shoulders. He's not bad-looking really, tall and rangy with nice brown hair and eyes that look green in certain lights. It's just that usually he looks so apologetic, walking with his head down and arms hanging. He wears terrible clothes too. One day Natalka will take him shopping.

They let themselves in without difficulty. The green-carpeted corridors are deserted. The whole place reminds Natalka of a film she once saw about an ocean liner that was really an outpost of hell, full of damned souls endlessly playing bingo and having three-course meals with a single complimentary glass of wine. She looks at the doors stretching in front of her – all painted a uniform green that still manages to clash with the carpets – and imagines that behind each one is a different reality: an ice-bound planet, a shadow realm, a world made entirely of library books. It must be because she read *The Magician's Nephew* at an impressionable age. The wood between the worlds.

They climb the non-slip, rubberised stairs and let themselves into Peggy's flat. Someone, probably Sally, has cleared away every vestige of the wake. There's not a plastic glass or a crumb anywhere. Peggy's chair sits by the balcony window pointing towards the sea. Her binoculars aren't there though. Even the pictures have been taken down from the walls. Everything has been packed into boxes, some marked 'Charity', others 'Keep'. They open a few at random, Natalka stabbing with a knife found in a box labelled 'kitchen equipment', Benedict carefully peeling off tape. It's clear that Nigel has decided to keep most of the hardbacks and give the others to charity. Many of the hardbacks are by Dex Challoner and the covers show urban scenes, gritty and mysterious, with the X in Dex like a gunsight in the sky.

'Some of the earlier ones are different though,' says Benedict. 'They have people on them.'

He's right. Earlier editions show a ruggedly handsome man, sometimes accessorised by a clinging blonde woman. But, about ten years and ten books ago, the publishers had decided to ditch the humans and go for buildings. Over this period Dex's name had got bigger and acquired the trademark X. Natalka opens *Any Port for a Murder*, showing a dockyard in a snowstorm. *For Peggy*, reads the dedication, *without whom . . .*

'Without whom what?' she says.

'Without whom this book would never have been written,' says Benedict. 'That's what they usually say.'

Natalka finds several more books dedicated to Peggy and, even when the dedicatee is different, she is always mentioned in the acknowledgements. *Thanks to Peggy Smith for her invaluable help. Thanks, as always, to Peggy for her advice and encouragement. Special thanks to Peggy, she knows why.*

'This is a good one,' says Benedict, who is looking at *Murder Market*, which shows Smithfield, complete with meat hooks. He reads aloud, '"For Peggy, with thanks for the murders."'

'Thanks for the murders,' says Natalka. 'That's the one I saw before. Is that an English phrase? Like some kind of code for something else?'

'Not one I've ever heard,' says Benedict. 'Are there any more?'

'Yes,' says Natalka, 'when I was packing them up, I saw books by other writers too. Try the charity boxes.'

These boxes contain well-thumbed paperbacks, mostly murder mysteries and nearly all with a dedication or an acknowledgement to Peggy. 'Thank you, Peggy, for all your help.' 'Special thanks to Peggy Smith.' 'PS: for PS.' This last is in a book called *Why Didn't You Take Me?*. Though recognisably a crime novel, it's very different from the Dex Challoners. Even the name, J.D. Monroe, is in a loopy 'feminine' typeface and the cover shows a Tuscan farmhouse with the title disappearing into the blue depths of the pool. Natalka rifles through the box and finds three others by the same author. *Why Not Me?*, *It Was You*, and *You Made Me Do It*.

'Lots of question marks,' she mutters. From the blurb she reads that Julie 'JD' Monroe divides her time between Tuscany and Brighton. And very nice too, thinks Natalka. Three of the books have the same 'PS' line in the acknowledgements.

'This one's in Latin,' says Benedict. 'Peggy Smith, *sine quibus*.'

'What does that mean?'

'Without whom.'

'Who's the book by?'

'Lance Foster. It's called *Laocoön* and *The Times* said it was a literary masterpiece.'

'Sounds shit.'

Benedict laughs, which surprises Natalka a little. 'It does indeed.'

'What does it all mean?' says Natalka. 'All the books. "Without whom". "Thank you for the murders". She called herself a murder consultant. Do you think she told these writers how to kill people?'

'But how would Peggy know how to kill people? She was a retired civil servant.'

'She lived through the war. She may have been a spy.'

'She was born in 1929. She was a child in the war.'

'Do you think children can't be spies?'

'No,' says Benedict. But he sounds uncertain.

'My country's at war,' says Natalka. 'The first thing you learn is that you can trust no one. Not that sweet old lady in the flat upstairs, not your old babysitter and not children. They see everything. They make excellent spies.'

'That must be terrible,' says Benedict.

'Yes,' says Natalka and finds that she doesn't want to talk about it any more. She turns her attention to a box of books marked *Charity*. These look very different from the Challoners. They are mostly paperbacks – smaller than the paperbacks Natalka sees in the supermarket – some with plain green and white covers, others with lurid pictures of dripping knives and smoking guns.

'Classic crime,' says Benedict. 'Peggy loved these writers. I do too. Margery Allingham, Ngaio Marsh, Dorothy L. Sayers, Agatha Christie. Sheila Atkins.'

'Who's Sheila Atkins?'

'She's a golden-age writer. Famous between the wars. No one really reads her these days, which is a shame. Look at this one.'

Benedict proffers a book with a cover showing a woman in a skimpy dress carrying a candle and a bloody knife. It's called *Give Me the Daggers*.

'Lots of them have titles from Shakespeare,' says Benedict. 'This one's called *The Prince of Darkness is a Gentleman*. I think that's from *King Lear*. It comes when—'

'Thanks, Benny,' says Natalka, because she's afraid he's going to tell her the plot. 'I have heard of Shakespeare. We even study him in Ukraine.'

'Sorry,' says Benedict. 'I was just going to say that the covers don't really do the books justice. They're very subtle. Almost psychological thrillers.'

'This is a waste of time,' says Natalka. 'We should be looking through her papers. Maybe there's another threatening note.'

Benedict looks hurt. 'You said to look through the books.'

'Well, now I'm saying to look through her papers.'

Natalka opens Peggy's desk. There are some letters there. Natalka wishes she had the time to read them. Should she take them away? But this seems wrong. In one of the drawers, though, she finds a large silver button and pockets it. For luck.

'There's nothing in any of these,' says Benedict, who is opening and shutting all the Challoners.

'We must . . .' begins Natalka and then she stops.

'What is it?' says Benedict.

'Can you hear something? Footsteps.'

But the footsteps have stopped now. There's silence. This, for some reason, is the scariest thing of all.

'I can't hear anything,' says Benedict.

'Shhh.'

A key turns in the lock. Instinctively, they move together into the centre of the room.

The door opens. And in walks a masked figure pointing a gun at them.

Chapter 7

Benedict: shiny shoes

At first Benedict can't quite take in the gun or the mask. He focuses on all the wrong things. The leather jacket, the dark jeans, the shiny shoes. Then he realises that his life is in danger. He wants to throw himself in front of Natalka but finds himself unable to move. Is this how it ends? Should he be trying to say a final, perfect act of contrition? 'Oh my God, I'm very sorry that I have sinned against you . . .'

Next to him, Natalka makes a sound that's almost a growl. He's not touching her but he can feel that she's tensed for action. It's as if she has a force field around her. Benedict reaches out, whether to hold her or restrain her he doesn't know, but, as he does so, the man grabs something from the floor and backs out, leaving the door open.

'Let's go after him,' says Natalka.

'Are you mad?' says Benedict. 'We need to call the police.' He already has his phone out.

'I'll call DS Kaur,' says Natalka. 'It'll be quicker.' While Natalka talks ('with a gun . . . in Peggy's flat . . . just now . . .') Benedict goes to the window. He hopes to see the man escaping but Peggy's sitting room overlooks the beach so all he can see is the blameless blue sea. A boat with red sails is moving smoothly across the horizon. Red sails in the sunset. It looks like it belongs in another world.

'She's coming,' says Natalka. 'She says not to touch anything. What did he take?'

'Who?' says Benedict, still looking at the boat.

'Benny! The gunman! What did he pick up from the floor?'

Benedict struggles to pull himself together. Usually, he likes it when Natalka calls him Benny but now she just sounds exasperated and he doesn't blame her. He thought that being in danger was meant to sharpen your reflexes but he feels as if he is underwater.

'A book,' he says, trying to come back to the surface. 'One of the old ones. A Sheila Atkins, I think.'

'Which one?'

Benedict looks at the books spread out on the floor. There were two of the three Atkins books, with their faded but still garish covers. He can see *Give Me the Daggers* and *The Prince of Darkness is a Gentleman*. There's something else on the floor too. A bookmark that must have fallen out when the gunman picked up the book. It's a picture of a saint – a holy picture, Benedict's grandmother would have called it. St Patrick, all in green.

'Which book?' says Natalka, her voice rising.

'I think it was *Thank Heaven Fasting*,' says Benedict. 'I don't see it anywhere.' He's pleased to have made this small breakthrough. 'It had a picture of a man and a woman embracing on the cover. It's a quote from—'

'We don't need to know where it's from,' says Natalka.

She's probably right.

'What was the book that Edwin had?' says Natalka. 'The one with the note inside?'

'*High Rise Murder*,' says Benedict. 'It was an advance copy. Not published yet.'

'"We are coming for you",' says Natalka. 'That's what it said. Do you think it came with the book?'

Benedict opens his mouth to answer and closes it again. Sirens are approaching. Such a familiar yet ominous sound. It seems incredible that it's actually heading their way. But, a few minutes later, they hear more footsteps on the stairs and DS Kaur appears, accompanied by a muscular man with a crewcut. She stops in the doorway.

'Are you both OK?'

'Of course,' says Natalka.

'This is DS Winston. He's going to guard the room until SOCO come. Come out now. Leave the room without touching the walls or the door.'

Scene of the crime, translates Benedict in his head. He's seen it on TV programmes. He has to suppress a twinge of excitement. This is serious, he tells himself. But he can't deny it's the most interesting thing to have happened to him since Brother Giles forgot the doxology in Matins.

Behind Harbinder, a door opens and Edwin's head appears. 'What's going on?' He sounds quavery and much older than usual.

'Can we use your flat?' says DS Kaur. 'Neil, you wait here.'

Neil Winston seems used to being ordered about. He nods and takes up his position by the door. DS Kaur ushers Natalka and Benedict into Edwin's flat. Benedict has known Edwin for two years but their relationship, though warm, consists mainly of coffee and remarks about the weather. When Peggy joined them their conversation was more wide-ranging, often straying to the picnic table and, once, to a fish and chip lunch at The Cod Father. But Benedict has never been inside Edwin's home and now, despite the circumstances, he looks around with interest. It's decorated in quiet good taste: cream sofas, wooden floors, oriental rugs, white-painted bookcases. There are racks of CDs too and enough vinyl to keep a collector happy for years. No photos, though, or anything personal. It's darker than Peggy's flat, partly because the curtains are half drawn. Of course, there's no sea view on this side of the building.

Natalka and Benedict sit side by side on one of the sofas, DS Kaur takes the armchair. Edwin bustles away to make tea, 'for the shock', and Benedict surprises himself with a fleeting, but acute, longing for brandy.

'So,' says DS Kaur, 'what happened?'

Natalka describes it all: the footsteps, the masked man, the gun. DS Kaur watches her intently, occasionally making a note in a pleasingly pre-digital jotter. She has a businesslike and competent manner but Benedict suspects that the detective could be as scary as Natalka if she tried. He studies her profile: dark hair pulled back into a ponytail, beautifully straight nose, large brown eyes with long eyelashes, determined lips, no make-up that he can see.

'Isn't that right, Benny?' Natalka gives him a nudge. Quite a hard one.

'What? Yes.'

'He's in shock,' says Natalka, giving him a look.

'Can you describe the man at all?' says DS Kaur.

'He had a mask on,' says Natalka.

'Tall,' says Benedict, 'wearing a black leather jacket, the blouson sort, black jeans, possibly Levi's, black shiny shoes.'

Natalka stares at him and Harbinder repeats, 'black shiny shoes.'

'I noticed,' says Benedict, almost apologetically.

'I always notice shoes,' says DS Kaur. She makes a note in her pad. 'Did he say anything?' she asks.

'No,' says Natalka. 'He just pointed the gun at us, then he picked a book up off the floor and left.'

'What was the book?'

'We think it was *Thank Heaven Fasting* by a writer called Sheila Atkins,' says Benedict.

'Why would he take that book?'

'We don't know,' says Natalka. 'That's why we were in Peggy's flat,' she adds, in a slightly accusatory tone, 'looking for clues.'

'And did you find any?' asks DS Kaur. Benedict admires the way that she gives nothing away. His voice trembles in moments of stress or emotion but Kaur keeps the same light, impersonal tone throughout. She has a slight accent that his mother would describe as 'estuary'.

'Lots of books,' says Natalka, 'all dedicated to Peggy.'

'Not all,' says Benedict. 'There were lots of classics too. Some out of print like the Atkinses. But there were lots of modern books that mentioned Peggy. All the Dex Challoner books and some by another writer, J.D. Monroe.'

Edwin comes in with the tea and Benedict sips his gratefully, even though Edwin has added sugar. He admires the cups, white china with a watery green rim. He always has cups and saucers in the café, never mugs, even though it doubles the washing up.

'I can't believe it,' says Edwin, who has obviously been listening. 'A gunman in Preview Court.'

'Seaview,' says Natalka.

'That's what I said.'

'It's a CID matter,' says DS Kaur, 'because of the gun. We'll see if there are any forensics in the flat. Was the man wearing gloves?'

'Yes,' says Benedict. 'Black leather.'

'Kinky,' says Natalka.

Edwin laughs and tries to turn it into a cough.

'We've put out an alert,' says DS Kaur, 'but it's hard because we haven't got a lead on the car. There's CCTV in the car park and in the lobby though. I'll look at that.'

'Do you think he'll come back?' says Edwin. He looks both nervous and excited, which Benedict thinks probably mirrors his own emotions. They both need to get out more.

'I wouldn't think so,' says Kaur. 'But there'll be a police presence here for the next twenty-four hours. Try not to worry.'

'I'm not worried,' says Edwin, fiddling with a button. He's obviously in his evening attire, leather slippers and a cardigan in place of his usual jacket.

'You should be,' says Natalka. 'They are out to get us.'

'Who?' says Edwin. 'Who is out to get us?'

'The people who killed Peggy,' says Natalka.

'Hold on a minute,' says DS Kaur. 'We don't know that Peggy was murdered. The death certificate says that she died of a heart attack.'

'Then how do you explain the gunman?' says Natalka.

Kaur gives Natalka a rather exasperated look. She's about to answer when there's a knock on the door. Edwin puts his hand to his chest and Benedict feels his own heart beating faster. Harbinder goes to the door.

'What's happening?' says a woman's voice. 'I got an alert from the emergency services.'

'Alison,' says Edwin. 'You'll never guess what's been going on.'

This must be Alison Slopes, the warden of Seaview Court. She doesn't live in but has an office on the first floor and is meant to be contacted in an emergency. Benedict met Alison for the first time at Peggy's funeral earlier. She's a pleasant-looking woman in her early fifties, still wearing her black suit but now accessorised by pink running shoes.

'There's been a report of a man with a gun,' says DS Kaur.

'What do you mean?' says Natalka. 'There's been a report? I saw him. Benny saw him. He pointed a gun at us.'

'A gun?' says Alison. She sits down heavily on Edwin's cream sofa.

'We were in Peggy's flat,' says Natalka, 'when a man came in and pointed a gun at us. Then he ran off with a book.'

'With a book?' says Alison.

'Some old book no one's heard of,' says Natalka.

'Not a Dex Challoner then?' says Alison. 'I love the Tod France books. I always treat myself to a hardback when a new book comes out. Dex was at the funeral, you know.'

'We know,' says DS Kaur, seeming rather impatient with this book club chat. 'And we're taking this report,' she glances at Natalka, 'very seriously. But there's no need for alarm. I was just telling Edwin that we'll keep the flats under surveillance for twenty-four hours.'

'Do you think he'll come back then?' says Alison, echoing Edwin earlier.

'We've no reason to think so,' says Kaur. But Benedict thinks that she looks rather worried all the same.

Benedict insists on walking Natalka home, even though she says it's not necessary. She rents a room in a house near the church. She complains because the family keep inviting her to share meals with them but Benedict thinks it sounds friendlier than his own bedsit where, sometimes, he doesn't hear a human voice from five p.m. (when the Coffee Shack closes) until seven the next morning, unless you count Radio 4, which he doesn't.

He says goodbye to Natalka in a porch full of bicycles and other detritus of family life. They hug, which is unusual for them, and the warmth of it carries Benedict along the high street and towards the river. His bedsit is on the top floor of a large Victorian house. It's a nice room, large and airy, overlooking the estuary. Benedict can look down on the masts of boats and on the fast-flowing water and sludgy mud. At night he can hear the boom of the fog horn and watch as the lighthouse beam flickers across his window. He likes the light; it's company. Some of the other residents complain about it and put up blackout blinds but Benedict keeps his curtains open, which is probably why he wakes up so early every morning.

This is the first time Benedict has lived on his own. He went straight from school to the seminary in Wonersh. He'd loved it, the place had been his university, but then he'd been sent to Rome. A compliment, everybody said; a sign that the church had him destined for higher things. But, although he'd loved the city, he found the work hard and he'd struggled because he didn't speak any Italian. He had Latin A-Level though, which had helped. It was Rome that had convinced him to become a monk, against his superiors' advice. They had wanted him for the hierarchy. Like the mafia, his friend Francis said. But the hours spent on his own in Roman churches, the only sounds distant bells and the sigh of his own breathing, made him yearn for the contemplative life. He joined the community at St Bede's as a postulant and, after nine months, started his novitiate. The ceremony that marked the beginning of this phase of his life remains etched on his mind. He entered the chapter house wearing his ordinary clothes – and very ordinary they were, too, after years in a seminary – to find the habit of the order laid out on the trestle table: tunic, belt, scapular and hood. Benedict had to signify his acceptance of monastic life by putting his hands on these clothes and, presently, changing into them. He remembers how thrilling, how *dramatic*, they had seemed compared with his drab everyday garb. The choice had been easy.

Then, six years later and a year after taking his solemn vows, Benedict had changed his mind again. This time it had not been easy. He had been so sure before that he doubted his own doubts. But his novice master, who had remained his confessor, supported him. It wasn't that he had been wrong the first time, Brother Damian said, it was that God now had a different plan for him. His years of training for the priesthood and monastic life hadn't been wasted; they were all part of a wider destiny. Benedict had clung to these words all through the trauma of leaving the community, with its comforting structure of chanting (eight times a day, starting at sunrise), physical work and prayer, for the daunting Outside World.

His parents, having been shocked at his vocation, were now shocked at his abandoning it. But they did help him buy the Shack, and the proceeds from it pay for this room overlooking the harbour. In those last months at St Bede's, the thought of being alone both terrified and thrilled him. The echo of your voice in an empty room, the freedom to wear pyjamas all day, to watch television, to eat cornflakes in bed. But, in reality, he still wakes up at five-thirty every day and is showered and dressed by six. That leaves a lot of hours to get through, even though he's at the Coffee Shack from six until five. He was delighted by television at first and was thrilled to discover whole channels devoted to crime drama. He watched reruns of *Morse*, *Vera* and *Midsomer Murders*. He watched *Father Brown*, *Monk* (ha!) and *Murder, She Wrote*. He became an armchair expert in forensics, untraceable poisons and wild guesswork. When he'd met Peggy at the café the conversation had naturally turned to detective fiction and who would kill who and why. Edwin hadn't shared their love of gore but his background in religious broadcasting meant that he and Benedict had some interesting chats about plainsong and polyphony. They had been happy times, Benedict realises now, sitting in the sunlight talking about Miss Marple and Gregorian chants. He wishes that, in true mindful, prayerful fashion, he had appreciated it more at the time.

Can he use his second-hand detective skills now? Back in his bedroom, Benedict takes out a sheet of paper and notes down all that he can remember about the gunman. DS Kaur had been impressed that he had noticed the shoes, he remembers. What about smells? Benedict is proud of his olfactory powers. He could recognise every herb in the monastery garden and can tell different coffee beans from scent alone. Did the gunman smell of anything? Benedict closes his eyes to relive the scene: 'Can you hear something?', the door opening, the gun, the moment when he proved himself incapable of throwing himself in front of Natalka and becoming a hero. Had there been a smell? He can only think of Natalka who wears a lemony Chanel scent called Chance. He can smell books too, the daffodil-stalk freshness of new books and the mustiness of Peggy's classic tomes. Why had the gunman picked up that particular book? *Thank Heaven Fasting*. It's a quote from *As You Like It*, as he'd been about to tell Natalka. *'Down on your knees And thank heaven, fasting, for a good man's love.'* Not a very feminist sentiment. Why was that dated, out-of-print book so important that Shiny Shoe Man came after it with a gun? Would he have shot Benedict and Natalka for it if they'd put up a fight? Benedict suspects so somehow.

He sits at his desk until it's quite dark outside and he can see the harbour lights glowing on the water. Should he make himself something to eat? There's a gas ring in his room, plus a microwave and mini-fridge, but Benedict doesn't feel hungry. Maybe staring down the barrel of a gun does that to you. He decides to go downstairs to see if he has any post. He doesn't get much, the occasional postcard from his mother or a letter from Francis, written in his careful Jesuit hand. Might as well check though. He pads down in his socks and sifts through the teetering pile of junk mail: takeaways, old political leaflets, the scientologists looking for new recruits. Then he sees something on the floor by the doormat. It's a flyer showing a book with a skyscraper on the cover.

Dex Challoner will be at Chichester Waterstones,
talking about his new book,
High Rise Murder.

7.30pm Friday 21st September.
All welcome.
£3 including complimentary glass of wine.

Chapter 8

Harbinder: Murder in the title

When SOCO have finished in Peggy's flat, Harbinder and Neil enter the airy room where, only a few hours earlier, Harbinder had chatted with the Rev. Jenny and co. about Peggy. Outside, the sun has set and the sky is almost navy blue. Harbinder puts on the light and surveys the piles of books on the floor.

'Jesus,' says Neil. 'Why would anyone have so many books?'

'She liked reading,' says Harbinder. 'She liked murder mysteries. I think she was a bit of an armchair sleuth.'

Some of the books are in boxes but others are lying on the floor. Clearly Natalka and Benedict had been in the middle of sorting them out. The desk – the sort with a lid that folds down – is open and there are some letters and papers visible. Why hasn't Nigel taken these away?

'Did SOCO find anything?' Harbinder asks.

'They were looking for fingerprints.'

'He was wearing gloves.'

'Oh well, he might have sneezed or something. Left DNA.' Neil is always vague about forensics. He would have preferred to live in one of those old-fashioned crime novels, where the detectives trample all over the crime scene, pausing only to beat up suspects and drink beer.

'What's going on?' says Neil, all twitching nose and ruffled whiskers. 'Who were those people in here just now?'

'Natalka, one of Peggy's carers,' says Harbinder, 'and her friend Benedict. He owns the Coffee Shack on the seafront.'

'I know it,' says Neil. 'Good coffee.'

'Natalka was the woman who first raised the alarm about Peggy,' says Harbinder. 'She found the "murder consultant" business cards.'

'Natalka,' says Neil. 'And what kind of a name is that?'

One, two, three, four, five, six ... 'She's originally from Ukraine,' says Harbinder. 'I'm sure that she thinks your name is equally strange.'

'Neil's not strange,' says Neil. 'Everyone's called Neil.'

'Only ex-footballers,' says Harbinder. 'The point is that Natalka thought there was something suspicious about Peggy's death and this rather proves her right. A man with a gun is certainly suspicious.'

'If there really was a man with a gun. We've only got their words for it, the carer and the coffee guy.'

Harbinder knows that this is true but somehow she believes them. It was the shoes, she thinks. Benedict had noticed the shoes. He'd given a pretty good description too. 'CCTV should have picked something up,' she says. 'There are cameras in the car park.'

'Why would a gunman threaten them? And then go away without doing anything?' Neil sounds aggrieved now, a squirrel deprived of its nut.

'Apparently he took a book,' says Harbinder. She checks her notebook. 'It's called *Thank Heaven Fasting* by someone called Sheila Atkins.'

'He took a *book*? Why?'

'Your guess is as good as mine. Peggy's neighbour, a chap called Edwin Fitzgerald, found a postcard in another one of her books. It said, "We are coming for you".'

'Do you think this is all mixed up with that "murder consultant" stuff? Was the old lady murdered after all?'

'I don't know. But something's going on. Dex Challoner, the author of these . . .' she points to the pile of books with Murder in the title, 'he was at the funeral. I think we should go and talk to him.'

'Dex Challoner,' says Neil, 'he's famous. Kelly read one of his books in her book club.'

'I'll tell him,' says Harbinder. 'Sure he'll be delighted.'

Neil nods in a satisfied way, taking this at face value. It's too easy sometimes.

Harbinder goes over to the desk. In the cubbyholes are pens, pencils, paperclips, stapler, a book of stamps. Peggy is obviously an organised person. Harbinder is wearing gloves so she pulls out the letters to examine them. They seem to be in the same handwriting, addressed, in formal style, to Mrs Peggy Smith. Harbinder puts the letters in an evidence bag to read later. As she does so a postcard falls out. It shows a cadaverous man, smiling in a sorrowful kind of way. Next to the man's face are the words: *A people who elect corrupt politicians, imposters, thieves and traitors are not victims, but accomplices.* Harbinder turns it over. *For Peggy, Love and thanks always. M.* This too goes in the bag.

The papers spread out on the writing surface seem to be from a manuscript, she can see dialogue, quote marks, words like 'suddenly' and 'ominous'.

'Listen to this,' she says to Neil. She reads in a deadpan voice.

'"*Ah, Mr France. I've been waiting for you.*"

'*Tod swings round, all his highly-trained senses on alert. The figure is in darkness but he recognises the voice. All too well. But how can Sergei have traced him here, to the top of the Gherkin in London? But it's him all right. He would recognise that lisp anywhere.*

'"*Sergei Baranov.*"

'"*You thought I was dead. How charming. Rumours of my death were . . . how does the phrase go? Premature.*"

'"*Reports of my death are greatly exaggerated. Mark Twain.*"

'"*Still the same Tod France. So erudite. So English.*"

'*All this time Tod has been moving forward, rearranging the molecules as the sensei taught him, all those years ago, high in the Himalayas. Now he's near enough to smell Baranov. Vodka and cigarettes and cheap scent. He can see the gun too. A limited edition [fill this in later] that looks as if it means business. And Baranov, he remembers, is a crack shot.*

'"*Stop!*" *The gun is pointing at him now. And he can see Baranov's eyes, ice green with the scar over the left that was the legacy of his last encounter with Tod France.*

'"*Go no further, Mr France.*"

'"*MI5 knows I'm here.*" *Tod risks a bluff.*

'"*No, they don't. I took care of them. And of your sidekick, the enterprising Miss Thomas.*"

'*Oh God. Not Tilly. Don't let him have hurt Tilly.*

'"*Can you think of any reason why I shouldn't just kill you now, Mr France?*"'

'Don't stop there,' says Neil. 'It's great.'

'That's all there is,' says Harbinder. 'But there's a handwritten note below it.' She passes the sheet of A4 to Neil.

Peggy, darling. Please help! I can't think of any reason why bloody Baranov doesn't kill Tod and get it over with. Tod has to have some cunning plan up his sleeve but I can't think what. Slow-acting poison? Have we done that before? Maybe it isn't Baranov at all? Maybe it isn't Tod? Twins or is that too much of a cliché? Do help me, darling. I've got to give Miles the rough draft next week.

'That must be from Dex Challoner,' says Harbinder, 'because that's a Tod France book. It looks like Peggy helped him with his plots.'

'He wouldn't need help,' says Neil. 'He's a famous author.'

'I think I should ask him,' says Harbinder.

Neil looks like he's about to argue but, luckily, Harbinder's phone rings. It's Olivia, at the station. Harbinder listens to her message then turns back to Neil.

'We've got a gunman,' she says. 'CCTV picked him up in the car park. Gun and everything. Let's go and talk to Donna.'

Neil looks at his watch. It's eight o'clock. Harbinder knows that he hates working late on a Netflix night.

Chapter 9

Natalka: buying and selling

'Is that you, Natalka?' Her landlady, Debbie Harper, calls from the kitchen.

'Yes,' says Natalka warily, her foot on the bottom step of the stairs.

'Do you want some supper? I've made lots.'

This should be Debbie's middle name. She has a husband and three children but she always ends up cooking for an army. She should try living in a country where food is rationed, thinks Natalka. Or where you don't know where your next supplies of bread are coming from. But then she feels guilty for these thoughts. Debbie is a very good landlady. And, besides, Natalka is hungry.

Natalka joins the family around the big kitchen table. Along with Debbie, presiding over the lasagne, there's her husband Richard, a teacher, and their children Lucy, Andrew and Sophie, ranging from fifteen to eight. There's a buzz of conversation that Natalka actually finds quite comforting. It reminds her of home, in those far-off days before her father left and reduced their family group to two sulky teenagers and their frazzled mother.

'How was the funeral, Natalka?' says Debbie. 'I was thinking of you this afternoon.'

Of course. This must be why Debbie was so keen for her to eat with them. She knew that it was Peggy's funeral today. Natalka herself can hardly remember it. So much has happened since then. She's hardly going to say, 'It was fine but afterwards a man tried to kill me.' So instead, she just says, 'It was OK. As good as can be expected. The vicar was nice.'

'Jenny,' says Debbie, who knows everyone. 'She's very good. She visits lots of people in hospital.'

'Do you have women priests in your church, Natalka?' says Richard, who is always trying to learn more about Ukraine.

'I don't think so,' says Natalka. She's pretty sure that, whatever else has changed since she left home, this won't have. 'I think you can be married though.'

'Oh, Natalka,' says Debbie, 'that reminds me. Someone was looking for you.'

Natalka freezes, a mouthful of lasagne halfway to her mouth.

'Two men,' says Debbie. 'They came to the door yesterday. I thought they might be Ukrainian.'

'Did they say what they wanted?' says Natalka.

'No,' says Debbie. 'They said they wanted to surprise you. They seemed like nice boys.'

This is no surprise. Everyone seems nice to Debbie. But, if Natalka is right about her mysterious callers, nice is definitely not the word to describe them.

In her room, Natalka opens her computer. This is often her favourite part of the day. After hours spent hoisting, toileting, chatting and preparing food in kitchens where she doesn't want to touch the surfaces, she looks forward to the moment where she can sit in her neat little room and lose herself in money. Natalka had been quick to appreciate the potential of bitcoin, a cryptocurrency that operates without a bank. In the old days you used to be able to 'mine' bitcoins and then trade them, creating what is called a blockchain. The biggest trading hub was called Magic, which seemed appropriate. It was all about numbers and algorithms, which played to Natalka's strengths. She had once studied pure maths at university. Nowadays, though, you need multiple computers, all of them spewing out numbers, to make any money from bitcoin. Natalka still makes the odd transaction, just to keep her hand in, but mostly she just looks at her bank account, Motherland, which now contains almost five hundred thousand dollars. The trouble is that every empire has to start somewhere and Natalka's started with a theft.

Downstairs, the doorbell rings. Natalka goes to the door and listens. She hears teenage voices and Debbie laughing. Then Richard says, 'Only if you've done your homework.' Thank God. It's just one of Lucy's friends calling for her. The Harper children are as sociable as their parents. The house is always full of youngsters, coming home from football practice with muddy boots, dumping violin cases and gym bags in the hallway or just hanging about playing computer games and eating crisps. Natalka doesn't mind this as long as she's left alone but the events of the afternoon have made her feel twitchy. She used to be gregarious. She had been popular at school, one of a trio with her two best friends and fellow blondes, Dasha and Anastasia. They had played havoc with the hearts of the boys in their year, secure in the knowledge that their friendship came first. 'A triangle is the strongest shape,' Natalka the mathematician used to say. She has no idea what Dasha and Anastasia are doing now.

Even at university in Bournemouth Natalka had a wide circle of friends, some of whom also doubled as lovers. But now she seems to have lost the desire to socialise. Occasionally she goes to London to meet with her uni friends but mostly she sits in her room counting her money. Her best friend in Shoreham is probably Benedict, which is depressing when you come to think of it.

Natalka goes to the window and sees Lucy and her friend setting off, shoving each other and laughing. Suddenly she remembers walking with Dasha and Anastasia, so close that she could feel their hip-bones jutting against hers. She can recall the exact smell of September evenings in Donetsk, grass and woodsmoke and petrol fumes. Natalka watches until the two girls cross the road by the church and disappear from view. She's just about to turn away when she notices a white car parked opposite, where there's usually a battered camper van.

Natalka can't see very well but she thinks that there are two people in the white car. Two men came to the house yesterday, asking for her. Are these the same people? Are they lying in wait for her, those nice boys who just wanted to surprise her? Of course, it might be nothing of the sort. The inhabitants of the car could be parents waiting for their child to come back from Scouts, they could be an adulterous couple, snatching a few minutes together before going back to their respective spouses. But something about the car — engine off, its occupants in shadow — makes her feel uncomfortable. She thinks of the man with the gun, of Benedict's lips moving in prayer, of the moment when she thought that she might see her brother again. Natalka goes back to her computer and makes herself stay there for ten minutes, staring at the screen.

When she returns to the window, the car has gone.

Chapter 10

Harbinder: Millionaires' Row

The CCTV shows him clearly, black leather jacket, black wool hat, mask covering his face up to the eyes. And there's the gun, held casually in the man's left hand before he threw it into the back of his car and set off.

'Left hander,' says Donna.

'Very sinister,' says Neil. 'That's what left means in Latin, you know. Sinister.'

'Left in Latin is "sinistram",' says Harbinder. 'Interesting how superstitions prevail amongst the uneducated.' She is left-handed, as Neil knows full well.

'Have you put a trace on the car?' says Donna.

'Yes,' says Harbinder. 'It was stolen from Shoreham High Street at approximately five-thirty this afternoon. The owner can't remember if she left the keys in when she popped into Tesco Metro.'

'Idiot,' says Neil. Though Harbinder thinks she may have done the same thing herself a few times. 'Shows opportunism though,' she says. 'Our man saw his chance and took the car. Might imply this is a spur of the moment thing.'

'What about the gun?' says Donna. 'They're usually traceable.'

'I asked Firearms,' says Harbinder. 'But it's not a good enough image to identify a make. They said it could even be a replica.'

'If it's a replica,' says Neil, 'then the gunman didn't mean to kill, just to scare people off.'

'But why?' says Donna. She always becomes peevish if criminals don't behave exactly as she expects them to. 'Why take a gun, even if it is a replica, to steal a book?'

'Why steal that particular book?' says Harbinder. 'Benedict Cole says that it was an old book called *Thank Heaven Fasting* by someone called Sheila Atkins.'

'Never heard of it,' says Donna.

Neil is looking at his phone. 'Amazon says it's out-of-print. Good thing too by the sound of it..'

'What about the postcard?' says Donna. 'That was in a book. Was it by the same author?'

'No,' says Harbinder. 'That was in a Dex Challoner book called *High Rise Murder*.' The postcard, in its evidence bag, is on the table in front of them. It's clear now that the handwriting is actually printed in a loopy font. *We are coming for you.*

'And one of Peggy's neighbours found this?' says Donna, frowning at the piece of white card.

'Yes, a man called Edwin Fitzgerald. He has the flat across the hall from Peggy.'

'And there's no address on the postcard?'

'No, so it must have come in an envelope.'

'I think we should talk to Dex now,' says Harbinder. 'If he was

involved, it's better to see him before he gets his story straight.'
Getting his story straight, she thinks, doesn't seem to have been his
forte, given his relationship with Peggy.

'You can't think Challoner was involved,' says Neil. Harbinder
waits for him to say 'he's famous' again but Neil meets her eyes
and subsides.

'Do you know where he lives?' asks Donna.

'There's only one place it could be,' says Harbinder.

Shoreham is almost the last place you'd expect to find a Millionaires'
Row and yet one exists. Harbinder knows it well. She's quite an
expert on luxury accommodation. She loves looking at house details,
the more expensive the better. She wonders if it's because, deep
down, she's scared of leaving her parents' house so she only looks at
places she can't afford. She'll save that thought for another day.

She's pretty sure that this is where Dex Challoner lives. She
looked on his Twitter account earlier and amidst the thinly disguised self-promotion ('Wonder what Tod would make of the
new flats in Docklands #highrisemurder #dexchallonerbooks') she
finds a picture of an artistically disordered desk #writeratwork.
Location: Shoreham. It has to be Millionaires' Row. She knows the
insides of the house very well from the website. White rooms with
doors opening out to the ever-changing sea, decks large enough to
host a cocktail party, breakfast islands, L-shaped sofas, modern art,
antique mirrors, Swedish lighting, car ports. But, when she parks on
the coast road, none of this is visible. The backs of the houses are
blank and intimidating, high walls with barred windows, security
gates bristling with intercom. You can't see the sea from this side
either but she can hear it whispering in the dark.

Harbinder doesn't know which house is Challoner's. She's quite prepared to press every intercom button shouting 'Police' but she sees immediately that this won't be necessary. The third house along has a flagpole and, lit up by judiciously placed floodlights, is a banner bearing the gunsight insignia that Harbinder has already seen on many best-selling books. What sort of person lives in a high-security house and then flies a flag with their logo on it? She's about to find out.

A man's voice answers the speakerphone and presses enter as soon as she says the magic word, 'Police'. Harbinder goes through the gate to find double doors opening of their own accord. Then she's in a hallway lined with (yes!) spotlit modern paintings. A chrome and glass staircase leads off to her right and, in the distance, she can see huge windows reflecting the darkness of the sea.

A man is standing at the foot of the stairs, glass in hand. Harbinder recognises him immediately as the author of *High Rise Murder*.

'Mr Challoner? I'm Detective Sergeant Harbinder Kaur of the West Sussex Police. I'd like to ask you some questions about Peggy Smith.'

Dex Challoner puts the glass down and runs his hand through his hair. 'Didn't I see you earlier? At Peggy's funeral?'

'That's right,' says Harbinder. 'Is there somewhere we can talk?'

Challoner leads her along a corridor to the room with the windows. It is, of course, furnished with huge white sofas and glass tables. The three non-window walls are all lined with books. Even so, Harbinder doesn't think that the family spends much time in this room. There's no TV, for one thing. She knows from Wikipedia that Challoner is married to an actress called Mia Hastings and they have two school-age children, Finn and Maisie.

'My wife and children live in London during the week,' says Dex, in answer to Harbinder's question. 'I need time alone to write.'

Harbinder can imagine that you need peace and quiet to write. For most authors, though, this probably means a computer terminal in their bedroom, not a five-bedroom seaside house (cost, approximately 3.4 million). She had no idea that writing could make you so rich. She thinks of her friend, Clare, who teaches creative writing. No wonder so many people shell out for her course.

They sit on the white sofa and Dex offers tea, coffee or 'something stronger'. At least he doesn't automatically assume that she's teetotal. Harbinder asks for tea, herbal if possible. According to the police manuals, it's meant to be a good thing to accept offers of food and drink as it makes the interviewee feel that they're in charge. Dex brings her peppermint tea in a Tod France mug. He has also topped up his own glass with what looks like whisky.

Harbinder asks how he knew Peggy. Dex looks surprised at the question but says, easily enough, that she was friends with his mother, who had also lived in Seaview Court.

'Ma wasn't the easiest of characters but she and Peggy hit it off immediately.'

He has a strange accent, partly upper-class English, partly something that could be Australian. He's dressed in jeans and black jumper and is wearing moccasins that probably double as slippers. Apart from the shoes, he could be wearing the gunman's clothes which is probably an indicator that he's innocent. Surely any self-respecting criminal would get changed, at the very least?

'Ma was from Poland,' says Dex. 'So she didn't suffer fools gladly.' The same phrase was used of Peggy at her funeral, Harbinder remembers. She can't quite see how an inability to suffer fools is linked to being Polish. In that case, maybe Harbinder has some Polish blood mixed in with that over-tolerant Indian stuff.

'What do you mean by that?' she says.

'She could be very touchy,' says Dex. 'Always thinking that people were being rude, cheating her out of money, that sort of thing. It made going to the shops with her rather a trial.' He smiles.

'Did you get to know Peggy through your mother?' asks Harbinder.

'That's right,' says Dex. 'Just popped in to see the old lady one day and there was Peggy sitting on the sofa, the two of them drinking sherry and talking about spies and contract killers and gruesome murders.'

This is interesting. Despite everything, Harbinder finds herself warming to Dex. There was real affection in the way he said 'the old lady' and at least he had popped in to see his elderly mother, unlike lots of adult children.

'Was Peggy interested in murder?' says Harbinder.

To her surprise, Dex laughs. 'Was she? She was obsessed with it. She'd read every crime novel going and she loved true-crime stuff too, even the podcasts. She and Ma used to watch *Midsomer Murders* together and Peggy always guessed who did it before the first ad break.'

Harbinder's mother also watches *Midsomer Murders*, but 'for the lovely old houses'; she doesn't seem to notice that most of them contain a corpse.

'I noticed that you credit Peggy on a lot of your books,' says Harbinder. 'In one of them it says "thank you for the murders".'

Dex laughs again. 'There was no one like Peggy for thinking up really gory ways for people to die. She was good on plotting too. She gave me ideas for quite a few of my books. It started out as a joke at first but then it became a tradition. I always send her an early manuscript of my books and I always credit her in the acknowledgements.'

'So she helped you?'

Dex bristles slightly. 'I wouldn't say "helped" exactly. She had some good ideas. I didn't always use them. It was really just something to keep Peggy entertained.'

Harbinder remembers the note. *Peggy, darling. Please help!* That didn't sound like keeping an elderly lady out of mischief. It sounded as if Dex relied on Peggy to get him out of plot holes of his own making. *Do help me, darling. I've got to give Miles the rough draft next week.* Miles is Dex's editor; Harbinder had noted his name in the acknowledgements. His agent was someone called Jelli Walker-Thompson. Could that really be a name? Harbinder thinks she prefers the Dex of the note – harassed, flippant, pleading – to the suave figure in front of her.

'Mr Challoner,' she says, 'today, when Peggy's carer was boxing up her books, a man broke into the flat and threatened her at gunpoint. Do you have any idea why this would have happened?'

Dex stares at her. 'Gunpoint? What are you talking about?'

'A man broke into Peggy's flat and threatened her carer with a gun,' says Harbinder. She knows that people often have to hear this sort of thing twice. 'The man then left, taking with him a copy of a book called *Thank Heaven Fasting*.'

'*Thank Heaven Fasting*?'

'Yes. Do you know it?'

'No, I've never heard of it.'

'It's by a writer called Sheila Atkins. Published in 1938.'

'Ah, well. I don't read much golden-age stuff.' Dex swallows the rest of his drink in one gulp. Harbinder notes that he holds the glass in his right hand.

'So you've no idea why that book could have been so significant?'

'No,' says Dex, putting the glass down on the coffee table. 'But like I said, Peggy read all sorts of stuff. She was a real crime addict.'

'Where were you at six o'clock this evening?'

Dex jumps as if she has hit him. 'You can't mean . . . you can't suspect . . .'

'Just to eliminate you from the enquiry,' says Harbinder.

Dex takes a deep breath and seems, consciously, to calm himself. 'I got back from the funeral, changed and went to the gym. I try to go every Monday, Wednesday and Friday.'

'What time did you get to the gym?'

'About five. I left at six-thirty. There'll be records. You have to sign in and out. You can check for yourself.'

Harbinder would definitely be checking. 'What time did you get back here?'

'About seven. I made myself some supper. Chicken and salad. Then I settled down to do some work. I often write at night.'

Gym visits, chicken and salad. Dex Challoner is certainly determined to stay fit. To be fair, though, he's quite trim and he doesn't look his age (sixty, according to Wiki).

'Do you have any idea who the gunman could have been?'

'No. I mean I write about things . . . I don't know these people in real life . . .'

He sounds genuinely rattled. Harbinder is about to ask more about how he researches his books when her phone buzzes. She ignores it at first but then thinks that it might be Donna.

But it's her dad. This is a surprise because Dad never texts. He only leaves sarcastic voice messages on the lines of, 'This is your poor white-haired old father. Have you forgotten me?'

The text is brief and to the point.

Mum injured. Can you come home?

Harbinder breaks the speed limit and gets there before the paramedics. The flat has its own entrance next to the shop. Harbinder opens the door and finds Bibi lying at the foot of the stairs.

'I tripped over Starsky,' she says, trying to smile.

'That bloody dog.'

'It wasn't his fault,' says Bibi, quick as ever to defend their German shepherd, often delusionally referred to as a 'guard dog'. 'He was lying on the bottom step, keeping watch.' Harbinder has no doubt that the animal was sleeping soundly in the most inconvenient place possible.

'I think she's broken her leg,' says Deepak, who is hovering in the background, uncharacteristically at a loss. Starsky is at his side, also looking worried.

'I think so too,' says Harbinder. Her mother's leg is bent at an angle that makes her feel slightly sick. She sits on the bottom step and puts her arm round Bibi. Her skin feels cold under the thin sari.

'Where's Kush?' says Harbinder. Her oldest brother, Khushwant, usually does the late stint at the shop, probably because he's scarier than the muggers.

'It's his kick-boxing night,' says Deepak. 'He's not answering his phone.'

'He shouldn't leave you here you on your own,' says Harbinder.

'I can cope,' says Deepak, squaring his shoulders. But her father is in his sixties now and, though he cuts a tall, dignified figure in his kurti and turban, he would be no match for teenagers high on lighter fuel and racism.

'Can you get a blanket for Mum?' says Harbinder but, before Deepak is halfway up the stairs, the blue light of the ambulance is shining through the bubbled glass of the front door.

Harbinder briefs the paramedics in what she hopes is a professional manner. They are brisk and kind, 'All right, love?' and Bibi responds with brave flirtatiousness, 'Aren't I lucky to have such handsome rescuers.' All the same, she cries out in pain when they lift her onto the stretcher. Harbinder sees her father clench his fists impotently.

'You go in the ambulance with Mum, Dad,' she says. 'I'll follow in my car.'

Chapter 11

Edwin: gin and tonic

Edwin surprises himself by looking forward to the event at Chichester Waterstones. It's because he doesn't get out much, he tells himself. In the old days at the BBC there was always something to do in the evenings: parties, drinks in the pub after work, intimate dinners in secluded Italian restaurants. In the sixties there had been things called 'happenings' where a group of people would gather in a space like an old cinema or empty swimming pool, take drugs and listen to sitar music. Edwin had never been very keen on the drugs but he had enjoyed the spurious sense of togetherness, of barriers coming down. They never came down far enough for him to kiss one of his lovers in public though. But it's different now. Edwin sometimes sees men walking along the seafront holding hands and the sight never fails to make him feel happy and also rather sad for his young self, who was never able to enjoy this simple pleasure. But he knows that homophobia still exists. He still sees and hears it everywhere, in code words like 'flamboyant' and 'outrageous', in assumptions and allusions and aspersions. There's still a long way to go.

Edwin doubts whether LSD and sitars will be on the menu at Waterstones but he dresses with care, wearing a silk cravat instead of his normal tie. He puts on his good winter coat because the September nights have suddenly become colder. He adds a trilby and is feeling rather dashing. It's only when he passes the door of number twenty-one that he remembers: Peggy is dead and they are trying to catch her murderer.

Natalka has offered to drive. Benedict doesn't own a car and it's been years since Edwin got behind the wheel. He's not surprised when Natalka roars up in a sporty red VW Golf. She's a hot-hatch girl, and no mistake, though he does wonder where she got the money on a carer's salary. They pick up Benedict outside the gas station and drive off in a definitely festive atmosphere. There's pop music on the radio and, even though Edwin doesn't recognise the words and can't identify a tune, he finds himself responding to the pulse of the beat. I'm going out with friends, he thinks, and the thought warms him even more than the VW's rather off-putting heated seat.

'Is DS Kaur coming?' asks Benedict, leaning forward from the back seat like a child.

'She's going to try,' says Natalka. 'Her mum fell over and broke her leg on Monday night so she's been busy trying to work and look after her.'

Edwin notes, with interest, that Natalka seems well-informed on DS Kaur's activities, also that the scary policewoman apparently lives with, and cares for, her parents.

'I told Harbinder to employ a carer, even for a few weeks,' says Natalka. 'She can't do everything. She's got two older brothers but they seem a bit useless.'

'That's always the way,' says Benedict, even though he'd once told Edwin that his older brother and sister were 'terrifying over-achievers'.

Edwin is rather disappointed by the venue. Not that the book-shop isn't lovely. The upstairs event space is surprisingly spacious and even boasts a beautiful chandelier. It's just that he would have expected a bestselling author to be appearing at the Dome or the Southbank Centre. This is, after all, just a room over the book-shop. Natalka and Benedict are the youngest people there by some margin. Edwin starts to feel younger by the second and embarks on a rather interesting chat with a retired GP from Steyning.

When Dex Challoner appears it's with little fanfare. He slides onto the 'stage', which is, in fact, just a slightly raised platform, and pours himself a glass of water. The manager gives a brief introduction and tells them where the fire exits are and then Dex stands up and talks for forty minutes about his books. It's a slick performance. Edwin is sure that he has given the same talk many times before but Dex manages to get in several topical jokes and a few naturalistic ums and ahs. Edwin has had plenty of experience of arts types who seem incapable of talking about their art and so is favourably impressed with the writer. There are a few clichés – 'a bad page is better than a blank page' – but the story of a lonely but bookish childhood is well told and Dex is generous about other authors and funny about his earliest efforts. '"The Cricket Stump Murders" will remain unpublished for ever.' When the questions come Dex answers with humour and eloquence, not even rolling his eyes when he is asked where he gets his ideas. Edwin claps loudly at the end.

The manager tells them to form a queue if they want to have

their books signed. Edwin tags on the end holding his proof copy of *High Rise Murder*. Looking round the room he sees that DS Kaur has arrived and that Natalka has somehow managed to procure another glass of wine. He hopes she remembers that she's driving.

Watching Dex work the queue, Edwin is, once more, full of admiration. Dex chats and smiles and poses for photographs (always managing to get the book in shot, Edwin notices). He catches snatches of conversation: 'I'm so pleased', 'What a nice thing to say', 'That sounds like a great book idea but it's for you to write not me,' 'I'm sorry, perhaps you'll like this one more.' Eventually Edwin reaches the table.

'Great to see another man here,' says Dex, with his professional smile. And it's true that most of the audience are women. 'Thanks for the solidarity.' Then he sees the book and turns it over, puzzled.

'A proof copy,' he says at last.

'It belonged to my friend, Peggy.'

'You were a friend of Peggy's?' Dex looks at him properly now. He has very dark brown eyes, shiny like a bird's.

'Yes,' says Edwin. 'I'm Edwin Fitzgerald. I was her neighbour at the flats.' He doesn't want to risk saying Peggy's name in case his voice wobbles.

'I think I saw you at the funeral,' says Dex. 'Did Peggy give you this book?'

'In a way,' says Edwin. 'Nigel, her son, told me to pick a keepsake and I chose this. I knew she was a great fan of yours.'

'That's nice,' says Dex, his bright eyes never leaving Edwin's face.

'When I opened the book, though, this fell out.'

Edwin holds out the postcard. *We are coming for you.*

Dex turns it over in his hands. 'What does it mean?'

'I was hoping you'd tell me.'

The manager is starting to get restive. 'We need to close at nine,' she says. Dex hands the postcard back and scribbles something in Edwin's book. Edwin finds himself walking back to the others.

'What did he write?' asks Benedict.

Edwin shows him the title page. *To Edwin, all will be revealed. Dex.*

'What does that mean?' says Natalka.

'I'm going to talk to him.' DS Kaur goes up to the table where Dex is posing for one last photograph with two excited-looking women. Edwin watches as the detective approaches and speaks quietly to the author. She's back in a few minutes.

'We're meeting him for a drink,' she says.

As they walk to the pub they pass the cathedral, floodlit and beautiful. Edwin remembers filming midnight mass there in the eighties. Producing religious programmes wasn't exactly cutting-edge TV but there had definitely been a few exciting moments, mostly when the cameras had stopped running. It feels rather exhilarating to be out with friends again and, when Dex asks what he wants to drink, Edwin asks for a gin and tonic, although he hasn't had spirits for nearly a decade. DS Kaur has orange juice and Edwin is relieved to see Natalka drinking Coke. Benedict and Dex have manly-looking pints.

The pub is cosy and old-fashioned. They find a table by the window and chat for a while about books and events. Dex is flatteringly interested in Edwin's BBC experiences. 'I'm always hoping that Tod will be televised. It's almost happened once or twice but we always seem to fall at the last hurdle.'

'TV is like that,' says Edwin, though he knows nothing about drama. The gin is making his eyes water slightly.

DS Kaur seems to want to get back to business. She's not exactly a cosy person, thinks Edwin. You can't imagine her relaxing on a sofa watching an old film. She always seems poised for action somehow.

'You were going to tell us about Peggy,' she says.

Dex takes a thoughtful drink of beer. 'Well, I told you that Peggy was a great friend of my mother's. Mum could be a difficult character. She didn't take to a lot of people. I had a fairly strained relationship with her too, sometimes. She sent me away to boarding school when I was just eight.'

'Me too,' says Edwin. 'They say it's character building but that depends on what sort of character you want to build.'

'Exactly,' says Dex, smiling at him so warmly that Edwin is sure that he is blushing.

'I was angry for years,' says Dex. 'After university, I went to live in Australia. I barely kept in touch with my parents. But, when I came back, I got close to my mother. My father had died by then and I'd got married, softened up a bit. I started to understand Mum a bit better. She had a pretty traumatic childhood herself.' He looks round as if to check that they're not being overheard but the pub is empty apart from a solitary drinker at the bar.

'Mum was only a teenager in the war. They were desperate years in Poland, of course. I knew that she'd been involved in the resistance in some way but I suppose I just thought she was running messages or something like that. Then, a few years ago, she told me that she'd been an assassin.'

'Oh my God,' says Benedict.

'Cool,' says Natalka.

'She said that they called her the schoolgirl assassin. She knew a million ways to kill people. Apparently she and Peggy talked about it all the time. There was another old dear too, can't remember her name. The stories they used to tell!'

Edwin feels slightly hurt that Peggy hadn't mentioned any of this to him. He never met Dex's mother, Weronika. She had died just before he moved to Seaview Court. But Peggy could have told him more about her. The schoolgirl assassin. He can't believe that never came up.

'Mum was a strange character in some ways,' says Dex. 'She told me this with no emotion at all. She wasn't proud, she wasn't sorry. It was just a fact. But then, a few weeks before she died, she told me that she was scared.'

He stares into his pint, apparently mesmerised. Eventually, DS Kaur prompts, 'Scared?'

'She thought that someone was spying on her. She complained about people stealing her stuff, said money had gone out of her bank account. The thing is, that wasn't unusual for Mum. She often thought that people were spying on her and cheating her. I put it down to her childhood. But now I'm wondering.'

'You're wondering if it was true?' says Edwin.

'When Mum died,' says Dex, 'I never thought that it wasn't of natural causes. I mean, she was ninety-five. But now, with Peggy dying and you finding that postcard in the book. And that story about the gunman.'

'It wasn't a story,' says Natalka. 'We could have died.'

'Well, I started to wonder. It sounds crazy to say it but, was Mum murdered? Was Peggy murdered?'

'I think so, yes,' says Natalka.

Dex looks at DS Kaur, obviously expecting her to dismiss this. But Harbinder just says, 'Did your mum ever tell anyone about her concerns?'

Concerns. It's a very official-sounding word. That's what Alison writes at the end of her weekly bulletins: *Let me know if you have any concerns.* But Weronika hadn't been concerned. It sounds as if she had been terrified.

'No,' says Dex. 'Mum didn't trust authority.'

'Peggy was the same,' says Edwin. 'She called the police "cossacks". It caused quite a stir at our neighbourhood watch meeting.' He stops, suddenly remembering DS Kaur's presence.

'Don't worry. I've been called worse,' she says. 'Did Peggy ever say she was worried?'

Edwin tries to remember. 'She didn't say worried, exactly. But, very recently, she did mention that she thought she saw two men in a car watching her.'

Natalka makes a sudden movement that knocks over her drink. This is most unlike her. Usually she's as neat as a cat. Edwin hopes that she isn't a bit drunk.

'Two men in a car?' she says, as Benedict goes to get a cloth. 'When did Peggy see them? What did they look like? How old were they? What car did they drive?'

'I can't remember,' says Edwin. 'But if I know Peggy, she wrote it down. She wrote everything down in her Investigation Book.'

'We looked through her papers,' says DS Kaur. 'We didn't find anything like that. Though we did find a note from you to Peggy,' she says to Dex, 'asking for her help with some Russian spies.'

Edwin thinks that Dex looks rather embarrassed. 'That was probably a bit of a joke,' he says. 'Peggy had a great sense of humour.'

Edwin remembers this too. Peggy had liked a joke. She read *Private Eye* and listened to *The Now Show* on the radio. She had quite a weakness for off-colour Carry On type humour too. Infamy, infamy. They've all got it in for me.

He realises Benedict is talking to him. 'Another drink, Edwin?'

It's a good evening. Edwin goes mad and has another G and T but when he offers to buy a third round Dex says that he has to be going. He has a driver to take him back to Shoreham, something that impresses Benedict hugely. 'But you have a driver too,' says Natalka. 'Me!' On the drive home, Edwin thinks about snowy woods, of bombs concealed in satchels, of tower blocks and ruined churches, of 'the schoolgirl assassin', of Peggy's face, bright-eyed under her pink beret. He thinks of Peggy and Weronika sitting by the windows at Preview Court talking about murder. In his imagination, the faces become shadowy and more sinister.

He must have fallen asleep because he wakes up when the car comes to a stop.

'You're home, Edwin,' says Natalka.

But Preview Court will never really be home. Especially now, without Peggy.

'Thank you for the lift,' he says to Natalka. Edwin raises his hat but Natalka is already backing out of the drive. Benedict waves from the passenger seat.

Edwin thinks that the sleep will have sobered him up but it takes him three goes to remember the passcode for the main entrance. He climbs the stairs slowly and has a similar problem fitting his key into his door lock. Once inside his flat, he makes himself drink a glass of water, even though he knows this will mean getting up for the loo in the night. He looks out of the window as he drinks. His flat doesn't have a sea view, except what the estate agents would call 'obliquely'. Instead, his kitchen looks out over the car park, lit now by sulphuric-looking security lights. As Edwin watches, a black cat walks slowly along the wall. Is that lucky or unlucky? It seems to be different in different countries. Edwin had once owned a beautiful Siamese called Barbra. He'd like to have a pet again but there's nowhere here to let a cat out. Maybe he should have a little dog, a Westie or a poodle. It would be a reason to get out, to walk along the promenade. Peggy once counted thirty-five dog-walkers in an hour. As he said earlier, Peggy wrote everything down, lists of names and dates and times. Dear Peggy. He still can't believe she's gone.

Edwin watches as the cat completes its circuit and then jumps nimbly into the night. No, dogs are too dependent. What did Nicky once say to him? 'People are either cats or dogs. I'm a dog, eager and loving. You're all cat, Edwin.' But Nicky is dead now. Another one to add to the list.

It takes Edwin a long time to wash, do his teeth and get into his pyjamas. When he finally lies down, the bed spins slightly, which is disconcerting but not actually unpleasant. He sleeps deeply and wakes to Radio 4 telling him that celebrated author Dex Challoner has died suddenly in the night.

Chapter 12

Benedict: Motive and means

Benedict doesn't hear the news until Edwin appears at the Coffee Shack at nine. Saturday mornings are always busy and Benedict suspects that he might also have a hangover. Can you get a hangover from two pints and a small glass of white wine? His rugby-playing elder brother would scoff at the idea but it's been years since Benedict has drunk enough to put him over the limit for driving. Last night, there had been a pleasingly macho camaraderie about it.

'What's yours, Benedict?' Dex had asked. 'Pint?'

'Yes, please,' Benedict had said and, when it was his turn to order, he couldn't quite face demoting himself to a half. Now he has a slight headache and his cappuccinos aren't quite as mindful as he would have liked.

He sees at once that Edwin isn't himself either. He hasn't shaved, for one thing, and the white whiskers are quite a shock. He's wearing a jumper rather than his usual shirt and tie and his jacket is buttoned up wrong.

'What's up?' says Benedict, putting a lid on a takeaway latte ('I like it extra hot,' the customer had told him firmly).

Edwin waits until the woman has taken her volcanic latte away. Then he leans forward. His eyes are red-rimmed. Benedict hopes he isn't ill.

'Dex Challoner is dead.'

'What?'

'I heard it on the news just now. "Found dead in his seafront home." That's what it said.'

'Jesus, Mary and Joseph.' It's a prayer, he tells himself, not an expletive.

'Exactly,' says Edwin, looking calmer now that he has passed on the shock to someone else.

'They didn't say how he died?'

'No, but he was in perfect health at eleven o'clock last night.'

'Have you rung Natalka? Or DS Kaur?'

'No,' says Edwin. 'I came straight to you.'

Benedict can't help feeling flattered by this. He rings Natalka and, when she doesn't answer, leaves a message. Then he makes Edwin a flat white with extra sugar. This seems to be happening rather a lot these days. How long ago was it that Edwin gave him sweetened coffee in an elegant cup?

Edwin drinks the coffee sitting at the picnic table. Benedict puts a brownie in front of him and, when there's finally a lull in the stream of customers, he rings DS Kaur.

'I'm not here at the moment,' says the now-familiar, no-nonsense voice. Benedict tries the other number on her card and a voice says, 'DS Neil Winston.' That must be the sidekick. The one Kaur had left waiting for the SOCO team at Peggy's flat.

'Is DS Kaur there?'

'She's not available at the moment. Who's calling?'

'Benedict Cole. Peggy Smith's friend.'

A pause and then Neil says, 'I'll make sure she calls you back.'

'Is DS Kaur investigating Dex Challoner's death?' asks Benedict.

'I'm afraid I can't give you that information,' says Neil. 'Someone will call you back.'

As soon as the phone goes dead, Natalka calls. 'Summit meeting in an hour,' she says, 'As soon as I've finished my morning calls. Looks like we have a serial killer on our hands.'

She sounds almost excited by the prospect.

Natalka turns up at the Coffee Shack at ten, bringing with her a palpable sense of action and energy. She's wearing a sweatshirt and leggings and looks as if she's just come from an expensive gym session rather than helping old people get showered and dressed.

'Now it's happening,' she says to Benedict. 'We have to act before he kills again.'

'How do we do that?' says Benedict, making Natalka her regular cappuccino with an extra shot. He notes that Natalka has somehow hypnotised him into thinking that they are now a crime-fighting unit. He draws a careful heart on the foam.

'We need to think,' says Natalka, once again drinking the coffee without noticing the decoration. 'Where's Edwin?'

'He went home to shave. I said we'd join him at the flats. I can shut the Shack for an hour.'

They walk across the coast road, carrying their coffees and a bag of slightly broken brownies. Benedict leaves a message for Harbinder telling her where they're going but he doubts that she'll have time to contact them. He imagines her at the crime scene: the outline on the floor, the white-suited figures, the yellow and black tape, the shouts of 'We've found a footprint/murder weapon/DNA.' But so far real policing has been disappointingly unlike the TV version.

Edwin opens his door looking more like his usual self. He has shaved and is wearing shirt, tie and cardigan with well-pressed trousers and slippers. They take the coffee and the brownies and sit at the round table by the window. There's a pleasingly businesslike feel to it – Edwin has even supplied paper and pens – it's hard to remember that a man has died.

'Bye, Dex,' Benedict had said last night, waving from the kerb as Dex got into his chauffeur-driven car. 'Good luck with the book.'

'Bye, Ben,' Dex replied, abbreviating his name with easy intimacy. 'See you around.' But no one will be seeing Dex ever again.

'Let's look at this logically,' says Natalka, drawing lines on a piece of paper. Her writing is slanting and bold. Foreign-looking, Benedict thinks.

Monday September 10th Peggy dies
Monday September 17th Funeral. Gunman threatens N and B
Friday September 21st Event in Chichester.
Saturday September 22nd Dex Challoner found dead.

'He could have died of natural causes,' says Benedict, more for form's sake than anything. It's rather thrilling to see the events written like this. *Gunman threatens N and B*. He's already forgotten how terrified he was at the time.

'Really?' says Natalka. 'A man steals a book at gunpoint and, a week later, Dex Challoner is dead. Does that sound like coincidence to you?'

'"No one knows the day or the hour,"' quotes Benedict, aware that he's risking Natalka's annoyance, '"not even the angels in heaven or the Son himself."'

'Matthew 24,' says Edwin.

'I know more about God than you,' says Natalka, with one of her sweeping, unanswerable statements. 'The question is, could Dex have been the gunman? He's about the right build.'

'And he wears shiny shoes,' says Benedict. 'I noticed yesterday.'

'But why would he do that?' says Edwin. 'I don't understand any of it.' He takes a peevish bite of brownie.

'The answer might be in the book,' says Benedict. 'I bought a copy of *High Rise Murder* yesterday. I'll see if I can get hold of the Sheila Atkins book, *Thank Heaven Fasting*.'

'*Reading* won't help,' says Natalka. 'We need action. What about those other authors, the ones who dedicated books to Peggy? They could be in danger too.'

'That assumes that Peggy is the centre of all this,' says Edwin. 'What about Dex's mother? She was a murderer. The schoolgirl assassin. Maybe Dex and his mother were both killed for revenge.'

'But then why kill Peggy too?' says Natalka. 'Why break into her flat and steal that book?'

'Could it have been the son, Nigel?' says Edwin. 'He seemed very keen to get the books boxed up and out of the way. And he told me at the funeral that he'd been an army cadet. Maybe that means that he has a gun.'

Benedict doesn't think that the cadets let you keep your own gun. But he's always avoided anything military, even the scouts.

His brother Hugo was the opposite, he'd been in the CCF at school before studying Economics at university and going on to make shedloads of money in the city. Even his sister, Emily, had been more macho than him. She'd played county hockey and is now a PE teacher at a private school.

'Are you still with us, Benny?' says Natalka.

'We need to think about who would benefit from Dex's death,' says Benedict. 'And Peggy's too, for that matter. Motive and means.'

Natalka and Edwin look gratifyingly impressed. Benedict doesn't tell them that this methodology comes straight from Jessica Fletcher in *Murder, She Wrote*.

'Who inherits Dex's money?' says Natalka. 'I bet he was rich.'

'Writing books doesn't necessarily make you rich,' says Benedict, thinking of Francis, who has written several tomes on the Holy Spirit.

Natalka is looking at her phone. She uses both thumbs to scroll, like a teenager. 'He's married,' she says. 'Wife Mia. She's an actress. She's in that doctor show on TV.'

'*Paradise General*,' says Edwin, betraying his daytime viewing. 'She plays Dr Diaz.'

'So presumably she's got money of her own,' says Benedict. 'What about Peggy? Who would benefit from her death?'

'Nigel,' say Natalka and Edwin together.

'Why would Nigel steal the book though?' says Benedict. 'Surely they were all his anyway?'

'He could be a spy,' says Edwin. 'He read modern languages at Cambridge. That's always a sign.'

'In Ukraine,' says Natalka, 'priests are often spies. That's you, Benny.'

'Except I'm not a priest any more,' says Benedict, hurt despite the 'Benny'. 'I sell coffee from a kiosk.'

'The perfect cover for a spy,' says Natalka.

Benedict is about to answer when there's a sharp tap on the door. They all look at each other.

'Who is it?' calls Edwin, rather querulously.

'DS Kaur,' comes the answer.

They all jump up to open the door. Natalka gets there first.

DS Kaur is wearing a black, official-looking jacket and looks more like a police officer than usual. Edwin bustles to make more coffee and Benedict pushes the brownies towards her.

'Thanks,' says DS Kaur, taking a bite. 'I'm starving. Haven't had time for breakfast.'

'What happened?' says Natalka. 'Is it murder?'

Kaur hesitates, as if wondering how much to share with them, but then she says, 'It's murder all right. He was shot in the head.'

From the doorway, Edwin gasps. Benedict finds himself making the sign of the cross but then stops when he sees both Natalka and DS Kaur looking at him.

'When did it happen?' asks Natalka.

'The cleaner found him when she came into work this morning,' says DS Kaur. 'Looks like he was shot when he got home last night because he was wearing the same clothes. Nothing stolen, as far as we can see, but I'll be paying close attention to the books.'

Edwin brings in a cafetière and some posh-looking biscuits. DS Kaur downs black coffee without waiting for it to cool.

'Thanks, Edwin. The press have been a nightmare, swarming over the place already. Someone leaked it early on.'

'I heard it on the *Today* programme,' says Edwin.

'Well, it's a very Radio 4 kind of murder,' says Kaur. 'Crime writer shot dead.'

'Any leads?' says Benedict. He can't believe he's asking such *a Murder, She Wrote* question. He can't suppress a twinge of excitement.

'Nothing that I can share,' says DS Kaur. 'I shouldn't really have told you this much. If it gets out that he was shot I'll have to kill you all.'

She looks as if she might do it too.

'I just came round to tell you to be careful, Edwin,' says Kaur, in a different tone. 'We've got plain clothes police watching this building and I'm sure the gunman won't come back but it might be wise to be extra vigilant. Don't let anyone in unless they have ID. You too, Natalka and Benedict. I've asked the local police to keep an eye on your houses too.'

'Two men came looking for me the other day,' says Natalka. Benedict and Edwin both turn to look at her. Benedict is surprised to see that Natalka looks very serious, twisting the silver ring she always wears on her little finger. She almost looks *scared*.

DS Kaur must sense this too because she says, gently, 'What do you mean, "looking for you"?'

'Debbie, my landlady, said that two men came to the door asking for me,' says Natalka. 'She thought they were Ukrainian. Apparently they said they wanted to surprise me.'

'And you've no idea who they could be?' says DS Kaur.

'No,' says Natalka, twisting the silver band. Suddenly Benedict is sure that she's lying.

Edwin says, 'Peggy thought that two men were spying on her. Two men in a car parked outside her window, by Benedict's café.'

'She told me too,' says Benedict, 'but Peggy did like to . . . to dramatise things.'

'But now she's dead,' says Natalka. 'That's dramatic enough, don't you think?'

'We don't know that Peggy was murdered,' says DS Kaur. 'Though, I have to admit, a gunman breaking into her house was suspicious. Especially when you think how Dex died.'

This has the effect of silencing them all. Benedict thinks of Kaur's words, 'shot in the head'. He tries to imagine the reality of this, as opposed to the Cluedo 'in the library with the revolver' scenario.

'Have you spoken to Dex's wife?' asks Natalka, so maybe she's thinking the same thing. 'It's usually the husband or the wife, isn't it? Where was Dex's wife last night?'

'At home in London apparently,' says DS Kaur.

'It's so awful,' says Benedict. 'Did they have children?'

'Two,' says Kaur, 'aged ten and thirteen.'

'What an age to lose your father,' says Benedict.

'I haven't seen mine since I was twelve,' says Natalka, 'he's no loss.' She tosses her hair back and turns to DS Kaur. 'What are you going to do now, Harbinder?' Benedict can't believe that Natalka is calling the detective by her first name, even though she invited them to do this last night.

'Go back to the station for a team briefing,' says DS Kaur, stifling a yawn. 'Then checking, checking and more checking. Then home to see my mum and bully my brothers into helping her more.'

'How is your mum?' asks Benedict.

'Not too bad,' says Kaur. 'She loved it in the hospital. You'd have thought it was a spa day. She's made Indian sweets for all the nurses, all tied up with ribbons. Drives me mad.'

Chapter 13

Harbinder: how the other half lives

In fact Harbinder is on her way to interview Dex Challoner's wife. She doesn't know why she didn't tell her new friends this. Partly it's just because they are civilians and this is a police matter and partly it's because they seem a little *too* interested in the case, especially Natalka. They are involved, because of the gunman, but it's probably best to keep them at arm's length.

At Millionaires' Row Neil is waiting for her by Dex's entry-phone. Harbinder wonders whether the gunsights flag will soon be flying at half-mast.

'The wife's just arrived,' says Neil. 'Someone from the Met drove her down.'

'Does she know we want to talk to her?'

'I don't know. She must be expecting it, surely?'

But Mia Hastings doesn't seem to be expecting a visit from the grandly named West Sussex CID. She looks quite shocked when Harbinder and Neil appear in the room with the sea view and the bookshelves. The woman sitting beside her also glares at them, as if they are intruding. She introduces herself as Helen Marks, a family liaison officer with the Metropolitan Police.

'It's great that you're here, Helen,' says Harbinder, though she'd rather it was their FLO. 'Can you stay while we have a chat with Mia?'

'Chat' always sounds better than 'interview'.

'I'll stay,' says Helen, managing to make it sound like a threat.

Mia Hastings is familiar to Harbinder because she stars in a medical drama beloved of her mother. In fact, it's an effort to remember that Mia is not Dr Diaz, who has recently survived both drug addiction and being stalked by a murderous ex-patient. This is the final straw, Harbinder wants to say, now your husband has been killed. But Mia is simply a forty-something actress, a slight woman with short dark hair and large, thickly lashed eyes. She's wearing an oversized jumper and shivering slightly.

'Are you warm enough?' says Harbinder. 'It's quite cold in here.' The day is bright but the sun hasn't warmed the room much. Helen Marks has kept her coat on.

'Dex never has the heating on during the day,' says Mia. 'He's got excellent circulation.' Her eyes fill with tears.

'I'm sorry,' says Harbinder, sitting beside her. 'Do you feel up to answering a few questions?'

Mia looks at her, eyes huge in her pale face. 'Was Dex murdered? I can't believe it.'

'We don't know what happened yet,' says Harbinder. 'That's why these first hours are so important. We have to put the picture together.'

'Like a jigsaw,' says Neil. Nibble, nibble, flicks tail.

'Can I see him? Dex?' says Mia, addressing the question to Helen.

'I'll take you,' says Harbinder. 'Just as soon as we've had a quick chat.' The cleaner, Reyna, identified Dex's body but they will need an identification from next-of-kin as well. Harbinder hopes that the mortuary has tidied him up a bit. 'When did you last hear from Dex?' she asks.

'At nine-thirty last night,' says Mia. 'He texted to say that his talk had gone well and that he was going for a drink with some friends.'

Neil looks rather accusingly at Harbinder but she doesn't feel that the time is right to out herself as one of Dex's drinking buddies.

'Nothing after that?' she says. The coroner estimated that Dex had been dead for between five and seven hours. Reyna discovered the body when she arrived at the house at seven. Harbinder had seen Dex drive away from Chichester at eleven last night; he would have been home by half past. This means that he must have been killed between midnight and two a.m. She assumes it was earlier because Dex was fully dressed and the whisky glass on the table still contained a generous double.

'No,' says Mia. 'Dex knows that I go to bed early when I'm on my own. Normally he comes home on Friday but he had the event and . . .' She stops, rubbing her eyes. Helen pats her shoulder.

'What time did you go to bed yesterday?' asks Harbinder.

'About ten,' says Mia. 'The children went at the same time. I let them stay up a bit later on Fridays and Saturdays. I watched a film on my iPad for a while and then I went to sleep. I think I was asleep by eleven.'

Harbinder supposes that it's not impossible for Mia to have driven down to Shoreham, while her children were asleep in bed, killed her husband and then driven back. Not impossible but pretty improbable.

'Where are the children now?' she asks.

'With my mother,' says Mia. 'I couldn't bring them with me. It would be too upsetting for them.'

'How did Dex seem when you spoke to him?'

'Fine. In good form. He was hoping that *High Rise Murder* would be number one for a second week. We'll find out on Tuesday and he won't be here.' Her face crumples again.

'Mia,' Harbinder leans forward, trying for her most soothing tone, 'has Dex ever mentioned a woman called Peggy Smith to you?'

She half-expects a denial but Mia says, 'The old lady in the flats? Yes, I met her once or twice when we visited Weronika.'

'Peggy helped Dex with his books, didn't she?'

Mia bristles slightly. 'I wouldn't say helped. He used to say that she was good at coming up with murders.' She looks at Harbinder. 'Peggy died recently, didn't she? You can't think . . . Is this connected in some way?'

'As I say, we're still putting the picture together,' says Harbinder. 'But there have been a couple of slightly strange events recently. Someone broke into Peggy's flat and stole a book called *Thank Heaven Fasting*. An old crime novel. Have you heard of it?'

'No' says Mia. 'But I don't really read crime fiction. Except Dex's books, of course.'

'We also found a rather strange note in Peggy's copy of one of Dex's books. Has Dex ever received a threatening letter from a fan? Something that seemed out of the ordinary?'

'You should see the nutcases who write to us,' says Neil. He smiles at Mia and receives a tremulous twitch of the lips in return. He's quite useful sometimes, bless his furry whiskers.

'Dex does get lots of emails from fans,' says Mia, 'but his personal assistant answers his book emails and messages to his Tod France Facebook account.'

'Who is his personal assistant?' says Harbinder.

'Cathy Johnson,' says Mia but doesn't offer contact details. Harbinder will have to get them later.

'What about Twitter?' says Harbinder. 'I've seen a few tweets from him.'

'Cathy mostly deals with that. He does tweet occasionally.'

Harbinder remembers the picture of the messy desk #writerat-work. If Dex had posted that, did he realise that it also advertised his address?

'Do Dex's publishers know?' she asks. She doesn't want to add 'about the murder'.

'I told Jelli,' says Mia. 'Dex's agent. She was devastated. She will have told them.'

'Jelli?' says Harbinder. She remembers the name but surely it can't be real?

'Short for Angelica,' says Mia.

Harbinder writes it down. She'll have to talk to these exotic creatures soon.

'Have you finished?' says Helen. 'Mrs Challoner wants to see her husband's body.'

Mia starts to sob, doubling over as if she's in pain. Helen looks accusingly at Harbinder, although it was actually her fault.

'Of course,' says Harbinder. 'We'll take her now. I'll ask our family liaison officer to meet us there.'

'The wife's in the clear then?' says Donna.

They don't have their briefing until five o'clock. Donna ordered in pizza at four and the grease-stained boxes are still on the table. Harbinder can tell that Neil is dying to clear them away.

'I think so,' says Harbinder. 'Of course, technically she could have done it but I can't see it somehow.'

'Of course she didn't do it,' says Neil. 'She was heartbroken.'

Neil has always been a sucker for a pretty face but Mia Hastings had seemed devastated at her husband's death. At the mortuary, she had actually thrown herself across his body, something Harbinder has only seen in films. It had taken Maggie, the FLO, almost ten minutes to get her out of the room.

'You saw him the night before,' says Donna. 'How did he seem?'

'Fine,' says Harbinder. 'He did his talk, he signed some books and then we went for a drink.'

'How the other half lives,' says Neil, as if he's never visited a pub.

'Anyone dodgy-looking in the audience?' asks Donna.

Harbinder remembers arriving late and seeing a sea of grey heads. 'Definitely not,' she says.

Donna finds a bit of pizza crust and chews it meditatively. Harbinder says, 'Dex talked about his mother last night. Her name was Weronika and apparently she was a spy in the war. The schoolgirl assassin, they called her. I think that might be the link. His mum knew Peggy Smith too.'

'Sounds a bit far-fetched,' says Donna, 'but let's get Intel onto it. There'll be records or something.'

But Harbinder doubts if there will be records of this desperate, murky period of history. She thinks of her grandparents' stories of the partition of India; of families split apart and never reunited, of unsolved murders and places that simply disappeared from the map. This was 1947, just after the war. Is there anyone alive who remembers the Polish resistance? Was Weronika the last of the freedom fighters?

'Anything from SOCO?' says Donna, turning to the present with what sounds like relief.

'He was shot in the head,' says Neil. 'One shot so it could be professional. No weapon found but, from the wound, it looks to have been a semi-automatic pistol. There's no sign of forced entry.'

'So Dex must have known the killer,' says Donna.

'Either that or they had a plausible story,' says Harbinder. 'Security's pretty tight in those houses.'

'CCTV?' says Donna.

'Lots of cameras,' says Harbinder. 'But most of them don't seem to be working, including the one over Dex's front door. We're working on it though. The neighbours' cameras might have picked something up. They're away on holiday at the moment.'

'Dex was shot as he sat on the sofa,' says Neil, 'and the bullet lodged itself in the cushions. The fact that he was sitting down implies he didn't feel threatened.'

'Or the killer ordered him to sit,' says Donna. 'Sounds almost like a punishment killing.'

Harbinder had thought this too but wondered if she was getting carried away with the schoolgirl-assassin stories.

'His phone was next to him,' she says. 'That might mean that he'd just made a call or sent a text.'

'Or played Panda Pop,' says Neil.

Harbinder ignores him. 'I've got onto the service provider but it's an iPhone and Apple often refuses to give up the password.'

'Maybe the wife will know,' says Donna. 'It's usually one of the children's birthdays or something. What are you doing tomorrow?'

Harbinder looks at her list of names. 'We're seeing Dex's editor and publicist,' she says. 'And his agent.'

'Do you think they'll have anything useful to say?'

'I don't know,' says Harbinder. 'But so much of this seems to come back to the books. That's the link between Peggy and Dex. That and her friendship with his mother.'

'What about the book that the gunman took?' says Donna. 'The one with the odd title.'

'*Thank Heaven Fasting*. Dex said he hadn't read it.'

'Have you?'

'No,' says Harbinder. 'I haven't had much time for reading, what with my mum and everything.'

'What about the other writers?' says Donna. 'The ones who mentioned Peggy in their books. Have you contacted them?'

'It's on my "To Do" list,' says Harbinder.

Back at her desk, Harbinder looks at her list. According to Natalka and Benedict, there are three writers who mentioned Peggy Smith in their acknowledgements: J. D. Monroe, Lance Foster and Eliza Bennington. Taking them in alphabetical order, she contacts Bennington's publishers to be told that the name is a pseudonym. The author is a man called Sage McGannon and he's currently 'at a writer's retreat in the South of France'. Nice work if you can get it, thinks Harbinder. Next she tries Lance Foster but his publishers, Cassowary, don't seem to exist any more. She has more luck with J. D. Monroe because there's an email address on her website.

Harbinder sends a message including her phone number and, ten minutes later, there's a call.

'DS Kaur? This is Julie Monroe.' It's a rather breathy voice, younger than Harbinder was expecting.

'Oh, hallo. Thank you for ringing back. I'm one of the detectives investigating the death of Dex Challoner.'

'Oh my God,' says Julie Monroe. 'It's so awful. I just can't believe it.'

'Did you know Dex?'

'A little. I just saw him at festivals and events. He was always so nice, so friendly. I just can't believe that he's . . . gone.'

Gone is one way of putting it.

'Ms Monroe,' says Harbinder. 'I understand that you also knew Peggy Smith.'

'Peggy?' Now she really does sound surprised. 'Yes, I knew her. Why do you ask?'

'You acknowledge her in your books. PS: for PS.'

'That's right. She gave me some advice. It was a joke between us.'

'You know Peggy died recently?'

'Yes. I came to her funeral. I had to leave before the wake though.'

'Well, we found a note amongst Peggy's things. A postcard really. It said, "We are coming for you." I just wondered whether you'd received anything similar.'

There's a long pause and then J. D. Monroe says, 'I think I did.'

'You *think* you did?'

'Well, I get all sorts of things sent to me. Books to review, flyers about new releases. I think I might have got a postcard saying that.'

'Can you find it? I'll have an officer go round to your house tomorrow.'

'The thing is,' says Julie, 'I'm going to Aberdeen tomorrow for a literary festival.'

Harbinder has no idea what a literary festival entails and she's not going to ask. She says that she'll send an officer round to look at the postcard and clicks the red button to end the call. She's feeling frustrated. A man has been shot dead and the only clues seem flimsy, insubstantial things – literally paper-thin. And, in a few moments, she's got to go home and probably cook supper, clean the house and help her mother to bed. What had Natalka said about getting a carer who might be able to help? She scrolls through her phone contacts until she finds N. Natalka has added the number herself, complete with disturbingly sultry selfie.

'Hallo?' That accent again.

'It's DS Kaur. Harbinder. I'm just ringing about carers. For my mum. You mentioned that you knew someone who might do private work.'

'Yes,' says Natalka. 'Maria. She's very good. Not a word to Care4You, though. Patricia hates people working freelance but you can't make ends meet otherwise.'

Make ends meet. Natalka's English is really very good. Harbinder wonders when she left Ukraine. When was the war with Russia exactly? Another desperate, murky conflict.

'Thank you,' says Harbinder.

'How is the investigation going?' asks Natalka. 'Have you found out who killed Dex?'

'I can't really say,' says Harbinder. 'It's at a very early stage.'

She expects Natalka to challenge this but instead she says, after a brief pause, 'You know I told you about those two men outside my house?'

'Yes.'

'Well, I didn't tell you that I thought they were waiting for me, watching the house where I live. Last night they were back again. A white Ford Fiesta. I've got the licence plate.'

And sometimes her vocabulary is American, thinks Harbinder. Licence plate instead of number plate.

'I'll run a check on it,' says Harbinder. 'Have you any idea why these men could be watching you?'

To her surprise, Natalka says, 'Yes. I'd rather tell you face to face though. What about tomorrow night?'

And Harbinder finds herself agreeing to meet Natalka in a pub near her parents' house.

Chapter 14

Natalka: tea and biscuits

Natalka is waiting in a car park. She feels as if she is on stake-out, waiting to exchange hostages, perhaps, or to pass on a sinister package, wrapped in silver foil. It must be thinking about the mysterious men in the Ford Fiesta. But also it brings back memories of clandestine meetings in the Ukraine, of passwords and burner phones and a churning feeling that could either be excitement or fear. But she's put all that behind her now. Tonight, she'll tell DS Kaur everything. Or nearly everything. But right now she has to get Harriet Hartington ready for bed. As Harriet is bed-bound this requires a winch and two carers. So Natalka is waiting for a colleague, wondering who Care4You will send. When she sees Maria's car drawing up, she's relieved. Maria is efficient and reliable. She's not the friendliest of the carers but some of the others are *way* too friendly, yacking on about their kids and their pets and their unreliable husbands. Maria's not a chatterer. Natalka knows that Maria is married with children but she doesn't talk about them unless she's asked directly. She's professional. Natalka thinks she'd be perfect for Harbinder's mother.

She tells Maria about the possible job as they climb the stairs to Harriet's flat. The Hartingtons live in Harbour Mansions, which used to have a sea view until Seaview Court was built. Now it looks out onto the back of the other building. It's quite the wrong place for an elderly couple with mobility problems but neither Harriet nor her husband, Douglas, complain about it, or about anything really. Douglas always greets them with tea and a KitKat. He's a small, frail man, unable to lift his wife on her own. He frets about this and about young girls like Natalka and Maria having to do such heavy work. Maria, in her turn, worries about Douglas's blood sugar level. He seems to have an endless supply of chocolate bars in a Charles and Diana Wedding Day tin. Natalka just eats the KitKats.

'How are you, Harriet?' says Natalka, entering the sitting room which is now dominated by a hospital bed. The room smells, as all the clients' rooms tend to do, of air freshener, urine and pre-cooked meals.

'Mustn't complain,' says Harriet. And, in her case, she really means it. 'Tell me about your day.' Harriet hasn't left the flat for five years and is always hungry to hear their news. Natalka wishes that she could tell her about Dex Challoner and a real murder case involving schoolgirl assassins and mysterious clues hidden in books. But she thinks that the excitement might kill the old lady.

'I went out for a drink with some friends last night,' she offers.

'With Benedict?' says Harriet. Natalka must have mentioned Benedict once and now Harriet and Douglas both seem obsessed with him. 'Pretty girl like you should have a boyfriend,' is what Harriet says.

'He was there,' says Natalka. 'And some other friends too. In Chichester.'

'We went to Chichester once,' says Harriet. 'We had fish and chips.'

Natalka and Maria use the winch to raise Harriet and give her a blanket bath. Then they slide the bedpan in (Douglas leaves the room at this point), change the sheets and lower Harriet into a more comfortable position. They have an hour, which isn't really long enough, but it's the time allotted by the local authority. Afterwards, they stay for a few minutes, chatting. This is strictly forbidden by Patricia but it's clearly Douglas's favourite part of the day. He brings in more chocolate and they sit around Harriet's bed, talking about *Coronation Street*, although neither Natalka nor Maria watches the soap opera. Natalka doesn't own a television and resists her host family's attempts to get her to join them in front of their set. Maria has three young children and no time for such frivolities.

'This is going to break Michelle's heart,' says Natalka, when Harriet recounts the latest Weatherfield scandal. She's never watched it but she knows the characters by now.

'No, she's tough,' says Harriet, biting a Mars bar in two.

Then it's time to go. They fill in the book, 'Washed, toileted, made bed. Meds given. All OK', and descend the stairs. At the door, they pause to check their phones. Both have several other evening calls to make.

'Will you call Harbinder?' says Natalka.

'Yes,' says Maria. 'I need the money.' All the carers struggle for money. They are paid the minimum wage and, even working extra hours, it's not enough to feed a family of five.

'She's a nice woman,' says Natalka. 'I'm sure the family is nice too.'

'I just need the money,' Maria repeats. She fiddles with her phone for a few seconds and then says, 'Did you see that Dex Challoner has died?'

'Yes,' says Natalka. 'It was on Twitter.'

'You know I used to look after his mum, Weronika?'

'Yes?' says Natalka, all her senses on alert.

'She was a funny woman but we got on well. We used to talk in Polish together. But Peggy said something odd about her once.'

'What?'

'It was after Weronika had died. I was saying how sad it was but Peggy said that she thought her death was suspicious. She wouldn't tell me any more. She said it was only a suspicion and she couldn't say more until she had proof. When I asked again she said the answer was in a book.'

'Which book?' asks Natalka, so urgently that Maria takes a step backwards.

'One of the old ones,' says Maria. 'I can't remember the title but I think it had two people cuddling on the cover.'

'*Thank Heaven Fasting*?'

'That was the one. It didn't have much about heaven in it, from what I could see.'

Natalka has four other clients to see. Once she's put the last one to bed she parks her car outside the Harpers' house, keeping a lookout for white Fiestas, and walks to the pub. It's a real drinkers' bar, dominated by a TV showing the snooker. Harbinder is already there, drinking a glass of red wine and reading a book. She puts it away when she sees Natalka.

'Do you want a drink?' says Natalka.

'I've got one, thanks.'

Natalka gets herself a large red and sits beside Harbinder on the slightly sticky bench seat. The policewoman has nice eyes, she notices, slightly shadowed as if she doesn't get enough sleep.

'How's your mum?' she says.

'She never complains,' says Harbinder, 'but I think she's in a lot of pain sometimes. And it means she can't do as much as usual so that's extra work for me. At least I don't have to walk the bloody dog. Dad does that.'

'What about your brothers? Do they help?'

'No, they're both selfish bastards.' Harbinder takes a swig of wine. 'Maybe that's unfair. They're both married with their own families. Kush works in the shop and Abhey's pretty busy being an electrician. It's just that they both think all the domestic stuff — cooking, cleaning and all that crap — is down to Mum or me. And I'm not good at that kind of thing. I'm good at being a detective.'

'I spoke to Maria just now,' says Natalka. 'She says that she'll help you. I'm not good at domestic things either. My brother was always better at cooking than me.'

'I didn't know you had a brother.'

'He's dead.' It seems easier than explaining.

'I'm sorry.'

'That's OK. It's all water under the bridge now.'

'You speak wonderful English,' says Harbinder. 'Did you learn it at school?'

'Yes,' says Natalka. 'We all had to learn English but I actually went to university here. At Bournemouth.'

'Bournemouth,' says Harbinder. 'I went there once. Sandy beaches.'

'It's a lovely place,' says Natalka. 'I enjoyed my three years there. I liked my fellow students too. So much that I married one of them.' She laughs at Harbinder's shocked expression.

'You're married?' Harbinder is jolted out of her low-pitched detective's voice. She almost sounds like a teenage girl, like Natalka's long-lost friends Dasha and Anastasia.

'It was really just so that I could get a British passport,' says Natalka. 'Have you ever been married?'

Harbinder laughs again. 'No. I'm gay.'

'But you can still get married, can't you? In Britain anyway.'

'There's the slight problem of finding someone to marry first,' says Harbinder.

'But there are dating agencies, aren't there? Online groups. Apps.' Natalka's fingers are itching for her phone. She has always enjoyed matchmaking.

'Don't worry about me,' says Harbinder. 'I thought you had something to tell me.'

'Yes,' says Natalka. 'But I might need another drink for that. But I've got something else to tell you first. Maria said something strange just now. Apparently Peggy said she thought Weronika's death was suspicious. You know, Dex's mother. She wouldn't say any more but she said the answer was in a book. The one that the gunman took.'

'*Thank Heaven Fasting*?'

'That's the one. Do you know anyone who's read it?'

'No,' says Harbinder, 'Benedict said it was out of print.'

'Do you like reading crime novels?'

'Sometimes. Horror's more my thing though.' She indicates her paperback which has a large, bloody-fanged rat on it. 'Especially when I'm stressed.'

'Benny said that he'd try to track down a copy,' says Natalka. 'He reads all the time. It's because he used to be a monk. Nothing to do except read and pray.'

'Benedict used to be a monk?'

'Yes. Didn't you know? He gave it up a couple of years ago, moved to Shoreham and bought the Shack. His family is quite rich, I think.'

'I can imagine him in a monastery,' says Harbinder. 'He does seem a bit like he's from another world.'

'He knows a lot about murder though,' says Natalka. 'It comes of reading all those crime novels and watching old TV shows.' She drains her glass of wine. 'Another?' she says.

'I shouldn't,' says Harbinder. Then, after what looks like a brief internal struggle, 'Oh, OK then. A small glass of red. Thank you.'

Natalka gets them both large glasses. When she comes back to the table, Harbinder looks at her expectantly. 'Now what did you want to tell me? Was it about the men who are watching you? The ones in the car?'

'Did you trace the number plate?'

'I've put our Intel team onto it.'

Natalka knows that Harbinder is watching her, waiting. She senses that Harbinder would be a hard person to fool. DS Kaur might live at home with her parents but she has a toughness about her that Natalka respects. After all, she's been dealing with a murder enquiry all day and she relaxes by reading about killer rats.

'Back in Ukraine,' says Natalka at last, 'before I came to England, I was studying maths at university in Kiev. I was good at algorithms and coding and I was short of money. So I got involved with something . . .'

She stops, wondering how much to say. Eventually Harbinder prompts her, 'What did you get involved with?'

'A cryptocurrency,' says Natalka. 'Like Bitcoin. I set it up with two friends. It wasn't illegal and we made lots of money at first. But then war was coming and I wanted to get out. So I took the money and I escaped to England.'

'You took the money?'

'Only a bit of it,' says Natalka. 'About ten per cent. All I needed to get to university in England. I had the authentication codes, you see, and API tokens.' She can tell Harbinder doesn't understand. 'It's hacking, really. I suppose you could arrest me for it.'

'I suppose I could but I can't see my boss wanting to get involved with cryptocurrency fraud in another country. Tell me about the two friends. Are they the people you think are watching you?'

'No,' says Natalka. 'There were others involved. Bad people. Like the mafia. That's what war does. It helps bad people make more money. Well, some of them were involved in our cryptocurrency. I think they've followed me to England.'

Harbinder looks a bit bemused but at least she doesn't seem incredulous. 'Why would they wait so long?' she says. 'You've been in England a long time. You went to university. You got married.' She does sound as if she finds this hard to believe.

'I don't know,' says Natalka. 'But Peggy said she saw two men waiting outside her house. Then I saw them outside my lodgings. It can't be a coincidence.'

'Do you think they could have been involved with Peggy's death? With Dex?'

'I don't know, but the way Dex was killed . . . You said he was shot in the head. That sounded professional. It sounds like them.'

'Do you have any names?'

'No,' says Natalka. 'You don't know the names of these people.'

This is true. The people who had invested in their company went by aliases, joke names, none the less sinister for being ridiculous. And, even if Natalka did know their real names, would she give them to DS Kaur? She seems sympathetic but presumably she has a boss who might start asking awkward questions. And speaking of questions, maybe she should ask a few of her own.

'Who do you think killed Dex?' she says. 'Have you got any leads?'

'You know I can't tell you that.'

'I was the one who came to you about Peggy. I was the one who gave you this case.'

Harbinder laughs. 'You make it sound as if I should be grateful to you.' She pauses, looking at her wine with half-closed eyes. 'One thing I suppose I could tell you. I got a call from Julie Monroe, J.D. Monroe. She's one of the authors who credits Peggy in her acknowledgements.'

'I remember,' says Natalka. '"PS: for PS."'

'That's right. Well, Julie received an unsigned postcard. On it were the words, "We are coming for you".'

'My God,' says Natalka. 'She's the next victim.'

'I hope not,' says Harbinder. 'But I should talk to her. The only problem is that she's going to a literary festival in Aberdeen tomorrow.'

'Are you going to go to Aberdeen to question her?' says Natalka.

'I'd love to,' says Harbinder. 'I went to Scotland last year and it was beautiful. But I've got too much work to do here.'

'Aberdeen *is* a long way away,' says Natalka.

She's wondering if it's too far for the white Ford Fiesta.

Chapter 15

Benedict: two candles

'We can't go to Aberdeen,' says Benedict.

'Why not?' says Natalka.

'We can't just go charging round the country interviewing suspects. Besides, it's miles away.'

'I think it would be fun,' says Edwin.

Benedict and Natalka exchange glances. Benedict knows that it hadn't occurred to either of them that Edwin would want to come too. Edwin is only with them because he suddenly decided to go to mass that morning, to light a candle for Peggy. Benedict met him at Seaview Court and they walked to church together. It had been a surprise to find Natalka waiting for them outside afterwards.

Benedict has been attending this church since moving to Shoreham two years ago. It's one of the things he likes about Catholics. He's been going every Sunday and, although the elderly Irish priest always smiles and says hallo, no one has tried to get him involved with parish life. His friend, Richard, a priest who was once a protestant vicar, says that, in the C of E, they have you arranging flowers and volunteering for Sunday School before you can say 'amen'. Benedict knows that, if he went for coffee in the parish hall after mass, people would be friendly to him and someone would definitely try to sell him tickets for the Catholaity bazaar, but the parishioners seem to understand that he wants to be left on his own. It's funny, Benedict is not normally a fan of his own company, but he has always liked hearing mass on his own. Even when he was a teenager, he used to sneak away to the Saturday evening service the way some of his contemporaries blagged their way into bars and nightclubs. When his mother found out about his mass habit, she threatened to take him to a psychiatrist.

It was very different going to church with Edwin. For a start, Edwin was tired after the walk and needed to sit down on a bench outside for five minutes. Several well-meaning people came up to them, asking if they were all right and offering helping arms. Then, when they finally got inside, Edwin wanted to sit at the front so he could hear. Benedict's usual seat is in the back row, near the exit and the holy water stoup. It felt much more public at the business end of the church. The two nuns in front of them turned round and said hallo. A family sat behind them and Benedict found himself returning dropped toys and children's missals. By the time the bell rang, he was on smiling terms with the whole family. Edwin and Sister Lucrezia were getting on famously.

After mass, they lit two candles for Peggy. Benedict put a pound coin in the slot marked 'offerings' and tried to say a prayer. 'Eternal rest give unto her, Oh Lord, and let perpetual light shine upon her . . .' But Peggy herself kept coming between him and the words: her dauntless gaiety, her double espresso with hot milk on the side, her pink beret, her way of saying his name with an Italianate emphasis on the first syllable. What would she be saying if she could see them now? 'Religion is the opium of the people', probably. But she would have been pleased that they were thinking about her. Next to him, Edwin's eyes are shut and his lips are moving.

Benedict said a prayer for Dex too. He remembered the confident, basso-profundo voice saying, 'Bye, Ben. See you around.' *No one knows the day or the hour, not even the angels in heaven or the Son himself.* He was glad, in a way, that Dex didn't know, that he had a convivial evening in the pub and then went home, expecting a peaceful night and another morning. But, if he had known, maybe he could have protected himself. Don't the Scriptures also tell you to 'stay awake' and 'be ready'?

'Shall we go?' said Edwin.

In the porch, Father Brendan came towards them, hell-bent on friendliness.

'Is this your father?' he said, shaking Edwin's hand.

'No, just a friend,' said Benedict.

'Sure, and friendship is very precious.'

It was at this moment that Benedict spotted Natalka, sitting on the wall and vaping furiously. She's trying to give up smoking.

They walked back together, stopping to look at the sea and for Edwin to get his breath back. It was a lovely morning and the promenade was busy: families with pushchairs, children on roller skates, elderly couples wrapped up against the autumn chill, a variety of dogs accompanied by a variety of owners. Benedict would like a dog but pets aren't allowed in his digs. Edwin watched the scene with a smile that was at once sweet and slightly sad. This was when Natalka suggested the Aberdeen trip.

'What about work?' says Benedict.

'I'm on a zero hours contract,' says Natalka. 'I can take time off.'

'What about me?'

'You can shut the Shack.'

'I never shut it.'

'It's shut today, isn't it?'

Benedict has no answer for this. He knows that he's almost alone in believing that Sunday is a day of rest.

'It's a long drive,' says Edwin, 'but we could stop for the night in Northumberland. I love the border country.'

'I don't mind,' says Natalka. 'I like driving.'

'Did you tell Harbinder that you were planning to see Julie Monroe?' asks Benedict. He is worried by how quickly Edwin is turning this into a road trip.

'We talked about it,' says Natalka evasively. 'She wanted to go herself but she's too busy with the Dex Challoner case.'

'Did you tell her what Maria said about Dex's mother?'

'Yes,' says Natalka. 'She thought it was an important clue. We both agreed that you should read the book and find out what it meant.'

'Thanks a lot,' says Benedict. He imagines the two women laughing about him, bookish ex-monk Benedict. For a moment, he surprises himself with a desire to impress them both with some reckless, mindless act of bravery. The trouble is he can't even imagine what this might be . . .

'You'll have to take regular breaks, Natalka.' Edwin is still thinking about the drive. 'We must stop at service stations. They even do quite good coffee these days.'

'I could share the driving,' says Benedict, although he hasn't driven in years. But it's his way of accepting the inevitable.

★

Benedict hopes that they might all have lunch together but, invigorated by the sea air, Edwin goes back to Seaview Court to research routes to Aberdeen (he is proud of his prowess as a silver surfer, even though he does refer to it as 'the interweb'). Natalka accompanies Benedict as far as the high street but then slouches away to meet unspecified 'friends'. Benedict goes to a café where he tries to eat a mushroom risotto mindfully. Even taking twenty seconds a bite, it's only one thirty by the time that he's finished. He walks slowly back to his digs, looking in the shops on the way. Most of them, unlike the Shack, are still open. He wanders into one of the many charity shops to look for a book. He's irritated to see that the books are artfully arranged by the colours of their jackets. Books should be arranged by size or author or genre, not just because the woman on the front is wearing a red dress. Then he looks closer. One red book has black lettering on the spine and he sees the word 'heaven' (he thinks that he has a particular antenna for cosmological language). *Thank Heaven Fasting* by Sheila Atkins.

Back in his room, he makes himself a coffee, sits at the desk by the window and opens a notebook. He's going to read this book in a methodical, Peggy-like way. Even so, he imagines his father saying, 'That's no way for an adult man to spend a Sunday.' His father had always disapproved of reading for its own sake, rather than as a means towards passing exams. Benedict's older brother, Hugo, did very well in exams (better than Benedict) but afterwards never opened a book in public. What is Hugo doing now? Probably playing rugby for the over thirties, before going home to roast beef with all the trimmings. 'Celia always does a proper Sunday lunch,' Benedict's mother said once, approvingly, and Benedict doesn't expect that his sister-in-law has let the fact that she gave birth to a son four months ago affect her domestic goddess status.

Thank Heaven Fasting is a strange book. It's about a woman called Adrienne who takes a job as a companion to a wheelchair-bound aristocrat in the South of France. There are some rather wonderful descriptions of the Riviera which make Benedict nostalgic for holidays that he has never had. The aristocrat, Lady Fitzroy (we never learn her first name), seems determined to make Adrienne marry her dissolute nephew, Giles. Adrienne, though reluctant, does so only to find Giles murdered and herself the main suspect. Benedict speed reads the next bit to find the twist in the tale. Lady Fitzroy and Adrienne planned it together so that Adrienne would inherit Giles' money and Lady Fitzroy would be free of her detested relative (it's never quite explained why she hates him so much). Lady Fitzroy was the killer, exploiting the fact – known only to Adrienne – that she was actually perfectly able to walk. The book ends with Adrienne emigrating to America and Lady Fitzroy walking to the beach where she is either going to swim or drown herself.

It's dark by the time that he has finished and the lighthouse beam is beginning its slow sweep across the harbour. Benedict looks down at his notes to see that he has only written 'France?'. There must be more to it than that. Why was this book so important that it was stolen at gunpoint? Why was Peggy's clue about Weronika to be found in its pages? Benedict tries to organise his thoughts, to approach things logically. On one level, the book is about the difficulties encountered by single women in the nineteen thirties. Benedict supposes this is where the title quotation comes in. In *As You Like It* Rosalind (disguised as a man) tells Phoebe the shepherdess to be grateful for Silvius's love: 'down on your knees,

And thank heaven, fasting, for a good man's love.' Giles isn't a good man but Adrienne is meant to be eternally grateful for the chance to marry him. Marriage and, soon afterwards, widowhood, gives Adrienne the status she craves. Lady Fitzroy is also a rich widow but, as an elderly woman on her own, she too is trapped. Benedict supposes that this is symbolised by the wheelchair. Both women achieve their freedom by murdering a man. On another level, it's a murder mystery with a thoroughly modern unreliable narrator. Sheila Atkins breaks several of the laws of crime writing, though, including having the narrator conceal things from the reader. As a Who Done It, the book is a failure. As a psychological thriller, it is slightly more interesting.

It really is an unusual book, thinks Benedict; even more extraordinary for having been published in 1938. What is the message? Is Peggy Lady Fitzroy? Is Dex Giles? But then who is Adrienne? He opens his laptop and googles Sheila Atkins. Sheila May Atkins, born 7 April 1912, died 10 October 2012. Goodness, she'd been a hundred when she died. There are very few biographical notes on Wikipedia. Born in Guildford, Surrey, the author of ten crime novels. The titles are listed below:

'Give Me the Daggers 1935
The Eye of Childhood 1936
A Painted Devil 1937
Thank Heaven Fasting 1938
Where Is Thy Lustre Now? 1950
The Prince of Darkness is a Gentleman 1952
Pale Hecate's Offerings 1955
A Burnished Throne 1960
Sea Change 1970

Rounded with a Sleep 1972'

All the books are now out of print but some of the covers are reproduced, garish images that Benedict is sure do not reflect the stories inside. The cover of *Thank Heaven Fasting* shows a blonde in a red evening dress (Adrienne is described as dark) embracing a moustachioed gallant in a dinner jacket. As far as Benedict remembers, there had been no such embrace in the book. Giles' proposal had been sealed by a 'chilly kiss on the cheek'. Is there a clue in the titles, in the first words or first letters? Benedict scribbles for a few minutes but the best he can come up with is *Give me the eye of a painted devil*. Peggy was the one who liked crosswords, anagrams and word puzzles. She would have solved it in minutes but, of course, if she were there she could just tell him the answer straight out. 'Oh, Peggy,' he says aloud, 'why did you have to be so clever?'

Sheila had started young, her first book published when she was only twenty-three. Then there had been several books, one a year for a while, and then a gap for the war years. Three books in the fifties, one in the sixties, then two in the seventies. Nothing else. Sheila Atkins had lived another thirty-odd years but had never written – or never published – another book. Is there a significance in the last two titles? Do they signify a change of some kind? They are both from *The Tempest*, Shakespeare's last play, and the final one is from Prospero's epilogue, often thought to be Shakespeare's farewell to the stage.

> *Our revels now are ended. These our actors,*
> *As I foretold you, were all spirits and*
> *Are melted into air, into thin air:*
> *And, like the baseless fabric of this vision,*

The cloud-capp'd tow'rs, the gorgeous palaces,
The solemn temples, the great globe itself,
Yea, all which it inherit, shall dissolve
And, like this insubstantial pageant faded,
Leave not a rack behind. We are such stuff
As dreams are made on, and our little life
Is rounded with a sleep.

It really is beautiful, thinks Benedict. Perhaps he should have studied English literature, as his teachers had wanted, rather than going into the priesthood. He had good enough grades, he could have gone to university. Maybe he still could? But now is not the time for thinking about Shakespeare's lyricism, now is the time for catching a murderer. He can't deny a twinge of excitement at the idea that he, the former Brother Benedict, could even be having such an internal conversation.

Could Peggy have known Sheila Atkins? It's possible although Sheila was at least twenty-five years older. Had they known each other during Peggy's time in the civil service? But there's no career history for Sheila. No husband or children either. Doesn't mean she didn't have them, of course.

Benedict googles 'Peggy Smith'. Once he has discounted *Peggy Sue Got Married* and several Peggy Lee clips, there are only a few Peggys left, mostly of a certain age. His own Peggy is not there. She's that rare creature, a person without a social media footprint. There's only one photograph, a blurry picture of a group of women around a table. 'Seaview Court Christmas Lunch 2008' reads the caption and it's been posted on the Seaview Court Facebook page. The page seems to have been dormant since 2009 and there are no more photographs. Benedict peers at the image of Peggy, who is wearing a pink paper hat. Next to her is another grey-haired woman who clearly has no truck with festive headgear. Is that Weronika? Benedict could imagine her being a resistance fighter.

He googles Weronika Challoner and the same picture pops up. There's nothing else apart from the fact that Weronika once addressed the Lancing WI on 'Life in Wartime Poland'. Benedict assumes that she missed out the part about being a schoolgirl assassin although, remembering his mother's stories of the WI, maybe not. Had Weronika and Peggy known Sheila Atkins? Why did Peggy say that she knew someone who would be glad that Weronika was dead? What was the clue hidden in these strange, out-of-print books?

He gives up and starts searching for cheap hotels in Aberdeen.

Chapter 16

Harbinder: TBR

'It's not what I was expecting,' says Neil.

'What were you expecting?' asks Harbinder. 'Solid gold books? People in togas declaiming poetry at you?'

'No,' says Neil, with dignity. 'I just thought that a publishing company would be more . . . well, bookish. More like a library.'

'When did you last go to a library?' says Harbinder. 'They're information hubs these days.' But she thinks she knows what Neil means. Seventh Seal was a small publisher that was bought by a much larger conglomerate, and now functions as an imprint within that company. Their offices are faceless and corporate. They wait in reception surrounded by low sofas and cases which display books behind glass as if they are dangerous reptiles. Neil is nervous, jiggling his leg and fiddling with his phone. To get away from him, Harbinder goes to look at the books. 'New Releases' says the sign. *High Rise Murder* is there. Will they take it down? she wonders. Maybe they'll drape it with black cloth like they do in churches. Then she sees the book beside it.

'Neil!'

'What is it?'

He lumbers over, more like a bear than a woodland animal.

She points at the book, which is displayed face outwards. *It Was You* by J. D. Monroe. It's the same loopy writing, the same vaguely Tuscan scene on the cover.

'J. D. Monroe,' says Harbinder. 'Julie Monroe. She got one of the threatening postcards too.'

'Excuse me,' says a soft voice. 'I'm Tamsin, Miles's assistant. Would you come with me, please?'

They pass through security gates that wouldn't be out of place in an airport and whoosh upwards in a glass lift. Then Tamsin uses her lanyard to let them into an open-plan office full of people staring at their computer screens. It could be a larger version of the West Sussex CID rooms. Tamsin ushers them into a glass-walled meeting room where a bespectacled man is waiting for them.

Miles stands up to shake hands and Tamsin offers drinks. Harbinder and Neil both ask for coffee and Miles for herbal tea. Harbinder notices that Neil is too intimidated to ask for his usual two sugars.

Miles Taylor is one of those perpetual schoolboys with floppy blond hair but is probably in his early thirties. His voice is posh enough to set Harbinder's teeth on edge but he does seem genuinely upset when he says, 'This is such an awful thing. We're all shattered.' Harbinder thinks of the silently typing figures. It doesn't seem like a place that's been touched by tragedy but she supposes that life must go on. Reading books, correcting spelling mistakes, whatever they do in publishing companies.

'Thank you for seeing us,' says Harbinder. 'I know it must be a difficult time for you. Were you close to Dex?'

'In a way,' says Miles, pushing his hair back. 'I hadn't been his editor that long. I was a fan though. It was partly why I came to Seventh Seal, to work with Dex.'

'Who was his editor before you?'

'Betty Champion. She was a legend in publishing, a great character. She was with Dex from the beginning. He wrote stand-alones at first. It was Betty who had the idea for the Tod France series and the rest is history. She and Dex were very close.'

'Is Betty still around?'

'No, sadly she died a few years ago. A real shock to everyone. I was Betty's assistant and I was promoted to work on the last three books.'

'Did you get on well with Dex?' asks Harbinder.

'Yes, very well. Dex was easy to work with. He never missed a deadline and he actually seemed to enjoy being edited. Unlike some writers.' He smiles but Harbinder is not sure what 'being edited' means. She's not sure that she likes the sound of it.

'When did you last see Dex?' asks Neil.

'He came into the offices last week to celebrate *High Rise Murder* going to number one. He seemed in fine form.'

'Did Dex ever mention the name Peggy Smith to you?'

'The old lady who used to help with the books?'

'Yes. Did you ever meet her?'

'Just once. Dex took me to meet her, we had coffee at a nice little place on the seafront. She was a great character.'

'Was that the only time you met her?'

'Yes, but we used to correspond. I sent her postcards and proof copies of books I thought she'd like.'

'Was this from you?' Harbinder shows him a photograph of the card she found in Peggy's desk.

'Yes,' says Miles. 'Peggy was a great admirer of George Orwell.'

'On the back it says, "For Peggy, Love and thanks always. M."'

'Well, I was grateful to her.' Is it Harbinder's imagination or does Miles sound slightly defensive? 'She was a great support to Dex.'

'Did Peggy write to you?' The letters in the desk are all from someone called 'Joan'. The writing is tiny and almost indecipherable. Harbinder has sent them to a handwriting expert.

'Sometimes,' says Miles. 'She used to recommend crime novels that I might not have read. Golden-age classics, mostly.'

Golden age. That rings a bell. Dex's voice, 'I don't read much golden-age stuff.'

'Did Peggy ever recommend books by Sheila Atkins?' asks Harbinder.

Now Miles does look surprised. He rubs his head again. 'Yes. How did you know? One of Peggy's last letters mentioned Sheila Atkins.'

'Was it a book called *Thank Heaven Fasting*?'

'Yes.' Miles's hair is standing up in a crest now. 'I think it was.'

'Was it a letter or an email from Peggy?'

'A letter. She was old-fashioned like that.' Harbinder, remembering the desk with its neat cubbyholes, can believe this.

'Do you still have the letter? she asks.

'No, I'm afraid not. I recycle everything.'

'Can you remember what was in it?'

'Just the usual, asking how I was and so forth. Then she asked if I'd read that book. *Thank Heaven Fasting*.'

'And had you?'

'No. I'm afraid not. People always expect editors to have read everything but I'm frightfully ignorant in some ways. Peggy was definitely better read than me.'

Miles says that he is 'frightfully ignorant' in a way only utilised by people who actually think that they are very clever. Harbinder doesn't want to tell him about the significance of the Atkins book just yet. She tries to signal this silently to Neil who nods and changes the subject.

'Peggy was a friend of Dex's mother,' he says. 'Did you ever meet her?'

'No,' says Miles. 'She died before my time. Sadly.'

'Apparently Peggy used to help Dex comes up with murders,' says Neil. 'Does that make sense to you?'

Miles smiles. 'He did once say that it's hard to find new ways of killing people.'

Once again, Harbinder thinks of the handwritten note. *Do help me, darling. I've got to give Miles the rough draft next week.* Had Dex tried to conceal the extent of Peggy's involvement from his editor?

'Peggy died recently,' says Harbinder. 'It's possible that there's a link with Dex's death.'

The smile vanishes. 'Oh my God,' says Miles. His hand shakes as he drinks his herbal tea.

Harbinder presses on. 'Do you know if Dex ever received any threatening messages?' she says. 'Any emails from fans that seemed a bit odd?'

'His personal assistant would know more about that,' says Miles. 'But, as far as I know, Dex's fans loved him. There's going to be real sadness in the book community.'

Miles says 'the book community' as if it's an actual place. Is there really a world where people care so much about books that they write to the authors and consider them friends? Harbinder thinks about the audience in Chichester on Friday, the expressions on people's faces when they queued up for Dex's signature. Those readers will definitely be sad today.

'Do you edit J. D. Monroe's books?' asks Harbinder.

'Julie?' Miles seems to brighten. 'Yes, she's a real sweetie. She had a huge hit with her first one, *You Made Me Do it*.'

'What about the others? Aren't they as successful?'

Miles looks slightly uncomfortable. 'Sometimes, when a writer's had a huge hit with their debut, it's hard to recreate the same success with the others.'

'J. D. Monroe also seems to have known Peggy Smith,' says Harbinder. 'She credits her in the acknowledgements. "PS: for PS".'

'Really?' says Miles. 'I suppose Dex must have introduced them.'

'Do you know what help Peggy gave J. D. Monroe?'

'I imagine it was a similar thing. Coming up with ideas for murders.' Miles laughs, then looks guilty. 'Julie's a lovely lady. I can imagine that she wouldn't find it easy to kill off her characters.'

'What about Lance Foster?' says Neil. 'Is he one of your authors?'

Now Miles does look surprised. He rears back in his chair.

'Lance? He used to be published by Cassowary but they were bought out by Seventh Seal. Then Seventh Seal were bought out too. That's what publishing is like sometimes, big fish eating smaller fish only to be swallowed by a whale.'

Miles smiles to show this is a joke but Harbinder wonders where he comes in the feeding chain. Is he a small fish in a big pool?

'So, did you ever work with Lance Foster?' she asks.

'No,' says Miles. 'He's technically one of my authors but I've never worked with him. He's only written one book.'

Harbinder looks at her notes. '*Laocoön*.' She's not quite sure how to pronounce it.

'Yes. It's very literary, not to everyone's taste, but it was very well reviewed, longlisted for the Booker.' Miles brings his chair back with a thump. 'Did Lance know Peggy too?'

'Well, he credits her in the book. Something in Latin.'

'That sounds like Lance.' Something tells Harbinder that Lance, unlike Julie, is not a real sweetie.

'Thank you,' says Harbinder. 'Could we speak to Dex's publicist now?'

Pippa Sinclair-Lewis is a surprise. From her name, Harbinder imagined a twenty-something beauty with swishy hair and a trust account. But Pippa seems to be in her mid-sixties, with grey, close-cropped hair and sensible shoes. She sits opposite them and gives them a no-nonsense look behind gold-rimmed spectacles that don't entirely hide red-rimmed eyes.

'I worked with Dex for fifteen years,' she says, 'so this is a bit of a shock.'

'I'm so sorry,' says Harbinder. 'This must be very difficult for you.'

'People are saying that he was murdered,' says Pippa. 'Is that true?'

'There are suspicious circumstances,' says Harbinder. 'That's all we can say.' A bullet to the head, she thinks. Suspicious in anyone's book. Especially one written by Dex Challoner.

Harbinder asks about the Chichester event and Penny says that it was part of a publicity tour to promote the new book. 'It's not a particularly big venue but it was near to home and Dex wanted to do it. He's a very good speaker. I mean, he *was* . . . God, I just can't get my head around it.'

'I was there,' says Harbinder. 'He was very good. Very interesting.'

'You were there?' says Pippa, rather rudely surprised. 'Why?'

'I live nearby,' says Harbinder. 'And I like crime novels.' Well, she likes horror, which is almost the same thing.

'Have you read any of Dex's books?' asks Pippa.

'No,' says Harbinder. 'But I'd like to.'

'I'll send you the first one in the post,' says Pippa. This seems very generous until the publicist spoils it by adding, 'We've just done a reprint with the new cover and we've got too many copies hanging round.'

'I talked to Dex a few days ago,' says Harbinder. 'We were investigating another suspicious death, someone Dex knew quite well. Have you ever heard of a woman called Peggy Smith?'

She expects Pippa to shake her head impatiently but, instead, the publicist smiles, changing her face completely. 'The murder consultant? Yes, I knew about her. I even met her once. I went down to Shoreham to see Dex and we took Peggy and Weronika out to lunch. The stories they told!'

'Murder consultant? Is that how Dex introduced her?'

'Yes. It was a joke between them. Dex even had some business cards made up for Peggy. It was because she was so good at thinking of gruesome ways for characters to die.'

'Do you know why she was so good at that?'

'Dex said something about her being an ex-contract-killer but I assumed that was a joke. Weronika had a fairly colourful past too. She was in the Polish resistance when she was only a teenager. I imagine that she saw some terrible things.'

'Dex told me that his mother was called the schoolgirl assassin.'
Pippa looks at Harbinder oddly. 'When did he tell you that?'

'After the Chichester event. We went for a drink. '

'He didn't mention it to me. I always text him after an event, if
I can't be there in person.'

'Maybe he didn't think it was important,' says Neil, soothingly.
But it was important, thinks Harbinder. A few hours after the
conversation in the pub, Dex had been murdered.

'What'll happen now?' she asks, really wanting to know. 'Do
you work with lots of other authors?'

'Yes,' says Pippa. 'But Dex was my biggest author and, anyway,
it's about time I retired. I'm getting out of touch. There are all
these new young publicists and marketeers now, mad keen on
building social media profiles and the like. They've got a new
person here called Dakota who has all these crazy ideas for mail-
outs and publicity stunts. Nothing as simple as telling people
about the book.'

So Pippa Sinclair-Lewis's career ends with Dex's death, thinks
Harbinder. She wonders what it will mean for Dex's agent.

Jelli Walker-Thompson's office is in Covent Garden. Neil says that
it's only a few stops away on the Tube but Harbinder suggests that
they walk. 'The carbon monoxide fumes will probably kill us,' says
Neil, but he agrees fairly readily. And it is a pleasant walk, along the
Embankment then across the Strand and up towards Covent Garden.
The river is sparkling and there are still tables outside cafés and
restaurants. There are many more homeless people than Harbinder
remembers though. This is a problem even in Shoreham. Harbinder
always tries to direct people towards hostels but she knows that there

are many reasons why rough sleepers can't use them; you need ID, for one thing. It feels wrong to walk past mattresses and carboard boxes that constitute people's homes. Neil doesn't seem to notice. He's probably concentrating on his daily step count.

The agency is called Walker and Hutchance. It's above a solicitor's office and reached by a concealed door in an alleyway. Inside, there are enough books to satisfy Neil's library-loving soul: books on every table, piled three deep on the stairs. Books even constitute the coffee table in Jelli Walker-Thompson's office.

'It's my TBR pile,' she says.

'TBR?' says Neil.

'To be read. If I'm ever killed, my TBR pile will be the murder weapon. Sorry, that's in terrible taste. Bad news takes me that way sometimes.'

This is a surprise and so is Jelli Walker-Thompson. She's black, for one thing, and Harbinder has already noted that people of colour are rather thin on the ground in the publishing world. Jelli is also comparatively young to have her name in gold letters above a business in Covent Garden. She tells them that she didn't take 'the conventional route' into publishing.

'I was brought up in South London,' she says. 'Left school at sixteen. Worked as a shop assistant and care worker. Even joined the army for a while. Then I went to Cambridge as a mature student. They were keen to improve their diversity quota.'

'How long have you been Dex Challoner's agent?' asks Harbinder.

'Five years,' says Jelli. 'He was with Ernest May for many years but decided to change his representation.' Harbinder wonders if this means that Jelli somehow lured Dex away. How? she wonders.

'How did you get on with Dex?' asks Neil.

'He was a nice man,' says Jelli, as if daring them to disagree. 'And a dream client.'

'When did you last see him?' asks Harbinder.

'Last week. They gave a little reception for him at Seventh Seal. He seemed very happy.'

'He didn't tell you that anything was bothering him?' says Neil. 'No strange emails or messages?'

'No,' says Jelli. 'He seemed very chipper. *High Rise Murder* was at number one and he was planning a new project.'

'The next book in the series?'

'No, he'd already written that. *Murder in the Park*. No, this was a stand-alone.'

Harbinder asks about Peggy Smith and Jelli says immediately, 'Oh, yes, the old lady in the flats. Dex was fond of her, I think. She was a friend of his mother's. He was good to his mum.'

'Did he ever describe Peggy as a murder consultant?' says Harbinder.

She's not prepared for the effect of these words on the agent. Jelli has been fiddling with a roll of elastic bands on her desk. Now she drops it and it bounces slowly across the wooden floor.

'What did you say?'

'Did Dex ever call Peggy a murder consultant?' repeats Harbinder, raising her eyes at Neil.

'No,' says Jelli. Then, collecting herself with an obvious effort, 'It's just . . . that was the name of Dex's next book, the secret new project. It was going to be called *The Murder Consultant*.'

'Dex was writing a book called *The Murder Consultant*? What was it about?'

'I haven't read it but I think it was about an elderly lady who solves crimes. But it wasn't cosy, he said.'

'Cosy?'

'That's what people sometimes call crime novels that aren't all blood and gore. Old-fashioned books.'

'Like Sheila Atkins?'

Jelli gives her a look that could also be described as old-fashioned. 'Yes. Those golden-age writers are sometimes described as cosy. I wouldn't agree myself. Some of those authors are dark as hell. Even Agatha Christie.'

Dark as hell. It's a phrase that, in the circumstances, strikes Harbinder as singularly ill-chosen.

They don't discuss the case on the train home because they are surrounded on all sides by jaded-looking commuters. Neil gives up his seat to a woman with grey hair who looks even fitter than him. Harbinder keeps hers, though she dreads seeing someone genuinely in need, a pregnant woman, say, even one wearing an irritating 'Baby on board' badge. The two people opposite are reading the *Standard* and the headline is 'Bestselling Writer Found Dead'.

As the train lurches through south London, Harbinder thinks about Dex and his secret new project. Did someone kill him to prevent *The Murder Consultant* being written? Did the same person kill Peggy, and maybe Weronika Challoner as well? She gets out her phone and checks her messages. Does she dare have a quick game of Panda Pop? She glances at Neil but he has his headphones on and seems in another world. She'd never live it down if he saw her popping those bubbles. She checks that the sound is off but, as she does so, a text flashes up.

On our way to Aberdeen! Will keep you posted. Nx

Chapter 17

Edwin: the Miners' Arms

Edwin makes a flask of coffee and some sandwiches for the journey. He knows that they'll stop at service stations but you never know when you might need some caffeine and a ham sandwich. He's brought a bag of mint humbugs too. He waits by the front door, so that Natalka won't have to ring the bell. It's very early, still dark, but there's a freshness in the air, a sense of the town waking up. He can smell the sea and hear the waves hissing over the shingle. He shivers although he's wearing his winter coat and a tartan scarf in honour of Scotland. He spent some very pleasant summers at the Edinburgh festival when he was with the BBC.

He sees Natalka's headlights sweeping through the gates. She gets out to help him with his case, which is a neat wheelie thing from his frequent-flier days.

'You travel light,' says Natalka. 'I like that in a man.'

She has a way of saying things that charges the words with innuendo, which has its effect even if you are eighty and gay. Edwin laughs rather wildly.

'Shall I get in the back?' he says. 'Benedict should have the front seat. He's got longer legs.'

'No, sit in the front,' says Natalka. 'You can change over when we stop for a break. First come, first served.' There it is again.

Benedict is waiting by the power station, carrying a Gladstone bag and a large packet of Haribo Sours.

'I've got humbugs,' says Edwin, by way of greeting.

'Great,' says Benedict. 'I'm looking forward to this. We can play word games.'

'God give me strength,' says Natalka.

They play Who Am I?, which lasts until the M25. It's not a complete success. Benedict's choices are too obscure and religious (St Thérèse of Lisieux, Thomas Cranmer, Padre Pio), Edwin's too old-fashioned (Marlene Dietrich, James Mason, Jacqueline du Pré) and Natalka's too modern (Dua Lipa, Stormzy, Jameela Jamil). They stop at a café near Oxford for a late breakfast or early lunch. Natalka goes outside to vape, leaving Edwin and Benedict finishing their food. Benedict seems to be eating his wrap maddeningly slowly. Edwin tries to make his sandwich last but he has still finished a good five minutes before Benedict. Maybe he was taught to eat slowly in the monastery. To distract himself from Benedict's eating, Edwin says, 'Have you thought about what we'll do when we actually get to Aberdeen?'

They have booked a Travelodge in Aberdeen, although Edwin has found a more picturesque-sounding B&B in the North Pennines for tonight, slightly off their route but worth it, he thinks. Benedict has been in charge of researching the festival. Now he puts the printed-out pages of the brochure on the table. Edwin is glad that he's not having to look at them on a screen. He has printed out the route, although Natalka is using her iPhone to navigate. It makes Edwin feel nervous if he can't see where he's going, or where he's been.

Benedict swallows his last mouthful and takes a long drink of water before replying. 'J. D. Monroe is on a panel at four o'clock tomorrow,' he says. 'The subject is "Deadlier than the Male?". Apparently it's about whether women crime writers are more violent than men. There are two other writers on the panel. Susan Blake, who writes the DI Mike Malone books, and a YA author called Becki Finch who's written a book about a homicidal vampire called Trevor.'

'Goodness,' says Edwin, feeling rather overwhelmed. 'You've done your research.'

Benedict looks delighted with the compliment. Edwin supposes that he doesn't get many. 'I've bought us weekend passes so we can attend all the talks,' he says. 'And I've been looking through the authors attending the festival. There are a couple of others who mention Peggy in their acknowledgements. Lance Foster is one. He wrote a book called *Laocoön*. He's on a panel on Wednesday morning called "Is *Hamlet* a Crime Novel"?'

'Clearly not,' says Edwin. 'Considering it's a play.'

'I think it's probably making the point that lots of literary classics are about murder,' says Benedict.

'Of course *The Mousetrap* is from *Hamlet*,' says Edwin, remembering an amateur production in Richmond, with a rather interesting Mr Paravicini.

Outside, they find Natalka walking up and down between the parked cars.

'Would you recognise a Ford Fiesta?' she asks them.

'I'm afraid not,' says Edwin. 'All cars look the same to me.' This isn't quite true. He'd driven a Fiat 500 when he lived in Brighton and he still smiles at the thought of its snub-nosed little face.

'I would,' says Benedict unexpectedly. 'My dad used to quiz us on the makes of cars.'

'Well, look out for a white Ford Fiesta,' she tells them. 'It can be another travel game.'

'Why?' says Edwin. 'Was that the car that Peggy saw outside her house?'

'That's right,' says Natalka, getting out her car keys. 'Come on, let's hit the road.'

Now Edwin is in the back seat and he finds himself drifting off at times. One minute he's chatting about Dex Challoner and speculating on whether he was killed by an ex-lover, the next he's in a barge with François floating down the Seine and his mother appears dressed as Marie Antoinette . . .

He wakes up to hear Natalka saying that their route tomorrow will take them past Gretna Green.

'Shall we get married, Benny? Edwin can be our witness.'

Benedict laughs but Edwin thinks that he can detect something wistful in the sound. Could Benedict be sweet on Natalka? She's far too wild for him, of course, but stranger things have happened.

They stop at Tebay services, which are surprisingly picturesque, complete with a duck pond and farm shop. Edwin has a sudden longing for tea and cake. That's how I know I'm old, he thinks. Because sometimes it does take him by surprise. He sees a wizened old man in the mirror and wonders whether a geriatric burglar has broken in. His hands, with their veins and liver spots, appal him. He thought that his voice was still the same but, the other day, in the chemist, he heard a querulous bleat asking for Gaviscon tablets. Could that really be Edwin Fitzgerald, who was once described by the *Radio Times* as 'mellifluous'? Get a grip, Edwin, he tells himself. You're on a road trip with two young friends. You're spending the night in a B&B and then you're going to Scotland, one of your favourite places on earth. What's more, you're on the track of a dangerous criminal. You're a detective, almost a *crime fighter*. He sits up straighter.

Benedict brings him tea and a rather delicious-looking scone . He divides the scone into three. Natalka eats hers in one bite. Benedict does his irritating nibbling again. Edwin tries not to look. It's quite exhilarating, being annoyed by someone, especially a friend. It's been a long time since he's spent so much concentrated time with other people. And, apart from those two years with Nicky, he has never shared a house with anyone. It's about time he became less precious, he tells himself, dusting crumbs off his lap. All the same, he's glad that Benedict has finished eating.

The next part of the journey is the most exciting. They leave the motorway and pass through grey stone villages where children are leaving school for the day and yellow-coated crossing attendants put up imperious hands to stop the traffic. It's quite a shock to see people going about their ordinary lives and something about the children, clutching bookbags and projects made out of cardboard boxes, makes Edwin's eyes grow misty. He'd been at an all boys prep school. Very elitist and snobbish, no doubt, but also the happiest educational experience of his life. He's in the front seat again now, partly because he's meant to know the way to the B&B.

'It's near Rookhope,' he says, trying to sound like he knows what he's talking about.

'There's a W. H. Auden poem about Rookhope,' says Benedict from the back seat. Edwin has no doubt that he will soon remember the poem.

They leave the houses and abandoned factories behind them and start to drive through truly stunning scenery; moors purple with heather, rocky outcrops that look like hands pointing to heaven, sudden waterfalls, dry-stone walls. They climb higher and higher. Edwin's ears pop and he can hardly hear Natalka singing along to a swoony ballad on the radio. The wilder the countryside gets, the more exhilarated she seems.

They pass stone arches that seem to be rising out of the ground, as if they are the remnants of an underground city.

'It's the Rookhope chimney,' says Benedict. 'Apparently it used to carry poisonous gases from the lead smelting works higher up on the moors.'

'Poisonous gases,' repeats Edwin. Suddenly the stone archways seem menacing rather than picturesque. He thinks of underground lairs, of Smaug the dragon hiding his treasure, of travellers who disappear on lonely moorland and are never seen again.

'In one mile,' intones Natalka's phone, fixed to the windscreen, 'you will arrive at your destination.'

'There are no houses anywhere,' says Natalka. 'What's this place called again, Edwin?'

'The Miners' Arms,' says Edwin. He's starting not to believe in the B&B himself now. He'd booked it partly because he'd liked the name. He imagined burly arms, callused hands clenched around a pitchfork or a pint of beer. He's always liked forearms.

'In Rookhope,' says Benedict suddenly, in what Edwin recognises as his poetry voice.

'"*In Rookhope I was first aware*
Of Self and Not-self, Death and Dread . . .
There I dropped pebbles, listened, heard
The reservoir of darkness stirred . . ."'

'Very cheerful, Benny,' says Natalka. *The reservoir of darkness.* The words echo in Edwin's head, adding to the dizzy feeling. He thinks of the spaces beneath them. Old mining tunnels. Caverns measureless to man. Death and dread.

'I think this is it,' says Natalka.

There's nothing else it can be. A row of three cottages, facing the moors, with the hills behind them. As they get closer, Edwin sees the welcome words on a roadside sign, 'The Miners' Arms, Public House, B&B, Free wi-fi.'

'Cosy,' says Natalka.

They ring the doorbell and are met by a flame-haired woman wearing an orange minidress and black boots. The effect, in the dark hallway, is enough to make Edwin take a few steps backwards.

'Edwin Fitzgerald?' he says at last, making it a question the way the young people do. 'I booked some rooms online.'

'Oh, hallo.' The vision shakes his hand. 'I'm Jess. I run the place. Welcome to the North Pennines.'

'It's very beautiful,' says Edwin, stepping into what looks like an old-fashioned parlour. 'But you must feel quite isolated here.'

'I don't mind,' says Jess. 'I'm from Leeds originally. I like the quiet.' There's a laptop on the table and Jess scrolls with an expert finger. Her nail polish is also orange.

'Yes, here we are. Two rooms for E. Fitzgerald. A twin and a double.'

Edwin can feel himself going red, something that probably hasn't happened since he was a teenager.

'No,' he says. 'I booked three rooms.'

'I'm sorry,' says Jess. 'The website is a bit confusing. The twin room comes up as two. The trouble is, we're full tonight. We've only got four rooms and backpackers have taken the other two.'

Edwin turns to Natalka and Benedict.

'I'm so sorry.' This setback, coming just when he thought he'd reached the journey's end, suddenly seems like a disaster.

'Where are the backpackers from?' asks Natalka.

Jess looks at her in surprise. 'I didn't ask. They're usually from Holland or Germany.'

Natalka takes a turn around the room. The cheery ballad-singer has gone. She looks almost manic.

'I'll take the double,' she says. 'You and Benny can share the twin.'

Edwin can't work out if Benedict looks relieved or disappointed.

'What's up with Natalka?' Edwin says to Benedict when they are alone in their room. Thank goodness, it's large and comfortable, with two beds covered in patchwork quilts. Edwin lets Benedict take the one by the window. As he does so he has a clear flashback to choosing beds in the dormitory. That's the second time he's thought about boarding school today. Maybe this journey is taking him back in time, as well as northwards. Maybe, by the time they arrive in Scotland, he'll be a schoolboy again, all spots and buck teeth, carrying a clarinet case.

Benedict puts his Gladstone bag on the bed.

'She seems fine,' he says.

'She seems on edge to me,' says Edwin. 'All that stuff about spotting Ford Fiestas. And she practically bit that nice landlady's head off about the backpackers.'

'A bit tired from the journey, that's all,' says Benedict.

Edwin gives up. At least they won't have to resort to his battered packet of ham sandwiches because the pub does food in the evenings. He's tempted to lie on his bed for a rest but knows that, if he does so, he'll fall asleep in an instant. Benedict is clicking his way through the TV channels.

'Ooh,' he says, in a pleased voice, '*Murder, She Wrote.*'

Edwin settles down in an armchair to watch.

When he wakes, it's dark outside and someone is knocking on the door.

'Edwin! Benedict!' Natalka's voice sounds high and impatient. 'Wake up! I want supper.'

'Coming!' says Benedict. 'Just give us a minute'. Benedict gets off his bed and Edwin wonders if he's been dozing too. Edwin goes to the bathroom to wash his face with cold water. He checks his reflection in the mirror. A bit crumpled but not too bad for someone who's been travelling all day. In the bedroom, he swaps his cardigan for a tweed jacket. Benedict is anxiously flattening his curly hair and brushing imaginary specks off his jumper.

'Do I look OK?' he says.

'Beautiful, dear boy.'

But, when Edwin opens the door, he's taken aback by the vision in front of him. Natalka has changed into different clothes, tighter jeans and a figure-hugging pink jumper. Her blonde hair is loose and her blue eyes glitter, enhanced by mascara. Edwin thinks that he can hear Benedict breathing hard in the background. Even he's not immune. He's always liked being around attractive women.

'You look lovely, my dear.'

They go downstairs in procession, Natalka followed by the two men. The tiny bar seems very full but, on closer inspection, this effect is achieved by just four people. These must be the backpackers and they all seem to be Dutch. Edwin watches Natalka and sees her visibly relax, her shoulders dropping. Benedict is watching her too.

Jess gives them menus and tells them that her husband, Jay, is the chef. Edwin asks how long they've been at the Miners' Arms.

'Two years,' says Jess, opening the bottle of red wine they have ordered. 'The place was quite run-down when we arrived. These used to be miners' cottages. There was a whole row of them but the others were demolished. You can still see their gardens, honeysuckle and apple trees, although everything else has gone. It makes me sad to think about them sometimes.'

Edwin thinks about them too. The ghost cottages with the gardens still in flower. He shivers although the room is warm. But it's a good evening. Edwin's steak and kidney pie is delicious and he drinks more wine than usual. Benedict has risotto and Natalka orders steak. Afterwards they drink brandy by the fire. It's noticeably colder here than in Sussex.

Somehow, the conversation gets onto marriage. Edwin says that he wouldn't have married Nicky, even if it had been legal at the time.

'Why not?' says Benedict. 'I'd love to get married.'

He sounds almost belligerent. Edwin realises that they are all slightly drunk.

'I can't imagine being contracted to another person like that,' says Edwin. 'It would make me feel claustrophobic.'

'I was married once,' says Natalka. 'It's not all that.'

Both men stare at her.

'You were married?' says Benedict. 'When?'

'After uni,' says Natalka. 'It was the only way I could stay in the UK. I think he was called Daniel.'

'You *think*?' Benedict sounds like he's about to cry.

'OK. He was called Daniel. Dan. He was nice enough.'

'Would you get married again?' asks Edwin. 'If Mr Right came along.' He tries to put ironic questions marks around 'Mr Right'.

'Or Miss Right,' says Natalka.

'Are you gay then?' asks Edwin. He can't believe that he says it straight out, just like that. It must be the brandy. It's been years since he drank spirits.

'Not always,' says Natalka. 'Another brandy?'

'Not always,' says Benedict. 'What does that mean?'

'It means I've slept with men and women,' says Natalka calmly. 'Haven't you?'

'No,' says Benedict. Edwin wonders if he's a virgin. Do you have to be a virgin to be a monk?

'I've only slept with men,' says Edwin. 'I knew I was gay from about the age of ten.' Prep school again, and seeing Crossland Major in the showers.

'I wish I could go back to when I was ten,' says Natalka. 'Before the war, before my father left, when my brother was still alive. I loved school so much. I was the best at maths in the whole district. My hair came down to my waist and every boy wanted to go out with me.'

'I didn't like school,' says Benedict, though Edwin can tell that he's thinking about the image that Natalka has conjured. 'I never felt I was as good as my older brother and sister. They were both much better at things than me.'

'You're really clever,' says Natalka.

Benedict blushes. Or it could just be the reflection from the fire. 'I like books and reading but I wasn't much good at exams and . . . you know . . . all the other things that are important at school. Hugo played rugby and Emily played hockey. We did Gilbert and Sullivan operas every year and they always had the main parts.'

Edwin can't let this pass. 'They're operettas, not operas.'

'You've got a good voice,' says Natalka. 'I've heard you singing in the Shack.'

Now Benedict is definitely blushing. 'I wonder if that's why I became a monk,' he says, 'just so that I could sing.'

'That seems a bit extreme to me, dear boy,' says Edwin.

Chapter 18

Benedict: Education, salvation and damnation

Benedict wakes early, wondering why there's a train running through the room. Then he realises it's Edwin lying two metres away from him and snoring loudly. Benedict closes his eyes and tries to get back to sleep. He thinks of Natalka in her pink jumper, of Jess telling them about the miners' cottages. *You can still see their gardens, honeysuckle and apple trees, although everything else has gone.* The snoring increases in volume then, maddeningly, stops and restarts again. Benedict decides to get up.

He has a quick shower, hoping that the hiss of the water doesn't disturb his roommate. Then he dresses quickly and goes downstairs. It's seven a.m. He can see Jess in the dining room, laying the table for breakfast. Benedict waves but walks past her and lets himself out the front door.

It's a beautiful morning, the grass glittering after the night's rain. The moor rises up behind the house, the passing clouds making shadows chase across the heather. A bird sings somewhere high above and even the air here smells different, sharper and zestier somehow. Benedict walks along the road, trying to find the ruined cottages. At the bend he sees a dry-stone wall enclosing a space of apple trees and wild roses. Natalka is sitting on the wall.

'You're up early,' he says.

'I couldn't sleep,' she says. She's holding an apple in one hand and the image she presents, with her blonde hair, framed by the fruit-laden trees, is like something from a classical painting. *The Judgement of Paris*, perhaps. Benedict is a bit hazy about the legend but he seems to recall that it involves the most beautiful woman in the world.

Benedict sits beside her. 'Are you OK? Edwin thought you were a bit preoccupied yesterday.'

'I'm fine.' Natalka takes a bite of the apple and makes a face. 'Sour.' She throws it into the air and it lands somewhere amongst the brambles.

'There'll be another apple tree there one day,' says Benedict.

'In hundreds of years,' says Natalka.

'That's something the monastery taught me,' says Benedict. 'Time isn't important. "A thousand ages in thy sight are as an evening gone."'

'You do like quoting, don't you?'

'I suppose it stops me saying what I'm really thinking.'

'What are you thinking?'

Benedict looks at her, a vision with the sunlight in her hair. 'I was thinking that it's still at least five hours' drive to Aberdeen,' he says. 'We should leave by nine at the latest. I can share the driving, if you like.' He doesn't know whether to be relieved or disappointed when Natalka declines his offer.

'It's OK,' says Natalka. 'I like driving.' She stands up and stretches. 'I'd better have a shower before breakfast,' she says. 'How's Edwin?'

'Dead to the world when I left.' Benedict wishes that he hadn't uttered the d word. He has a sudden urge to cross himself.

'You'd better go and wake him up,' says Natalka. 'I think he was a bit tipsy last night.'

But, when they get back to the Miners' Arms, Edwin is just sitting down to a full English breakfast. He looks his usual perky self in a tweed jacket with his pink bow tie. Natalka goes upstairs to shower so Benedict joins Edwin at the table by the window. The backpackers, according to Jess, have already left.

'Did you sleep well?' says Edwin.

'Yes,' lies Benedict.

'So did I,' says Edwin. Benedict knows that this is true. Jess comes over and he orders toast and coffee.

'You should have a proper breakfast,' says Edwin, cutting his black pudding into quarters. 'We might not get lunch. When's this panel again?'

'Four o'clock. At the library,' says Benedict.

Natalka appears, her hair wet. Benedict tries not to stare as she, too, demolishes eggs, bacon and black pudding.

'So what's the plan for today?' he says.

'We go to the event,' says Natalka, 'and afterwards we talk to J. D. Monroe, ask her about Peggy and about the postcard. You'd better do that, Edwin. You're the least threatening.'

Benedict isn't sure but he *thinks* this might be a compliment.

It's another beautiful drive. Moors, mountains, lakes (lochs?). As promised, they pass through Gretna Green, 'Home of Love since

1754' according to the sign. It's pleasingly picturesque, with low white houses nestling under green hills.

'Ready, Benny?' says Natalka. 'With this ring and all that.'

'I will if you will,' says Benedict, trying for a casual note.

'My dear boy,' says Edwin, 'you sound positively terrified.'

Clearly, the devil-may-care voice needs work.

After Gretna Green is Lockerbie, another place whose name is larger than the town. It looks peaceful today, grey brick and Gothic towers, but no one speaks as they pass through. This route will also take them through Dunblane, where sixteen children and their teacher were shot dead in 1996. So much tragedy in this beautiful world, thinks Benedict. He says a prayer under his breath when he sees the signpost and Natalka surprises him by crossing herself.

They cheer up when they stop for coffee on the M9. Even the motorway service station seems exotic to Benedict. It's full of tartan shortbread and woolly Highland cows. They buy sandwiches for the journey and Natalka texts Harbinder.

'Just keeping her in the loop.'

'What does she think about us going to Aberdeen?' says Benedict. 'Does she think we're interfering?'

'I don't think so,' says Natalka, but she sounds evasive. 'I went for a drink with her the other night.'

'Did you?' says Benedict. He can't imagine it somehow, the two of them together, serious Harbinder and mercurial Natalka. But then he remembers what Natalka said about being attracted to both men and women. Was the drink actually a date?

'Did you tell her that we were going to Aberdeen?' says Benedict.

'I texted her,' says Natalka. 'She didn't say not to go.'

This, Benedict thinks, is far from approval.

They get caught in traffic around Stirling and again in Dundee. By the time they enter Aberdeen it's three-fifty. J. D. Monroe's panel starts at four.

'We'll have to ask the way,' says Natalka. She pulls into a bus stop and calls to a grey-haired passer-by.

'Excuse me, sir. Do you know the way to the library?'

'Ah, well now,' says the man, twinkling at her. He is clearly going to take his time. 'Are you wanting the Central Library?'

Benedict consults the programme. 'Yes, please.'

'Right at the crossroads and straight along Skene Street. It's next to the church and the theatre. Do you know what folk here call them?'

'No,' says Natalka, twinkling back. 'Tell me.'

'Education, salvation and damnation,' says the man. 'Have a good day now.'

Benedict still has these words in his head as Natalka drops him and Edwin at the library saying that she'll find somewhere to park the car. Education, salvation and damnation. He can almost hear it said in Abbot Michael's Irish accent rather then the Scots burr of the passer-by. The three buildings look suitably imposing, grey stone with domes and turrets. The Granite City, Aberdeen is sometimes called. A vast statue of William Wallace is pointing at His Majesty's Theatre, as if he is making his choice, but Edwin and Benedict ascend the steps to the library. The talk is about to start.

It's a large library and there are still seats at the back next to a tea urn and a plate of cup cakes sweating under cling film. Benedict looks out over the sea of heads and thinks of Chichester, Dex Challoner talking so fluently and humorously about his writing. It's such a civilised world; books, libraries, tea and cakes. How can it possibly also be a place where you can be murdered for the sake of a few words?

With a jolt, Benedict realises that someone is saying Dex's name. A young librarian standing at the front is calling for, 'A minute's silence in memory of the brilliant Dex Challoner who was to have attended this festival.' Benedict remembers seeing Dex's name in the programme. He bows his head and silently recites the prayer for the dead. 'Eternal rest give unto him, Oh Lord.' It occurs to him that he's been saying those words rather a lot in the last few days.

The librarian, who introduces herself as Moira, starts off the discussion with brisk biographies. 'J. D. Monroe, author of the best-selling *You Made Me Do It*. And also *Why Not Me?*, *Why Didn't You Take Me?* and, the latest, *It Was You.*' Presumably the last three didn't sell quite so well, thinks Benedict. Moira mentions a couple of awards, which makes JD blush furiously. She's younger than Benedict expected, probably in her mid-thirties, with fair skin and blonde hair that seems to be escaping from its clips.

'Susan Blake is the author of twenty-five DI Mike Malone books and has an army of fans.' But no awards, thinks Benedict. Susan has short pink hair and a truculent expression. Benedict guesses that she's in her fifties. Presumably she's been writing about Mike Malone for over twenty years. What must it be like to live with a fictional character that long?

'Becki Finch's debut novel, *My Boyfriend the Vampire*, has sold over a million copies worldwide and is being made into a film starring Timothee Chalamet. She's currently working on a sequel.' Becki is the youngest panellist. In fact, she looks about fifteen, with long dark hair and a nose ring. She's wearing ripped jeans and a leather jacket and seems singularly out of place in the room. Benedict assumes that she's the most successful author present. In monetary terms, at least.

The first questions are the basic 'what's your book about?' sort. Benedict finds himself dozing slightly. Natalka appears and slides into the seat next to him.

'What have I missed?' she whispers.

'Nothing much,' says Benedict.

Susan Blake is explaining that Mike Malone is her ideal man, 'he's tough and macho, acts first and asks questions later.' Benedict starts to feel rather depressed. Moira asks the other authors if they have ever written their ideal man into their books.

'Oh no,' says J. D. Monroe, 'my ideal man doesn't exist.'

'Yeah,' sneers Becki Finch, 'my ideal man is a long-dead vampire.'

The debate only warms up when Moira asks the panellists if they think that women are particularly attracted to violent books. 'I don't know about other women,' says Susan, 'but I love a bit of blood and gore. There are lots of people who I'd like to hit in real life but I'm not allowed to. So I do it in my books.' There's some laughter and Susan grins at the audience in what Benedict feels is a rather disconcerting way.

'Women write about violence because women experience violence,' says Becki. This simple truth has the effect of dissolving any remaining laughter in the room. 'Men hate us. Books are a way of getting our own back.'

'What do you think, JD?' asks Moira. Benedict has already noticed that she tends to answer questions last. 'Are crime novels a form of revenge?'

'I don't know,' says JD, twirling a stray strand of hair. Stop it,

Benedict wants to say. They were taught public-speaking skills at the seminary and he still remembers being criticised for fiddling with his glasses while giving a sermon on the repentant thief. 'I don't have much actual violence in my books,' JD goes on, 'it's all implied, but, of course, murder *is* violence, however it's described. I struggle a bit with the murders, to be honest. I once knew this wonderful old lady who could think up incredibly bloodthirsty ways of killing people.'

There's another ripple of laughter in the room. Moira says, 'Tell us more about this wonderful old lady.'

'Well . . .' JD is now twisting her bracelet round and round. 'It's very sad actually because she died recently but I think she had been involved with the Cold War in some way. She often talked about Russia and spies and espionage . . .' Her voice dies away. The atmosphere in the room has grown tense, almost hostile, Benedict thinks. He imagines the grey-haired crime fans thinking 'Why bring real-life death into the conversation? That's a bit tasteless, isn't it?' Certainly Moira moves them quickly onto the Q and A session. Most of the questions are for Susan. There are obviously lots of Mike Malone fans in the audience. Becki, perhaps sensing her demographic is elsewhere, leans back and stares at the ceiling. J. D. Monroe tries harder to look interested but Benedict catches her looking at her watch once or twice.

But one person has a question for J. D. Monroe. A male voice from the back of the library says, 'Who do you think killed Peggy Smith?'

JD puts her hand to her throat while a livid flush is rising. Moira says brightly, 'Is that a character in one of your books?'

'No,' says JD. 'It's . . . I don't know . . . I . . .'

Moira waits for a second and then brings the proceedings to a close. Natalka stands up to look for the questioner. 'He's leaving,' she says. 'I'm going after him. You and Edwin talk to JD. Don't let her get away.'

And she's gone, leaving Benedict and Edwin to approach the signing table.

There's a long queue in front of Susan Blake. Becki seems to have disappeared. One person is talking to JD. Benedict overhears, 'always wanted to write but haven't had the time . . .'

When the would-be writer goes away, Edwin put a copy of *You Made Me Do It* on the table. They agreed that it would be impolite not to buy a book.

'Would you put "Dear Edwin"?' says Edwin, with all his old-school BBC charm. 'I was a friend of Peggy's.'

JD puts her hand to her throat again. 'Was it you who asked that question? I didn't see who it was.'

'No,' says Edwin. 'But we would like to talk to you. This is my friend Benedict Cole. We've come all the way from Sussex. We know Harbinder Kaur.'

'DS Kaur?' JD seems to relax slightly. 'Are you with the police?' This is said on an incredulous note and Benedict is sure that Edwin, in his pink bow tie, is not everyone's idea of an undercover detective.

'No,' says Edwin, with a reassuring chuckle. 'We're just friends of Peggy's.'

It sounds a bit like 'Friends of Dorothy', thinks Benedict, and JD may well be forgiven for confusing the two.

'Could we have a coffee?' says Edwin. 'After you've finished signing?' This is said for politeness' sake only. There's no one else in the queue.

'OK,' says JD. 'But let's go to a pub. I need a drink.'

They go to the Rob Roy, which is on the corner of a nearby street, all dark wood and polished brass. Benedict offers to buy drinks. JD and Edwin both ask for gin and tonic but Benedict has a pint of something called Windswept Wolf. He texts Natalka to tell her where they are and joins the others at a secluded table, separated from the rest of the room by a high-backed wooden settle.

JD takes a gulp of her drink.

'Thanks,' she says. 'I needed that. I hate those things.'

'Panel discussions?' says Edwin. 'Why? I thought you were very good.' Benedict assumes that he's being polite because JD honestly hadn't been very good; she had either spoken too much or too little and had singularly failed to mention her latest book.

'Publishers expect it,' says JD. 'It's not enough to write a book, you have to go out there and sell it. I'm just not good at it. I rehearse all these witty anecdotes and then can't find a way to bring them into the conversation. Or I do and I forget the punchline. You've got to be like Susan today, always on message. Or interesting, like Becki. I'm honestly not very interesting. All I do is sit at home, writing books and eating biscuits.'

Benedict thinks of the biography on the inside cover of *You Made Me Do It*. There had been no mention of a husband or partner that he can remember. He does recall something about JD dividing her time between Tuscany and Brighton but, when he asks about this, JD laughs, a surprisingly robust sound.

'I once told my editor that I was going on holiday to Tuscany and somehow that became "divides her time". Mostly I divide my time between the sofa and the fridge. As you can see.'

JD made similar comments on the panel, about wanting to see women in her books who were 'overweight and unglamorous, like me'. Why do people put themselves down like this? thinks Benedict. It's rather boring. JD is tall but she's not at all overweight. Then he thinks, is that what he does? Puts himself down in the hope that someone will disagree with him? If so, perhaps it's about time he stopped.

Edwin has obviously decided to get down to business.

'How did you know Peggy, JD?' he asks.

'Oh, do call me Julie.' Julie gives him a smile which, like her laugh, is surprisingly warm. 'Dex told me about Peggy. We got chatting at a crime-writing festival and I told him that I had problems with plotting. It was all right with the first book. That almost seemed to write itself. But with the next one I got into real difficulties. I knew there had to be a murder but I just couldn't think of an original way to do it.'

'And Dex suggested that Peggy could help?' asks Benedict.

'Yes. He made a joke about her. He said that she was a born assassin.'

Benedict and Edwin exchange looks.

'He said that she had the soul of a killer hidden in the body of a sweet old lady. He was joking, of course. Anyway, he suggested that I should contact her. He was generous that way, Dex. He always helped other writers, even if there was nothing in it for him. I wrote to Peggy and she came up with some great ideas for the books.'

'Did you ever meet Peggy in person?' asks Edwin.

'No,' says Julie, regretfully. 'But we sent each other lots of emails and letters. Peggy was a great letter writer. And I always mention her in my acknowledgements.'

'PS: for PS,' says Benedict. 'Postscript for Peggy Smith.'

'Yes,' says Julie. 'She liked that. She loved codes and puzzles. She did the cryptic crossword every day. Sorry, I'm sure you knew that.'

'We used to do it together,' says Edwin. 'But she was much quicker than me. I can never work out anagrams. You said something about Peggy being involved in the Cold War. I had never heard that story.'

'I'm trying to remember how I heard it,' says Julie. 'I think Peggy hinted at it once. She also mentioned Russia rather a lot.'

'The *kulaks*,' says Edwin.

'Yes,' says Julie, smiling. 'That was what she called her son. He sounded very dull. I don't know how she knew so much about Russia. I really don't know anything about her past. I'm sure you know more,' she says to Edwin.

'Not really,' says Edwin. 'I know that her husband had been in the navy. She didn't talk about him much but she once said that he'd been the love of her life. After him, she wasn't interested in men. I mean, she was only in her early sixties when he died. She could have married again. I thought that was very sweet. I think she liked working in the civil service and she retrained as a librarian later. She worked part-time in the library when she first moved to Shoreham.'

'You don't know if she ever went to Russia?' says Benedict.

'No,' says Edwin. 'I think Peggy did most of her travelling in books. Anyone want another drink?'

'It's my round,' says Julie. But, at that moment, Natalka appears from behind the settle, accompanied by a tall man in glasses.

'This is Lance,' she says. 'He was the man who asked the question. He's a writer. He also knew Peggy. He's going to help us.'

Lance looks like he's not too sure about that. There's a rather awkward discussion about Peggy and then Lance offers to buy drinks. There's further discussion about whose round it is but, eventually, Lance and JD go to the bar, Edwin disappears to find the loo and Benedict finds himself sitting next to Natalka. There's a silence broken only by voices murmuring on the other side of the wooden settle.

'We're getting somewhere,' says Benedict. 'With the case, I mean.'

'Maybe,' says Natalka. 'Lance also had one of those notes. He didn't want to come here at first but I persuaded him.'

Benedict wonders why Lance hadn't wanted to come. Is it just because he doesn't want to socialise with them or is he hiding something? Why did he leave the library event immediately after asking his question? He's about to ask Natalka what she thinks when her face changes, so immediately and so completely that it's almost shocking.

'Listen,' she says, pointing to the partition.

'What?'

'Those men. I think they've come to kill me.'

Chapter 19

Harbinder: parathas

Harbinder is, in fact, absolutely furious about the trip to Aberdeen.

'How dare they?' she says to Neil. 'How dare they go off like that? As if this is some sort of game . . . some sort of . . . *road trip*. Don't they know this is a murder investigation?'

Neil is silent for a moment because he is driving. They are on their way to interview Nigel Smith who lives in a village near Lancing. Neil is always extra careful on winding country roads.

Eventually he says, 'Why *did* they go?'

This, unfortunately, is the key question and the answer is going to put Harbinder in the wrong.

'I met Natalka for a drink,' she says. 'Just to discuss a carer for my mum. I told her about J.D. Monroe, about her getting one of the postcards and being on the way to Aberdeen.'

'Why would you do that?'

Harbinder tries to answer honestly. Partly it was because Natalka had opened up to her about the cryptocurrency fraud but partly, she knows, it's because she had let her guard down, enjoying having

ELLY GRIFFITHS

a drink with an attractive woman. She can't say this to Neil. He knows she's gay, of course, but she's pretty sure that he's never actually equated this with fancying women.

'I was trying to find out if she knew any more about Peggy,' she says. It sounds feeble in her own ears. Neil seems to accept it though.

'So Natalka's gone to Scotland with the coffee guy,' he says. 'Are they an item then?'

An item. Who says 'an item'? But, hard though this is, Harbinder doesn't take the opportunity to mock Neil's vocabulary.

'They've taken Peggy's elderly neighbour Edwin with them,' she says. 'It's hardly a romantic trip.'

'They're just playing amateur detectives,' says Neil. 'Don't worry about them.'

She has to hope that he's right. They have reached the village which is so pretty that it makes Harbinder's teeth ache. Neil, of course, is in heaven as they circuit the duck pond looking for the house, which is far too grand to have a number.

'It's a perfect English village.'

'Probably full of racists and fascists,' says Harbinder, who is trying to track their progress on her phone.

'Why would you say that?' says Neil. 'I'd love to live somewhere like this. It's like a Christmas card.'

'Exactly,' mutters Harbinder. She's being unfair, she knows. Neil isn't a bad sort, it's just he's in thrall to a certain idea of Englishness, one that still isn't available to people whose skin isn't as white as Bing Crosby's Christmas.

Eventually they track down the house, High Trees, which is set back from the village green and, yes, surrounded by both a high wall and high trees. Nigel obviously isn't much of a one for droppers-in. He's expecting them, though, so opens the door with an attempt at bonhomie. Sally is hovering behind him.

'You've found us all right, then?'

'No problem,' says Harbinder, fending off a rather overweight spaniel. She's slightly off dogs after Starsky broke her mother's leg. This creature, who seems to be called Ozzy, reminds her of her friend Clare's dog, Herbert, an overindulged fluffball who enjoys invading your personal space.

'Down, Ozymandias,' says Sally, in a rather ineffectual way.

Ozymandias. Of course.

Nigel leads them into his study, a room full of leather-bound books. Harbinder is ready to bet that Dex Challoner's oeuvre is not represented. In fact, the whole room looks like one of those show homes in Harbinder's favourite property magazines. There's even a display of antique suitcases and an oversized station clock.

Sally bustles off to make tea, accompanied by Ozymandias.

'We wanted to talk to you about Dex Challoner,' says Harbinder. 'You've heard what happened to him?' In all honesty, Dex's death would be hard to miss. The author's murder has been on every news programme and has dominated the local press.

'Yes,' says Nigel, sinking into what looks like a very expensive office chair. 'Ghastly thing to happen.'

'I know that your mother and Dex were friends,' says Harbinder. 'And we're looking into the possibility that the two deaths were connected.'

'Now hang on a minute,' says Nigel, switching into bluster mode. 'My mother's death was from natural causes.'

Harbinder thinks it's interesting that this legal phrase comes so easily to Nigel's lips when talking of his mother's demise.

'We're not suggesting anything different,' says Harbinder, although they are, really. 'It's just that your mother was involved with Dex Challoner's books.'

'I don't know that I'd use the word "involved",' says Nigel. 'Mum knew Dex's mother Weronika. That's all.'

'She used to think up murders for Dex,' says Sally, coming in with a tray. 'She was very proud of that. She loved murder mysteries.'

Nigel shoots his wife a look that could've come straight from a crime novel.

'I don't know why,' he says. 'She was an intelligent woman.'

'Don't intelligent people read crime fiction?' asks Harbinder. 'Dex went to Oxford, after all.'

'That's different,' says Nigel. Of course it is, thinks Harbinder. Dex was a man, for one thing.

'Did Peggy talk to you about her consultancy on Dex's books?' says Harbinder, directing her question to Sally, who is still hovering by the door.

'A little bit,' says Sally. 'As Nigel says, she got to know Dex when he visited his mother at Seaview Court. He was impressed by her knowledge of crime fiction. She'd read it all. From the golden age right up to the very newest stuff, some of it quite violent. Apparently, Peggy suggested a way of killing someone that hadn't been done before – poisoned incense, I think – and Dex used it in a book. He acknowledged her in the author's notes and, from then on, he always sent her his work in manuscript and often took on her suggestions.'

'Poisoned incense,' says Harbinder. 'Was that in *Murder at Matins*?'

'I don't know,' says Sally. 'I haven't actually read any Dex Challoner. I'm more of an Agatha Christie girl myself.'

Harbinder thinks that Sally Smith is the sort of woman who calls herself a girl to deflect attention from her intelligence. She detects the same tendency in her own mother.

'I'm not much of a reader,' says Neil, with the sort of bluff good-humour that he does well. It's a deflection tactic too, in its way. 'I was totally out of my depth at the publishing place. We went to see Dex's editor and publicist. The publicist, Pippa, remembered meeting Peggy and Weronika together. She thought that they might have had some knowledge of Russia, perhaps during the Cold War?'

'My mother worked for the civil service,' says Nigel, in a voice that is meant to shut down the conversation.

Luckily, Sally has other ideas. 'I always thought she was a spy,' she says brightly. 'The conversations she used to have with Weronika. And there was that business in Moscow, with the Ukrainians.'

'That's not relevant,' snaps Nigel.

We'll be the judge of that, thinks Harbinder. 'What business in Moscow?' she asks.

'Oh, just something that happened to Peggy in Russia. She went on holiday with a friend. They were both in their seventies. It was a real adventure for them. Anyway, they seem to have got caught up with some Ukrainians who may or may not have been spies. This was before Russia annexed the Crimea. Anyway, I think Peggy and her friend let these men stay in their rented apartment. It got them into trouble with the Russian authorities but the embassy stepped in – Nigel has some friends there – and it all turned out happily in the end.'

'That's very interesting,' says Harbinder. 'Do you have this friend's name?'

'She's called Joan Tate,' says Sally. 'She's still alive but I think she has Alzheimer's. She's in a home near Lewes. I've got the address somewhere. I still send her Christmas cards.'

'That would be very helpful,' says Harbinder. 'Thank you.'

'There's no point,' says Nigel. 'She's out of it. Completely dool-ally. I really wouldn't bother.'

I'm sure you wouldn't, thinks Harbinder. She has noticed before that Nigel gets an odd facial twitch when he's talking about his mother. Right now, his face is like a pulsating orange.

'He's hiding something,' says Neil, driving carefully over the speed bumps that surround the perfect village.

'You think?' says Harbinder.

'Yes, I do,' says Neil, who can't do irony and drive at the same time. 'Don't you?'

'Yes,' says Harbinder patiently, 'I do. The question is, what?'

'Something about his mum,' says Neil.

He's a little woodland animal, Harbinder tells herself. A cute squirrel nibbling on a nut that is rather larger than he is.

'Nigel was very cagy about Russia,' she says. 'Dex wrote about Russian spies, Peggy actually met some spies in Moscow. Now they're both dead.'

'The Russians would hardly bother to kill an old lady living in sheltered accommodation in Shoreham.'

'Really? What about those poor people poisoned in Salisbury earlier this year? Or did you miss that?'

'Oh yeah. Poisoned at Pizza Hut, weren't they?'

'I think it was Zizzi's,' says Harbinder. 'But that's hardly the point. The point is that the Russians are perfectly capable of killing people living quiet lives in England. Dex wrote about Russians. Remember that extract I read you? The one we found in Peggy's desk? I think that was from his new book, *Murder in the Park*. And, in the desk, there were all those letters from Joan.'

'Do you think it's the same Joan?'

Climbs tree, examines fur for fleas.

'It's certainly a theory,' says Harbinder.

'You couldn't read her writing though, could you?'

'None of us could. I'm hoping the graphologist gets back to me soon.'

She waits for Neil to ask what a graphologist is but, instead, he says, 'And there were those men watching Peggy. Maybe they were Russians too?'

Harbinder is pleased that he has come up with this connection on his own. 'Natalka thought they might actually be after her,' she says. 'She got involved with something dodgy back in Ukraine. Cryptocurrency fraud.'

'Cryptocurrency? Is that like bitcoin?'

'That's right. Natalka claimed to have been in on the early days of it. She was studying maths at university in Kiev.'

'You friend Natalka is a bit of a dark horse.'

'She's not my friend,' says Harbinder. She wonders if Neil, in his whimsical woodland way, is trying to imply something. 'But she did say something else. Apparently Peggy told Maria that a clue about Weronika's death was hidden in the book. You know, *Thank Heaven Fasting*. Benedict emailed me a synopsis of it. Sounded ridiculous.'

'Who's Maria?'

'A carer. In fact, she's caring for my mum at the moment. Do you mind if we pop in on our way back?'

'I don't mind,' says Neil. 'Do you think she'll have made some of those flatbread things?'

'She's on crutches,' says Harbinder. 'She hasn't got time to make parathas.'

In fact, she's very much afraid that, not only will her mother have been cooking, she'll give Neil a care package of food to take home.

Sure enough, Bibi is cooking. At least, she is sitting at the kitchen table chopping onions furiously while Harbinder's brother Abhey stirs something on the stove.

'Abhey's being so helpful,' says Bibi. 'He's turning into a very good cook.'

Harbinder can only see Abhey's back but she knows that he's smirking.

'Man stirs food for ten minutes and suddenly he's Jamie Oliver,' she says. 'I know the syndrome.'

'When did you last do any cooking, sis?' asks Abhey. 'Hallo, Neil.'

'Hi, Abhey.' Neil's voice drops an octave. Harbinder knows that he finds her brothers intimidating. They're both over six foot and look even taller with their turbans on.

'Are the kids here?' asks Harbinder. In her opinion, Abhey and his wife Cara mostly visit when they want free babysitting.

'No,' says Abhey, virtue emanating from him like the aroma from the curry. 'I just popped in to see Mum. I had a job in the area.' Abhey, Bibi tells everyone, employs three people and *has his own business cards*.

'Where's Starsky?' says Harbinder, looking around for the dog. She wouldn't put it past him to trip her mother again.

'Downstairs. Helping Dad in the shop.'

'Stacking shelves, is he?' But Harbinder's heart isn't in it. For some reason, her parents really believe that the dozy animal is their best friend and helpmate.

'Give Neil something to eat,' says Bibi. 'I've made parathas.'

'He's not hungry,' says Harbinder. 'We just popped in to see how you are. Like Abhey did. We're pretty busy trying to catch a killer at the moment.'

'I'm sure he could manage a plate of something,' says Bibi. Neil assures her that he could.

Soon Neil is sitting down, nibbling his way through samosas, parathas and chakli. Harbinder wants to say that she hasn't got time to eat but, unfortunately, her mother is an excellent cook so soon she's chomping too. Bibi tells Harbinder how happy she is with Maria. 'Such a sweet girl. You know she's got three children and still finds time to care for people like me.'

'It's her job, Mum,' says Harbinder. She decided to employ Maria legitimately, through Care4You, because it might be embarrassing otherwise. Natalka will think that she's a mug. Thinking about Natalka makes her irritated all over again. What on earth was Natalka doing, haring up to Aberdeen to see J. D. Monroe? This isn't a game, a crazy road trip. It's a murder enquiry. Dex was shot in the head by someone who knew how to kill. Peggy may well have been murdered too. Harbinder feels guilty for telling Natalka about J. D. Monroe's threatening message. But how was she to know that Natalka would drop everything and drive six hundred miles in the company of an ancient TV producer and an ex-monk-turned-coffee-shop-owner? Right on cue, her phone pings.

Harbinder clicks onto the text. In the background she can hear her mother saying, '. . . always on her phone. I bet you're not like that at home, Neil.' Luckily, Neil's mouth is too full for him to answer.

It's from Natalka. *Met Lance Foster. He had postcard too. Plot thickens!*

For some reason, the exclamation mark makes her angriest of all.

Chapter 20

Natalka: voices

Natalka likes Lance from the start. She even liked his voice when she heard it echoing from the back of the library, asking the question about Peggy. It was deep and authoritative, not prim BBC like Edwin or posh overlaid with embarrassment like Benedict. The face, what she could see of it, matched the voice and so it was curiosity as much as anything that sent her charging out of the library in pursuit of the mysterious stranger.

She catches up with him in a kind of sunken garden. He is walking quickly, head up, as if he sure of his direction. But Natalka is quicker, flying down the granite steps in her performance trainers.

'Hi! Wait!'

He turns. He's tall with a beaky nose, heavy brows and horn-rimmed glasses. He looks slightly as if the nose, glasses and brows might all have come in a set but otherwise he's rather attractive. Older than Natalka first thought, though. Mid-forties, maybe even fifty.

'You were in the library,' says Natalka, panting slightly despite her twice-weekly kick-boxing. 'You asked the question about Peggy Smith.'

'Who are you?' says the man, which seems like the wrong question.

'I'm Natalka Kolisnyk. I'm investigating Peggy's death.'

'Are you a police officer then?' Something is flickering in the man's face. Not fear, something more subtle, maybe even amusement.

'No. I was a friend of Peggy's. We're private investigators.' That sounds good, she's rather proud of it.

'We?'

'I'm here with two friends. We think Peggy's death is mixed up with this.' She waves her hand towards Education, Salvation and Damnation, towering above the perimeter of the park. 'With the crime-writing world.'

'I don't want to be rude,' says the man, though he probably does, 'but I think you've been reading too many crime novels.'

'What about you?' says Natalka. 'You asked the question and then you walked out. Maybe you've been reading too many judgy things.'

'Judgy things? Do you mean courtroom dramas? Where are you from anyway?'

'Ukraine. How do you know Peggy?'

The man sighs and pushes his glasses further up his nose.

'It's complicated but, basically, she advised me on a book.'

'Are you a crime writer then?'

'Not exactly. I'm a literary author. My novel took certain elements from the crime genre though.'

Thinking that these were probably the best bits in the book, Natalka asks his name.

'Lance Foster. I wrote a book called *Laocoön* that some people seemed to rather like.'

'I know. *The Times* said it was a masterpiece.'

Lance raises his eyebrows. 'You've heard of it?'

'I came across it when I was clearing Peggy Smith's flat. There was a dedication in it to her.'

'"Peggy Smith, *sine quibus*." That means . . .'

'I know what it means,' says Natalka. Although she hadn't until Benedict translated. 'Why did you ask J. D. Monroe if she knew who killed Peggy?'

'I was looking in one of her books. I saw the line in the acknowledgements. PS: for PS. Then she actually mentioned Peggy on the panel. I couldn't help myself.'

'Why do you think that Peggy was murdered?'

Lance gives her that half-amused look again. 'You do say what you think, don't you?'

'You're the one who said it. You said, "Who do you think killed Peggy Smith?"'

Lance shrugs. 'It was just a joke.'

'I don't think so.'

Lance is silent while a woman passes them, pushing a buggy containing a wailing baby. Two children in school uniform trail behind her. It must be about six o'clock, thinks Natalka. The skies are already darkening. Evening comes quicker here than it does in Sussex.

'I didn't think anything about it at first,' says Lance at last. 'I didn't even know that Peggy was dead until I saw Dex Challoner at a festival. And then Dex was killed in that awful way and I got this postcard. It was in an envelope and the only message was—'

'"We are coming for you."'

Now he really does stare. 'How did you know?'

'J. D. Monroe had one too.' Natalka's phone buzzes. She consults it briefly. 'Let's go and have a talk with her,' she says.

Lance doesn't want to come at first. Strangely, it seems to be the presence of his fellow writer that's putting him off. 'One does rather try to avoid the social side of these festivals.' Natalka has never heard any English person use the indefinite pronoun before.

'You need to come,' she says. 'We have to solve the mystery.' And, in the end, curiosity prevails. They set off to find the pub, an old-fashioned building on a street corner. It's very crowded inside but, in a cosy high-sided booth, JD, Edwin and Benedict are talking about Italy. In fact, it's Benedict who's talking. '. . . the monastery of Santa Maria delle Grazie,' he is saying. 'At dawn prayers the only sounds are the cries of eagles and falcons, you can see the River Tiber far below, dark green against the purple rocks . . .' His face is glowing and he looks quite transformed. Natalka finds herself oddly unwilling to interrupt. But JD has looked up and registered their presence. Edwin, too, turns round.

'You found him, I see,' he says.

'Yes, this is Lance Foster,' says Natalka. 'He was the man who asked the question. He's a writer. He also knew Peggy. He's going to help us.' If she says this upfront, she thinks, Lance can hardly disagree.

'Hi,' says JD. 'I'm Julie Monroe. I think we've got the same publisher.'

'Really?' says Lance, raising his eyebrows as if doubting this.

'Yes,' says Julie. 'Seventh Seal. I've seen your book in my editor's office. Why did you say the thing about Peggy? Do you really think that she was killed?'

Natalka is rather impressed by such plain speaking. She begins to suspect that Julie is not as mild-mannered as she appeared on the panel.

Lance looks discomforted by the direct question and deflects matters by offering to buy drinks. Natalka asks for a large glass of red. Benedict says that he's fine. He's only halfway down his pint. JD says it's her round and the two writers argue their way to the bar. Edwin has gone to the loo. Natalka and Benedict find themselves alone, sitting side by side on the high-backed bench.

Maybe it was hearing him talk so lyrically about the monastery in Rome but Natalka thinks that Benedict looks slightly different. He's silent for a few minutes, drumming his fingers on the table and then he says, 'We're getting somewhere.' It's a few minutes before she realises that he's talking about the case. Benedict loves murder mysteries, she knows. She thinks that he's enjoying this one, even though it started with the death of a friend.

'Lance also had one of those notes,' she says. 'He didn't want to come here at first but I persuaded him.'

And then it happens. It's as if the car radio has suddenly tuned in to a new wavelength. The mutterings on the other side of the sofa become words and those words are in a language that doesn't need the internal translation that has become second nature to her.

'*Are you sure?*'

'*I'd know that face anywhere.*'

'*Be careful.*'

'*Don't worry about me. I'm not the one who's going to get hurt.*'

Natalka grasps Benedict's arm. She hardly knows what she's saying. 'Those men. I think they've come to kill me.'

'What? Where?'

He gets up to look over the partition but she pulls him down. 'No! I don't want them to see me. I've got to go. Now!'

'I'll come with you.'

'All right,' says Natalka. And, pulling up her hood to cover most of her face, she weaves her way through the pub, just as Lance and Julie finally manage to attract the attention of the barman.

Without really knowing where she's going, Natalka leads Benedict through the streets of the granite city. She looks round a few times but the men don't seem to be following her. Could she have been mistaken? But they were definitely speaking Ukrainian and how many Ukrainians do you get in north-east Scotland? Are they the men who were waiting outside her house in Shoreham? The ones Peggy saw outside her apartment? Natalka hurries on, pulling Benedict after her.

More by luck than judgement, they reach the place where she has parked the car. They get in but Natalka doesn't start the engine. They sit looking out at the streetlights reflecting unfamiliar buildings. Natalka is wondering how much to tell Benedict. She doesn't want to terrify him and she's not even sure she understands it all herself.

'What's going on?' says Benedict. But his voice isn't querulous or frightened. It's kind and surprisingly calm.

'Those men,' she says. 'I think they're after me.' She twists her ring, the silver ring that Dmytro gave her for her sixteenth birthday.

'Why are they after you?' says Benedict.

Natalka takes a deep breath. 'Back home in Ukraine, I got involved with something. A cryptocurrency. I went into it with two friends from university. We made a lot of money. But we also borrowed money from some . . . some bad men. I wanted to get away, to go to England, so I took some of the money.' She waits for Benedict to exclaim in horror but he stays silent. 'Not all of it, obviously,' she says, 'but enough to pay for my fare and my tuition. I meant to pay it back but then war broke out and my brother went missing. My mother's on her own. I need to send her money.' She realises that she's crying.

Benedict reaches out and touches her shoulder. 'It's OK.'

'It's not OK, Benny. I think those men are criminals, from the Ukrainian mafia. I think they want to kill me. And if I die my mother will have no one.'

'Why do you think they were the men?'

'I heard them talking in Ukrainian.'

'Did you recognise them?'

'I didn't get a proper look at them. I panicked.'

'I managed to take a quick photo as I was leaving,' says Benedict. 'It may not have come out too well.'

'You took a photo?' Benedict is becoming cooler by the second.

He proffers his phone. The picture is dark but Natalka goes into Edit and lightens it. She sees two men sitting at a pub table. They look youngish, probably both in their thirties. Both are wearing Harrington jackets and have cropped hair. It's too dark to read their expressions.

'They're not drinking alcohol,' says Benedict. 'I thought that was a bit suspicious. In Scotland anyway.'

Sure enough, there are several empty bottles of Coke on the table.

'Short hair,' says Natalka. 'They could be military.'

'What do you want to do now?' asks Benedict.

Natalka can only think of one thing she wants to do. And she wants to do it very badly.

'Eat,' she says. 'And have some more wine.'

'Let's find a restaurant then,' says Benedict.

They take the car back to the Travelodge first then look for somewhere to eat nearby, 'So I can drink,' says Natalka. They find an old-fashioned Italian restaurant in a basement, reached by steps down from the pavement. Inside, it's dark and conspiratorial, with candles in Chianti bottles and oil paintings of Vesuvius and the Colosseum. The waiter, who has a strong Scots accent, tells them that there's a big Italian community in Aberdeen.

'Lots of Italians who were prisoners of war in Scotland stayed. My *nonno* was one of them.'

'Do you get many Ukrainians here?' asks Natalka.

'I don't know about Ukrainians,' says the waiter, 'but you get a few Russians. The Russian department at Aberdeen University is famous. I'm studying there too. Modern history.'

'Could your men have been from the university?' says Benedict, after the waiter has gone. 'They could be mature students.'

'I don't know,' says Natalka. They've ordered red wine and she takes a gulp. 'Benny! Have you told Edwin that we left the pub?'

'Gosh. No.' Benedict types out a text message. 'Shall I tell him where we are?'

Natalka hesitates. 'Sure.'

But a few minutes later Benedict gets a message back that Edwin has gone to get a pizza with 'Julie'.

Natalka is surprised how pleased she feels to have a meal alone with Benedict. It's because she's feeling stressed, she tells herself. It's a strain being with too many people.

'Edwin is obviously getting on well with Julie Monroe,' she says.

'Yes,' says Benedict. 'He gets on with most people, though. You should have seen him at church. I've been going there for two years and I've never spoken to anyone. Edwin was the life and soul of the party.'

Natalka discovers that her glass is empty and fills them both up again.

'Why did you become a monk?' she asks.

Benedict looks surprised but he answers readily enough. 'I fell in love. That was what it was like. I used to go to mass without telling anyone. God was like my secret relationship. Then I went to the seminary and I struggled a bit; it was all so rational and logical. We had to do something called apologetics, refuting arguments against Catholicism. I just wanted to say, "You can't prove it, you just have to feel it."'

'That's how I feel about maths,' says Natalka. 'I know maths is meant to be all about logic and proof but for me it was more about the feeling. I love the way numbers work. It's as if they exist on a higher sphere.'

'Like God,' says Benedict. He too seems to be drinking his wine very fast. 'I suppose that's why I went into the monastery. Unlike the seminary it was all about experiencing the love of God.'

There's a silence broken only by the waiter bringing their plates of pasta. Natalka adds cheese to her ragu and says, 'Why did you leave then?'

'I fell out of love,' says Benedict. He looks, momentarily, so stricken that Natalka doesn't feel like she can ask him any more. They move on, with what feels like mutual relief, to murder.

Chapter 21

Edwin: footsteps in the dark

It takes a while for Edwin to realise he's been abandoned; he's been enjoying his second G and T and listening to Lance and Julie talk. It's nice to be out for the evening in a new city, to be in the company of attractive young people (his definition of young is rather elastic), to be talking about books. Julie and Lance seem to be getting on well but Edwin can tell that they're not attracted to each other. He tries to work out why. Maybe Lance is gay? But Edwin has become good at spotting closeted gay men. It's self-preservation, really, and Lance is not giving off the vibes. Maybe they're both happily married to other people, but that would be very dull.

Lance and Julie are discussing Peggy, her encyclopaedic knowledge of crime fiction and how she always knew what was wrong with a plot.

'Of course, plot is overrated,' says Lance. 'I try to get beyond describing what happens next.'

Edwin reminds himself never to read Lance's book.

'Surely your readers want to know what happens next,' says Julie. 'It keeps them turning the pages.'

'Oh, readers,' says Lance. 'I never worry about *them*.'

'I worry about readers all the time,' says Julie. 'I worry whether they'll like my new book as much as they liked the last one. I worry whether there's too much sex and violence, then I worry that there's not enough. Sometimes I'm so paralysed with worry that I can't write at all.'

'You should free yourself,' says Lance. 'For me there's nothing but the author and the page.'

But Lance has written one book to Julie's four, thinks Edwin. And Dex Challoner had written more than twenty. He tries to remember the J. D. Monroe titles. They all seem to involve 'Me' and 'You'. He realises that Lance is addressing him.

'Where's Natalka?' Lance is saying.

Edwin looks round as he if might be able to spot her hiding behind a pot plant. The pub has thinned out slightly. There are two foreign-looking men at the next table, a group of people who could be crime writers milling around the bar, and a couple of elderly drinkers by the pool table. No sign of Natalka or Benedict.

'Is that Miles over there?' says Julie. 'I wonder who he's talking to?'

Lance ignores this. 'Natalka insisted that I come here,' he says, 'and now she's vanished.'

'Perhaps she went for a meal with Benedict,' says Julie. 'He was lovely, I thought.'

'They were with me,' says Edwin, trying not to sound hurt. Then he thinks of checking his phone. He prides himself on his computer skills but he can't get used to having his phone switched on all the time, much less displayed on the table like the youngsters do. At present Julie's pink sparkly case sits cosily beside Lance's battered but expensive-looking model. It's almost like foreplay.

Sure enough, he has a message from Benedict.

Natalka feeling a bit faint. Better now. We've gone for a meal. Romano's. Car at Travelodge. 5 min walk from pub. Have left your suitcase at reception. Bx

There's one of those location thingies attached. Edwin is initially irritated and only slightly mollified by the kiss. But then he thinks: maybe this is his chance to leave Benedict and Natalka alone together. If there is a possibility of Eros's arrow striking, Edwin wants to give him room to take aim.

'Feeling faint?' says Lance. 'She was fine earlier.' He sounds rather possessive, thinks Edwin, considering that he's only just met Natalka.

'Speaking of meals,' says Julie, 'I could do with mopping up some alcohol.' She looks expectantly at Lance.

'I'm going back to my hotel,' says Lance, with what Edwin considers spectacular lack of gallantry. 'I've got some writing to do.'

So Edwin ends up having a pizza with the author of *You Made Me Do It*.

It's a surprisingly pleasant evening. Julie is a good companion, chatty without being overbearing, and a good listener too. She tells Edwin that she's single, lives in Brighton, and worked as a nurse before becoming a teacher.

'That was all the careers advice we got at school. Become a nurse or a teacher. Well I did both.'

'I wanted to study music at university,' says Edwin, 'but my father said there was no money in it. I was lucky though. I got a job at the BBC in the days when all you needed to do was make teas and run errands. I started as an errand boy and never left.'

'That's very cool though,' says Julie. 'Would I have seen you on TV?'

'I've never been in front of the camera,' says Edwin. 'But I was a presenter on Radio 3 for a while.'

'That's my favourite radio station,' say Julie. 'That and *The Archers* on Radio 4.'

'How did you become a writer?' asks Edwin. It's something that lots of people want to do, he imagines, but very few seem to manage it.

'I used to write short stories,' says Julie, 'but I never got any of them published. I was living in West London, looking after my mum, working in a school I hated and feeling very depressed. Then my mum died and, somehow, the grief process gave me an idea for a book. I took a big chance, and left my job and spent six months writing it. I was lucky. I sent it to an agent and she loved it. I know that doesn't happen to most people.'

'And that was *You Made Me Do It*?'

'Yes. It won prizes and everything. The trouble is, none of my other books have sold half so well.'

She smiles as she says this but Edwin thinks that she looks genuinely upset.

'Does it matter?' he says. 'If the first one did so well?'

'Of course it matters,' she says. 'One book won't keep you all your life. Unless it's *To Kill a Mockingbird* or something like that. But it's more that . . . I don't know . . . I want to be a proper writer. I don't just want to be someone who got lucky once.'

'Writing a successful book isn't just getting lucky,' says Edwin. 'And you have had other books published. I gather that's more than Lance can say.'

Julie grins. 'What did you make of him?'

'He seems pleasant enough. Takes himself a bit seriously.'

'That's because he thinks of himself as a literary author. He never said exactly how he knew Peggy either.'

'Didn't he?' Edwin hadn't noticed this.

'And if he does publish another book,' says Julie, 'everyone will be all over it. Reviews in *The Times*. Interviews on Radio 4. Even if nobody buys it.'

Edwin thinks that Julie sounds rather bitter. Their coffees arrive and Edwin manages to change the subject to the glories of Brighton. Edwin says he still misses his house in Kemp Town and is suitably scathing about Seaview Court.

'I love Brighton,' says Julie. 'The first thing I did, when I got my advance for my first book, was buy a flat there. Well, in Hove.'

'Hove actually,' says Edwin, which is a very Brighton joke.

'I walk along the promenade every morning,' says Julie, 'from the peace statue to the pier. Just me and Arthur. My dog,' she adds hastily, as if she doesn't want Edwin to get the impression that there's a man in her life.

'I was thinking that I'd like a dog,' says Edwin. 'It would be a reason to go out for a walk every day.'

'Arthur's great,' says Julie. 'He's a Jack Russell so he's got loads of personality. He's quite a handful, though. My previous dog, Wilbur, was a mongrel. I still miss him.'

'I still miss my cat, Barbra,' says Edwin. 'It's the space that they occupy. That region near the skirting boards. I keep expecting to see Barbra stretched out by the radiator. Not that she ever lived in Preview Court, of course. She would have hated it.'

'I still think I see Wilbur,' says Julie, draining the last of her wine. 'He was a very different character from Arthur, more self-contained, more like a cat. Sometimes I think I catch a glimpse of him, just out of the corner of my eye, and then he vanishes.'

'Maybe you do see him,' says Edwin. He's aware that he's rather drunk, a large glass of red after those two gin and tonics have put him in a dreamy, slightly maudlin, mood. Pull yourself together, he tells himself. He takes a long drink of water and suggests that they ask for the bill.

Edwin insists on walking Julie home. 'Always be a gentleman,' his mother used to say and, even in the days when he thought that he hadn't lived up to her idea of what a man should be, he tried to be a gentleman. Julie is staying at the Majestic, with most of the other festival-goers. As they approach the hotel, lights blazing in almost all the windows, Edwin thinks it looks like an ocean-going liner, the band playing on, the passengers heedless of the danger out there in the dark sea . . . But no, now he's thinking of the *Titanic*. This is simply a conference venue, probably half-empty most of the year, coming to life for a few nights.

'It's very jolly,' says Julie. 'The writers all stay drinking in the bar until the early hours. You should come in for a nightcap.'

'That's kind,' says Edwin, wishing he had a hat to doff, 'but I'd better get back to my hotel.' It's pushing it to call the Travelodge a hotel, he thinks, especially when he can't break himself of the habit of pronouncing it 'an 'otel'.

Julie shows him the location on her phone but Edwin goes to reception and gets a real map, on paper with street names and everything. The Travelodge looks to be only a few minutes away. Edwin kisses Julie on both cheeks and they arrange to meet for coffee tomorrow, then he sets off through the dark streets.

He thought that he'd feel rather scared, walking through an unfamiliar city at night, but the alcohol gives him courage. He strides along like a man half his age, remembering wandering the Paris boulevards with François, or Edinburgh with Nicky. It's as if their stalwart bodies are marching alongside his aging frame. He can almost hear . . . Hang on, there *is* someone following him. Definite footsteps, getting nearer and nearer. And is that a man's voice calling his name?

The footsteps start running. Edwin stops. He can't possibly outrun his pursuer so he might as well meet his mugger with dignity. Though, he can't quite work out how a mugger would know his name.

'Edwin?' The figure comes alongside. Dark jacket, jeans, longish hair and, illumined by an iPhone torch, a familiar, slightly ursine, face.

'Freddie Fanshawe.'

'Edwin Fitzgerald. Fancy seeing you here.'

Freddie Fanshawe is a BBC arts correspondent who once worked for Edwin. He was a graduate intern then and looks barely older now, although he must be in his forties.

'I'm on holiday,' says Edwin. 'I love Scotland.'

'I'm here to cover the literary festival,' says Freddie. 'I wouldn't normally bother but what with the Dex Challoner business . . .'

'I can see that would give it a newsworthy edge,' says Edwin. 'Are you on your way to the Travelodge?' He can just see the blue-lit sign at the end of the road.

Freddie pulls a face. 'Yes. Not like the old days, is it? A week in the Balmoral, all expenses paid.'

'No, there's no luxury today,' says Edwin. 'Although the authors seem to be having a good time at the Majestic.'

'I've just been there,' says Freddie. 'Had to leave before they drank me under the table.'

They've reached the Travelodge, fluorescent lighting showing an empty reception desk and a vending machine containing chocolate bars and miniature bottles of shampoo.

'Can we meet for a coffee tomorrow?' says Edwin. 'I might have something for you about Dex Challoner.'

He'll wait until he's sober to decide exactly how much to tell Freddie but it occurs to him that an information exchange might be mutually beneficial. Freddie looks gratifyingly curious as he heads towards the lift. Edwin presses the bell for attention. He needs to collect his bag and have a long lie-down with a flannel over his eyes.

As he waits at the desk, the doors swoosh open behind him and a man enters. He must already have his room key because he walks straight past Edwin to summon the lift.

Edwin doesn't know what surprises him most: the fact that Nigel Smith is in Aberdeen, or the fact that he's staying at a Travelodge.

Chapter 22

Harbinder: not a good son

Harbinder makes an appointment to see Joan Tate at the grandly named Highcliffe House. 'She won't know who you are,' says the cheerful voice on the phone, 'but she does love having visitors.' On the way to collect Neil, Harbinder calls in at the address given for Cathy Johnson, Dex's assistant. They have already spoken over the phone but Harbinder wants to meet the woman for herself. Surely no one could be as sunny as Cathy sounds. Dex was 'lovely', Mia was 'lovely', Dex's books were 'ever so lovely'. Maybe the sweet-toned voice is hiding a red-eyed monster with dripping fangs.

But it seems that the voice hadn't lied. Cathy is a kind-faced woman in her early fifties. Her house, a bungalow on the strip of land between Ropetackle Bridge and the sea, is neat and orderly. The sitting room has pink walls and a flowery purple sofa. There are no books to be seen anywhere.

'I answered an advertisement in the local paper,' says Cathy. 'I'd never had anything to do with authors and publishing before.'

'What were your main duties as Dex's assistant?'

'Mainly answering letters. He got so much fan mail. But also booking hotels and travel. Sending out books as prizes in competitions. That sort of thing.'

'Did you run his Twitter account?'

'No, he liked to do that himself. Said it was the personal touch. I was relieved. I don't know much about social media.'

Looking round the room, Harbinder can't see any evidence of teenagers who might be able to provide social media tips. It's very much the house of a single person.

'Did Dex ever receive any unpleasant letters or postcards?' says Harbinder. 'Anything threatening?'

'Oh no.' Cathy looks shocked. 'All the letters were lovely. Everyone loved Dex.'

'So he never received a postcard saying "We are coming for you"?'

'No. That would have made me feel quite nervous.'

Although J. D. Monroe had practically ignored it, thinks Harbinder. She asks Cathy what Dex was like to work with.

'He was lovely.' Cathy's eyes fill with tears. It's a predictable answer but quite moving, nonetheless.

Outside, she looks at the street name and realises that she is a few doors from the headquarters of Care4You. Does Patricia Creeve run the company from a private house? If so, maybe Harbinder should drop in and ask a few questions about Natalka. There just seem to have been too many mentions of Russia and Ukraine in the last twenty-four hours. Does Harbinder believe Natalka's story about the cryptocurrency and the theft, not to mention the mysterious men who are supposedly following her? And now Natalka has hared off to Aberdeen on the slimmest of pretexts. Maybe Natalka's employer will have some insights. Surely Patricia runs checks on anyone who works for her as a carer?

Patricia Creeve seems surprised to see her but is welcoming enough. She shows Harbinder into a room that was once a small bedroom and is now full of filing cabinets and flowcharts. There's still a single bed, though, and Harbinder sits on the edge of it. She has to move several large stuffed toys first.

'I won them on Brighton Pier,' says Patricia. 'I proved surprisingly good at Buffalo Bill's Rifle Range.'

Did she go on the pier by herself? wonders Harbinder. Like Cathy's place down the road, the house bears all the signs of single occupancy.

'Have you always worked from home?' she asks.

'I used to rent an office,' says Patricia, taking the desk chair and sitting up very straight, 'but the overheads got too much. Commercial rents have gone sky high in Shoreham. It's because everyone comes here from Brighton.'

This, Harbinder knows, is the perpetual refrain on the lips of every Shoreham resident. They all resent their glamorous, raffish neighbour.

'Are you very busy?' asks Harbinder.

'Frantic,' says Patricia. 'Carers come and go all the time and I get referrals from the hospital every day. They can't let elderly people go home without a care plan and, of course, they're desperate to clear the beds.' She shows her mobile phone where a steady stream of messages from 'NHS' scrolls past. 'I've had to see two clients myself this morning because Natalka suddenly took off like that.'

'I wanted to talk to you about Natalka,' says Harbinder. 'How long has she been working for you?'

'Two years,' says Patricia. 'She's very reliable normally. One of my best workers. That's why this is such a shock.'

'How did she come to work for you?' asks Harbinder. 'Did she have any previous experience?'

'No,' says Patricia. 'No experience necessary. A car and a clean driving licence is all you need.'

'I thought you'd need a health qualification of some kind.'

'I like my workers to have an NVQ in Health and Social care,' says Patricia, 'but it's not essential. I've got some nursing experience and so has Maria but most of the girls are just looking for a job to fit in around their families.'

'What about Natalka?' she says.

'Natalka's a clever girl,' says Patricia. 'She's got a degree. I think she does this because it leaves her free for other things.' Her face is bland but Harbinder gets the impression that Patricia has more to say. She'd like to tell Patricia not to call women girls but maybe that would sound too aggressive. She would say it if Neil were here, just to annoy him.

'What other things?' she asks.

'Well, she seems to have quite a lot of money,' says Patricia. Her professional stance relaxes somewhat and she leans back in the chair. 'Nice car, expensive clothes. She didn't earn that here, believe me.' She laughs, rather bitterly. 'I thought at first that she had a rich boyfriend but that's another thing: she's a really pretty girl but there's never a mention of a man. I did wonder if she was . . . you know . . . *gay*.' She lowers her voice although there's no one listening, unless you count the stuffed toys.

'It's hard to tell who's gay and who's not these days,' says Harbinder. 'What do you know about Natalka's background?'

For the first time Patricia looks slightly alarmed. 'Why do you want to know? Are you investigating her or something?'

'No,' says Harbinder, trying to sound soothing. 'It's just something that's come up in connection with Dex Challoner.'

'Dex Challoner? It was so awful him dying like that. We looked after his mother, Weronika. She was a character, I can tell you.'

'I've heard,' says Harbinder. 'Natalka is Ukrainian, isn't she?'

'I think so,' says Patricia.

'Do you know if Natalka is in contact with anyone from Ukraine?' asks Harbinder.

'I think she hears from her mum. She showed me a picture of her once. She looked just like anyone.'

Imagine that, thinks Harbinder. 'Weronika was Polish, wasn't she?' she says. 'Did she ever talk to you about what she did in the war?'

'No. She might have spoken to Maria though. They were quite close; Maria's Polish too, and I think they enjoyed being able to speak to one another in their own language.'

'At Peggy's funeral Maria said that Peggy knew a lot about Poland. Did she ever talk to you about Poland? Or Russia?'

'Not really. I only visited Peggy a few times. Natalka and Maria were her regulars. We do try to stick to regulars because the clients prefer it.'

'Does Natalka ever go back to Ukraine?'

'Not that I know of. She said once that she was saving for her mother to come here.'

'Does she have any other family?'

'She mentioned a brother once but I think he might be dead.'

'Do you know his name?'

'Mm, I think it's something like Dimitri. Something foreign.'

That narrows it down, thinks Harbinder. She remembers a primary school teacher who tried to call her Sarah because she couldn't pronounce 'Harbinder'. Her father had visited the school to explain that, unlike Sarah, Harbinder was perfectly phonetically regular.

Patricia's phone starts buzzing angrily and Harbinder thinks it's time to leave. She hasn't got much from the interview apart from the fact that Natalka has a mother and maybe a brother, and the reassuring thought that, if policing goes wrong, she can always apply for a job as a carer.

Even if Harbinder does have to become a carer, one thing is for sure: she's never going to work at Highcliffe House. It's not that bad from the outside, not the Gothic castle its name suggests but a pleasant detached house set back from the road. Inside, though, it's a nightmare of silent figures in wipe-clean armchairs, blaring TVs and low-level muttering, permeated with the scent of urine and cabbage.

'If I ever end up in a place like this,' mutters Neil, as they follow the care assistant to Joan Tate's room, 'shoot me first.'

'I'm not your next of kin,' says Harbinder. 'I'll leave that to Kelly.'

'She'd do it too,' says Neil. 'Of course, you do things better in your culture.'

'My culture? You mean people from Shoreham?'

'You know what I mean. You look after your old people.'

He's got a point, though Harbinder would never tell him so. Her maternal grandmother lived with them until she died, a revered figure, waited on hand and foot, even when she couldn't quite remember who they all were. Harbinder, who was eight when Nani died, remembers talking to her about horses (a brief infatuation), secure in the knowledge both that her grandma adored her and that she couldn't understand a word.

The staff at Highcliffe House don't seem cruel, just overworked and harassed. The carer greets Joan affectionately and rearranges the orange cardigan around her shoulders.

'It's not hers,' he says. 'Clothes get mixed up.'

Harbinder looks around the room, wondering if the possessions displayed on the small table belonged to Joan or not. There's a wedding photograph, a china horse and a vase of plastic flowers. Joan herself, a small woman with a birdlike face, says, 'Are you the doctor?'

She's addressing Harbinder. 'No,' says Harbinder. 'Not all Indian people are doctors.' All the same, she's pleased that Joan asked her the question and not Neil. It predisposes her to like the old lady.

'We're friends of Peggy's,' she says. 'Your friend Peggy Smith.'

Joan's face lights up immediately. 'Peggy! Is she here?'

'I'm afraid not,' says Harbinder. She's not about to tell Joan that her friend is dead, even if she'll forget it in seconds.

'Hallo, love,' says Neil, sitting beside Joan. 'I like your cardy.'

Harbinder thinks that he sounds very patronising but Joan positively beams. 'It's not mine,' she says. 'I'm an Autumn not a Spring.'

'You look lovely anyway,' says Neil.

'Are you my grandson?' says Joan. 'He doesn't come often.'

'I'm sure he'll be here soon,' says Neil. 'I'm Neil and this is Harbinder. We wanted to have a chat about Peggy. You had a lovely holiday with her in Russia, didn't you?'

'Russia,' says Joan, as if it's a new word.

'Do you remember the young men you saw?' says Harbinder. 'They stayed at your apartment.'

Joan stares at her; her eyes are very pale blue but they look as if they are still keen. 'We had fun, didn't we?' she says.

'Yes,' says Harbinder. Does Joan think she is Peggy? She's heard of people being colour blind but this seems extreme.

'You said they were students,' says Joan. 'Such nice boys.'

'Were they Russian?' asks Harbinder.

'Miles,' says Joan. 'They were miles from home.'

'I know,' says Neil. 'It must have been such an adventure. Can you remember anything else about the men?'

'We took them to the ballet,' says Joan. 'Such nice boys.'

'What were their names?' says Harbinder again. 'Dimitri? Ivan? Vladimir?' She can't think of any other eastern European names so says, rather desperately, 'Nigel?'

'Nigel wasn't a nice boy,' says Joan. 'Not a good son.'

Harbinder and Neil exchange glances. 'Why not?' says Neil.

'He took all Peggy's money,' says Joan. 'He said she gambled too much. She gambles too. Peggy said so.'

'Who?' says Harbinder. 'Who gambles?'

'On the horses,' says Joan. 'Oh, we did like the horse races.' Then, with no warning at all, she falls asleep.

'Is she OK?' says Neil. He touches the orange cardigan. 'Joan?'

Joan's chest is rising and falling. She looks very peaceful but, just to be sure, Harbinder goes into the corridor and finds someone who looks like a nurse. The woman comes into the room, checks Joan perfunctorily, and says that she sleeps a lot. 'She might be like this for hours.' But, when Harbinder leans over to say goodbye, Joan opens her eyes. 'Red Rum!' she says. And then she's asleep again.

Chapter 23

Benedict: a damn good mystery

Benedict wakes up with a momentary panic thinking that he's in his attic room in Shoreham and the door and window have changed places. But then he remembers. He's in a Travelodge in Aberdeen. He's with Natalka (presumably sleeping on the other side of this plasterboard wall) and Edwin (presuming that he got back safely from his tryst with Julie). They are investigators on the trail of a murderer. They might also be being followed by the Ukrainian mafia.

Strangely exhilarated by these facts, Benedict gets up and goes to the loo. Then he searches for the kettle and finds it cunningly hidden in the bedside cupboard. He makes himself tea and settles back on the bed. Today they are going to see Lance Foster in action. Is there something odd, suspicious even, about the author of *Laocoön*? Why did he ask Julie if she knew who killed Peggy? Surely that was an odd thing to do? Benedict realises that he never got the chance to ask Lance how he knew Peggy. He'd been too focused on Natalka. And what about Natalka's story, the cryptocurrency and the 'bad men' who were out to get her? When she had talked about her mother and brother it was as if a different Natalka was emerging, younger and more vulnerable, but also more foreign and unknowable. Who knew that she had studied maths, for example? Benedict barely scraped a pass at GCSE. He is aware that he is ignoring the fact that Natalka is also, by her own admission, a thief.

Benedict showers, feeling a slight frisson at the thought of being naked only a few metres from Natalka. When he emerges, his plugged-in phone is buzzing with a message. It's from Edwin. *Breakfast at 8? There's a nice café opposite, 'The Rowan Tree'.* There's no one like Edwin for using proper punctuation in texts. He sounds in good spirits anyway. Benedict sends a text to Natalka and starts to get dressed.

Edwin is sitting in a window seat demolishing a plate of kippers. He certainly seems on fine form. He says that he noticed the café when he walked home last night after having dinner with Julie.

'Did you have a good time?' asks Benedict, ordering coffee and a bacon sandwich. He feels slightly hung-over and the sight of Edwin expertly filleting his fish makes him feel rather queasy.

'Very pleasant,' says Edwin. 'Julie was good company. I think she might be rather lonely. She looked after her mother until she died and now she lives in Hove with just her little dog for company.'

'At least she's got a dog,' says Benedict. 'Remember the way Peggy used to make lists of dog-walkers?'

'Yes,' says Edwin. 'Two collie-crosses, three spaniels and one unidentified long-haired mongrel.' They both laugh.

Edwin says, 'I met a friend last night too.'

'A friend?'

'Yes, someone I used to work with at the BBC. Freddie Fanshawe.

I knew him when he was a graduate intern but he's a news reporter now. He's here because of Dex's murder. I thought he might have some information for us.'

'Information?'

'Yes, about the investigation. Speaking of which, I've got some news. I'd better wait until Natalka joins us.'

As he speaks, the door swings open and Natalka appears. She's wearing a black jumper and black jeans and her hair is wet from the shower. She looks like a beautiful assassin, thinks Benedict.

Natalka orders black coffee.

'You ought to eat something,' says Edwin.

'I can't face breakfast.' Maybe Natalka is hung-over too, thinks Benedict. The thought makes him feel rather cheerful.

Edwin glances round the empty café as if checking for eavesdroppers. Benedict thinks that he's milking his moment.

'So,' says Edwin. 'My news is . . . Nigel Smith is here.'

'Peggy's son Nigel?' says Natalka.

'The very same. And staying in the Travelodge, no less. I saw him come in last night. I'm pretty sure he didn't recognise me.'

'Perhaps he's come for the festival,' says Benedict.

Edwin treats this idea with the contempt it deserves. 'Nigel despises crime fiction. I heard him say so. He's here for some other reason.'

'Maybe he's got a mistress,' says Natalka. 'That's usually the explanation.'

'You don't take a mistress to a Travelodge,' says Edwin. 'Why do people stay in Travelodges? Usually because they're on business of some kind. What's Nigel's business?'

'I think his wife said that he worked in the City,' says Natalka. 'They seem pretty rich.'

'That could mean anything,' says Benedict. 'If the Shack was in Mansion House I could say that I worked in the City.'

'But would you be rich?' says Natalka.

'Probably not.'

'Maybe Nigel isn't rich,' says Edwin. 'Maybe he's lost all his money. That's why he wanted to sell Peggy's flat off so quickly. Money's a pretty good motive for murder.'

'Do you really think Nigel could have murdered his own mother?' says Natalka. Benedict wonders if she's thinking of her mother, at home in Ukraine. It was mentioning her mother that made her cry last night.

'The murderer is usually a member of the family,' says Benedict. 'In real life anyway, not in crime fiction. Then it's always the most unlikely person.'

'And, in real life, it's the most likely,' says Edwin, buttering his last piece of brown bread.

'We'll need to watch Nigel closely,' says Natalka. Benedict wonders if she's going to tell Edwin about the Ukrainians but she doesn't and Edwin, with his usual tact, doesn't mention their disappearance last night.

After breakfast, they walk to the Majestic. Lance's panel is at eleven in the hotel itself. Edwin has arranged to meet his BBC friend afterwards.

'You've been busy,' says Benedict.

'It's what you do at festivals, isn't it?' says Edwin. But Benedict has never been to a festival, unless you count seeing Pope Benedict in Hyde Park in 2010, which he doesn't.

★

The venue for Is *Hamlet* a Crime Novel? is the Conservatory, a smallish room off a cavernous ballroom. Windows on one side look out onto a somewhat windswept garden, and chandeliers, shrouded in cloth, hang like growths from the ceiling. Benedict, Edwin and Natalka sit on spindly gilt chairs at the back of the room. It's like a wedding, thinks Benedict, although he has only been to two, Hugo's and the nuptials of two ex-classmates who broke up six months later. This is a sparsely attended wedding, though, with a much smaller turnout than at yesterday's event. There are only fifteen people in the room. Julie Monroe, arriving a minute before the start, makes it sixteen.

'Sorry,' she whispers, although Benedict doesn't know why she is apologising. 'I was working on my edits.'

Lance makes his entrance in the company of three other men. After noticing the preponderance of women at the other literary events, Benedict wonders why this one is so different. The chair introduces himself as Hamish Macleod, a lecturer at the university. The other two writers are a tattooed young man called Simon Stevens, whose debut novel *Chip Rapper* was shortlisted for the Booker Prize, and Cymbeline Blake, an author who was once very famous and whom Benedict had assumed was dead. Hamish gives brief résumés for the three writers, adding that Lance Foster is a creative writing tutor, something Benedict hadn't known.

Hamish asks whether crime fiction is underrated by critics.

'I don't write crime fiction,' says Lance. 'I write literary fiction.'

'To be honest, mate, I don't know what it all means,' says Simon, whose accent is heavily disguised public schoolboy. 'I just write books.'

'It's all bollocks,' says Cymbeline Blake.

Hamish, who is now sweating slightly, asks them which classics they consider to be crime novels.

'*Heights*,' says Lance, 'and *Floss*.' After a few minutes Benedict translates this as *Wuthering Heights* and *The Mill on the Floss*.

'I don't read much,' says Simon. 'But I like a good gangster film.'

'The classics are crap,' says Cymbeline. 'I prefer a porn mag.'

There's a sound of people leaving the room. Hamish is starting to look really nervous but Lance, unexpectedly, leans forward and says, 'Jane Austen too. *Emma*'s a damn good mystery. Lots of clues in Miss Bates' monologues. I teach a course on the golden age. Christie, Marsh, Allingham, Atkins. Never ignore old ladies. I once knew an old lady who was just like Miss Marple.'

Benedict, Edwin and Natalka exchange glances. When the chair invites questions from the audience, Benedict puts up his hand. 'I was interested to hear Lance mention golden-age writers,' he says. 'What are the panel's views on writers like Sheila Atkins?'

'Never heard of her,' says Simon.

Cymbeline seems to have sunk into a coma.

'I'm an Atkins fan,' says Lance. He seems to be laughing at some private joke. 'She's very dear to me. Atkins knew how to plot too. You'd be surprised.'

'Have you read *Thank Heaven Fasting*?' says Benedict.

'Yes.' Lance looks rather surprised and is about to say more but Hamish interrupts to ask if there are any other questions. There aren't, so Hamish asks the three writers what they're working on.

'Another crap novel,' says Cymbeline. 'People will buy it though.'

'Nothing,' says Simon. 'If *Chip Rapper* is my only book, my only chance at immortality, then I'm happy.'

'I've just finished a book. Something completely different,' says Lance. 'I'm very excited about it.'

But he doesn't sound excited. In fact, he sounds almost as bored as the audience feels. Hamish calls time, ten minutes early.

'That was fun,' says Natalka.

'Shall we go and talk to Lance?' asks Benedict.

'I'm going for a coffee,' says Edwin. 'There's only so much literary chat I can stand. Reminds me of the old days in the BBC.'

'I'll come with you,' says Julie.

Natalka and Benedict make their way to the signing table. Surprisingly, there is a long queue in front of Cymbeline Blake. Next to him, Lance and Simon are chatting self-consciously.

'That was very interesting,' says Benedict to Lance.

'Do you think so?' says Lance. 'It seemed a bit of a car crash to me.'

Benedict warms to the writer. After all, he had been the least offensive person on the panel. 'Was Peggy Smith the lady who reminded you of Miss Marple?' he says.

'Yes,' says Lance. 'She was a born sleuth. That's what my old mum always said.'

This is interesting, thinks Benedict. It's the first mention of any close family.

'You never told us how you knew Peggy,' says Natalka. 'You just said it was complicated.'

'You disappeared last night,' says Lance. 'That's why.' He sounds rather annoyed and, again, more proprietary than Benedict likes.

'Let's meet later for a drink,' says Natalka.

Lance looks at his watch. 'OK. I'm meeting my agent for lunch. Why don't we have a drink in the hotel bar tonight? Say seven o'clock?'

'OK,' says Benedict. They watch as Lance gathers up his things and leaves the room, skirting the queue that still surrounds Cymbeline. Benedict wonders if the agent lunch really exists.

The hotel lobby suddenly seems very full of people. Benedict sees Edwin and Julie, nose to nose on a sofa. They are drinking coffee but many other delegates are already hitting the bar. Benedict moves out of the way for a man carrying three brimming pint glasses. Is he going to drink them all himself?

'Fancy a drink?' says Natalka.

'Why not?' Natalka seems quite calm this morning but he scans the room for the Ukrainians, just to be on the safe side. As he does so, he sees a large man in a blazer heading for the swing doors.

He touches Natalka's arm. 'Look.'

'Who is it? Oh, it's Nigel. Who's that with him?'

'I think it's Lance,' says Benedict.

Chapter 24

Natalka: not a good room

Natalka feels calmer in the daylight. There had been a bad moment when she woke up, feeling dehydrated and slightly sick, and thought that there was a man sitting on the end of her bed. She'd jumped up, heart thudding, but it was only her jacket hanging on the back of a chair and the strangeness of the hotel room, with its clean lines and primary colours. The room at the Miners' Arms had been different, cosy and cluttered with a sloping ceiling, but she hadn't slept well there either.

Benedict had been kind, though. He'd seemed different last night. Maybe it was his surprising initiative in taking a photo of the men or maybe it was because he hadn't seemed shocked at her revelations, but he'd suddenly seemed less of a joke – funny ex-monk Benedict who spends ages trying to make the perfect cappuccino – and more like a man, someone she could have known in her former life. They'd had two bottles of wine too. No wonder she feels slightly delicate this morning.

Lance's panel was strange. The writers all seemed determined to prove that they're not crime writers. Why, when it's clearly a great thing to be? Dex Challoner was extremely wealthy and even J. D. Monroe seems to have a good life: flat in Hove, Tuscan holidays, cute dog. Although, come to think of it, her clothes weren't much to write home about. Writing one 'literary' novel doesn't seem to have made Lance rich. He told Natalka last night that he has to do two teaching jobs in order to make ends meet. And his clothes, though cool, have seen better days. He's still attractive though, even when he's spouting some nonsense about Jane Austen. And he seemed quite pleased to see them afterwards, although that could be because he wanted it to look as if he has fans.

In the lobby afterwards, she'd suddenly been afraid. What if the Ukrainians from last night were here? What if they're out to hurt her, maybe even kill her, a single bullet to the head like Dex? She wanted a drink but, just as she suggests it, Benedict sees Nigel leaving the hotel with Lance and is full of sleuthing enthusiasm.

'Let's follow them.'

'We'll never get through this crowd,' says Natalka. It's true that the Majestic suddenly seems very full; people are moving from one panel to the next, others are heading to the bar for some serious drinking. Benedict has to admit defeat and buys them both a glass of wine. He's getting less monk-like by the second.

They retreat to a quiet corner behind some potted palm trees, where they are soon joined by Edwin and Julie.

'Did you see Nigel and Lance?' says Benedict. 'They left together.'

'That's interesting,' says Edwin. 'How do they know each other?'

'Through Peggy?' suggests Julie. She seems to be up to date with the whole investigation. Natalka has noticed before that Edwin is a terrible gossip.

'Have you ever met Nigel?' Natalka asks Julie.

'No. I saw him at the funeral. He didn't talk to me. I thought he seemed a bit stuck up.'

'Maybe Lance and Nigel are having an affair,' says Natalka.

'Impossible,' says Edwin. 'No gay man would fancy Nigel.'

'We should tell DS Kaur,' says Benedict. 'I mean, it's pretty suspicious, isn't it?'

'Let's send her a selfie,' says Natalka. She gets them all together and orders Benedict, who has long arms, to press the button. The resulting picture is slightly blurred and Julie has her eyes shut but it's quite good of Natalka. She texts it to Harbinder.

They have lunch in the hotel and share a bottle of red wine, which makes Natalka feel quite sleepy. She goes back to the Travelodge for a nap while Edwin meets his BBC friend and Benedict and Julie attend a panel on 'Detective Duos: from Holmes and Watson to Bryant and May.'

The bed is very comfortable and the black blinds make the room satisfyingly dark but somehow she can't sleep. She keeps thinking about Dmytro, his sweet, funny face with its snub nose and guileless blue eyes, the way that he used to give names to every living creature, even spiders, the way that he would blink when he was telling you a funny story. She hasn't seen him for six years. Eventually she gives up, gets up and has another shower. Then she puts on her best jeans and a new, ruffled top. She doesn't know who she's trying to impress but she always feels better when she thinks she's looking good. She puts on make-up too.

It's six o'clock and almost dark by the time that she leaves the Travelodge. The day had been fine but now it's raining, a thin persistent drizzle that is definitely making her hair frizzy. The lights of the Majestic seem cosy and welcoming, rows of golden windows like an advent calendar. As soon as Natalka pushes through the swing doors, she can hear voices from the bar area. Someone says loudly, 'You're an absolute shit, Rupert.' Someone else laughs and there's the unmistakable sound of a champagne cork popping. Natalka makes her way through the throng and orders a glass of red. She finds a deserted table but soon she's joined by three friendly women who call themselves book bloggers. It's a new term to Natalka but she doesn't like to ask what it means. She chats to the bloggers until Benedict and Edwin appear at five to seven.

'Any sign of Lance?' Benedict asks.

'Not yet,' says Natalka. She's suddenly feeling very nervous. She looks round the room. The occupants are almost all middle-aged and mostly women. There's no one who looks like a Ukrainian gangster.

'Are you all right?' says Edwin. 'You've gone very pale.'

'I'm fine,' says Natalka. 'How was your BBC contact?'

'Not that helpful really,' says Edwin. 'Freddie didn't seem to know that much about Dex Challoner. I told him all about Peggy being Dex's murder consultant. He was fascinated.'

At seven-thirty there's still no sign of Lance. The bar is very full now and the noise level is rising. The bloggers are raving over the latest Ian Rankin book. Natalka goes to the reception desk to ask for Lance's room number.

'I'm not supposed to give it,' says the receptionist, a spotty youth with an accent that Natalka assumes is Scottish.

'I arranged to meet him,' says Natalka, with her most sultry smile. 'We're good friends.'

The man blinks and hands over a post-it. 'Room 315.'

The lift, the old-fashioned sort with criss-crossed metal doors, is extremely slow but eventually it creaks its way to the third floor. The hotel is far bigger than it looks from the outside, a maze of corridors and meaningless little flights of stairs that go up and down for no discernible reason. Stags' heads watch gloomily from panelled walls. Room 315 is in a tiny alcove of its own, near a store cupboard.

'It's not a good room,' says Natalka. 'I've been a chambermaid and I know.'

She goes to knock on the door but sees with surprise that it's open. She stops on the threshold, suddenly afraid to go further. It's Benedict who edges past her. 'Lance?' Then Natalka hears him say, 'Holy Mary Mother of God.'

It has to be something serious to make Benedict take Our Lady's name in vain. Natalka and Edwin look at each other and follow Benedict into the room.

Lance is sitting in a chair by the window. Natalka thinks of Peggy sitting sightless beside her binoculars and her view of the sea.

Chapter 25

Benedict: looks like a crime

Benedict knows immediately that he's dead. He touches Lance's hand. It feels clammy and sweaty as Benedict checks for a pulse.

'Holy Mary Mother of God.'

He doesn't even know that he's said the words aloud but then Edwin appears at his side saying something that sounds like 'murdered'.

'Is he dead?' asks Natalka, her voice shaking. Somehow, that makes Benedict pull himself together.

'I think so, yes.' Lance's head is back against the chair but his eyes are open, pupils dilated. 'Call an ambulance,' he says, but he can already hear Edwin on the phone, giving directions in an admirably clear voice.

'Is there a pulse?' asks Edwin, who is speaking to the operator.

Benedict lowers his head to Lance's chest to listen for a heartbeat but he already knows. Lance's body has a horrible leaden quality to it.

'He's dead,' says Natalka, sounding like she's crying. 'Someone killed him.'

'We don't know that.' Benedict tries to take in everything about the room. The door had been open but Lance was just sitting in his chair. If he'd seen his death approaching, it had been in a form that hadn't, at first, alarmed him. Could he have died from natural causes? It's possible but Lance had seemed fine earlier that day, talking about *Heights* and *Floss*, saying that he was excited about a new book project.

'The ambulance is on its way,' says Edwin. 'We should tell the concierge. I'll go.' He leaves the room.

'Concierge,' says Natalka. 'It's a very Edwin word.'

'It is,' agrees Benedict. Natalka is half-laughing, half-crying. Benedict puts his arm round her, smelling that familiar lemony scent.

Edwin reappears, accompanied by two security guards and the spotty youth from reception.

'Jesus Christ,' says the first security guard, entering the room. 'Have you touched the body?'

Lance, thinks Benedict, has become 'the body'.

'Just to check if he was breathing,' he says.

'He's dead, all right,' says the guard. 'Do you know this guy?'

'Just vaguely,' says Benedict. 'He's one of the crime authors.'

'Well, this looks like a crime,' says the second guard.

No one has anything to say to that and they wait, in a rather uncomfortable silence, until blue lights are reflected in the window and the ambulance arrives.

The paramedics confirm that Lance is dead. They then have to wait for a private ambulance to take him away. 'We cannae take a dead body,' one of the paramedics explains. While they are waiting, the police arrive, having been called by the security guards. There are four of them. First two men in uniform, then a tall man who introduces himself as DI Harris, and a woman called DS Macready. They are very efficient. They herd everyone into a nearby room. Someone even brings in tea and biscuits, on an actual trolley.

It's strange, being in what is a standard hotel bedroom. Benedict, Natalka and Edwin sit in a line on the double bed. DS Macready takes a seat at the desk. DI Harris stands in front of them, his head almost brushing the light fitting, a chandelier apparently made of velvet antlers.

'Who found him?' says DI Harris. He has red hair, cut very short, and a manner that's brusque but not impolite.

'Me,' says Benedict.

'And you are?'

'Benedict Cole.'

'Are you a friend of the deceased?'

The deceased. Lance has moved on from being 'the body' to 'the deceased'.

'Not really,' says Benedict. 'I only met him yesterday. He's one of the writers at the crime-writing festival. His name is Lance Foster.' He has already given Lance's name to the paramedics.

'How come you were in his room?' says Harris. It's said in a flat voice, without a hint of suggestion.

'We'd arranged to meet him for a drink,' says Natalka. 'When he didn't arrive, we went to find him. I'm Natalka Kolisnyk and this is Edwin Fitzgerald.'

Harris looks at the three of them and Benedict tries to read his expression. He knows that they must seem an ill-assorted group: a glamorous woman, an awkward bespectacled man and an elderly gentleman in a cravat.

'Are you on holiday?' asks Harris. 'We're here for the festival,' says Natalka. She pauses. 'And to investigate a murder.'

'What?' For the first time, Harris's voice rises. DS Macready looks up from her notes. She's rather attractive, with pale skin and dark hair pulled back into a ponytail.

'Say that again,' says DI Harris.

Benedict thinks that he ought to speak before Natalka mentions the Ukrainian mafia.

'We were friends of Dex Challoner,' he says, 'the writer who was killed in Shoreham. We know that Dex had received a threatening letter and we found out that another writer, Julie Monroe, had also received an anonymous note, so we decided to come to Aberdeen to talk to her.' He tries to make it sound as if this is perfectly rational behaviour but he thinks that he can sense an invisible 'Nutter' sign hovering over his head.

'Why didn't you go to the police?' says DS Macready.

'The police know about it,' says Benedict, 'but DS Kaur said—'

To his surprise, DI Harris takes a step forward, '*Who?*'

'DS Kaur of the West Sussex police.'

'DS Harbinder Kaur?'

'Yes.'

'Well, well, well,' says DI Harris. 'What a small world.'

DS Macready looks completely baffled. She turns to Benedict. 'Tell us about these threatening notes.'

'They were postcards,' says Benedict. 'No address or stamp so we think they were sent in an envelope. They all had the same message printed on them. "We are coming for you." We knew that Dex, Julie and Lance all had links to a woman called Peggy Smith, who had also died recently.'

'Peggy was a murder consultant,' says Natalka. 'We think she was murdered too.'

'A *what*?' says DI Harris.

'A murder consultant,' repeats Natalka patiently. 'Peggy helped crime writers come up with new ways to kill their characters. We found one of the postcards in one of Peggy's books. *High Rise Murder* by Dex Challoner. Then, when we were sorting out Peggy's belongings, a gunman burst in and stole one of her books.'

'A gunman,' repeats Harris, sounding rather stunned. Benedict thinks that the 'Nutter' sign must be flashing neon red by now.

'So,' Natalka continues, 'when Dex was murdered, we thought the deaths must be connected. Then, when we found out that J. D. Monroe had also received a postcard . . .'

'J. D. Monroe?'

'Julie Monroe. She's another one of the writers.'

Macready makes a note. Harris turns to Edwin. 'Where do you fit in, Mr Fitzgerald?'

Benedict thinks that Edwin is rather magnificent. He uses what Peggy used to call his 'radio voice' and it seems to soothe even DI Harris's savage breast.

'I was a friend of Peggy's,' he says. 'I'm retired and I like reading. I fancied a trip to Scotland. I used to visit Edinburgh quite a lot in my younger days. Such a beautiful city.'

'And how's the trip working out for you?' says Harris.

'Slightly more eventful than I might have wished,' admits Edwin.

'Do any of you know anything about Lance Foster?' asks Harris. Benedict thinks he looks hardest at Natalka, maybe suspecting that the drink in the bar was a lovers' tryst. Though why she would have brought Benedict and Edwin along, he doesn't know.

ELLY GRIFFITHS

'He was divorced,' says Edwin. 'He mentioned an ex-wife.' He turns to Benedict and Natalka. 'That was in the pub yesterday after you left.'

'He had the same publisher as Dex Challoner,' says Benedict. 'Seventh Seal, I think it was.'

'Thank you,' says Harris. 'You can all go now. Don't leave town though.'

When they get downstairs, there's still a party roar coming from the bar. The police have sealed off the area around Lance's room but, as Natalka had pointed out, it's an out-of-the-way corridor and many of the hotel guests aren't aware of the drama going on upstairs, despite the police cars outside. Benedict is surprised to see that it's only eleven o'clock. It feels as if days have passed since they sat waiting for Lance, listening to the bloggers talk about Ian Rankin.

Outside, the night is cool and blessedly quiet. They walk in silence for a while and then Edwin says, 'Do you think Lance could have died of natural causes?'

'It's possible,' says Benedict. 'He could have had a heart attack or an allergic reaction. Anything, really.'

'I think he was murdered,' says Natalka. 'When I saw him, in the chair by the window, it made me think of Peggy.'

This reminds Benedict that Natalka had been the one to discover Peggy's body. No wonder she's so shaken. 'Peggy could also have died of natural causes,' he says.

'You don't believe that, Benny,' says Natalka. 'We are looking at a serial killer. And we don't know who will be next.'

Unconsciously they increase their speed until they see the Travelodge sign, the illuminated blue sleeping profile. It suddenly looks sinister to Benedict. Is the figure asleep or dead? Maybe he is blue because he's stopped breathing? The red background is rather terrifying too, come to think of it.

There's nobody at the reception desk and they climb the stairs in silence, eschewing the lift by mutual consent. On the landing, Natalka kisses both men on both cheeks.

'Goodnight,' she says.

'Goodnight, darling,' says Edwin.

Benedict says nothing.

He thinks that he will lie awake for ages but the bed comes up to greet him and he sleeps deeply with no dreams.

Chapter 26

Harbinder: good old-fashioned detective stories

Harbinder hears her phone buzz as she drives away from Highcliffe House. She doesn't look at it until she's back at her desk. The selfie doesn't make her smile. Benedict, Edwin and Natalka are grinning like loons and brandishing wine glasses. There's another woman with them, a blonde with her eyes shut. Benedict looms too close the camera which makes his nose look alarmingly large. Edwin is a blur of grey hair and pink bow tie. Natalka looks annoyingly glamorous. She probably chose that picture because it flattered her.

She shows it to Neil. 'What the hell do they think they're playing at?'

'Natalka looks like a model,' says Neil. 'Is there a message?'

'No. Oh, hang on, there's another text. "Guess who's here? Nigel!" Nigel who? Does she mean Peggy's son?'

'Can't be. We saw him only yesterday.'

But Harbinder remembers the pile of suitcases in the study. Maybe they weren't just an interior decorating feature? It would be easy to get a plane to Aberdeen. She's flown to Scotland herself and was amazed at how easy it was. Quicker than catching the train to London.

She scans through her emails. The forensics on the Dex Challoner case have come through but there's frustratingly little. The murderer must have stood in the doorway and fired from there; no fibres, no fingerprints, no tell-tale droplets of DNA. There is a footprint, size eight, in the garden which suggests that the assailant approached by way of the French windows at the back of the house. There's no CCTV either, although they haven't managed to trace all the home-owners. Many of the houses on Millionaires' Row are only occupied for a few weeks a year.

The briefing is at five. Harbinder reports of their meetings with Dex's wife, editor, publicist and agent.

'Dex was a big money-earner for the publishers,' she says. 'There's no incentive for them to kill him. Besides, he doesn't seem to have been too much of a diva. They all seemed rather fond of him.'

'The killing looks professional,' says Donna. 'I can't see some booky type carrying that off.'

Harbinder thinks about Benedict, surely the epitome of a 'booky type'. What are the three musketeers up to now?

'We've discovered a tenuous Ukrainian link,' she says. 'Peggy Smith went on holiday to Russia some time in the noughties and may well have accidentally got involved with some Ukrainian activists. We've visited Joan Tate, the friend who was with her, but she has Alzheimer's now and couldn't tell us much.'

'Apart from some out-of-date racing tips,' says Neil.

'She loved Neil,' says Harbinder, 'thought he was her long-lost grandson.'

'It all starts with Peggy Smith,' says Donna, chewing on her pen. 'I mean, as far as we know her death was from natural causes. What was on the death certificate? Heart failure?'

'Yes,' says Harbinder, 'and we know Peggy suffered from angina. But, according to her carer, she'd been in good health on the morning of her death. Then there was the gunman at Peggy's flat and the threatening postcard Peggy received. The one that was hidden in the Dex Challoner book. Another writer, J. D. Monroe, received the same note.'

'Really?' says Donna. 'Have you been to see her?'

'She's in Aberdeen at a crime-writing festival at the moment,' says Harbinder. 'Another writer at the event, Lance Foster, has also had the postcard. Oh, and guess who's just turned up in town? Peggy's son Nigel.'

'How do you know all this?'

'The carer, Natalka, is there with some friends.' Harbinder doesn't look at Neil.

'This carer seems very involved. What's her story?'

That's the trouble with Donna; she doesn't miss much.

'She's called Natalka Kolisnyk and she's Ukrainian,' says Harbinder. 'I've looked into her background. She's been working for the care company for two years and has a mother back in Ukraine. Natalka told me that she'd been involved in some cryptocurrency fraud and she thought that some Ukrainian heavies might be after her.'

'Do you believe her or is she a bit of a nutcase?'

Harbinder doesn't look at Neil. She is honestly trying to think. 'I think she's genuinely scared,' she says, 'but she could just be dramatising things. I don't know why she went dashing off to Aberdeen like that. She sent me this selfie today.' She shows her phone to Donna who scrolls back through the texts, frowning.

'She seems very pally with you,' she says. 'Be careful.'

Neil unexpectedly comes to Harbinder's aid. 'Natalka's with her boyfriend and some old bloke who knew Peggy. The three of them are just on some sort of road-trip,' he says. 'We haven't allowed ourselves to become distracted.'

'That's good,' says Donna. 'For now, let's concentrate on Dex Challoner. A well-known writer murdered in his own home. There's lots of press interest and we need to get a result. Look again into his movements on the night before the murder. Have we got his phone records?'

'Not yet.'

'Get onto the provider. There's usually a clue in the texts. Remember his phone was on the sofa beside him when he died.'

Harbinder goes back to her desk to chase the phone provider but, as she does so, she sees an email from Sandy, the graphologist.

I've managed to transcribe most of the Joan letters, but there are a few gaps, here and there. Hope this helps.

She has sent the letters as a document attached to the email.

Dear Peggy,

How lovely to hear from you. I'm glad the move to Shoreham is working out. It's hard to time these things right, isn't it? But you are still healthy and can enjoy the [illegible, possibly 'sea'] and the walks. I'm finding walking a little difficult these days. Hazel (Jason's wife) says I need to lose weight. Bloody cheek! I'm glad you've found congenial friends though. Fancy Weronika knowing about [illegible]. There aren't many of us left.

Much love

Joan

Dear Peggy,

I'm sorry about Weronika. You must miss her. Surely you can't [illegible] your carer? Can you send me a list of books, some good old-fashioned detective stories. I need something to keep my brain alive. I can't even do the quick crossword these days, let alone the cryptic.

Much love

Joan

Dear Peggy,

Edwin sounds fun. I wish I had a neighbour like him. Days, weeks, go by sometimes without me seeing anyone. Don't want to be a [illegible – misery guts?] but it gets me down sometimes. Jason comes when he can but he's very busy at work. Hazel says I should have carers in but I don't fancy it somehow. Did you say you were thinking of employing carers? How I wish I was [illegible]. They knew how to live!

Much love

Joan

Dear Peggy,

It's so funny, I was thinking about the boys only the other day. Fancy you running into one of them! What a time that was! Can you believe that we took them to the Bolshoi that night as if nothing had happened? Do you know what happened to the others? I've always been afraid that they ended up in prison after all. The Crimean situation is so terrible. I've always felt that Putin was [illegible]. Jason says that I don't understand about politics but he's a kulak, just like your Nigel. Have you read [illegible]. Fascinating insights, I thought.

Much love

Joan

Dear Peggy,

Sorry for the delay in writing. I've been finding it hard to concentrate somehow. I'm sure Jason thinks it's Alzhimers (sp?). He can't wait to put me in a home and forget about me. I wish I could see you again. What fun we had.

Much love

Joan

The first letter is dated June 2006, the last October 2015. They strike Harbinder as incredibly poignant. 'I wish I could see you again.' But the two old friends never had met again. The unpleasant-sounding Jason was right; Joan did have Alzheimer's. And he had put her in a home and, if he hasn't forgotten her, he certainly doesn't visit very often. Harbinder thinks of the shrunken woman in the orange cardigan. It's hard to imagine her exclaiming 'Bloody cheek!', doing the crossword or talking about the Crimean situation, yet she had once done all this, and more.

The gaps are annoying. *Surely you can't . . . your carer? How I wish I was . . . They knew how to live!* Sandy has sent scans of the original letters and Harbinder squints at them now. Could one of the words be Russian? *How I wish I was Russian. They knew how to live!*

But the big revelation is surely that Peggy met one of the students whom she and Joan had helped in Russia. Surely this is what she means about Peggy meeting one of the 'boys'? When was the

Russian trip? Sally had said that Peggy was in her seventies at the time, which puts it between 1998 and 2008. Peggy must have moved into Seaview Court just before 2006. Edwin, she thinks, arrived about six years later. The letter about meeting one of the boys is dated 2014, which must mean that he got in touch four years before Peggy died and maybe as much as sixteen years after the trip.

The mention of Weronika is interesting too, although Joan mentioned congenial friends, in the plural. What did Peggy say to Maria? That Weronika's death was suspicious? Are there any clues in the letter?

'What are you peering at?' Neil has made one of his surprisingly soundless entrances.

'The letters from Joan to Peggy. The ones we found in Peggy's desk. Sandy's transcribed them. Have a look.' She shifts her chair back so Neil can see.

He reads quickly. 'Bloody hell,' he says, 'poor old Joanie.'

'Yes.'

'She was getting Alzheimer's. No wonder she couldn't do the crossword. And Peggy did meet one of the Ukrainians again.'

'Looks like it.'

Neil is still gazing at the screen. Harbinder wonders if he needs glasses. Then he says, 'I wonder what this means. "There aren't many of us left."'

He's right, Harbinder has to admit. That is a significant line. And she has no idea what it means.

Rather than going straight home, where she'll probably be confronted with all sorts of domestic chores that somehow only a woman can do, she decides to call in on Clare. Harbinder met Clare

Cassidy on a murder case last year. She's head of English at a local comprehensive school (Harbinder's old school, in fact) and is not, on paper, the type of person Harbinder would normally associate with. For one thing Clare is tall, thin and effortlessly elegant, for another she is going out with a Cambridge don and loves talking about books written by dead white men. But, somehow, they have become friends and Harbinder is also very fond of Clare's teenage daughter, Georgie.

Clare, stylish even in sweatpants and an oversized jumper, greets Harbinder warmly. Georgie, who is watching TV in the sitting room, waves and Herbert, Clare's lunatic dog, acts as if he hasn't seen Harbinder for years and must compensate for this by running round in circles and barking shrilly.

'Quiet, Herbert,' says Clare. 'Would you like a cup of tea or a glass of wine? Let's go into the kitchen. Georgie's busy watching *Queer Eye*. I think it's one of her set texts for A Levels.'

Despite claiming that she is opposed to competitive exams, Georgie got a string of A stars, or 9s as they are now inexplicably known, for her GCSEs in the summer. She's now at sixth-form college where she's studying English with a woman who claims to be a white witch. Schools have certainly changed since Harbinder's day.

Harbinder loves Clare's kitchen. It's all sleek lines and concealed lighting, unlike her parents' house where, on top of everything, there's something. They sit at the table overlooking the garden, which is also subtly spotlit, and drink red wine. Harbinder tells Clare about the case, aware that Donna probably wouldn't approve.

'I don't expect you've read Dex Challoner,' she says. 'He's not a Victorian with a beard.'

'I love his stuff,' says Clare. 'I'm a big crime fiction fan. Wilkie Collins wrote detective stories. So did Dickens.'

'If you say so.'

'Have you got any idea who killed Dex?'

'Not really. We've got a few leads but they're all rather far-fetched. Literally far-fetched. Russia and Aberdeen.'

'I love Scotland,' says Clare, as Harbinder knew she would. Clare's grandmother lives in Ullapool.

'I might have to go up there,' says Harbinder. 'There's a mad Ukrainian girl who keeps sending me texts.'

'A girlfriend?' says Clare.

'No,' says Harbinder.

'I'd love to go if it wasn't term time,' says Clare. 'I need a holiday. Work is mad at the moment.'

'How can English teaching be hard work?' says Harbinder. This is a joke between them. 'Just tell them to read silently for half an hour.'

'The students are fine,' says Clare. 'It's everything else. Targets and tracking and triangulation.'

'Alliteration,' says Harbinder. 'Things must be bad.' She occasionally likes to remind Clare that she's not totally illiterate.

'Have you ever read J. D. Monroe?' she asks. 'She wrote a book called *You Made Me Do it*.'

'I don't think so,' says Clare. 'Doesn't sound my sort of thing.'

'What about Lance Foster, *Laocoön*?'

'I've read that. I thought it was brilliant. A bit pretentious, but brilliant.'

'What's it about?'

'It's about a man with locked-in syndrome, you know, where

you're conscious but you can't move at all. He knows that someone has tried to kill him but he doesn't know who. Eventually he works it out but he can't stop the person trying again and succeeding.'

'So he dies in the end?'

'The ending is ambiguous but I think so.'

'It sounds a bundle of laughs.'

'It's not very jolly, no. Why are you asking? Is there a link with Dex Challoner?'

'I don't know,' says Harbinder. She's thinking of Natalka's text. *Met Lance Foster. He had postcard too. Plot thickens!*

When Harbinder finally arrives at her parents' house, a woman in a vaguely nurse-like uniform is letting herself out.

'Can I help you?' says Harbinder, hearing the officious note in her own voice.

'Oh, hi. I'm Vicky. Maria can't make it today so she asked me to pop in on your mum.'

'Very kind of you,' says Harbinder. She thinks that Maria should have cleared it with her first.

Vicky clicks to open her car door. 'Your mum's fine,' she says, 'but she's doing too much. I caught her vacuuming today. I told her to leave that to me.'

'Thank you,' says Harbinder. She's pretty sure that vacuuming is not one of Vicky's appointed tasks. Or Maria's, come to that. She suspects that it might become her job in the near future.

Inside, her mother is preparing supper. Her father is reading the paper. Starsky is lying at his feet like a hearthrug.

'Who's in the shop?' asks Harbinder.

'Kush,' says her father. 'How's my little girl?'

'Catching a murderer,' says Harbinder, although the murderer is far from caught. She tells her mum to sit down and takes over the food preparation, with only slightly bad grace.

'Leave that to me,' says Deepak. 'You go and have a shower. You've had a hard day.'

Deepak thinks that a shower is the answer to everything. He has about five a day. Harbinder almost refuses, just for the sake of looking martyred, but suddenly she craves the hot, steamy water.

'OK,' she says and heads up to her bedroom. When she moved back in with her parents, the best thing was inheriting the second-largest bedroom with en-suite bathroom. She showers and then lies on the bed wrapped in a towel to play a few restorative games of Panda Pop. It's only then that she realises that her phone is still switched off.

There are three messages to call Donna. She knows it's important as soon as she hears her boss's voice. 'I've had a call from the Aberdeen police,' says Donna. 'Lance Foster is dead. Looks like he may have been murdered. They think there could be a link with Dex Challoner. Anyway, your presence is requested. The DI asked for you by name.' Donna sounds quite impressed.

Harbinder flies from Shoreham Airport at ten p.m. 'There are always flights to Aberdeen,' Donna told her. 'It's because of the oil rigs or something.' Shoreham, officially now called Brighton City Airport, is a pretty art deco-style building which doesn't look, from the outside, as if it could possibly be concerned with anything as mundane as air travel. But the woman at security tells Harbinder that it's actually very busy. 'It's not just the riggers. We have lots of essential workers coming through here. Doctors, nurses, fire-fighters, police.' She glances at Harbinder's warrant card but is too discreet to say more.

Harbinder is rather startled to see that her plane actually has propellers but it's a smooth flight and she arrives in Aberdeen at ten minutes to midnight. She feels rather lost when she emerges into the rain. Donna told her to go straight to her hotel (a Travelodge, natch) and start the investigations in the morning but how does she get there? She can't see a taxi rank and maybe they're called something different in Scotland. Should she save police funds and get a bus? But they might not be running at this time of the night. She stands, holding her bag, feeling unpleasantly at a loss.

'Harbinder!'

She turns. A man is calling from a police car. He looks oddly familiar and, as she gets closer, the features slide into focus. Red hair, dark eyes, aquiline nose.

'Jim!' She'd met Sergeant Jim Harris last year, when they'd both been on the track of a killer. She'd thought he was based in Ullapool though.

'I've moved to Aberdeen,' he tells her, as they drive away from the airport. 'Promotion. It's DI Harris now.' The penny drops. This is the DI Donna mentioned.

'Congratulations,' says Harbinder, happy for him yet she feels a familiar sour taste in her mouth. When is she going to become DI Kaur? She passed the inspector's exam earlier in the year but there are no vacancies in West Sussex. Maybe she *should* move.

'Tell me about Lance Foster,' she says.

'Lance Foster, aged fifty-five, found dead in his hotel room. We're treating it as suspicious.'

'Who found him?' says Harbinder, although she thinks she can guess the answer.

'Well, this is the interesting thing. He was found by a very odd trio who claim to be friends of yours. They say they'd arranged to meet Lance for a drink in the bar. When he didn't turn up, they went to his room to find him.'

'Natalka Kolisnyk, Benedict Cole and Edwin Fitzgerald,' says Harbinder.

Jim shoots her a sidelong glance. 'Aye. Want to tell me where you fit into all this? I couldn't believe it when your name came up.'

Harbinder sighs. 'It's a long story.'

She tells him about Dex and Peggy and the mysterious postcards. She tells him about Joan Tate and the Ukrainian students. She tells him about Natalka's fears and Benedict's knowledge of out-of-print books. The unfamiliar streets slide past, the rain reflected in the car's headlights. Harbinder stops speaking just as Jim parks in front of the Travelodge.

'Bloody hell,' he says. 'It's like an episode of *Taggart*.'

Harbinder wonders if this is a joke. She's too tired to tell.

'I've set up an incident room at the hotel,' says Jim. 'See you there tomorrow at nine.'

'OK,' says Harbinder. 'Thanks for the lift.'

She checks in, takes the lift to the third floor, finds her room, lies down on her bed and falls asleep almost immediately.

Chapter 27

Harbinder is tucking into the full Scottish when Benedict appears in the dining area.

'Morning, Benedict,' says Harbinder.

'Harbinder! DS Kaur, I mean.' Benedict looks very surprised to see her. He takes off his glasses and polishes them as if it were their fault that she has suddenly appeared in front of them.

'I hear you've been having an exciting time,' says Harbinder.

'I don't know if you'd call it exciting,' says Benedict. He seems to have recovered his self-possession and goes to the counter to fill his plate before joining her at the table.

'Why are you here?' he says. Then, perhaps realising that this doesn't sound very polite, he says, 'Did DI Harris . . .?'

'Jim sent for me,' says Harbinder. 'We worked together on another case.'

'I thought he seemed to recognise your name.'

'Well, it was you who told him about the Dex Challoner link,' says Harbinder. 'Jim got in touch with my boss and asked if I could help on this case. I flew up last night. From Shoreham.'

'From that little airport?'

'Yes. My plane had actual propellers. It was terrifying.'

There's a short silence. Harbinder thinks that Benedict looks different somehow, more assured, despite the events of the last twenty-four hours. She wonders if Natalka is about to make an appearance. Will she be in her cheery, detective mode or will she be dramatising Lance's death, making it all about her?

It's Benedict who speaks first. 'Does DI Harris . . . goodness, it's hard to think of him as Jim . . . think that Lance was murdered?'

'He's treating the death as suspicious,' says Harbinder. She thinks there's no harm in telling Benedict this much. 'I understand that you found the body.'

Yes,' says Benedict, with a slight shudder. 'We were due to meet him for a drink. When he didn't turn up, we went to his room. He was just sitting there in his chair . . . dead.'

'How did he seem? Peaceful?'

'I don't know.' Benedict rubs his glasses again. 'He was very sweaty,' he says at last. 'I noticed that. It was odd because the room wasn't hot.'

'It's a lot colder here than in Sussex,' says Harbinder. She remembers how cold she'd felt last night, even in her puffer jacket. 'Why were you meeting Lance anyway?'

'We'd met him the night before,' says Benedict. 'I think Natalka told you. He was at Julie— J. D. Monroe's event and he asked a question about Peggy. He came for a drink with us later and it turned out he'd had one of the postcards too. We went to his panel this morning.'

'Panel?'

'An interview discussion with two other writers. Lance never really explained how he knew Peggy but he said that, if we met him in the bar at seven, he'd tell us the whole story.'

'But he never turned up?'

'No. Unavoidably detained by death.'

Harbinder suspects Benedict of practising that line. She's not quite sure how to cope with the new, confident Benedict.

'And I gather you've seen Nigel Smith too?'

'Yes,' says Benedict, looking round rather furtively. 'He's actually staying here. Well, he was yesterday. And, guess who he had lunch with?'

Benedict has rather given away the punchline.

'Lance Foster.'

'Yes. I mean, that's strange, isn't it?'

'It certainly is.' Harbinder remembers Nigel's scathing comments about crime fiction. What, then, is he doing at a crime-writing festival? She senses that Benedict has a theory.

Sure enough, he says, 'I've been thinking about it and there are only three explanations that make sense . . .' But Harbinder never gets to hear what they are because, at that moment, Natalka and Edwin appear from the outside doors. Natalka is in her jogging gear, leggings and hoodie, and Edwin is carrying a paper.

They both express surprise/shock/pleasure at seeing Harbinder. She briefly tells them the Jim/airport/propeller story.

'So DI Harris must definitely think that Lance was murdered,' says Natalka, sitting down with a plate full of eggs and bacon.

'I don't know what he thinks,' says Harbinder, 'but I'm due for a briefing at the Majestic Hotel now.' She gets up.

'Will we see you later?' asks Edwin. He too looks none the worse for his experiences. He is smartly dressed as usual, with a spotted scarf tucked into a navy blue cardigan. He is spreading marmalade on his toast with great concentration.

'I'm sure DI Harris will want to interview you again,' says Harbinder.

'He did tell us not to leave town,' says Benedict.

'There you go then,' says Harbinder.

Aberdeen looks different this morning, the grey buildings sparkling after the night's rain. 'They call it the granite city,' said the receptionist at the Travelodge, 'but I like to think of it as the silver city.' Harbinder approves of the place, the buildings seem solid and substantial, bristling with spires and turrets. It's like a city in a story book.

The Majestic is a large, dour-looking hotel built of dark stone. There are police cars outside and, when Harbinder goes through the swing doors, the first person she sees is Miles Taylor, Dex's editor. He is on his phone and doesn't recognise her at first. The lobby is full of people trying to check out of the hotel, suitcases and tote bags full of books everywhere. A sign pinned to an easel says that the crime-writing festival has been cancelled 'due to tragic and unforeseen events'. Two police officers stand guard at the foot of the stairs.

Miles looks up and half-smiles, not able to place Harbinder. Then he seems to register the police lanyard around her neck.

'I know you, don't I?' he says. 'You came to see me about Dex.'

'That's right. I'm DS Kaur.'

'Was Lance murdered? That's what everyone is saying.'

'I can't say,' says Harbinder. Miles looks younger than ever with his backpack and headphones. He's wearing black and white

Vans trainers, too, like a student. But there's something about him, in this milieu, that seems to command respect. Harbinder notices people looking over to him, obviously wondering who he is talking to.

'The police want to talk to me,' says Miles. 'I don't know why. I wasn't Lance's editor. He hasn't published anything for years.'

'You were Dex's editor though.'

'So this is connected with Dex's death?'

'Again, I can't say. I'm not in charge of this investigation.'

'Such an awful thing to happen,' says Miles, almost to himself. 'Jelli will be devastated. Jelli Walker-Thompson. She was Lance's agent.'

And Dex's too, thinks Harbinder.

'Excuse me,' she says. 'I need to be going.'

Jim has set up his headquarters on the first floor. The lift looks grand but ancient. It's the open sort, with an elaborate bronze surround and wires and pulleys that look as if they've been there since Queen Victoria's time. Besides the lift itself is nowhere to be seen. Harbinder can hear it groaning somewhere on the upper storeys. So she takes the stairs, which are carpeted in deep red with tiny gold antlers on them. The corridors have red flock wallpaper and the main interior decorating theme seems to be death: more antlers, stuffed animals, crossed swords, hunting scenes. Occasionally there's an attempt at irony, a purple velvet deer peering out from an alcove, a painting of foxes chasing a man. Harbinder walks quickly, looking at room numbers. She passes a door marked 'Prayer Room' and can't resist looking inside. It's completely empty apart from a table containing the Bible and the Koran. She shuts the door quickly and, after a couple of meaningless twists and turns, finds the suite. It's called 'Darnley' which strikes Harbinder as ominous, though she can't think why.

'You've found us,' Jim greets her. 'This place is a rabbit warren.'

He performs brisk introductions. 'DS Sheena Macready, my number two. Tom McGrath, crime scene investigator. Doug Waterford, pathologist. Selma Francis, data.' There's another man called either Brodie or Brady, Harbinder never does discover which it is. It seems very odd to see the investigating team occupying a bedroom, complete with Day-Glo antlers and a giant photograph of the Forth Bridge over the bed. The door to the bathroom is open and she can see one of those free-standing baths, lonely on a plinth.

'This is DS Harbinder Kaur,' says Jim. 'She's from West Sussex CID. I've asked her here because there appear to be some links to the death of another writer, Dex Challoner. Does everyone know the case? Dex was a well-known crime writer, shot dead in his Shoreham home last Friday. Single bullet to the head, no signs of forced entry.'

'Are you treating Lance Foster's death as murder then?' asks Harbinder. She could have guessed as much from the police presence outside but she wants to know the evidence.

Doug Waterford answers her, 'I can't conduct a full post-mortem until we have an official identification.'

'Foster's ex-wife is due in Aberdeen today,' says Jim.

'Nevertheless,' says Doug. He has one of those Scottish voices that seems to make each word a yard long. 'My initial examination did yield some findings that might be of interest.'

'Of interest.' It's a very pathologist term.

'Specifically,' says Jim, maybe wanting to speed things up, 'the marks of a hypodermic syringe injection on the deceased's arm. This, together with an unusual amount of sweat on the surface of the skin, suggests death by insulin poisoning. Benedict Cole, who found the body, reports that the pupils were dilated, which is another sign. He was a surprisingly good witness.'

Harbinder feels oddly proud of Benedict. He is observant, she has noticed before. He would actually make a good detective.

'It's a very different MO from this Dex character,' says Brodie or Brady.

Maybe, thinks Harbinder, but this could be the way that Peggy Smith had died. There had been no post-mortem and no opportunity to study the body for puncture marks.

'Insulin poisoning is difficult to detect after death,' Doug is saying, 'but blood taken from the deceased shows an abnormally low glucose content.'

'So someone injected Lance Foster with insulin,' says Jim. 'It's very different from a gun to the head.'

'There is a link to Dex,' says Harbinder. 'They were both writers, for one thing, and Dex and Lance both knew a woman called Peggy Smith, who died a few weeks ago. We know that Dex, Lance and another writer, J. D. Monroe, all received threatening notes saying, "We are coming for you." Also, they all have the same publisher, Seventh Seal.'

'Natalka Kolisnyk mentioned this Peggy Smith,' says Jim. 'She said something about being held at gunpoint in her apartment. It all sounded a bit far-fetched to me.'

'Peggy was an elderly lady living in sheltered accommodation in Shoreham-by-Sea,' says Harbinder. 'Natalka was her carer. Peggy used to advise crime authors on their books. Apparently she was good at thinking up murders. Dex Challoner called her his murder consultant.'

Someone laughs and then tries to turn it into a cough.

Harbinder continues. 'When Natalka and Benedict were sorting out Peggy's books, a gunman did burst in and steal a book. We've got the gunman on CCTV but haven't been able to identify him.'

'He stole a *book*, you say?' Jim sounds astonished. Harbinder doesn't have him down as much of a reader.

'Yes, an out-of-print book called *Thank Heaven Fasting* by Sheila Atkins. We don't know its significance but we do know that Peggy's son Nigel was seen in Aberdeen yesterday. He was staying at the Travelodge but I checked this morning and there's no Nigel Smith on their records.'

'Are you sure it was him?' says Jim.

'I can't be completely sure,' says Harbinder, 'but Natalka and Benedict both recognised him.'

'Those two,' says Jim. 'I can't make them out at all. What's their game? And the other one too, Edwin Fitzgerald. I liked him though. Nice polite old chap.'

'They're here for the book festival,' says Harbinder. 'But they do fancy themselves as amateur detectives. They seem to have befriended Lance Foster, and J. D. Monroe too.'

'We're interviewing her in a few minutes,' says Jim. 'Harbinder, perhaps you'd like to sit in on that? Tom, anything from the scene?'

The crime scene investigator speaks from amongst a pile of deer-themed cushions on the bed. 'We haven't got all the results back yet but there's a mark on the doorframe that looks as if it was made by a gloved hand. I don't think we'll find much in the room itself.'

'It was the same with Dex Challoner,' says Harbinder. 'The killer fired from the French windows. Nothing from the room. Lots of CCTV cameras around but none of them working.'

'Similar thing here,' says Sheena. 'There's CCTV in the lobby but so many people came in and out all day that it's going to be hard to spot anyone who shouldn't be there. According to the receptionist, the only people on the third floor at the time Lance was killed were the cleaners. With so many guests, they were still doing the rooms in the evening.'

'So the killer simply took the lift up to the third floor, injected Lance and walked away again,' says Brodie/Brady.

'Actually, we think they took the stairs,' says Tom. 'There are some prints that look as if they were made by someone moving at haste. I've got a forensic podiatrist coming to look.'

That's a new one on Harbinder. She stores it up to tell Neil.

She says, 'If the killer didn't come into the room, did Lance let them in and then go back to sitting in the chair? It seems odd.'

'Maybe they came in, spoke to Lance and then killed him as they were leaving,' says Jim. 'In which case there will be forensics in the room. Good point, Harbinder.'

Harbinder tries not to look smug. Jim is the sort of boss who makes you want to please him. But he's not her boss; she must remember that.

'We think Dex Challoner knew his assailant,' says Harbinder, 'or, at least, wasn't threatened by them, because he was sitting on the sofa when he was killed. You'd think that, if someone turned up at your back door unannounced, in the middle of the night, you'd get to your feet at least.'

There's a discreet knock at the door. Sheena goes to answer it.

'Julie Monroe is here,' she says.

They talk to Julie in one of the connecting rooms, a small sitting room with a sofa, which probably doubles as a pull-out bed, two chairs and another giant TV. Sheena makes tea and coffee from the hospitality tray.

'No biscuits?' says Jim. 'I love a shortbread.'

'You're on a diet,' says Sheena, which implies a certain level of intimacy. Harbinder seems to remember that Jim is married, but not to anyone in the force.

Julie Monroe is blonde and rather attractive, with long legs in tightish jeans. Harbinder, who is not tall (her brothers often sing 'Hi ho, ho ho' as she approaches), can't stop herself looking at them enviously.

Sheena asks a few questions which establish that Julie is thirty-five, unmarried and lives in Hove. She's the author of four published books 'and several unpublished ones'. She's the same age as me, thinks Harbinder, but she seems to have accomplished a hell of a lot more, not least living on her own and not in her parents' spare room.

Jim asks her about the threatening note. 'It was printed,' says Julie, 'and said, "We are coming for you." I didn't think much about it at first but, then, when Dex was killed . . .'

'Did you know Dex Challoner well?' says Jim.

'Not really. I saw him at crime-writing festivals because you do see the same people again and again. He was always friendly. Not at all stuck-up, although he was nearly always the most famous person there. I told him that I sometimes had trouble thinking of murders and he told me about Peggy.'

'And this Peggy thought up murders for you?' Scottish people are very good at sounding incredulous, thinks Harbinder. Jim gives a particular sardonic emphasis to the word 'murder'. Murr-dah.

'I know it sounds odd,' says Julie, 'but Peggy had a very analytical mind. She read a lot and she was good at plotting. I'm better at people and relationships. Also, I get fond of my characters and don't want to kill them off. Peggy was tougher than me.'

'Did you know Lance Foster at all?' asks Jim.

'Slightly,' says Julie. 'We have the same agent and I saw him at Jelli's Christmas party and events like that. We didn't really chat. I didn't realise that he knew Peggy until he asked a question about her after my panel. Apparently he acknowledges Peggy in his book but it's in Latin. I didn't go to that sort of school.'

Another thing Julie and Harbinder have in common.

'So what did you do when you received the anonymous note?'

'I didn't realise what it was at first but then DS Kaur contacted me.' She smiles at Harbinder. 'She told me about Dex receiving the same message. I was really shocked. DS Kaur wanted to interview me but I was on my way to Aberdeen the next day. She sent a local police officer round, though, and I gave him the note. He didn't seem too interested, to be honest.'

Jim asks for details and scribbles them on his notepad.

'Did you see Lance in Aberdeen?'

'Yes. I went for a drink with some people that I met after my panel. Benedict and Edwin.'

'Benedict Cole and Edwin Fitzgerald?'

'That's right. Lance turned up later with a woman called Natalie . . . no, Natalka. We talked about Peggy for a bit and then I went for a meal with Edwin. I went to Lance's panel yesterday morning but I didn't speak to him afterwards.'

'Who were you with last night?' Sheena's casual voice keeps her from sounding like she's asking for an alibi.

'I ended up having dinner with a couple of other crime writers, Susan Blake and Helen Cray. I got back to the hotel at about midnight. I saw all the police outside and knew something was up but not what. I didn't hear until this morning.' She runs her hands through her hair and, for the first time, looks scared. 'I mean, Lance had one of those notes too, didn't he? Did Dex? Am I in danger?'

'We've no reason to believe that you're in danger,' says Jim, 'but there's no point in taking any risks. I'm going to put you up in a safe house for tonight. DS Kaur and her friends will be there too.'

It's the first that Harbinder has heard of it. She's beginning to think that promotion has gone to Jim's head.

Miles Taylor is next. He looks ill at ease, lowering himself onto the sofa as if unsure that it will bear his weight. He pushes back his hair with one hand and crosses his legs, black Vans jiggling. As Jim asks the preliminary questions, Harbinder notices that Miles starts to take on the timbre of his voice. It's probably unconscious but Harbinder thinks that it irritates the hell out of Jim.

'Did you know Lance Foster?'

'Hardly at all. I really don't know why you wanted to talk to me.'

'We spoke to Lance's agent.' Jim looks at his notes. 'Angelica Walker-Thompson. And she said that you were his editor.'

'In name only. Lance only wrote one book and I inherited him when his publisher was absorbed by Seventh Seal. I suppose my name was given to Jelli . . . Angelica . . . as a contact.'

'So you never really worked with Lance?'

'No.' Miles hesitates, raises his hand to his hair and then seems to think better of it. 'But, funnily enough, Lance got in contact a few months ago. He said he was writing something new. He seemed very excited about it.'

'Do you know anything about Lance's background?' says Sheena. 'We know that he's divorced. Do you know if he has any parents still alive? Siblings?'

'Sorry. No. Jelli would know more than me.'

But Harbinder knows that the police have already spoken to the agent who, apparently, was not in Aberdeen for the crime-writing festival.

'What about Dex Challoner?' says Jim. 'Were you close to him?'

Miles glances at Harbinder. 'As DS Kaur knows, I was Dex's editor for the last three books.'

'Did Dex know Lance Foster?'

'He never mentioned him to me but writers tend to know each other. Especially crime writers. It's a small world. And a sociable one.'

Thinking of the people milling about downstairs, Harbinder believes him.

'Did you see Lance Foster last night?' asks Jim.

'No. I went out for a meal with some colleagues and a couple of our authors.'

'What time did you get back to the hotel?'

'About midnight, I think.'

Jim asks for the names of Miles's colleagues and Sheena writes them down. Harbinder would have made notes herself, even if she was a DI.

'Lance Foster had apparently received a threatening letter,' says Jim. 'Do you know anything about that?'

'No,' says Miles.

Before he can say again that he didn't really know Lance, Harbinder says, 'The message is, "We are coming for you." We found a similar postcard in Peggy's flat, in one of Dex's books. Did Dex ever mention receiving a message like that?'

'"We are coming for you",' Miles repeats. 'It sounds familiar. Is it a quote? Dex never mentioned a threatening letter to me.'

'J. D. Monroe received one too.'

'Julie?' Now Miles does look shocked. 'Who would threaten Julie?'

He doesn't, Harbinder thinks, sound surprised that anyone would threaten Lance. Or Dex.

They break for lunch at one. Jim has sandwiches sent in for the team but Harbinder decides to go down to the hotel restaurant. The Majestic is providing a cold meal for any of the guests still in residence and Harbinder thinks that she might find Natalka and co. there. But, when she gets to the dining room, the huge room is empty apart from Julie Monroe sitting at a table under the glass roof, typing furiously into her laptop. Harbinder doesn't know whether to interrupt or not but Julie looks up and smiles.

'Do join me. It's quite spooky in here on my own.'

'I don't want to interrupt your work.' Harbinder finds it hard to think of writing books as work but this seems the polite thing to say.

'It's a way of escaping,' says Julie, shutting her laptop. 'Just for a moment, I can disappear into a different world. Of course, it helps that my books are all set on sunny beaches in beautiful parts of the world. It might be different if I was writing about the grim streets of Aberdeen.'

'Can you really write here,' says Harbinder, 'in the middle of a restaurant?'

'With all these crowds, you mean?' says Julie, looking round at the empty tables. There must be at least fifty of them. 'But, yes. I can work anywhere. In cafés, on buses, on the beach. I like to hear people around me, the buzz of conversation. Maybe it's because I live alone. You have to escape the silence.'

'I live with my parents,' says Harbinder. 'The house is always full of people. My brothers, their children, my parents' friends, their idiot dog. Silence sounds wonderful to me.'

'You see, your house sounds wonderful to me,' says Julie. 'I'm an only child and my parents are dead. I'd love to be surrounded by people.'

Harbinder wonders how they have got to this point so quickly. Normally, it takes her several weeks of acquaintance to admit to living with her parents.

'Do you know anything about this safe house?' says Julie.

'Not really,' says Harbinder. 'But Jim – DI Harris – said that it was on the coast near here.'

'Of course, you must be used to all this,' says Julie, 'but it seems rather terrifying to me.'

She doesn't look terrified, thinks Harbinder, particularly when you think that Julie is the one who has received a threatening note and the other two recipients of similar notes are dead. But Harbinder quite likes the idea of herself as a hardened veteran.

'I've been involved in a few murder cases,' she says. 'One up in Scotland, actually. That's how I know DI Harris.'

Luckily, because she shouldn't really say more, they hear voices in the lobby and Natalka, Benedict and Edwin appear, accompanied by two uniformed police officers.

'Edwin!' Julie waves. 'Natalka! Benedict!' Harbinder wonders how they have all got so friendly so quickly. Then she remembers the selfie. Julie is obviously the sort of person who forms instant relationships. She probably forgets people at the same rate.

'So exciting,' says Edwin, coming over and kissing Julie on both cheeks. 'We got a police escort here. Even though it's only five minutes' walk away.'

'They're putting us up in a safe house,' says Natalka to Harbinder. 'Did you know about this?'

'I've only just heard,' she says.

'The Aberdeenshire coast is beautiful,' says Edwin, as if this is a mini-break.

'They can't force us to go,' says Natalka. 'I've got my car. I could just drive home.'

Harbinder thinks that Natalka is the only one who looks properly shocked. She wonders why. After all, this road trip was all Natalka's idea. Why does she want to give up now? Natalka didn't show any squeamishness at Dex's death. Maybe she had really liked Lance Foster.

'We're all in this together now,' says Edwin. He looks positively thrilled at the thought.

The lunch of cold meat and salad is unappetising. Harbinder suspects that most of the catering staff have gone home. Julie is a vegetarian and, after a while, someone provides her with a wrinkled-looking baked potato. Inevitably, the talk turns to the case. Harbinder is forced to drop some of her professional detachment. After all, she wants to know what they have discovered. There's no point in keeping Julie out of the loop either. She's obviously avid for news.

'Edwin,' says Harbinder. 'You saw Nigel Smith at the Travelodge, didn't you? It's just that there's no record of him staying there.'

'Yes,' says Edwin. 'It was definitely him.'

'And I saw him yesterday,' says Benedict, 'having lunch with Lance. I told DI Harris.'

'Maybe Nigel is having an affair,' says Natalka, brightening slightly, 'like I always said.'

Could that be the answer? thinks Harbinder. She wouldn't put it past Nigel, although his wife is far more attractive than he deserves.

'I've been doing some research,' says Benedict, 'and Nigel and Lance were at school together.'

Harbinder was right; Benedict would make a good detective.

'That can't be right,' says Natalka. 'Nigel is much older.'

'They're both fifty-five,' says Benedict. 'And they both went to Denham College in Tunbridge Wells. It's a private school. Fees ten grand a term. Lance is on the alumni page and there's a picture of Nigel at one of the reunions.'

'Ten thousand a term,' says Natalka. 'That's two hundred and ten thousand pounds for seven years.' Harbinder remembers that she used to study maths.

'Were they just having an old school reunion?' says Harbinder. 'But why all the secrecy? I saw Nigel on Tuesday morning and he didn't say anything about going to Aberdeen.'

'I still think he's having an affair,' says Natalka. 'That's why men stay at hotels under assumed names.'

'I can't imagine any woman looking twice at Nigel,' says Harbinder.

'Maybe he was having an affair with Lance,' says Julie.

'That's what I said,' says Natalka.

'He's not the sort of man a gay man would fancy,' says Edwin firmly.

'There's still the school link though,' says Benedict, who seems reluctant to give up on his lead.

'Yes,' says Harbinder. 'I'll tell the investigating team. It's suspicious too if Nigel checked in under a false name. And Nigel was in the cadets at school. He probably knows how to fire a gun.'

'I don't think they let cadets near real guns,' says Benedict. 'My brother Hugo was in the CCF. All they did was throw smoke pellets at the local comprehensive school.'

After lunch, the amateur sleuths sit in the lobby and try to think of motive and means. The police officers watch them gloomily from another table. Harbinder is about to go back upstairs when her phone buzzes. It's Neil so she finds a discreet corner, framed by potted palm trees, to answer it.

'How's bonny Scotland?' says Neil.

'Cold,' says Harbinder.

'Thought you'd like to know,' says Neil, 'we looked into Peggy Smith's bank account, like you said. And, guess what?'

'What?' says Harbinder. She doesn't know why Neil seems to expect praise for perfectly normal CID procedure.

'Someone's been withdrawing money from Peggy's account, just a little each week, but it adds up to quite a lot.'

'Nigel?' says Peggy. 'Remember Joan said that he took all her money?'

'But why would Nigel want money? You've seen his house.'

She doesn't want Neil to start going on about the perfect all-white village so she says, quickly, 'Apparently Nigel was here, in Aberdeen, yesterday. He stayed at the Travelodge but there's no record of him. And he was at school with Lance Foster.'

'Should I pay him another visit, do you think?'

'I think you should. Edwin is sure that he saw him in Aberdeen.'

'Edwin is about a hundred though.'

'He's eighty and he's got all his marbles. Go and see Nigel.'

Harbinder clicks off before Neil can remind her that she's not his boss. As she does so, another message flashes up. Natalka.

Can I talk to you. In private.

Chapter 28

Edwin: the wind in the door

Edwin feels rather guilty at enjoying himself so much. Of course, he's very sorry that a man has died. Lance Foster was young (by Edwin's standards anyway) and pleasant enough. He certainly didn't deserve to be murdered in a depressing hotel room. If he was murdered, of course, but the way the police are fussing round them now certainly seems to suggest that was the case. But, all the same, the horror of the discovery, the interest of the investigation and now the prospect of moving to a safe house in an unspecified location, have had a remarkably rejuvenating effect on Edwin. He feels full of energy. At lunch he finishes off Natalka's roll and has two cups of coffee. He's positively buzzing.

Natalka, on the other hand, seems distinctly out of sorts. Of course, finding a dead body would upset anyone. Once or twice Edwin thinks he notices Benedict looking at Natalka with a worried expression. They must both look after her, he thinks, feeling pleasantly protective. She's only young, after all.

Benedict seems intrigued by the whole thing. Of course, he

loves detective fiction – he was even enthralled by a late afternoon showing of *Murder, She Wrote* that day at the Miners' Arms – but now Edwin detects a gleam in his eyes that Sergeant Cuff in *The Moonstone* would identify as 'detective fever'. 'The clue is in the books,' he keeps saying, 'it must be. I bought *Laocoön* yesterday. I must read it carefully.'

'I couldn't get past the first page,' says Julie. She, too, seems surprisingly cheerful. No one mentions the obvious fact that what links Dex, Lance and Julie are the anonymous notes and two of the recipients are now dead. Julie says a couple of times that she is 'really scared' but she doesn't look it. She goes to the kitchens to look for more coffee and comes back with a thermos and a tin of biscuits. Julie, Benedict and Edwin repair to a sofa in the lobby for more detecting. Natalka seems to have disappeared with DS Kaur.

Benedict draws a chart with the names Dex, Lance and Peggy on it and lots of connecting arrows. It's making Edwin's head swim. Plus, all that coffee has necessitated several trips to the loo which is an unreasonable distance away, along corridors with dado rails, clashing wallpaper and a preponderance of stags' heads, through several swing doors and past a room marked 'Electricity. Do not enter.' A few years ago, Peggy gave Edwin a Fitbit for Christmas and he had briefly been obsessed with doing his ten thousand steps a day. He's pretty sure he's done most of them today, to and from the Gents. There a strange moustachioed face on the door, to differentiate it from the Ladies which has a woman in a poke bonnet, and it's starting to look rather demonic.

On his last trip back to the lobby, he's surprised to hear someone hailing him from behind a palm tree.

'Edwin!'

It's Freddie Fanshawe with a manbag slung across his chest and a wheelie suitcase at his feet.

'Are you off?' says Edwin.

'Yes. Seemed easiest to get a taxi from here. What about you?'

'I'm staying for a day or so,' says Edwin. He can't resist adding, 'The police are putting me and some friends in a safe house.'

Freddie looks at him with mingled respect and, it seems, amusement.

'Good grief, Edwin, you do live, don't you?'

'I do,' says Edwin. 'I wish I could say the same for Dex Challoner and Lance Foster.'

'Is this because of the Dex Challoner connection?' says Freddie.

'In a way,' says Edwin. He doesn't want to admit to finding Lance's body. That would seem a bit *too* connected.

'You might be interested in something I heard about Dex Challoner,' says Freddie. 'Apparently he had delivered the next Tod France novel. Then he was going to write a stand-alone and then he wanted to give up writing altogether. I hear his agent was furious.'

'Why would a writer give up writing?'

'I don't know. I mean, they hardly ever do, do they? They keep on writing the same old stuff until we're all thoroughly sick of them.'

Edwin thinks that Freddie sounds far too cynical for an arts correspondent. He should try being a sports reporter, like Nicky, spending hours on some freezing touchline pretending to care whether someone-or-other United beat so-and-so Wanderers. That would show him how lucky he is. All the same, the news about Dex is interesting.

'How do you know this?' he asks.

'Can't reveal my sources,' says Freddie, putting a finger along-side his nose. 'Oh, there's Ginny waving. My taxi must be here. Goodbye, Edwin. Try not to get mixed up in any more murders.'

He trundles away, leaving Edwin feeling thoughtful. When he gets back to the sofa, he almost tells Benedict and Julie, but they are deep in a discussion about means and motive. 'But what's Nigel's motive for Lance? Maybe he bullied him at school?' Eventually Edwin falls asleep.

He is woken by a voice saying, 'Sleep, little Three-Eyes.' A face is bending over him and, for a wild moment, Edwin thinks it's his mother, who died more than thirty years ago. Thank goodness he doesn't say anything embarrassing like, 'Mummy'. Instead, he rubs his eyes and sees that it's Natalka. Funnily enough, something in her face, maybe its extreme symmetry, does recall Edwin's mother, who was a famous beauty in her day.

'We're off,' says Natalka. Edwin sees that DS Kaur is there, accompanied by a tall, blond man.

'This is Miles Taylor,' she says. 'He was Lance's editor. And Dex's. He's coming with us.'

'I really don't think it's necessary.' Miles looks extremely put out.

'It's just a precaution. Just for one night.' The red-haired policeman, DI Harris, has joined them. 'The house is in Cove Bay. It's a bonny place.'

Edwin doesn't think he's heard the word 'bonny' used in conversation before. He thinks it's charming. Harris is rather attractive in a bony, cadaverous way. He notes that Natalka and Julie are gazing up at him as if he is about to impart the secrets of the universe.

'If you want to take your car,' Harris is saying to Natalka, 'I'll send an officer to go with you.'

'I'll be OK,' says Natalka. 'Benny can come with me.'

'Nevertheless,' says Harris, 'an officer will accompany you.'

Even Natalka does not argue with that.

Edwin, Miles, Julie and DS Kaur are driven by Harris himself, DS Kaur in the front, as befits her status. It's a beautiful drive. They cross a bridge and leave the town behind them, passing between stone houses, softened by the afternoon light. After about fifteen minutes they reach the sea, mossy cliffs heading straight into water, waves crashing against the rocks.

'There's the house,' says Harris.

It's a modern, white-walled building, perched on the very top of the cliff. Below it, a concrete slope leads down into the water. When they get out the car, the strong, salty wind almost takes Edwin's breath away. He wraps his tartan scarf round his neck. Natalka is parking in the driveway. Harris gets out the keys. 'It's quite basic,' he says, 'but I think you'll be comfortable.'

The house is perfect: wooden floors, white walls, minimal furniture. From the sitting room, you can hear the waves slapping against the harbour wall. There are four bedrooms upstairs and one downstairs.

'I can't share a room,' says Miles immediately. 'I have space issues.'

That probably means Miles snores, thinks Edwin. Thank goodness I don't.

'Julie and I will share,' says Natalka. The two women seem to have become close quite quickly. They take a room that looks like it was decorated for children, complete with bunk beds and Tintin wallpaper. This leaves two singles upstairs and one double, plus a smaller double downstairs.

'I don't mind sleeping downstairs,' says Edwin. He has already worked out that this means easier access to the loo. Upstairs, DS Kaur gets the double, to her obvious satisfaction, and Miles and Benedict the two singles.

'I hope the curtains are dark enough,' says Miles. 'I'm used to blackout blinds.'

Miles is obviously going to be a trial.

'There'll be a patrol car outside all night,' says Harris. 'Any problems, Harbinder, just call me.'

'I will,' says DS Kaur, who is examining the TV.

'Is there any food?' says Natalka.

'I almost forgot.' Harris goes to the car and comes back with two carrier bags. 'Sheena went shopping for you.'

Edwin notes that macho Mr Harris didn't do the shopping himself. He's pleased to see that Sheena has included a couple of bottles of wine.

Benedict and Natalka cook them spaghetti bolognaise for supper, with a vegetarian version for Julie. It's very good, helped down by the red wine. They talk about Scotland, food, holidays – anything but murder. Edwin is surprised to find out that Miles went to university in Aberdeen. That hair is so very Oxbridge. But Miles is actually rather interesting when he's talking about Scottish history and his voice takes on a distinctly Highland lilt. He's talking about Mary Queen of Scots when Harbinder says,

'Who was Darnley?'

'Why do you ask?'

'I saw it on a hotel room.'

Miles looks surprised but says, 'Charles Darnley was Mary's second husband. He was murdered at Kirk O'Field.'

'I heard he was gay,' says Edwin.

'There's no evidence either way,' says Miles. 'Darnley was the father of Mary's son, who became James the first of England.'

'Doesn't stop him being gay,' says Edwin.

'No, it doesn't. Anyway, Darnley came to a horrible end. His house was blown up. Darnley and his valet were found dead in the adjoining field. Of course, it's believed that Darnley murdered David Rizzio, the Italian musician who may or may not have been Mary's lover.'

'So many murders,' says Edwin, thinking that Scotland hasn't changed.

It seems that DS Kaur – Harbinder to them now – is thinking along the same lines.

'Last time I was in Scotland,' she says, 'I was on the trail of a murderer, a very dangerous character. I arrived just as he was about to stab this teenage girl. I jumped on him and Jim, DI Harris, came flying through the door and took him down with a rugby tackle.'

'Goodness,' says Edwin, 'you do have an exciting job.'

'It's not usually that exciting,' says Harbinder. 'Mostly I'm sitting outside Shoreham power station looking for non-existent terrorists.'

'I can just imagine DI Harris charging in like that,' says Julie. 'He's very macho, isn't he?'

Harbinder agrees that he is, although her voice implies that this isn't necessarily a good thing.

'I saw lots of macho men back home in Ukraine,' says Natalka. 'When the war came they all turned out to be cowards.'

Miles turns to look at her. 'Oh, are you from Ukraine? Do you know . . .' He mentions a name but his accent is so heavy (pretentious, Edwin thinks) that it's incomprehensible.

'Yes,' says Natalka. 'How do you know it?'

'I studied Russian at university and spent a year in Moscow.'

'You didn't mention that before,' says Harbinder.

'It didn't seem relevant,' says Miles.

Edwin thinks that Harbinder looks rather irritated but he can't think why.

'I heard something interesting today,' he says. 'Freddie Fanshawe, my BBC friend, said that Dex Challoner was planning to give up writing for good.'

'That's not true,' says Miles quickly. 'Dex had already delivered the next Tod France and he was very excited about a new project.'

'*The Murder Consultant*,' says Harbinder.

Miles gapes at her in a very uncouth way. 'How did you know that?'

'His agent told me.'

'Jelli Walker-Thompson,' says Julie. 'She's my agent too.'

'And Lance's,' says Benedict. He's been very quiet throughout the meal but Edwin thinks that his mind is working furiously. Another sign of Detective Fever.

'Remember the panel yesterday?' says Benedict. 'Lance said that he was working on something new. He said that he was very excited about it.'

'Well, he won't write it now,' says Natalka.

'Two writers who were excited about starting new projects and now they're both dead,' says Benedict. 'It makes you think, doesn't it?'

This has the effect of silencing the supper party.

Harbinder hasn't been able to make the TV work so, after supper, they play cards. Benedict finds an ancient pack of cards in the dresser, the joker marked up as the ace of hearts. They play rummy, which Harbinder has never played before.

'We didn't really play cards in my family,' she says apologetically.

'My family played all the time,' says Natalka, 'even on the beach. My dad was a real card expert . . . What do you say here? Card sharp?' And it seems that Natalka takes after him; she wins round after round. Harbinder learns quickly but makes mistakes, Benedict is surprisingly reckless, Miles methodical, Julie very careless. Edwin finds it hard to concentrate. The picture cards look up at him with their cold profiles: king, queen, jack. Which is which? Natalka is undoubtedly the queen of hearts, Harbinder the queen of diamonds. Does that make Julie a club or a spade?

'This is so strange,' says Julie. 'It's almost like being on holiday but we're in a police safe house hiding from a murderer.'

Her words make them all pause, cards in hand. The table is lit by a standard lamp but otherwise the room is in shadow. The wind has grown stronger over the course of the evening and, occasionally, the windows shake and the curtains fly inwards.

'We're not exactly hiding,' says Natalka. 'Living in a white house on the top of a cliff.' Even so, Edwin thinks that she is the one who is most spooked by Julie's words.

Benedict says, soothingly, 'We're quite safe. I mean, there are police outside.'

Harbinder had offered the officers some of the pasta but reported that they were eating fish and chips in the car. Edwin hopes that the heavy meal hasn't sent them to sleep.

'Lance thought he was safe,' says Natalka. 'Then he was murdered.'

'We don't know that he was murdered,' says Edwin.

'Of course he was,' says Miles, shuffling cards rather clumsily. 'Why do you think we're here?'

Outside, the wind howls.

In his downstairs room, which is actually very comfortable, Edwin puts on his pyjamas and gets into bed. He has a book with him, *The Mating Season* by P. G. Wodehouse, which always cheers him up, but somehow he can't lose himself in the wonderful world of Bertie Wooster. The wind is still making a nuisance of itself. The door is rattling away as if a madman is trying to gain admittance. Suddenly Edwin thinks of a quotation, from Malory, he thinks, probably *Le Morte d'Arthur*. *What, nephew, said the king, is the wind in that door?* He thinks of the cards: king, queen, jack. Hearts, clubs, diamonds, spades. He can hear the waves crashing against the harbour wall. Something is knocked over outside, probably a dustbin. Edwin gets up and goes to the window. The road is empty. Where's the police car that's meant to be protecting them? The pampas grass in the garden is waving furiously. Edwin gets back into bed.

A few seconds later, he puts Bertie down again. He can hear another noise, a scrunching regular sound that stops and then starts again. Someone is unmistakably walking on the gravel path around the house. Edwin puts on his dressing gown and goes out to the hallway. There he meets Harbinder, who is still fully dressed.

ELLY GRIFFITHS

'Did you hear that?' he says.

'Yes,' she says. 'Could be nothing. Could be a cat.'

'A cat wearing hob-nailed boots,' says Edwin.

Harbinder opens the front door. A blast of cold air blows her hair back.

'The squad car isn't there,' she says. 'They must have driven round the block.'

There's no block here, on the very eastern edge of Scotland, but Edwin doesn't say so. Harbinder switches on her phone torch. 'Is anyone there?'

The wind takes the power from her words. Harbinder sounds scared and, suddenly, very young. Edwin joins her in the doorway.

'I'm going to look,' she says.

'I'll come with you.'

'No, you stay here. We can't leave the door open.'

Harbinder is only gone for a few minutes. When she gets back, she says, 'There's no one there and the squad car is back. Everything's OK.'

But she double-locks the door carefully.

Chapter 29

Harbinder: amanuensis

Harbinder goes slowly back upstairs. The noise outside could easily have been the wind, or an animal like a fox or a cat, but she can't help thinking about her conversation with Natalka earlier.

They had found a little sitting room in the hotel, complete with stag's head and several bird collages made from actual feathers. Natalka, curled up in an armchair, looked pale and heavy-eyed.

'Why did you want to see me?' asked Harbinder.

'You know I told you about the two men in the car?' said Natalka. 'Well, I think they followed me here. The other night, in the pub, I heard two men talking in Ukrainian. They were talking about me.'

'Are you sure?'

'They said, "I'd know that face anywhere."'

'Do you recognise them?'

'Benny managed to take a photo but it was hard to see. They were youngish, maybe in their thirties, with short hair. I don't think I recognised them. But how many Ukrainians do you get in Aberdeen?'

'Have you told DI Harris?'

'No. He already thinks we're all crazy.'

Harbinder thought that this was probably true.

'Well, we're going to a safe house tonight,' she said. 'They can't follow you there.'

Natalka had looked unconvinced and now Harbinder doesn't feel quite so confident. What if the mysterious men *have* followed her? The unarmed officers outside will be no match against the Ukrainian mafia. Harbinder can hear conversation and muffled laughter coming from the room that Natalka and Julie are sharing. For a moment she's almost tempted to join them but she's never been one for girl talk, even when she was a girl.

There's a murmur coming from Miles's room, as if he's speaking on his phone. No sound from Benedict. Maybe he's praying? But it's hard to keep thinking of Benedict as an unworldly, monk-like figure. He seems different in Aberdeen, more definite somehow. He has obviously been supporting Natalka, and probably Edwin too. Not that Edwin needs support. He'd been very calm just now when any of the others would probably have freaked out. Harbinder goes into her room. She's so pleased to have scored the double bed and en suite. Well, she deserves it, she tells herself. After all, she's the only one who is actually still working. With this in mind, she checks her email before getting into bed and playing Panda Pop for half an hour.

She wakes up early the next morning. The sun has made its way through the thin curtains. Miles won't have slept a wink. Harbinder lies completely still for a few moments enjoying the warmth and the sound of the seagulls. She wonders what's going to happen today. Jim must be certain that Lance was murdered, otherwise why go to the expense of a safe house? Will he want to interview them again? She thinks that he's rather intrigued by Natalka and Benedict, although he seems to have convinced himself that Edwin is a prince amongst men. And what's her role in this, other than to provide some background about Dex Challoner and Peggy Smith? She told Jim her suspicions that Peggy might have been murdered by the same method used to kill Lance Foster. Jim had listened politely but she's pretty sure he has discounted her theory. An old lady dying alone in Shoreham doesn't interest him. He's only really concerned with his own dead body. How come Jim is a DI and Harbinder isn't? But she can't waste time thinking about this. She's got a job to do and, it's time to get up.

She showers in her posh en suite. Should she have offered this room to Edwin, as the oldest? Her mother would definitely think so. But Edwin had seemed perfectly happy with his allocation. She dresses quickly in jeans and a jumper and goes downstairs.

Sure enough, Miles is in the kitchen, moodily eating toast. Edwin is also there, gazing at the kettle as if willing it to work. There's a cafetière beside him and a delicious smell of coffee in the air. The clock has hands in the shape of carrots chasing sundry vegetables around the dial. It's seven-thirty, a carrot past a radish.

'Morning,' says Harbinder. 'Did everyone sleep well?'

'Like a log,' says Edwin, pouring boiling water onto the coffee.

'Very fitfully,' says Miles. 'I think I'm allergic to the pillows here.'

Harbinder ignores this and gratefully accepts a cup of coffee from Edwin. She makes herself some toast and spreads it with butter and Marmite. As she does so, she can hear her father's voice. 'Marmite is just one reason why the British will never be a civilised nation.'

Absorbed in her breakfast, it's a couple of seconds before she realises that Miles is talking to her.

'. . . like to talk to you,' he is saying. 'Shall we have a walk on the beach?'

Harbinder looks at Edwin who raises an eyebrow at her. 'Don't mind me,' he says, 'I'm quite happy here with P. G. Wodehouse.'

The squad car is outside and Harbinder stops to talk to the occupants, a different pair from yesterday. She offers them coffee but they say that they have already stopped at McDonald's. The car smells faintly of waffles.

'Anything to report last night?' she says. 'I thought I heard someone moving around out here.'

'That'll be the wind,' says one of the policemen. 'It was a wee bit blashie last night.'

That must mean windy, thinks Harbinder. It's a good onomatopoeic word but she doesn't think that it explains the sounds outside the house.

Harbinder and Miles walk along the shingle beach. It's another beautiful morning, the air fresh and smelling of the sea. There are a few fishing boats moored above the tide line and a fisherman sits mending his nets on the harbour wall.

'I've got friends who live near here,' says Miles. 'The landowner keeps trying to stop the fishing but it's been happening for hundreds of years. It's a way of life for these folk.'

'That's tough,' says Harbinder. She has noticed before that Miles seems more approachable when he's talking about Scotland.

They continue walking towards the end of the bay, slipping a little on the wet pebbles. Miles finds a flat stone and attempts to skim it. Harbinder wonders when he's going to tell her what's on his mind.

'You wanted to talk to me?' she prompts.

'It might not be important,' says Miles, 'but I had a rather strange email last night.'

'Strange in what way?' says Harbinder. She is thinking of the postcards. *We are coming for you.*

'An unsolicited manuscript,' he says. 'A book from someone I don't know.'

'But that must happen all the time.'

'Seventh Seal only accepts manuscripts via agents,' says Miles. 'This one's from an address that I've never heard of.'

'Is that so unusual?' asks Harbinder. She watches as a seagull swoops low over the waves. The sky is cloudier now and the wind stronger.

'Not necessarily,' says Miles, 'but when I looked at the synopsis, it's an exact copy of a Dex Challoner novel.'

Harbinder still doesn't see why this is so surprising. Surely plagiarism, conscious or unconscious, must be part of a fiction editor's life. She says as much.

'It's a copy of an *unpublished* Dex Challoner novel,' says Miles. 'In fact, it's one that Dex hadn't written yet. Now he never will, of course.'

Harbinder thinks that she gets it now. '*The Murder Consultant*?'

'Yes. It was a top-secret project. Only Jelli and I knew about it, as far as I know. I suppose Dex might have told Mia and his closest friends, though he wasn't the sort of writer who talked much about his work in progress.'

'He talked to Peggy,' says Harbinder, thinking of the note she had seen. *Do help me, darling. I've got to give Miles the rough draft next week.*

'I meant he didn't have hundreds of beta readers out there.'

'Beta readers?'

'People who read an author's book before the publisher sees it. Often they're friends of the author. They pick up mistakes, offer suggestions, that sort of thing. It can be a useful process but Dex didn't work like that. Apart from Mia, Jelli and I were always the first people to see the manuscript. It was the same with Betty, his previous editor.'

'How similar is this book to the one that Dex was planning?'

'According to the synopsis, it's almost identical. It's about an old lady living in sheltered accommodation who solves murders. Based on Peggy, of course.'

'What's it called?'

'*Amanuensis*. It's trying quite hard to be literary and cool but it's the same plot, all right.'

'And you don't know who sent it?'

'No. It's a Gmail address. Someone who calls themselves Booksdofurnish. It's from an Anthony Powell novel, "Books do furnish a room".'

Why do people insist on telling her this sort of stuff?

'Did Peggy know that Dex was planning to write about her?' says Harbinder.

'Yes,' says Miles. 'Dex said that she was chuffed to bits about it.'

Chapter 30

Natalka: blue blistering barnacles

The first thing that Natalka sees when she wakes up is Tintin. His oval face with black dot eyes is right next to hers. She blinks and tries to focus. It's the wallpaper, an endless parade of cartoon characters. Tintin and his dog. What was its name? Snowy. Those two identical detectives. The Captain. Captain Haddock. He was Natalka's favourite character, with his pipe and his whisky and his grand house in the country. Perhaps he was an idealised father figure. Certainly he was nothing like her own.

Natalka is in the top bunk. She had thought it nice of Julie to offer her the prime position but now she feels rather trapped. She can't get up without waking her room-mate and she can hear Julie snoring gently in the bed below. She had talked in her sleep last night too, though Natalka couldn't make out the words.

It feels wrong just to lie here; normally she does yoga in the mornings or goes for a run. Natalka can't remember the last time that she shared a bedroom. Lovers – and husbands – don't count. She wonders who decorated this room with the Tintin wallpaper and why. Who slept here? Siblings certainly. Maybe twins. People used to say that she and Dmytro were like twins because there were only eighteen months between them. The only time she remembers sharing a room with Dmytro was on holiday. Her father used to borrow a caravan from a workmate and they'd drive to the coast. Natalka and Dmytro were meant to take turns with the top bunk but somehow it was always Natalka's turn. She was the oldest and she supposes that she was a bit of a bully. She wishes that she could see Dmytro again, even if only to say sorry. The wallpaper blurs before her eyes. Tintin, Snowy, Thomson and Thompson, Captain Haddock.

She tries to climb down quietly but Julie hears her.

'Morning.'

'Morning. Sorry. Did I wake you?'

'I was awake anyway.' Natalka thinks she's just being polite.

'I was looking at the wallpaper,' says Natalka. 'I love Tintin.'

'Could you get the books in Ukrainian?'

'We read them in English. I always thought they were English. I was quite shocked when I found out that Hergé was Belgian. Captain Haddock always seemed like a typical Englishman to me.'

'Billions of bilious blue blistering barnacles,' says Julie. 'That what he used to say.'

'I remember,' says Natalka. She always liked the phrase though she found it hard to say. She whispers it now, looking out of the window. She can just see the sea, glittering away to the left. She remembers those caravan holidays again. Odessa, Koblevo, Skadovsk. Golden sand, theme parks, the smell of pine leaves.

'I wonder what we'll do today,' says Julie.

'I think we should go to the beach,' says Natalka.

★

By the time Natalka gets downstairs, Harbinder and Miles have already been out for a walk and Edwin is dozing over a P. G. Wodehouse. Benedict is in the kitchen eating toast and reading a book. Natalka thinks it's one of Julie's, she recognises the swimming pool on the cover. What must it be like to see people reading something you've written? Nerve-wracking, she imagines. Like watching a teacher read your English essay.

'Morning,' says Benedict. 'I've made fresh coffee.'

'Great.' Natalka pours herself a cup. 'Not as good as yours,' she says.

Benedict actually blushes. 'It's never as good in a cafetière.'

'That sounds like code for something.' Julie appears, wearing one of those floaty tops beloved of women who think that they're overweight.

'Just talking about coffee,' says Benedict. 'There's some freshly made.'

'Thank you.' Julie gets a mug and notices Benedict's reading matter. 'Oh my God. You're reading my book.'

'Yes,' says Benedict. 'I bought it before I went to your panel. It's really good.'

'Thanks so much.' Julie sounds genuinely pleased. 'I can't watch you read it though. I'll keep worrying if you're looking bored. I once sat opposite a woman reading one of my books on the Tube. It was torture.'

'I think we should go for a walk on the beach,' says Natalka.

'I went earlier,' says Harbinder from the doorway. 'It's very pretty but the wind's getting stronger.'

'We should get some fresh air,' says Natalka. She's already feeling claustrophobic.

'It's cloudy now,' says Julie, looking out the window.

'That's the best time to see the sea,' says Natalka. 'In the wind and the rain.'

'I agree,' says Benedict. 'I love the sea in all weathers. It's the best thing about my job.'

'What do you do?' asks Julie.

'I own a café,' says Benedict, colouring again. 'Well, a shack really.'

'Benny makes the best coffee on the south coast,' says Natalka.

'I think I went there with Peggy once,' says Miles suddenly. 'The coffee was really good.'

'Really?' says Benedict. 'Actually, I remember. I thought you must be a relative of hers.'

'Did you?' says Miles. He sounds more offended that the remark warrants, thinks Natalka. Surely anyone would be proud to be related to Peggy?

In the end, there are just the four of them on the walk. Miles says that he's had enough exercise for one day and Edwin says that it looks as if it's about to rain. Sure enough, when they go outside, the clouds are low over the sea. The wind has picked up and the seagulls are calling. The tide is out, exposing rocks shiny with seaweed.

'We shouldn't go out of sight of the squad car,' says Harbinder. She's obviously not off duty, thinks Natalka. She notices how Harbinder scans the road outside before taking the path to the beach. She, herself, is feeling calmer today. They are in a safe house on the Aberdeenshire coast, miles from nowhere, there's a police car outside. Surely the Ukrainians can't follow her here?

They walk across the beach. Julie slips in her smart, ankle boots but Natalka's trainers have better grip. Benedict goes to the water's edge and skims a stone. It skips over the waves, once, twice, three times, four, five.

'You're really good at that.'

Benedict grins, the wind whipping back his hair. 'My dad taught me. I was always better than Hugo. It really pissed him off.'

Natalka thinks it's the first time she's heard Benny use anything even close to a swear word.

Harbinder and Julie are examining the rock pools. Natalka notices that they're walking close together, but not talking. Occasionally, Julie's hand just brushes Harbinder's. Julie turns and waves at Natalka. 'We might see blue blistering barnacles!' The wind throws her words into the air.

'More likely just beadlet anemones,' says Benedict. How does he know these things? 'You get velvet swimming crabs too,' he says. 'They're very aggressive.'

Julie is now climbing on the rocks. She teeters on the black seaweed. 'You can see for miles from here.'

'Careful,' says Harbinder. Julie turns to look at her, smiling, and then seems to fall forwards, putting out a hand to save herself. Natalka hears the crack from where she's standing.

'Julie!' shouts Harbinder. She scrambles over the rocks and helps Julie to her feet. Julie rests her head against Harbinder's shoulder, just for a second. Benedict and Natalka hurry towards them.

'Are you OK?' Harbinder is saying.

'I'm fine,' says Julie, rather breathlessly. But, as Natalka gets closer she sees that Julie's right wrist is already starting to swell.

Benedict and Harbinder help Julie back over the rocks. Her face is alarmingly pale.

'You need to go to the hospital,' says Harbinder.

'It's probably only a sprain,' says Julie. 'I just need an aspirin and a lie down.' But her lips are blue and her wrist is beginning to discolour alarmingly.

'I think it's broken,' says Harbinder.

Benedict obviously thinks so too. 'Natalka and I will drive you,' he says.

'No,' says Harbinder. 'You ought not to leave the house. I'll take her.'

They walk up the concrete ramp, Harbinder and Benedict supporting Julie. One of the officers has got out of the car. Edwin comes out of the house, looking concerned.

'You need to go to A and E,' says the policeman, looking at Julie's wrist. 'We'll take you. That way DS Kaur can stay here with the rest of you.'

'I'll go with you,' says Edwin.

'There's no need,' says Julie, but her lower lip is trembling.

'It's wretched being in A and E on your own,' says Edwin. 'I'll just get my coat.' This takes some time but eventually he emerges wearing a coat and tartan scarf and carrying Julie's jacket. Edwin and Julie get into the back of the car. Natalka, Benedict and Harbinder watch as the police car drives away. Then they turn back to the house.

'Edwin left the front door open,' says Benedict. 'He must have been in a state.'

Natalka feels her heart beating in her chest. 'Don't go in!' she wants to say. But she follows Benedict and Harbinder into the safe house.

To find a strange man in the sitting room pointing a gun at Miles.

Chapter 31

Benedict: murder backwards

Benedict has always wanted to be a hero. How would it feel, he used to wonder, to emerge from a burning building with a body in your arms? Or to take a bullet for the girl you love? But, when it comes to it, the thing proves surprisingly simple.

Miles is on the sofa, chalk white, hand shielding his face. The man stands in front of him, gun pointing at the editor's chest.

'Put the gun down,' says Harbinder, her voice admirably steady.

The man says something in a language Benedict doesn't understand.

Natalka answers.

The man swings round and points the gun at her.

Benedict shouts 'No!' and throws himself in front of Natalka.

The gun goes off.

Silence. Seagulls calling.

Is he dead? Is this what dying feels like? If so, it's not too bad. A rush of blood to the head, a feeling of euphoria and a sense of having done this, not once, but many times before. It's funny, being shot doesn't hurt at all. Then he realises that he is still standing, Natalka is holding him from behind, and the foreign man is still pointing the gun at Miles. There's a hole in the wall where the first bullet has lodged itself.

'You betray us,' says the gunman, in English. Automatically, even in this terrifying moment, Benedict looks at his shoes. Scuffed white trainers. Not shiny shoe man then.

'I didn't mean to,' says Miles. 'We were students. We didn't know what we were doing.'

'Give me the gun,' says Harbinder, 'then we can talk about this.'

'He betrayed us,' says White Trainers. 'We went to prison for years and he just went back to his cosy university.'

'I know,' says Harbinder. 'Peggy helped you both, didn't she? But then the police came after you and Miles got safely back to England.'

'How did you guess?' says Miles. He is still sitting, looking stricken, on the sofa.

'You studied Russian at university,' says Harbinder. 'I suppose you were on a year abroad when you met Peggy. I remember the thank you card that you sent her. And there was something else, something an old lady said.'

'And now I'm going to kill him,' says the gunman. 'I've waited a long time.' He levels the gun again.

'Andriy,' says a new voice. 'Put the gun down.'

Andriy turns and Harbinder lunges forward to knock the gun from his hand. Benedict goes to help her and, as he does so, Natalka launches herself into the new man's arms. Benedict lets go of Andriy but all the fight seems to have gone out of the man. He just sits there on the floor. Miles starts to sob.

Natalka is still embracing the stranger.

'What's going on?' says Harbinder, taking the bullets out of the gun.

Benedict looks hard at the second man and back to Natalka. And suddenly he understands.

'I think that's her brother,' he says.

'This is Dmytro,' says Natalka. Her eyes are shining and she looks more beautiful than ever. Transfigured.

'Who's that?' says Benedict, gesturing towards the man on the floor. Andriy.

'We're both studying at the university here,' says Dmytro. 'They have a special programme for political refugees. I arrive two weeks ago. I've been trying to find Natalka and then she appears in front of me.'

'Were you in the pub that night?' asks Natalka. 'I didn't see you. Why didn't you speak to me?'

'I wasn't there,' says Dmytro. 'I couldn't believe it when Andriy showed me the photograph.'

'What photograph?' says Benedict, thinking of the picture he had taken of the two men drinking Coke. Was one of them the man who had tried to kill Miles?

'I was in the pub with Sergei,' says Andriy. 'He was the other one who was in Russia that time. We are having a drink and we see *him*.' He points at Miles. 'I know I must have my . . .' He clicks his fingers for the word.

'Revenge?' says Natalka helpfully.

'Yes, my revenge. I take a photograph and she . . .' he points at Natalka, 'she is in the background.'

'It wasn't my fault,' says Miles, sounding, for the first time, sulky rather than scared.

'No? Why you not in prison?' returns Andriy. 'I go to prison for *ten years*.'

'I'm sorry,' says Miles.

Harbinder is on her phone. Benedict hears her say, 'Armed assailant. Back-up needed urgently.' It sounds almost like a betrayal, now that Andriy has started speaking, has become a person rather than a gunman.

'Did you try to find Peggy?' says Natalka to Andriy. 'Did you come to Shoreham?' She is standing beside Dmytro, holding his hand. Side by side there's a resemblance that wasn't as noticeable before. Dmytro is taller and thinner, his cheekbones almost painfully chiselled, but his eyes are Natalka's, deep, dark blue.

'Yes,' says Andriy. 'Sergei and me, we drive to Peggy's house. We see her but there are people there. We come back the next day but she is dead.'

'I saw you,' says Natalka. 'I saw you from my window. You were in a white car.'

'Yes. We saw you at Peggy house. We follow you.'

'You knocked on my door, of the house where I live. You said you were friends of mine.'

'I wanted to talk about Peggy,' says Andriy. 'I don't know . . . you and Dmytro . . . are brother and sister. Then he sees the photo. He tells me.'

'I recognised you immediately,' says Dmytro. His English, like his sister's, is excellent. He says something in Ukrainian. Natalka takes his hand, wiping away tears.

'You see, Benny,' she says, 'my brother is alive.'

'I'm very glad to meet you,' says Benedict. He gets up from the floor and extends his hand. Dmytro shakes it.

'You're a very brave man,' says Dmytro. 'You put yourself in front of Natalka. You are a hero.'

'I'm not,' says Benedict.

'You are a hero, Benny,' says Natalka softly.

When Edwin and Julie return, with Julie's wrist in plaster, Andriy has been taken into custody and Harbinder is still at the police station. Benedict, Natalka and Dmytro are eating fish and chips at the kitchen table. They suddenly realised that they were very hungry and the squad car, abashed at missing all the action, went out for supplies. It's four o'clock in the afternoon, the carrot pointing to an aubergine. Miles, who has given a lengthy statement to the police, is lying down in his room.

'This is my brother,' says Natalka proudly.

'Your brother?' says Edwin. 'I thought he was . . .' He stops.

'I thought you were dead,' says Natalka to Dmytro. 'I told everyone that you were dead.'

'I was a prisoner of war in Russia,' says Dmytro. 'I send letters to Mama via Amnesty but I never had a reply.'

'She's moved,' says Natalka. 'She was scared to stay in the old house. She travels around, looking for you. She never believed you were dead.'

'How did you get out of Russia?' asks Benedict.

'There was an exchange of prisoners on 7th September this year,' says Dmytro. 'A swap with the separatists. President Trump said it was "a giant step to peace".' He smiles, rather sardonically.

Natalka says something in Ukrainian. Dmytro replies. They are both crying. And, at this moment, Harbinder arrives, carrying several greaseproof bags. 'I was starving,' she says. 'I stopped

ELLY GRIFFITHS

at the chip shop on my way back.' Everyone falls on these fresh
supplies.

Dmytro has wiped his eyes. He turns to Harbinder. 'What has
happened to Andriy?'

'He's in custody,' says Harbinder. 'Jim wants to charge him with
attempted murder but Miles doesn't want to press charges. He
might get off with possessing an illegal weapon.'

'Andriy is not a bad man,' says Dmytro. 'I think seeing Miles
again just sent him . . .' He looks at Natalka.

'Over the edge,' says Natalka. Benedict guesses that she probably
finished his sentences even when they were children.

'Tell us about Miles,' says Edwin. Benedict thinks he sounds
annoyed at being out of the loop. 'How did he know this Andriy?'

'As far as I can make out,' says Harbinder, glancing upwards,
probably wondering whether Miles can overhear. 'Peggy and her
friend Joan met Andriy and Sergei in Russia in 2005. They were
students but they had got themselves involved with some espionage
business. They were hiding from the KGB – or FSB as it's now
called – and met Miles, who was in Russia as part of his university
course. Miles translated for them and he found a place for them to
hide, in Peggy and Joan's apartment. It seemed to go well, Peggy
and Joan even took them to the ballet. But, a few days later, Andriy
and Sergei were arrested. They were convinced that Miles had
betrayed them. I think he did, unwittingly, tell the KGB where to
find them. He was young and he probably panicked. Andriy and
Sergei were sent to prison but released three years ago. They came
to Aberdeen as part of the refugee programme. They were in the
pub one evening and who should walk in but Miles. He was out
for a drink with some of his authors.'

280

'Not me,' Julie says. 'He completely blanked me.'

'Dex Challoner's editor was the man Peggy helped,' says Edwin. 'It seems such a coincidence.'

'Not really,' says Harbinder. 'I think Miles wanted to work with Dex because of the link with Peggy. Remember we found that thank you card from him in one of Peggy's books? It was sent before Miles became Dex's editor.'

'How did you guess about Miles?' Benedict asks Harbinder. 'You seemed to know immediately.'

'Peggy's daughter-in-law told us about the students she had helped,' says Harbinder. 'And we found some letters from Joan that mentioned meeting one of "the boys", as she called them. But, when I saw Andriy pointing a gun at Miles, something else suddenly came into my head. I went to see Joan, Peggy's friend, in her care home. She's got Alzheimer's and wasn't making such sense. But, when I asked her about the students, she said, "Miles from home." Miles.' She looks round the table.

'That's very clever,' says Edwin.

Harbinder makes a self-deprecating noise but Benedict thinks that she looks rather pleased with herself. Remembering the way Harbinder had tackled the gunman, calmly taking the bullets from the lethal-looking weapon, he thinks she has every right to feel smug.

'Joan also said that Nigel wasn't a good son and that he'd taken all Peggy's money,' said Harbinder. 'She said that Peggy liked to gamble.'

'That's not true,' says Edwin. 'In all the years I knew her Peggy only made one yearly bet on the Grand National.'

'Joan said that she liked horse-racing,' says Harbinder. 'Or that someone did. And, just before we left, Joan woke up – she'd been dozing – and said "Red Rum". Then she went back to sleep.'

Everyone laughs but Benedict is thinking of old films, of a spooky hotel, of Jack Nicholson, his eyes wild. *The Shining*. Here's Johnny. He says, 'Red Rum is an anagram for murder. It's murder backwards, actually.'

'I hadn't thought of that,' says Harbinder.

'I'm terrible at anagrams,' says Edwin. 'I wouldn't have thought of it either.'

'All Dex's books had the word "murder" in their titles,' says Natalka.

'Maybe Joan was trying to send us a message,' says Harbinder.

'Maybe,' says Julie, slowly. She hasn't spoken much during the meal and Benedict wonders whether her wrist is hurting. It's her right hand so maybe she's worrying about her writing. Now Julie says, 'My mum had Alzheimer's and sometimes she seemed to speak in code, saying things that seemed weird and disconnected but made sense later.'

'Peggy liked codes,' says Natalka. 'Mysteries too.'

'I wish she was here to solve this one,' says Edwin.

No one stays up late that night. After supper Natalka and Dmytro shut themselves in the bunk-bed room to telephone their mother but Dmytro reappears at ten and announces his intention of sleeping on the sofa. This encourages everyone to go to bed. Miles still hasn't emerged from his room.

Benedict has only exchanged a few words with Natalka since the scene with the gun. It's as if she's a different person now that Dmytro has appeared. She is glowing, so incandescent that, a couple of times, when they were eating fish and chips, Benedict had to look away from her. It's as if, like the sun, it's dangerous to look at her for too long. They say goodnight on the landing and Benedict hears Natalka's door shut. There's a gentle snore from Miles's room and the faint bleep of an electronic game from Harbinder's.

Benedict should be exhausted but, when he gets into bed, he finds he can't sleep. This room was obviously once a study, with IKEA desk and chairs and a corkboard on the wall. There's no bedside light so he lies in the darkness, listening to the wind and the sound of the sea on the shore.

This is my brother.

Murder backwards.

Thank heaven fasting for a good man's love.

I once knew an old lady who was just like Miss Marple.

Thanks for the murders.

He must have closed his eyes because, when he opens them, his door is open and a sliver of light falls across the bed. He can smell Natalka's perfume.

She drifts across the room like a dream and sits on the end of his bed.

'You saved my life.'

'I didn't,' says Benedict. 'He wasn't trying to kill you.'

'You didn't know that,' says Natalka. 'I think you're the bravest person I have ever met.'

Benedict tries to speak, to remonstrate, but Natalka leans over and silences him with a kiss.

Chapter 32

Harbinder: miles from home

When Harbinder comes down to breakfast she finds Edwin and Dmytro having a lively conversation about Dynamo Kyiv. She is impressed by Edwin's knowledge of football; she thought that he only knew about classical music and P. G. Wodehouse.

Dmytro stands up when she comes in. He's very polite. It's rather exhausting.

'Can I get you some coffee?'

'Thank you.'

Harbinder makes herself some toast and sits opposite Edwin.

'Do you think we'll go home today?' says Edwin, spreading marmalade with a careful hand. Harbinder has noticed before that it irritates Edwin when Natalka uses the same knife for marmalade and for butter, and when Benedict eats too slowly. That's what living on your own does for you, she thinks. That'll be her in a few years' time.

'I hope so,' says Harbinder. 'I can't see that there's any point in keeping us here. If Julie needs police protection, that can happen just as easily in Brighton. And safe houses and surveillance teams are expensive. Jim must be wanting to get rid of us.'

'Do you think DI Harris will charge Andriy?' says Dmytro.

'He'll charge him with something,' says Harbinder. 'After all, he had a gun. And he fired it, even if the bullet did hit the wall.' Was he aiming for Miles, she wonders, or was the first shot simply a warning? She thinks that Jim could still charge Andriy with attempted murder even if Miles doesn't want to press charges.

'I don't think Andriy would have hurt Miles,' says Dmytro.

Harbinder isn't so sure. The gun had been loaded. She took the bullets out herself.

Just as they are finishing breakfast, DI Jim Harris himself appears.

'Bit of a mad night last night,' he says. 'Is there any coffee going?'

Edwin pours some out. Jim looks totally at ease, leaning back in his chair enjoying his coffee, but Harbinder thinks that the presence of the police officer makes Dmytro feel nervous. He gets up, muttering about needing a shower. Jim drains his mug and Edwin fills it up.

Jim turns to Harbinder. 'Good work yesterday. I've written up my report. You could be in for a commendation.'

Harbinder tries to look modest. She'd *love* to receive a commendation.

'How did you guess that Miles Taylor was the target?' says Jim.

Harbinder tells him the story about Joan and 'miles from home'. It had gone down well last night and she expected Jim to be similarly impressed but he smiles, rather irritatingly. 'So it was just a hunch then.'

'Maybe not,' says Edwin. 'Maybe Joan was also thinking about Miles. She also said "red rum" which is an anagram for murder.'

Now Jim laughs aloud. 'We need to have a quick chat, Harbinder,' he says.

Edwin stands up. 'I'll leave you to it.'

'No, stay,' says Jim, unexpectedly. 'You've been involved with this thing from the start and I'd like your input.'

Edwin sits down, looking immensely gratified.

'We've charged Andriy Avramenko with possession of a lethal weapon,' says Jim, 'but I'd like to add attempted murder to that. By his own admission, he came here to kill Miles Taylor until he was disarmed by DS Kaur here.' He makes a mock bow in Harbinder's direction. It does sound rather heroic, put like that.

'Avramenko must have followed us on Thursday evening and been hanging around ever since. I'll have a word with the uniforms about that.'

He sounds very grim. Harbinder can't believe how quickly time is moving all of a sudden. Lance was killed on Wednesday night, they moved to the safe house on Thursday. Today is Saturday, a busy day for her parents in the shop. She must go home and help them.

'Harbinder and I thought that we heard someone prowling round the house on Thursday night,' says Edwin.

'Yes. DS Kaur mentioned that.' Jim pauses for a moment to finish his second cup of coffee. When he looks up, his face has changed. It's as if he has made up his mind up about something. 'The thing is,' he says, 'I don't think there is a link between the murder of Lance Foster and that of Dex Challoner.'

Edwin and Harbinder look at each other. 'What?' says Harbinder.

'The two deaths are completely different,' says Jim. 'Lance was killed by a lethal injection of insulin, Dex was shot in the head. I don't think they're connected.'

'But what about the threatening notes?' says Harbinder. 'What about Peggy Smith? What about the gunman who burst into her flat?'

Jim makes an impatient gesture. 'I think we're in danger of complicating things. I've got a man killed in a hotel room and now I've got a crazed gunman wandering around. I don't need extra complications. All this stuff about books and anagrams, it's just conjecture. It doesn't add up to anything.'

Harbinder thinks that this is very unfair. It was Edwin who mentioned anagrams, not her. The rest is fact. A gunman did burst into Peggy's flat, Dex Challoner was murdered, three threatening notes have been received, Miles received a manuscript based on Dex's next book. It all has to connect somehow.

Jim says, in a more conciliatory tone, 'It certainly looked as if there was a link with the Dex Challoner case. That's why we got you up here, Harbinder. After all, they were both crime writers. But it's just as likely that we're looking at two different killers. Challoner could have been killed by a jealous girlfriend or a literary rival.'

'What about Lance?' says Edwin. 'Who killed him?'

'You tell me,' says Jim. He looks at Edwin as if this is a real request but Edwin just stares back at him.

'I don't have any suspects,' says Jim. 'There's nothing on the CCTV as yet but we're hopeful that something will turn up. I'll be looking into Lance Foster's private life too. Ten to one he was killed by someone he knew well.'

'Another jealous girlfriend?' says Harbinder.

Jim ignores this. Maybe, like Neil, he's bad at sarcasm. 'Aye. Maybe. Any road, we've got a long day of interviews ahead and you guys must be keen to get home.'

'Yes we are,' says Edwin, 'but—'

Jim stands up. 'I'll send a car for DS Kaur and for Miss Monroe. Miss Kolisnyk and Mr Cole can follow behind. Mr Fitzgerald, you can choose.'

'I'll go with Harbinder,' says Edwin. 'I don't want to be a gooseberry.'

Right on cue, Benedict and Natalka appear, both looking flushed and slightly sheepish.

Now that they know they're leaving, it seems a long wait for the police car. Dmytro is coming with them. He wants to spend some time with his sister. 'I can't wait to see Shoreham,' he keeps saying. Harbinder hopes that he isn't too disappointed.

They sit with their bags around them, Julie tapping with one hand on her laptop, Benedict reading *Laocoön* by Lance Foster. Natalka stares out of the window and Edwin reads a copy of the *Cove Bay News*, which came through the letter box that morning.

Harbinder tries to read her emails but can't concentrate. She is furious with Jim. How dare he dismiss their whole case as 'conjecture'? Lance's killer could still be in Aberdeen and now the police are concentrating on a Ukrainian man who, although admittedly rather hot-headed and murderously inclined, had no link with Lance Foster at all. She decides that a game of Panda Pop will calm her down but, before she can help Mama Panda defeat the Badboon, her phone pings. It's Neil.

'Hallo,' says Harbinder. At least this is someone who doesn't think that her case is pure fantasy.

Neil sounds excited, which means that he thinks he's made a breakthrough. It'll be tough to disillusion him but someone has to do it.

'We've had a lucky break with the CCTV at Millionaires' Row,' says Neil. 'One of the neighbours has just got back from holiday and their camera overlooks the patio at the back of Dex's place. Dex had a visitor at ten past midnight on September the twenty-second.'

According to the coroner, Dex Challoner had been killed some time between midnight and two a.m. on Saturday the twenty-second. Harbinder feels her heart beating faster. Detective fever, Edwin would call it.

'Who is it?'

'I'll send you a screenshot. We're hoping to get some more pictures from another neighbour.'

Neil is stringing things out but it's only a few seconds before the email flashes up on Harbinder's screen. She clicks on the attachment. It shows a woman looking straight into the lens of what she doesn't realise is a camera.

Maria.

Maria, who is currently looking after Harbinder's mother.

Harbinder rings Neil back immediately.

'It's Maria. The carer. She knew Peggy too. And Weronika. Natalka might have her contact details. I'll ask her. In the meantime, get onto Patricia Creeve who runs Care4You. She'll know for sure. And, Neil, go round to Mum's. Stop Maria getting anywhere near her.'

'Will do,' says Neil. 'Don't worry.'

Don't worry. Jesus.

'I'll be home as soon as I can.'

Jim gets her onto a flight at midday. He drives her to the airport himself. Harbinder doesn't know if the latest lead has blown his two murderers theory out of the water. She hopes so.

'This Maria,' says Jim, as they speed over the bridge, 'what do you know about her?'

'She's a carer,' says Harbinder, 'originally from Poland. She's married and has three children. My colleague has just been round to her house and there's no one there. Apparently they haven't been seen Tuesday.'

'So this Maria could have been in Aberdeen and, in theory, could have killed Lance Foster?'

'Yes. Remember the receptionist said that the only people on that floor were cleaners? Maria could easily have passed as a cleaner in her carer's overalls. She could even have worn her old nurse's outfit. People never notice foreign-looking women. I know that for a fact.'

'You can't get a rise out of me on that one,' says Jim. 'But why would Maria kill Lance?'

'I don't know. Maybe because he knew that she killed Dex.'

Harbinder is leaning forward, willing the car to go faster. Jim drops her outside the airport. That's the beauty of small airports, you can almost park on the runway.

'Your plane's in forty minutes,' he says. 'Good luck.'

Harbinder feels as if she's been holding her breath for the whole flight. When she arrives at Shoreham Airport, Neil is waiting for her.

'Olivia's with your mum,' he says. 'Everything is fine.'

Olivia Grant is one of their best young constables. Harbinder starts to breathe again.

'Still no sign of Maria?'

'No. We've got a car waiting outside her house. Patricia says that she hasn't been to work since Tuesday. She's very put out, what with Natalka and Maria going missing at the same time. She's had to visit a lot of their clients herself.'

Neil drives quickly and efficiently to Harbinder's house. She finds Olivia and her mother sitting on the sofa watching *Celebrity Antiques Roadshow*.

'Hallo, Harbi,' says her mother, looking round. 'Do you want something to eat?'

Chapter 33

Benedict: matching pyjamas

This time the drive through the Scottish hills is pure bliss. The sun shines on distant lakes and stone castles, on bosky woods and low-lying villages. Natalka is driving and she and Dmytro sing along to Radio 1. Benedict is in the back, dreamily listening to the lyrics. Maybe pop music is the reason both siblings are so good at English. Dmytro even has a slight American accent.

Benedict still can't quite believe that last night actually happened. He slept with Natalka. He, who honestly thought that he would die a virgin. He had sex with a beautiful woman and it hadn't been stressful at all, just miraculously and wonderfully right. Are they now going out together? Surely they're too old to be called boyfriend and girlfriend? Are they – the very word gives him a distinct thrill – in a *relationship*? Natalka and Dmytro sing about love and being closer to you. Benedict thinks of the future. Of waking up next to Natalka every morning, of shopping in the open market with her, going on boat-trips, celebrating Christmas together, possibly wearing matching pyjamas . . .

'Can you see what's happening in the other car?' says Natalka.

Benedict turns. The black Nissan Qashqai, driven by a taciturn young man called Duncan, is directly behind them. He can see Julie in the passenger seat. It looks like she's on her phone.

'Edwin's probably asleep in the back,' says Benedict.

'Don't you believe it,' says Natalka. 'He only pretends to go to sleep. He's the sharpest of all of us.'

'He is a very wise man,' says Dmytro. 'And he knows a lot about football.'

They stop at Tebay services again. This time they are attempting to do the ten-hour drive in one go, so rest stops are essential. Benedict, Edwin and Julie sit outside the farm shop drinking coffee. Ducks patrol the grass in search of crumbs. Natalka, Dmytro and Duncan are smoking and vaping at a different table..

'Why did Harbinder dash off like that?' says Julie. 'She hardly said goodbye.'

'She asked Natalka for Maria's home address,' says Benedict. 'Maria's one of the carers. I think she's doing some freelance work for Harbinder's family at the moment. Maybe Harbinder's mother has taken a turn for the worse. I hope not.'

'I must say, I was surprised that Harbinder didn't share the news with us,' says Edwin. 'Even DI Harris talked quite openly in front of me. He said he valued my input.'

This is the third time Edwin has mentioned this remark. Benedict is pleased that Jim recognised Edwin's contribution but, even so, try as he does to be charitable, it's a little galling. After all, Benedict is the one who likes solving mysteries. He was the one who spotted Nigel leaving the hotel with Lance, who worked out the old school connection. He's been wracking his brains over the case. And he has a flow chart to prove it.

'I wonder when we'll get back,' says Julie. 'I told the dog-sitter about ten. I can't wait to see Arthur again.'

'I'll get some coffee for Natalka,' says Benedict, before Julie can start showing him dog pictures. 'I know how she likes it.'

'I bet you do,' says Edwin.

Natalka lets him drive for the next stretch. It's been years since Benedict has been behind the wheel of a car. He passed his test at seventeen because his father informed him 'that's what men do'. Benedict had actually enjoyed driving and was rather pleased to pass his test first time, unlike Hugo who took three attempts. But there hadn't been much opportunity to drive at the seminary or, later, in the monastery. And now he can't afford a car. Hugo, of course, owns some four-wheel-drive monster with blacked-out windows.

It's quite scary at first but he soon gets the hang of it, enjoying the sensation of speed and autonomy. The huge sign saying 'M1 and The South' makes him laugh out loud.

'The south,' he says. 'It's such an over-simplification.'

'I like the south,' says Natalka and the words sound incredibly sexy in her incredibly sexy accent: palm trees, hammocks, drinks with umbrellas in them. 'I live in the south of Ukraine. You must visit one day.'

'I'd love to,' says Benedict hoarsely.

'We'll all go together,' says Dmytro.

'Is it all right for you to go back?' asks Benedict. He can't see Dmytro but he can hear him sigh.

'One day,' he says. 'One day I'll go back. When the Russians have gone.'

'It's incredible how long wars go on,' says Benedict. 'I was reading Conan Doyle the other day and he says that Dr Watson has just got back from the war in Afghanistan. Awful to think that there's still war there.'

'Crimea too,' says Natalka. 'You learn about Florence Nightingale in history books but it's still going on. Do you know, I read that animals are thriving in the area of Ukraine around Chernobyl. Anything, even deadly radiation, is better for animals than living near people.'

'Human beings are monsters,' says Dmytro, but he says it with a laugh in his voice. A few seconds later Natalka switches on Radio 1 again.

Even when you're sitting beside the woman you love, the M1 is a dreary motorway. They stop for lunch (toasted ciabattas with molten mozzarella) and, afterwards, Natalka takes the wheel again. Now they don't seem to feel like talking. Natalka listens to music, Dmytro snoozes in the back and Benedict reads *Laocoön* until it's too dark to see.

'Doesn't it make you feel sick to read in a car?' says Natalka.

'No,' says Benedict. 'It's one of my few super powers.'

He loves it when he makes her laugh.

They stop again for coffee and chocolate brownies that taste of charcoal. Benedict reads the acknowledgements page of *Laocoön* while Edwin and Julie queue up for refills.

'Lance doesn't thank many people,' he says. 'Nothing about his agent or editor.'

'What was the thing he said about Peggy?' says Natalka, finishing off brownie crumbs with a moistened finger.

'Peggy Smith, *sine quibus*.'

'Without whom.'

'Yes. There's only one other acknowledgement. 'Love and thanks to the bay window set.'

'Bow window set?' says Julie, putting her tray down. 'That's in Georgette Heyer. They were dandies who used to sit in the window seat of their club. On St James's Street, I think. Sophy, in *The Grand Sophy*, shocks everyone by driving her high-perch phaeton down St James's Street.'

'Lance Foster didn't strike me as a Georgette Heyer fan,' says Benedict. 'I wonder what he meant by "bay window set". Although . . . I wonder . . .'

'What?' says Natalka.

'Bay window can be an answer to a cryptic crossword clue,' says Benedict. 'The clue is something like "having a sea view perhaps" because, you know, bay and sea.'

'Please tell me that you're not going to start talking about anagrams again,' says Edwin, sitting down with his tea. 'I'm too old.'

'It's not an anagram,' says Benedict, 'but it might be a clue. Come on, Edwin, what comes to mind when I say "Seaview"?'

'A particularly depressing block of flats,' says Edwin.

'Exactly. What if Lance's mother – or relative, at any rate – lived in Seaview Court? What if she knew Peggy and Weronika? What if they were the bay window set? There are bay windows in Seaview Court. Peggy had one.'

'And that's how Lance knew Peggy,' says Natalka. 'He never did tell us.'

'We should tell Harbinder,' says Benedict. 'It's a link.'

'I don't think I'll ever see Harbinder again,' says Julie. She sounds rather fed-up and gets out her phone, maybe to cheer herself up with pictures of Arthur.

Edwin comes with them for the last leg of the journey. Duncan is going to take Julie to her flat in Hove, stay at a B and B nearby, and then drive back to Aberdeen the next morning. This explanation is the most any of them have heard him speak the whole day.

It's quite cosy to finish the journey with Edwin, the way they started it. It seems much more than six days ago that they set out in the dawn playing Who Am I and talking about Gretna Green. In that week, Benedict has discovered a dead body, thrown himself in the path of a bullet and had sex. A pretty memorable few days in anyone's book, even one written by a crime writer. He looks at himself in the passenger mirror, wondering if the change in him would be visible to an outsider.

'What are you smiling at?' says Edwin from the back seat. 'I could do with a laugh.' Edwin seems rather depressed at the thought of returning to Seaview Court.

'Just thinking about everything that's happened.'

'Yes, it's been a strange few days,' says Edwin.

'It's been wonderful,' says Natalka.

She must mean finding Dmytro, thinks Benedict, but it would be nice to think that last night played some part in Natalka's positive assessment.

'I wonder if we'll ever know what happened to Lance Foster,' says Edwin. 'I got the impression that DI Harris wasn't going to keep Harbinder informed. Mind you, he did say that he valued my input . . .'

'Let's play Who Am I?' says Benedict.

It takes them some time to explain the game to Dmytro and almost the whole of the M25 to guess Benedict's choice of Sammy Davis Junior. Then Edwin has a similar success with Joan Bakewell. By now they are on the Shoreham Road, the sea ink-black in the distance.

'I can't wait to see where you live,' says Dmytro.

'It's nothing special,' says Natalka. 'My landlady's looking forward to meeting you though. Her husband will probably ask you lots of questions about Ukraine.'

Benedict feels his heart sink. Natalka will drop him at his digs and then this adventure will be over. Maybe he and Natalka will go back to being just friends, meeting at the Shack for a comradely cappuccino every day.

Seaview Court is the first stop. Edwin looks rather sad wheeling his suitcase up to the front door but, once he has keyed in the code, he looks round and gives them a jaunty wave.

'Poor Edwin,' says Natalka. 'He'll be lonely after this. We must look after him.'

She really is an angel.

Natalka yawns as she backs out of the car park. It's nearly eleven o'clock. All too soon they are outside Benedict's apartment.

'See you around, Benny,' says Natalka.

'Sure,' says Benedict. He gets his Gladstone bag out of the boot. Isn't she even going to get out of the car?

But then, just as he is fumbling for his keys, Natalka is beside him. She kisses him on the cheek.

'I'll miss you tonight,' she whispers.

'Me too,' says Benedict. 'We must do it again sometime.'

'We will,' says Natalka. 'We are lovers now.' And she waves him goodbye as she gets into the car.

The house is silent as Benedict climbs the stairs. He opens the door to his bedsit which, flooded with moonlight, now looks like a magical bower, full of possibilities. He has a shower but, even though it's now nearly midnight, finds himself unable to sleep. He looks out of the window as the lighthouse beam sweeps across the harbour, illuminating ships and masts and the dark water. Maybe he should say his prayers. After all, he's got a lot to be thankful for. He remembers, with a sudden rush of affection, the evening prayers at the monastery, vespers, a litany of praise and thanksgiving. He doesn't kneel but stays sitting at his desk, staring dreamily in front of him. The surface is as neat as usual, just a book, a notepad and a bookmark. The book is *Thank Heaven Fasting* by Sheila Atkins and the notepad just has one word on it: 'France?' The bookmark is actually a picture of St Patrick, showing the saint in bishop's green, holding a shamrock and a staff. Then Benedict remembers. This was the bookmark that fell from Peggy's copy of the book, the one that was snatched by the gunman. He'd kept it because he'd always had a fondness for the patron saint of Ireland, even though he was never formally canonised. He likes holy pictures too. His grandmother, more Catholic than the rest of the family, had collected them.

The light falls on the picture. St Patrick. Pray for us. Then Benedict hears Peggy's voice. *Religion is the opium of the people.* Why had Peggy, who despised formal religion, kept a holy picture in a book?

Natalka's voice: *Maria said that the clue was in the book*. Benedict had read *Thank Heaven Fasting* from cover to cover and found nothing significant. But what if the clue was actually *in* the book? What if Patrick himself was the clue?

The searchlight moves on, leaving the room in darkness.

Chapter 34

Harbinder: church bells

Harbinder wakes early but her mother is already in the kitchen, preparing breakfast. Her father is at the table, eating a plate of dalia and reading yesterday's local paper. *Dex Murder: Police Baffled*. Starsky sits beside him, looking stoical. He's waiting for his morning walk.

'Isn't a carer meant to come in the morning?' says Harbinder, putting the kettle on for coffee. Her mother only ever makes tea or haldi doodh. Harbinder still remembers being asked, in primary school, to describe a typical breakfast. 'First you make the makki roti . . .' Kevin Brewster had laughed so much that he'd had to leave the room.

'I haven't seen Maria for a few days,' says Bibi. 'I hope she isn't ill. Patricia said that she'd try to send Vicky later. Or she might even come herself at midday. She's so kind.'

'Why aren't you the shop?' says Harbinder. It's only seven-thirty but the shop opens at seven.

'Kush is there,' says her father. 'I'm going to watch Kiaan play football.' He tries to sound casual but Harbinder knows that he loves watching his grandson play. Kiaan is only eight but, according to Harbinder's mother, that well-known football pundit, he has 'already been scouted'. It's funny, Deepak is scathing about Indians who try too hard to assimilate but there's nothing he likes better than watching Sunday morning football, yelling from the sidelines and complaining about the referee. If there's a more typically English pastime, Harbinder would like to see it.

'Give him my love,' she says, because she's very fond of her nieces and nephews. 'Tell him to score a hat-trick.'

Bibi rolls her eyes. 'He's a *defender*, Harbi.'

'I'm going into work,' says Harbinder.

'On a Sunday?' says Bibi, as if she's a devout Catholic about to drag them all to mass.

'I'm working on a murder case,' says Harbinder. 'If the carers don't come, ring me. And, Mum, if Maria comes round, ring me immediately.'

'Why?' says Deepak, looking up from the paper. Starsky goes to fetch his lead.

'I need to talk to her,' says Harbinder grimly.

Neil and Donna are both at the station, Donna finishing her morning doughnut, Neil flexing his biceps.

'How was bonny Scotland?' says Donna. 'Did you bring us back any shortbread?'

'Sorry,' says Harbinder. She always forgets to bring presents, although she hardly ever goes anywhere. Neil brings sweets even if he goes to Bognor for the day.

'This came for you,' says Neil, proffering a jiffy bag. 'I opened it in case it was a bomb but it's just a book.'

'Glad to see that you're following safety procedure,' says Harbinder. The book is a paperback copy of *A Town Called Murder* by Dex Challoner. Inside there's a note from Pippa Sinclair-Lewis, the publicist.

> *As promised this is the first in Dex's Murder series. Enjoy!*
> *Best,*
> *Pippa.*

It's a nice thought, thinks Harbinder, but she doesn't know when she's going to find the time to read a tome like this. She puts the book in her bag.

'What have we found out about Maria?' she says.

Neil turns to his notes. He writes everything down in his big, careful handwriting. It drives Harbinder mad but it's also useful sometimes.

'Maria Holloway, nee Lipska. She's thirty-five, married to Lee Holloway, a carpet-fitter. Born in Kozlowo but has lived in England for ten years. Used to work as a nurse at the Princess Royal. Good references from there. Patricia Creeve says that Maria left nursing for a job that she could fit round childcare. Maria and Lee have three children, Michael, Lucy and Jamie. The eldest two are at St Mark's in Steyning and they haven't been in school since Tuesday. Lee works at Carpet Kingdom in Shoreham and he hasn't been to work either. They live just outside Steyning. We've had a car posted outside their house all night but there's been no sign of life.'

No sign of life. Harbinder thinks of Peggy sitting in her chair with the view over the beach and the harbour. Had Maria, the ex-nurse, killed her? But why?

'Maria could have been taking money from Peggy's account,' she says. 'And Dex said that Weronika always thought that people were cheating her. Maybe she was right. Maybe Maria was stealing from her.'

'Why would she kill Dex though?'

'Maybe he found out that she'd killed his mother. Remember what Maria told Natalka? That Peggy said she knew something about Weronika's death?'

'Why would Maria say that if she was the one who killed her, though?' says Donna. She is staring at a picture on her laptop of Maria, taken from Facebook. Maria has her arms around two children. Her hair is loose and she is relaxed and smiling. Donna then clicks onto the still from the CCTV. Maria is looking straight into the camera, hair pulled back, eyes steely.

'Maria visited Dex at ten past midnight,' says Harbinder. 'It fits with the time of death.'

'Would she shoot him, though?' says Neil. 'I mean, I can just about see Maria killing two old ladies. Injecting them or something. But to shoot a man in cold blood . . .'

Neil never thinks that women are capable of extreme violence. It's quite sweet but not accurate, in Harbinder's experience.

'Could she have killed Lance Foster too?' says Donna.

'It's possible,' says Harbinder. 'The hotel receptionist says that there were cleaners in the vicinity. Maria could have posed as a cleaner in her carer's outfit.'

'What about Nigel Smith?' says Donna. 'If money was the motive, he stood to gain most from Peggy's death.'

'And Joan, Peggy's friend, said that Nigel had taken her money,' says Neil. 'He wasn't a good son, that's what she said.'

'Are we sure that Nigel was in Aberdeen at the time of Lance's death?' says Donna.

'I think so,' says Harbinder. 'Edwin was certain and he knows Nigel quite well. Benedict saw him too, going to lunch with Lance. Apparently Nigel and Lance were at school together.'

'I went to see Nigel on Friday,' says Neil. 'He wasn't there. His wife said that he was in Frankfurt. On business.'

'Sally might not know,' says Harbinder. 'Or she might be hiding something. Let's go to see her again. And, on the way back, we can call in at Maria's, talk to the neighbours, try to get some idea about where she might be.'

'OK,' says Neil. Harbinder thinks that he's dying to see the perfect village again.

The church bells are ringing as they approach the Smiths' house. This is probably the only place, aside from Ambridge, where people still attend the village church, thinks Harbinder. Her mother listens to *The Archers* sometimes, despite not being able to tell any of the characters apart. Will Sally, a Shula-type if there ever was one, be attending the Sunday morning service? But, no, Sally opens the door immediately, holding onto Ozymandias's collar. She's wearing wellingtons and has clearly just come back from a dog walk.

'Oh,' she says. 'It's you.' It seems that the veneer of civility is wearing thin.

'Can we come in?' says Harbinder. 'Hallo, Ozzy.' She tries, simultaneously, to pat the dog and push it away from her.

'It's not a very convenient time . . .' says Sally. But Neil and Harbinder are already sitting at the breakfast bar with Ozymandias frisking fatly around them.

'Where's Nigel today?' says Harbinder.

'As I told your colleague,' says Sally, 'he's in Frankfurt. On business.' She has taken off her boots and looks somehow diminished in fluffy pink socks. She doesn't offer them tea or coffee.

'We've got several witnesses who saw Nigel in Aberdeen on Tuesday and Wednesday last week,' says Harbinder. 'Do you know what he was doing there?'

'He wasn't in Aberdeen,' says Sally, but she turns away to fiddle with some roses in a vase. She's a very bad liar.

'Mrs Smith,' says Harbinder. 'Sally. We know that Nigel saw Lance Foster in Aberdeen. We know that Nigel and Lance were at school together. Lance was murdered on Wednesday evening. Unless you want your husband to be the number one suspect, you'd better tell us what Nigel was doing in Aberdeen.'

Sally turns. There's a smear of mud on her cheek and she suddenly looks small and vulnerable. The cuckoo clock in the hall strikes ten, a raucous and somehow sinister cacophony.

'I promised I wouldn't tell.'

Don't say anything, Harbinder warns Neil silently. Just wait. The clock continues to tick. Ozymandias licks his empty bowl in a meaningful way.

'Nigel's written a book,' says Sally suddenly. Harbinder and Neil exchange glances. Whatever Harbinder expected, it wasn't this.

'It only took him a few weeks ,' says Sally. 'But it's awfully good. Nigel didn't want people to know about it. I think he was a bit superstitious, not wanting people to know until it was actually published. I proofread it but I'm not clever enough to offer any real editorial advice. So Nigel thought of Lance. Like you said, they were at school together. They weren't close friends but they kept in touch and Lance offered to read the book. For a fee, of course. Nigel sent Lance the manuscript and, a few days later, Lance sent back some notes. Nigel wanted to discuss them in person. He wasn't sure that Lance had grasped quite what he was trying to do in the book.'

'This book,' says Harbinder. 'Is it called *Amanuensis*?'

Now Neil and Sally both stare at her.

'How could you possibly know that?' says Sally. She sounds rather scared.

'Miles Taylor told me about it,' says Harbinder. 'He seemed to think that it owed a lot to a book that Dex Challoner had been planning. Did Nigel overhear Dex discussing it with Peggy?'

'He might have done,' says Sally, her poise returning, 'but *Amanuensis* was an utterly original piece of work.'

If you say so, thinks Harbinder. She doesn't know if Nigel consciously copied Dex's idea or whether he has convinced himself – and his wife – that it's a unique work of staggering genius.

'Nigel sent the book to Miles,' says Sally. 'Such a nice man. Peggy liked him too. You know, Miles was one of the students that I was telling you about? The ones Peggy helped in Russia. Nigel sent the manuscript to Miles anonymously so that Miles wouldn't feel under any obligation to him.'

Or so that Miles wouldn't make the link with Dex, thinks Harbinder. She is pretty sure that Nigel wants Miles to feel under a huge obligation to him.

'I expect Miles will make Nigel an offer for the book,' says Sally. 'Nigel said that we could expect quite a sizable advance. I must say, we could do with the money.'

Really? thinks Harbinder, looking round at the kitchen, space-age cabinets nestling next to a classic Aga. If Sally and Nigel are hard-up, they must have a different definition of poverty. Then she thinks of Joan. *He took all Peggy's money. He said she gambled too much. She gambles too. Peggy said so.* Who is the 'she' here? Sally?

'Is that all?' says Sally. 'I really need to get on.'

And do what? thinks Harbinder. Aloud she says, 'Thank you. You've been very helpful. We'll see ourselves out.'

But Ozymandias accompanies them to the door, obviously under the illusion that they are all now best friends.

Driving through the country roads to Maria's house, Neil says, 'I honestly think that you're a witch sometimes, Harbinder. How the hell did you know about the book?'

Harbinder can't help feeling pleased. 'Miles Taylor told me about it. I knew that he was one of the students in Russia too.'

She tells Neil about Andriy, the Ukrainian gunman, and his search for revenge.

'Jim Harris, the DI in Aberdeen, doesn't think there's a link between Dex's murder and Lance's death but I do. I think the link is back here, in Shoreham.'

'Maria?'

'Maybe. Is this her house?'

It's a row of small terraced houses on the outskirts of Steyning. Very near Clare, in fact. But whereas Clare lives in a smart townhouse that has inexplicably transplanted itself to the Sussex countryside, these are small and boxy with pebbledash walls and woodwork in need of a coat of paint. Maria's house has a neat front garden with roses growing on a trellis, a few still clinging on to life. But her next-door neighbour has two rusting cars on the drive and, on the other side, hens cluck in a makeshift coop.

'I wouldn't like to live here,' says Neil, predictably.

'Presumably it's all they can afford,' says Harbinder. Is this why Maria stole, and maybe also murdered? To get away from the used-car salesman and the chicken farmer? 'Have you spoken to the neighbours?'

'Not personally. I think a couple of PCs called round.'

'Let's try them now.'

There's no one in the house with the cars on the drive but a woman answers the door of the hen house.

'I've already told the other policemen,' she says. 'I haven't seen Maria and Lee for days.'

'They didn't tell you that they were going away?'

'No, which is odd, because we get on well. Usually, if they go away, we look after their cat, Puzzle.'

'Who's looking after Puzzle now?'

'I think they've taken him with them.' The woman blushes slightly. She's youngish, about Harbinder's age, with short hair and tattooed forearms. 'I've got a key so I let myself in to see if the cat was OK. It looks as if they've taken him. The cat basket wasn't in its usual place.'

This is interesting. If you take the cat with you, things are really looking serious.

'And you've no idea where they've gone?'

'No. I told the others. Lee's parents live in Kent somewhere but I don't think they're close. Maria's family are all in Poland. I hope they're OK. They're such nice people. The kids are lovely too. Michael helps me collect eggs sometimes. I pay him 10p an egg.'

Harbinder and Neil sit in the car, watching the woman, Fliss, feeding the hens.

'It really looks like Maria's done a bunk,' says Neil. 'She must be guilty.'

'Or scared,' says Harbinder.

'Do you really think that Sally and Nigel are short of money?' she asks, after a pause.

'Of course not,' says Neil. 'Did you see that Aga? Kelly would love one of those. So would I, even though I can't cook.'

'Aga can't,' mutters Harbinder. 'Joan mentioned that someone gambled. Edwin said that it wasn't Peggy. Maybe it was Sally?'

'Joan was out of it, poor old dear. Hang on. I've got a text.'

Neil fumbles with his phone, scrabbling away with his little paws. It always annoys Harbinder to see him do this. He should use his thumbs like a normal person. She looks out at the row of houses, the dying roses, the rusting cars. Fliss, egg basket in hand, sees her looking and waves.

'Harbinder,' says Neil. The tone of his voice makes her turn instantly.

'I've got some more CCTV from Millionaires' Row,' he says. 'And look who it shows outside Dex's house.'

The picture is grainy but unmistakable. Patricia Creeve. With a gun in her hand.

'Where is Patricia now?' says Neil.

Harbinder looks at her watch. Twelve o'clock.

'She's with my mum,' she says.

Chapter 35

Harbinder: Indian summer

Harbinder rings home but gets no answer. Her mother doesn't have a mobile phone and her father is out watching an Under 10s football match. She calls Kush but he must be busy in the shop. She then rings control and tells them to send an officer round to her home address.

While she does all this, Neil is speeding towards Shoreham. They pass Clare's house and the old cement factory, they pass the flat, green fields, idling cars, a single-decker bus, lyrca-ed types on racing bikes. The siren is on and everyone gets out of their way.

'Go faster,' says Harbinder.

'Don't worry,' says Neil, arms straight at the wheel. 'We'll be there in ten minutes.'

But ten minutes is enough time for Patricia to give her mother a fatal injection. Bibi wouldn't even ask what it was for. She wouldn't want to be any trouble. She'd probably roll up her sleeve for the needle. Harbinder clenches her fists. If Patricia harms her mother she, Harbinder, will tear her apart. She'd enjoy doing it.

'Calm down,' says Neil. 'You're making this weird growling noise.'

The roundabout by the bypass is the usual snarled-up nightmare. In the centre of it all, horses graze, entirely oblivious. Neil changes lanes, passes on the inside, floors the accelerator. Harbinder wouldn't have thought that he was capable of driving like this.

But, once in the town, it's impossible. Every road seems to be choked with traffic. The high street has been closed for a Harvest Festival fête. Harbinder grinds her teeth and curses churches, fêtes and every human being alive. Neil turns into a side street and finds it blocked by a recycling van.

Harbinder opens the door. 'I'll be quicker on foot. Follow me as quickly as you can.'

She runs past the van and through the churchyard, elbowing aside children carrying balloons and toffee apples. Her mum always used to take them to the fête. People whispered about them because of Bibi's sari and Deepak's turban, but Bibi had been determined to enjoy every community event she could find. She'd even had a go on the carousel, sitting on one of those grinning painted horses, holding her sari with one hand and waving energetically with the other. Harbinder – God forgive her – had been embarrassed and refused to join her. It was Abhey who had sat on the adjoining horse, not caring that his entire class was laughing and pointing at the boy in the top-knot. If her mum survives this Harbinder will go anywhere with her, even to Harry Potter World or the gurdwara.

Finally she's at the corner of her road, past the pub where she drank red wine with Natalka. There's a car parked outside the house. Is it Patricia's? As she lurches across the road, Natalka's car draws up and Benedict almost catapults out. He's waving a tiny picture and not making much sense.

'Patrick. Patricia. It's her. I tried to ring you but you're not answering—'

'I haven't got time for this, Benedict.' Harbinder searches in her shoulder bag for her house key but, of course, for the first time, they are not where they should be. Harbinder bangs on the window of the shop.

'Kush! Let me into the house.'

Her brother emerges with maddening slowness from behind the counter.

'What's the matter, sis? The carer's with her. I saw her go up. Big, tall woman.'

'The carer's a psychopath,' pants Harbinder. 'Let me in.'

Something in her tone must have conveyed urgency to Kush because he not only opens the door but follows her upstairs too. Benedict tags on behind, still babbling about St Patrick.

'Mum?' shouts Harbinder. 'Mum!'

Silence.

'Mum!' Kush yells. Surely her beloved son's voice will rouse Bibi but there's only more silence, echoing off the walls.

Harbinder bursts into the sitting room. Her mother is sitting motionless in her chair.

'Mum!' Harbinder feels for a pulse and – thank the gods – it's there. Her mother's skin is warm too. She opens her eyes.

'Harbinder. Khushwant. What are you doing here?'

'Where's Patricia? The woman from the care agency?'

'She's in the kitchen, making tea.'

'Stay with Mum,' says Harbinder to Kush. She pushes open the kitchen door.

And finds Patricia Creeve backed up against the kitchen counter, while Starsky growls at her from across the room.

'I still can't believe it,' says Neil. 'I thought that Patricia was one of the good guys.' They are back at the station eating pizza. Patricia Creeve has been charged with the murder of Dex Challoner but Harbinder is confident that she will also admit to killing Peggy Smith and Lance Foster. Probably Weronika Challoner too.

'She needed the money,' said Harbinder. 'It was Patricia who gambled. That's why she had to move out of her office and run the business from home. Patricia had been taking money from Weronika for years but, when the old lady started to suspect, Patricia killed her. Peggy must have suspected something. Remember, she was the one who was so good at thinking up murders and plots. But she can't have had any proof. She told Maria that Weronika's death was suspicious. She said that the clue was in the copy of *Thank Heaven Fasting* but it wasn't in the book itself, it was the picture of St Patrick. Patrick. Patricia.'

'It might have been more helpful just to tell the police,' says Donna.

'She wasn't sure,' says Harbinder. 'She didn't have any proof.'

'So Patricia was the gunman who threatened Natalka and Benedict at Peggy Smith's flat?' says Neil. 'I thought they were sure it was a man.'

'Patricia is a tall woman,' says Harbinder. 'My brother said so earlier. She must have size eight feet too because there was a footprint outside Dex's window. We'll have to get a forensic podiatrist in.' She's pleased to have remembered this impressive-sounding job.

'Maria went to see Dex ,' says Neil. 'Which is why she was caught on CCTV at his house.'

'Yes,' says Harbinder. ' Peggy's death – and seeing Dex at the funeral – must have made Maria think about what she'd said that time: that Weronika's death was somehow suspicious. Maria went to Dex's house and told him, not realising that Patricia was the person Peggy suspected. Dex rang Patricia immediately. I'm not sure why. Maybe just to ask if he should believe Maria.'

'His phone was on the sofa next to him,' says Neil. 'That was the call he made. Patricia came straight over and shot him.'

'She was a good shot,' says Harbinder. 'She told me so. She said that she always won prizes at the rifle range on Brighton Pier.'

'So Maria didn't know it was Patricia?' says Neil.

'No,' says Harbinder. 'But she knew there was a murderer out there and she got scared.'

Maria has been found. She had taken refuge with her in-laws in Ashford. 'I was frightened,' she told the Kent Police. 'So I ran away. I'm sorry. I thought the killer would come for me next because I knew all of them. Peggy, Weronika and Dex.' She probably wasn't wrong, thinks Harbinder.

'What about Lance Foster?' says Donna.

'His mother was friends with Peggy and Weronika,' says Harbinder. 'Benedict told me just now. Apparently they called themselves the bay window set because they used to sit by the windows at Scaview Court enjoying the view. Lance mentions them in the acknowledgements in his book. Maybe there's a link there.'

'Could Patricia have got up to Aberdeen in time?' says Donna.

'It's possible,' says Harbinder. 'You can get from Shoreham to Aberdeen in a few hours. The woman at security said that nurses

ELLY GRIFFITHS

often took that flight. She might have been thinking of Patricia. Maybe Patricia travelled up that morning, wearing her old nurse's uniform. She could have caught the plane to Aberdeen, killed Lance and still have got home by midnight.'

'It's very cold-blooded,' says Neil.

'I think Patricia was cold-blooded,' says Harbinder. 'The care agency was only ever a way of making money. She told me that she was always short of cash. She had a gambling addiction too. That might have been what Joan was trying to tell us.'

'What about all the rest of it?' says Donna. 'The anonymous notes, the men who were spying on her?'

'The men turned out to be Ukrainian students,' says Harbinder. 'And one of them became Dex's editor. I think Nigel Smith is hoping he'll publish his book too.'

'Why is everyone writing a book?' says Donna. 'I can't see the appeal myself.'

'It passes the time, I suppose,' says Harbinder. She thinks of Julie saying, 'It's a way of escaping.' She imagines Julie sitting in a Brighton café, the chattering crowds around her, lost in her own sunlit world.

'You look tired,' says Donna. 'You should go home.'

'I'll drive you,' says Neil.

'My parents are probably still having a party for the dog,' says Harbinder.

But, when she gets home, her mother has gone to bed and there's only her father and Starsky waiting up for her.

'Come and sit with me, Harbi,' says Deepak. He's watching the news. It's still only ten o'clock.

316

Harbinder sits next to her father, breathing in the familiar smell of clean linen and aftershave. After a while, just because she's very tired, she tells herself, she lets her head rest on his shoulder.

'You must be exhausted,' says Deepak. 'You've had quite a time of it. I got in from the football to hear that you saved your mother's life.'

'That was Starsky really. He had Patricia pinned against the kitchen counter.'

She can feel her father's chest swell. 'Didn't he do well? You know, he must have understood the whole thing. He must have suspected that terrible woman from the start. That's why he started growling at her when she made the tea. He really is a first-class guard dog.'

Let's just give Starsky the Nobel peace prize right away, thinks Harbinder. But she reaches out to stroke Starsky's ears. 'He was a hero,' she says.

They watch the television in silence for a while. The weather forecaster tells them that the Indian summer will continue in the south of England. 'Indian summer,' says Deepak. 'That's racist in itself.' There's another pause and then he says, 'You know, I'm very proud of you, Harbi. I hope you know that. I know it's difficult sometimes, living with your old parents.'

'You're not that bad really,' says Harbinder.

'It's not easy. You're an adult now. A woman with a responsible job.'

Blimey. Can she have this in writing?

'I hope you know that . . . that you can always invite your friends here.'

Harbinder's heart seems to have stopped. Is her father saying what she thinks he's saying?

'You can always invite boyfriends home. Or girlfriends.'

There it is. What should she say? Maybe best to keep quiet. Deepak seems to have been preparing this speech for a while.

'We just want you to be happy. We don't care if it's with a man or a woman.'

Harbinder feels her heart fluttering as if it is about to fly away, taking her body with it. On her phone there is a text from Julie.

Fancy a walk in Brighton one day?

Harbinder and her father stare at the screen as the wave of high pressure swoops across Europe.

Chapter 36

Benedict: A Seaside Lady's Diary

It's Alison, the warden, who tells Benedict that Peggy's flat has been sold. 'I wondered if you and Natalka wanted to go in and see if there's anything left of Peggy's. The son and daughter-in-law took most things away but I think there's a box or two left.'

'They'll only have left things that have no value,' says Natalka. 'I know what those two are like.'

'You always say that you think the worst of people,' says Benedict. 'But you don't really.'

He feels that he can say things like this to Natalka now. They've been seeing each other almost every day for nearly two weeks now. Dmytro has gone back to Aberdeen and Natalka has been spending most nights at Benedict's flat. They have even talked – briefly – about getting a place together.

'There will be nothing left at Peggy's,' says Natalka. 'Nothing worth anything.'

But, when they open the door to the familiar apartment, there is a large box in the middle of the room. It's mostly full of old notebooks and Benedict gets these out now and spreads them on the floor. It's odd, being back here, with the sunlight streaming through the bay window. Benedict thinks of Peggy's funeral, the room full of people in dark suits, Nigel standing apart, glowering. He thinks of the footsteps on the stairs and staring down the barrel of a gun. Was that really Patricia Creeve behind the mask? Harbinder says so. It still doesn't seem possible to Benedict. But Patricia has been charged with the murder of Dex Challoner, having been caught on CCTV with a gun in her hand. Harbinder says more charges will follow. Natalka and Maria are running Care4You until a new manager can be found.

'Look at this,' says Benedict to Natalka, who is sorting through postcards. 'It's Peggy's Investigation Book. I wondered where that was. She's written it in this book. *A Seaside Lady's Diary*.' The title of the book is written in loopy writing, surrounded by pallid marine life.

Benedict flicks through the pages, marvelling at Peggy's neat writing and her meticulous lists of joggers, cyclists and people with dogs. September 2018, Peggy's last month on earth. Did she really die of a heart attack or did Patricia kill her? According to Harbinder, insulin poisoning is almost impossible to prove without a post-mortem.

Tenth of September 2018. The day Peggy died. What had Peggy seen that day?

2 x women with pushchairs

1 x priest (vicar?) eating an ice-cream

11 x dog-walkers. 6 lone women: 4 x indiscriminate breed, 1
   x pug, 1 x Jack Russell

1 man with greyhound, 2 x couples with doodle types.

5 cyclists

6 joggers

1 Unicyclist

Benedict looks at the list again. *11 x dog-walkers. 6 lone women: 4 x indiscriminate breed, 1 x pug, 1 x Jack Russell.*

'Natalka?' he says. 'What sort of dog does Julie have?'

'A Jack Russell,' says Natalka. 'Remember, she showed us a picture.'

'Look at this,' he says. He shows her the list.

'Unicyclist,' says Natalka. 'Probably from Brighton.'

'No. Lone woman with Jack Russell.'

'That could be anyone.'

'I know but Julie said that she'd never met Peggy. And there's something else that's been bugging me.'

'What?' says Natalka. She sounds exasperated but not entirely unaffectionate.

'When I read Julie's book *You Made Me Do It*, it reminded me of something. I've just realised what it was. The plot was exactly like the plot of *Thank Heaven Fasting*.'

'The book the gunman took.'

'Exactly.'

Natalka looks at him. They were both sitting on the floor but now they are standing.

'Where does Julie live?' says Benedict.

'Hove,' says Natalka. 'But she's out today. She's gone out with Harbinder.'

★

Natalka's car is outside her house and they are held up by Debbie who insists on discussing Dmytro and how charming he is. When they set out they are further hampered by the Saturday afternoon traffic on the coast road. Natalka weaves in and out of lanes as Benedict tries to call Harbinder and Julie. Neither of them are answering their phones.

'Do you really think that Julie killed Peggy?' says Natalka, over-taking an open-topped bus. 'She seemed such a nice person.'

'Means and motive,' says Benedict. 'Julie had both. She could have killed Lance too. She was right there in the hotel.'

'And now Harbinder's on a date with her,' says Natalka. 'I know where they'll go. Harbinder said they were taking the dog for a walk. Edwin said that Julie always walks between the peace statue and the pier.'

'Are they seeing each other then, Julie and Harbinder?'

'This is their first date, though Harbinder insists it isn't a date. I think they like each other though. I first noticed it at Cove Bay. When Julie broke her wrist.'

'I had no idea. I didn't realise Julie was gay. I didn't know Har-binder was until you told me.'

'I'm good at sensing these things. I've told you I've slept with men and women.'

'Yes. Thanks. Always good to hear.'

'Don't be sarcastic, Benny. Look for a parking space.'

It's easier said than done. The seafront in Hove seems to be full of people enjoying the beautiful autumn weather. Eventually Natalka squeezes into a space vacated by a motorbike. She negates all those jokes about women being bad at parking. Not that Bene-dict believed them anyway. He's always suspected that women were the superior sex.

They race along the promenade. Past the angel of peace, the café, the remains of the West Pier, like the skeleton of a vast sea creature. This boardwalk has changed since Benedict used to come here as a boy. Now it's all landscaped and manicured: pebbles embedded in concrete, skateboard areas and basketball nets, shops selling dream-catchers and animals made out of shells. There are countless women with dogs but none of them are Julie and Arthur.

'We'll never find them,' says Benedict, stopping to get his breath beside a whelk stall with a pink plastic lobster on its roof.

'Look over there,' says Natalka.

Harbinder is sitting alone on a bench, looking out to sea. She's holding a lead which is attached to a small dog. Benedict and Natalka stumble over the stones towards her. Harbinder looks up but doesn't seem that surprised to see them. Nor does the dog. Natalka and Benedict sit on either side of her.

'We want to talk to you about Julie,' says Benedict.

'She's not here,' says Harbinder, her voice flat. 'She's at the police station.'

Benedict and Natalka stare at her. Harbinder goes on, still gazing out to sea, 'I know Julie killed Peggy. Lance Foster too. I've suspected for a while. Patricia killed Dex because she thought Maria had told him about her stealing from Weronika. But Jim was right. That murder was very different from the other two. Then I remembered that the person who stole the book held the gun in their left hand. Patricia's right-handed. Julie broke her right wrist but she could still type. Then I read that book, *Thank Heaven Fasting*. Julie took the plot from it for her first book. Peggy must have known. She didn't advise Julie on her first book, according to Edwin. Maybe she read it later. That's why she asked Miles if he'd read *Thank Heaven Fasting*. Miles must have told Julie. So Julie killed Peggy.'

'Just for that?' says Natalka.

'It was Julie's big break,' says Harbinder. 'Her only really successful book. I think she would have killed to protect the secret.'

'That must have been why she killed Lance,' says Natalka. 'He asked her that question about Peggy. He must have suspected. And he mentioned *Thank Heaven Fasting* on his panel. That must have been aimed at Julie.'

'Yes,' says Benedict. 'He specifically mentioned Sheila Atkins' plotting skills. But, surely, if Julie had stolen the plot, she must have known someone would find out one day.

'Maybe,' says Harbinder. 'I just think, when it came to it, she found it surprisingly easy to kill Peggy.'

'Julie had been a nurse,' says Natalka. 'Edwin told me. She would know how to inject someone with insulin.'

'The Brighton police are interviewing her now,' says Harbinder. 'I said I'd take Arthur to some friends of hers. She was really worried about him.'

Benedict reaches out his hand to the little dog, who ignores him.

'I think she'll confess,' Harbinder continues, still in that odd, expressionless voice. 'There might be other evidence too. CCTV from the Majestic. Forensics from the room.'

Benedict thinks of Lance sitting in his chair by the window. He wouldn't have felt threatened when Julie appeared at his door, even if he'd guessed that she'd come to talk about Peggy. He would have sat down, almost looking forward to the conversation. Had Julie then stabbed him in the arm with a needle? As Harbinder says, the forensics will probably show.

'I've told Jim,' she says. 'That's the second case that I've solved for him. Not that he's grateful.'

For a few minutes, they all sit looking out over the beach. The sea is very blue, flecked with tiny white waves. Even though it's October, people are still swimming. A jet ski cuts its way across the horizon. From the undamaged pier they can hear music and shouts of laughter.

'I'm sorry,' says Natalka.

'It's OK,' says Harbinder. 'At least my parents know I'm gay now. I think they may have known for a while. I just hope my next prospective girlfriend doesn't turn out to be a murderer too.'

They all sit in silence, looking at the crowded blue sea.

Chapter 37

Harbinder: influencers

'So this Julie person confessed to killing Peggy as well as Lance Foster?' Donna sounds almost irritated but this is probably because she's had to come in to work on a Saturday.

'Apparently so,' says Harbinder. She had asked the Brighton police to wait at the peace statue but not to approach until she gave the signal. The café had its tables out and business was brisk but Harbinder found a spare seat and waited. As she saw Julie coming towards her, wearing a stripy top and blue trousers, with an excitable white dog on a lead, Harbinder had a sudden violent hope that it wasn't true. Julie was simply a thirty-something woman out walking her dog. An attractive, intelligent thirty-something woman with whom Harbinder could have her first adult, sanctioned-by-her-parents affair. Julie's wrist was still in plaster, she was holding Arthur's lead in her left hand. Julie waved, smiled and, when she reached Harbinder, kissed her on both cheeks. Harbinder's heart had sunk. She's no Christian but she remembered how Judas had greeted Jesus.

'Am I late? Sorry.'

'You're not late. I was early.' What should she say now? *Did you kill Peggy Smith? Did you kill Lance Foster and then spend two cosy days in a safe house laughing, chatting and playing cards?*

'How are you?' said Julie. She sat next to Harbinder at the café table. Arthur strained at his lead, anxious to continue the walk.

'OK. Still working hard on the case.' Was it her imagination or did Julie suddenly grow still beside her?

'I thought that was solved. I thought the manager of the care place did it. You said you had CCTV footage of her.'

'We've got CCTV footage of Patricia Creeve at Dex's place. She killed him, all right. The thing is, though, we've got CCTV of the person who threatened Natalka and Benedict with a gun. It's a different person.'

Harbinder remembers now that Julie had said nothing.

'It was you, Julie. You went to Peggy's flat with a gun – probably a replica – and you stole that book. There aren't many still in print and you wanted it out of the way. You'd already killed Peggy, hadn't you?'

When Julie finally spoke it was to say, 'You've got no proof.' And Harbinder's last gleam of hope faded. No innocent person would ever say those words.

'There's always proof,' said Harbinder. 'If not at Peggy's, there'll be forensics in Lance's hotel room. You know that. We always leave a trace of ourselves behind. Mind you, there's not much about police procedure in your books, is there? Or in Sheila Atkins's.'

She'd gestured then to the PCs who were trying, unsuccessfully in Harbinder's view, to blend in with the day-trippers. They had taken Julie away for questioning. Harbinder had said that she would follow them after she'd taken Arthur to Julie's friends but, actually, she had walked a little way along the promenade and sat on a bench looking at the sea. It was there that Benedict and Natalka had found her.

She'd rung Donna from Holland Road police station.

Now Donna and Neil are trying to process this latest development.

'Julie Monroe killed Peggy because she knew that she'd copied the plot of her book from some old murder mystery?' That's Neil, putting it in subtitles for the hard of hearing.

'Yes,' says Harbinder. 'I thought it might be impossible to prove. There wasn't a post-mortem and so many people have trampled through that flat. But Julie confessed. She'd confessed by the time I got to Hove police station. She confessed to Lance's murder too. Both by insulin injection. The forensic psychologist who interviewed her said that she thought Julie might have killed her own mother too. That's what gave her the idea. Apparently that's how the victim is killed in Julie's first book, with an insulin injection. No wonder she didn't have any trouble with that murder.'

'Did you have any idea?' says Neil. 'I mean, you must have known this Julie quite well. You were all held in the safe house together, weren't you?'

He's looking at her intently, quite unlike his usual darting squirrel gaze.

'I had my suspicions,' says Harbinder.

'Then you should have shared them with us,' says Donna, but quite mildly.

'They were just suspicions,' says Harbinder. 'I didn't guess until I finished *Thank Heaven Fasting* last night.'

'All this reading,' says Neil. 'You'll be joining a book club soon, Harbinder.'

'If I do,' says Harbinder, 'you have my permission to shoot me.'

It's early evening by the time she gets home. Her father is in the shop so Harbinder helps her mother prepare supper, watched drool-ingly by Starsky. Harbinder is glad that she didn't tell her mum about the date with Julie. Bibi is so keen to show that she isn't prejudiced that she will probably shower any prospective girlfriend with rose petals and Indian sweetmeats. It'll be even worse than the times when her brothers brought their girlfriends home.

After supper, Harbinder watches Saturday evening television with her parents, listening to their ritual comments on *Britain's Got Talent*.

'Look at that, Deepak. I couldn't do that.'

'Why would you want to, Bibi?'

As early as she can, Harbinder excuses herself and goes upstairs. After her shower, she gets into bed, picks up her phone and puts it down again. She's trying to wean herself off Panda Pop. She remembers Neil's comment about the reading. Maybe that's what she needs to do now. Read and take her mind off Julie's face when she saw Harbinder this afternoon. If this hadn't happened, could she have had a relationship with her? Maybe, thinks Harbinder, and, after their first row, Julie would have approached her with a loaded syringe. She's safer staying single.

She looks around her room for possible reading matter but there are only her old school and university books, plus a full set of James Herberts. But she isn't in the mood for horror tonight. On her desk is the jiffy bag from Pippa Sinclair-Lewis, containing Dex Challoner's first book, *A Town Called Murder*. She gets the book out now and flips through the pages. Death, guns, sex, murder. Looks like the perfect comforting read. As she opens the book at Chapter One, a postcard falls out. Pippa Sinclair-Lewis has written, *Enjoy! P*. Harbinder turns the card over and reads the words: *We are coming for you*.

Harbinder doesn't think that Pippa will answer an 'unknown number' call on a Saturday evening but she does.

'Sorry to ring you so late.'

'Don't worry. I'm a night owl. I was just reading.'

'Me too. I was reading *A Town Called Murder*.'

'Oh good. Do you like it?'

'I haven't really started it yet. I was just looking through it when a postcard fell out. It says "We are coming for you".'

To her surprise, Pippa laughs. 'Oh, that was one of Dakota's ideas. You remember I told you about Dakota, the new young publicist? Well, she had the cards made up to go with proof copies of a debut novel called *The Debt Collectors*. Crazy, really, because it doesn't even have the book's title on it. And she sent the cards before she sent the books. I suppose it's meant to create a "buzz".' Harbinder can imagine Pippa putting fastidious quotation marks around the word.

'Who would you send these cards to?'

'Oh, anyone who might talk about the book. Or give a quote that we could use on the cover. Reviewers, bloggers, authors.'

'People like Dex Challoner, Lance Foster and J. D. Monroe?'

'Yes. They'd be the sort of people. Influencers, you know.'

'I know,' says Harbinder. 'Well, I won't keep you any longer. Good night.'

'Good night,' says Pippa. 'Happy reading.'

But Harbinder has no intention of doing anything as dangerous as reading. She switches off the light and goes straight to sleep.

Chapter 38

Edwin: time and the hour

Edwin is back to his old game of trying to fill in time. As he goes about his daily routine, some lines from *Macbeth* keep coming back to him.

> *Come what come may,*
> *Time and the hour runs through the roughest day.*

Edwin remembers going to see an experimental production at the Edinburgh Festival with Nicky. The witches had been played by break-dancers dressed as chickens. He can't quite recall where these lines come in the play but, clearly, Macbeth had been having a tough day. So many people to murder, so little time. Edwin has too much time, it's soft-sift in the hourglass, trickling out a grain at a time. But, come what may, it will run out in the end. Sundays are OK because he's taken to going to mass. He likes Father Brendan and he likes the fact that some of the parish stalwarts now know his name and ask his advice on the pronunciation of difficult names in the readings. And the best thing is that Sunday morning mass, and the walk there and back, takes up two hours, three if he stays for coffee afterwards.

The trouble is that he wakes up too early, at about five a.m. That leaves far too many weekday hours to kill. Hours to kill. Since Aberdeen he's been noticing the murderous nature of the English language. Killing time. Getting slaughtered. A stab in the dark. Taking a pot shot. Patricia had shot Dex, Julie had stabbed Peggy with a needle. Edwin still can't believe that these women, both of whom he had liked, were capable of such things. But doesn't *Macbeth* warn you to ignore women at your peril?

Edwin doesn't let himself get up until six. Then he makes himself a cup of tea and a piece of toast, eating almost as maddeningly slowly as Benedict. Then it's time for the bathroom. If he tries really hard, Edwin can make his morning shower last two hours. After all, as the years go on, getting wet at all is a risky business. He always makes sure that the non-slip mat is in place and he uses the handrails thoughtfully provided by the people who converted Preview Court into a posh halfway house on the road to death.

Then he gets dressed. Edwin always takes care with this, trousers pressed, shoes polished, jumpers arranged by colour. Old age is no excuse for looking scruffy. Edwin has always prided himself on his dress sense. He would never have gone about like Benedict in shapeless jumpers and ill-fitting jeans. Mind you, Benedict's appearance has improved tremendously since he's started seeing Natalka. Benedict now wears well-made clothes in natural fabrics, greens and blues to bring out the colour of his eyes. He even has new glasses and a haircut that doesn't look as if he did it himself, with nail scissors and no mirror. No doubt about it, Benedict is a new man. About time too, Edwin thinks with satisfaction. He has managed to convince himself that he personally engineered the romance between Benedict and Natalka.

By the time that Edwin is fully dressed, with cravat or tie neatly tied, it's time to go to Benedict's coffee shack. This is Edwin's favourite time of the day. It's pleasant to think that, just a short walk away, there's a place where he will always get a warm welcome, a good coffee, and a chat about mutual friends. The danger is making it last too long. Benedict has other customers, after all. Edwin makes it a rule never to stay for more than half an hour. Besides, it's too cold to sit at the picnic table for longer. The fine weather has continued but it's October now and the morning air is a little chilly.

This morning, though, just as Edwin shrugs on his coat, there's a knock at the door. This in itself is rather worrying. People usually have to press the entryphone so that residents can let them in. A knock means that a stranger is actually inside the building. Briefly Edwin imagines himself facing a gunman, something that has happened twice to Benedict and Natalka. He is, not jealous exactly, more *curious*, about how he would respond in the same situation. Well, he might be about to find out.

Edwin flings open the door with unnecessary bravado and finds Sally Smith waiting outside.

'Hallo, Edwin,' says Sally. She's wearing a red jacket and a beret that suddenly reminds Edwin poignantly of Peggy.

'Were you on your way out?' says Sally, indicating Edwin's coat and hat.

'Just over the road to Benedict's café,' says Edwin. He can't bring himself to call it a shack, not out loud anyway.

'That's nice,' says Sally. 'Is it true that he and Natalka are a couple now? Alison mentioned it.'

'Yes,' says Edwin, thinking that this is an odd way of putting it. The tune 'We're a couple of swells' appears, unbidden, in his head. He will have to stop himself humming it.

'How lovely,' says Sally. 'I'm glad Natalka has found a nice chap. She was so kind to Peggy.'

'Benedict's a thoroughly nice chap,' says Edwin.

'You know that the police say that Peggy was murdered?' says Sally. 'Isn't it terrible?'

'Really terrible,' says Edwin.

'Nigel is very upset,' says Sally. 'He's burying himself in his writing.'

From what Edwin's heard, Nigel's writing would be better off dead and buried. He finds it rather sinister that Nigel Smith has suddenly reinvented himself as an author.

'Anyway,' says Sally. 'I came to tell you that we've sold Peggy's flat.'

'Yes,' says Edwin. 'Alison told me.' He had known that it would happen, of course, but now that it has, he feels unexpectedly sad.

'The new owner, Mrs Shepherd, will move in in a few weeks,' says Sally. 'And I thought, why don't you, Natalka and Benedict have a final tea party there first? Just as way of saying goodbye to Peggy. I think Natalka still has a set of keys. She can post them back to the estate agent afterwards.'

'I wonder how she knew I'd kept a set of keys,' says Natalka. She's in her running clothes and sitting on the picnic table, as if she's too athletic to use anything as prosaic as a seat.

'Maybe Alison told her,' says Edwin. 'She seems to know everything. Anyway, I thought a tea party was a rather nice idea.'

'I could bring some cakes,' says Benedict, coming over with a plate of broken brownies.

'Shall we ask Harbinder?' says Natalka.

'How is she?' says Edwin. 'After Julie, I mean.'

'OK, I think,' says Natalka. 'She's tough.'

'She was shocked though,' says Benedict. 'I mean, we all were.'

'Yes,' says Edwin. 'I really liked Julie.'

'I never trusted her,' says Natalka, though this is the first time she has said this. 'When I shared a room with her, she talked in her sleep.'

Lady Macbeth again, thinks Edwin.

'I think we should invite Harbinder,' says Benedict. 'Peggy would like us to celebrate the end of the case. I remember she always said she hated crime novels that didn't tie up all the loose ends.'

'I suppose we're the loose ends in this story,' says Edwin.

'No,' says Natalka. 'We're the main characters.'

Edwin thinks of this as he walks back to Preview Court. He wonders if he's been the main character in his own life. If his story was made into a film probably Nicky and his mother would have the biggest parts, or at least the roles most likely to win an Oscar. Well, the Peggy mystery would make an interesting last chapter anyway. Penultimate chapter, he tells himself firmly.

What should he do when he gets in? It's only eleven o'clock, far too early for lunch. If the paper has been delivered, he'll do the crossword. It's a kind of tribute to Peggy, trying to get his head round the cryptic clues. He thinks of anagrams, the right letters but in the wrong order. There are a few that crop up fairly often in crosswords. Edwin has been making a list.

Debit card — bad credit
Orchestra — carthorse
Dormitory — dirty room
Schoolmaster — the classroom
Astronomer — moon starer.

He lets himself into the flats and picks up the *Guardian* from the pile of papers on the hall table. *EDWARD FITZHERBERT*, it says in capital letters on the front. The newsagent never gets his name right. Typical really.

He's just about to start up the stairs when someone calls his name. His actual name. Edwin turns. Alison is standing in the doorway of her office.

'Hallo, Edwin,' she says. 'How are you?'

'Not bad,' says Edwin. 'Can't complain.' Well he can, but who would listen?

'I've been thinking about our new resident,' says Alison. 'The lady who's moving into Peggy's flat. Her name is Belinda Shepherd. She's coming down from London, recently widowed. She used to work for Radio 4. I thought it might be nice if you called in on her. She'll probably be lonely at first. You should have things in common, both working for the BBC.'

'I could bring her some of Benedict's brownies,' says Edwin.

'That would be lovely.'

Time and the hour, thinks Edwin, as he climbs the non-slip stairs to his flat. Time and the hour. But now the words have a jaunty, rhythmic feel.

Chapter 39

Natalka: back to usually

Natalka is trying to run every morning. The weather is still fine and it's a joy to pound along the path above the beach, the sea doing its blue sparkly thing in the background. Natalka thinks of Cove Bay, of the fishing boats coming in to shore, of Benedict skimming stones, of closing her eyes in terror, then opening them to see Dmytro standing in front of her, like a vision. She had thought that she was alone in the world, staring at her bank account every night, pursued by nameless enemies, but now she has her brother, her almost-twin. They text and Skype every day. Their mother, almost delirious with happiness, is planning to come to England to see them.

And Natalka has a boyfriend. That's what she called Benedict in her head, thinking of Dasha and Anastasia and their relentless acquisition, and disposal, of teenage boyfriends. She has a crazy desire to ring them and tell them about Benedict.

But that's another reason for running. She's worried that being with Benedict has made her soft. She used to do yoga every morning but now it's too easy to lie in bed watching Benny make her morning tea. He even goes out to buy her croissants, although he has fresh pastries in the shack. They're still spending most of their time in Benedict's bedsit but Natalka thinks that they should find a place of their own. Together they have enough money, even with her new business expenses.

Natalka is running Care4You. It seemed wrong to let the clients suffer just because the boss turned out to be a murderer. Natalka finds that she quite enjoys the administration side. Maria is a great help and Natalka has also employed several more carers, making sure that each one has a police check first. Maybe she should buy Patricia out, or maybe she should become a sleeping partner and let Maria take over. Or should she do something else entirely? Benedict keeps saying that they should visit Ukraine. Natalka says there's no point because her mother is coming to England. Natalka has met Benedict's parents a couple of times and it was awkward only because they were so obviously relieved to see Benedict with a woman. 'We never thought he'd catch someone like you,' said Benny's oafish brother, Hugo. It was obviously meant to be a compliment even if it did make Natalka sound like a virus. 'Benny has hidden depths,' Natalka told Hugo, who did not look delighted to hear it.

She has reached the shack. Benedict has a queue of customers, probably because he insists on making coffee in what he calls a mindful way, which actually means taking twice as long as a normal person. But Natalka finds herself smiling as she approaches. There's a lot to be said for sleeping with someone who tries to do everything in the best way possible. Tantric sex has nothing on it.

'Look, Benedict, it's your lovely girlfriend,' says one of the regulars. There's no point hiding anything from old people, that's something Natalka has learnt in her job. Look at Edwin, he had worked out that she and Benedict were a couple before they knew it themselves.

'Don't know what she sees in you,' says a spritely octogenarian in a baseball cap.

'Nor do I,' says Benedict, giving Natalka one of his beautiful smiles. He has made her a cappuccino too, just the way she likes it, with an added espresso on top. He always draws a heart in the foam too. He says that he's been doing that for a long time, since they first met, in fact. But, if so, Natalka has only started noticing now.

'I can't stay long,' says Natalka, drinking her coffee while doing leg stretches. 'I've got a lot of paperwork to get through.' She has rented an office; she's not working from Patricia's creepy spare bedroom.

'Don't forget that we're meeting at Peggy's at three.'

'I won't,' says Natalka. 'Back to usually.'

She'd said this to Benedict one day and now it's become a catchphrase between them. Natalka hates getting English phrases wrong but somehow she doesn't mind Benedict teasing her. It must be love, she thinks. Although she isn't sure that she believes in love, even now.

Natalka goes home to change so the others are already there when she gets to Peggy's. She gave the keys to Benedict and he has made the empty sitting room look quite cosy with deckchairs, a picnic rug and fairy lights around the bay window. As Natalka opens the door she hears a champagne cork pop, a sound that reminds her, momentarily, of the bar at the Majestic.

'I thought it might be nice to drink Peggy's health,' says Edwin. 'She loved a glass of bubbly. Her phrase, not mine,' he adds hastily.

Edwin has been looking rather more cheerful lately. Natalka thinks it's the prospect of a new neighbour. And the adulation of all the old ladies at mass. Benedict says that Edwin has become quite a celebrity at church.

'It's a safe-house reunion,' says Edwin.

'Happy days,' says Harbinder drily. She looks tired, thinks Natalka, but maybe that's because she has such dark, deep-set eyes. Or maybe it's just the contrast with her red jumper. Natalka has never seen Harbinder wear any colour other than black.

They talk about Peggy. It feels odd at first, with the marks on the walls where her pictures once hung and the scent of her special ground coffee still somehow in the air. But soon, it feels natural, as if Peggy is still in the room. Benedict shows them a picture that he's printed out from the internet. It's a Christmas party of some kind. Peggy is wearing a pink paper crown and is smiling directly at the camera.

'I think that's Weronika Challoner next to her,' says Benedict. 'Lance's mother is probably in the picture too.'

'I wish I'd met Weronika,' says Natalka. 'I'd love to have heard her stories about the war.'

'Peggy knew all about the war,' says Edwin. 'Far more than I did. Of course, I was ten years younger than her,' he adds hastily. 'Peggy knew all about the Middle East too. And the Balkans. I mean, nobody understands the Balkans.'

'What I can't work out,' says Benedict, 'is how Peggy knew all the things she did. She knew about Russia, Maria says she knew all about Poland. There wasn't a place in the world that she hadn't heard of. But she actually hadn't travelled much. I think that holiday to Russia was almost the only time she left the country.'

'Her husband travelled,' says Edwin. 'He was in the navy.'

'I think she kept one of his uniform buttons in her desk,' says Natalka. 'I found it when Benny and I were here that time. The time when the gunman – I mean Julie – burst in. I put it in my pocket. For luck.'

'And it's brought you luck,' says Edwin, smiling at her.

'Peggy didn't get all that knowledge from her husband,' says Harbinder. 'I think she got it from books.'

'You're right,' says Edwin. 'You can travel the world in books.' Natalka thinks it sounds like something he may have said in a BBC programme once.

'Talking of books,' says Benedict. 'I've discovered something.'

Natalka suppresses a smile. There's nothing Benny enjoys more than a bit of detective work and, like his favourite screen sleuths, he likes to make the revelation as dramatic as possible.

'What is it?' says Edwin. 'I think I've had enough shocks to last me a lifetime.'

'It's not a shock exactly,' says Benedict. 'But it is a surprise. I've been doing some research into Sheila Atkins. You know, the author of *Thank Heaven Fasting*.'

'We're not going to forget that book, Benny,' says Natalka.

'There's nothing about her on the internet,' says Benedict, 'but I found this book in the library.'

He's brought it with him just so that he can flourish it now.

'It's called *Heroines of the Golden Age*,' says Benedict, 'and it's about forgotten women crime writers. One of them is Sheila Atkins. Well, listen to this. "Atkins wrote many books while still in her twenties. During the Second World War she is popularly believed to have been in the secret service. In 1955 she married David Foster and they had one child, Lancelot."'

He pauses for effect. Edwin gets there first: 'Oh my goodness. Lance Foster. Sheila Atkins was his mother.'

'Yes. Later on it says, "Lancelot later became a writer and his first novel *Laocoön* was longlisted for the Booker Prize."'

'Why didn't he tell us?' says Natalka.

'Maybe he would have,' says Benedict. 'If we'd ever met up for that drink. I remember he laughed when I asked if he'd read Sheila Atkins and said that she was very dear to him. I think Sheila came to live here and was friends with Peggy. Sheila was older, of course. She lived to be a hundred.'

'It was one of the first things I heard about this place,' says Harbinder, 'that one of the residents celebrated their centenary.'

'Lance got his writing skills from his mother,' says Edwin. 'Even though he only wrote one book.'

'Actually,' says Harbinder, 'Pippa Sinclair-Lewis told me that Seventh Seal are publishing Lance Foster's posthumous novel. It's called *The Bow Window Set* and it's about a group of old ladies in a care home who solve crimes. Pippa thinks it'll do very well. Cosy crime, she called it.'

'Cosy crime,' says Edwin. 'That's an oxymoron, if you like.'

'Peggy would be pleased though,' says Benedict. 'I'll always think of her, sitting at this window, writing things down in her Investigation Book.'

'It was that book that helped solve her murder,' says Natalka.

'Well, it was Harbinder really,' says Benedict.

'No, it was Peggy,' says Harbinder. She raises her plastic champagne flute.

'To Peggy,' she says.

'To Peggy,' the others reply. And the sun streams in through the bay window.

Acknowledgements

The Postscript Murders is, in a way, a book about acknowledgements and I have many people to thank. First my wonderful editor, Jane Wood, and all at Quercus Books who worked so hard to produce this book while in lockdown. Particular thanks to Hannah Robinson, Ella Patel, Katie Sadler, Bethan Ferguson, David Murphy and Florence Hare. I mention in the book that copy-editors hardly ever get acknowledged so I'd like to thank the meticulous and all-knowing Liz Hatherell. Thanks also to Naomi Gibbs, my editor at HMH in America, for her contributions and support. Thanks to my amazing agent Rebecca Carter and all at Janklow and Nesbit. Thanks also to Kirby Kim at Janklow US.

The Postscript Murders contains a number of real places and entirely fictional events. Shoreham is real, as is Aberdeen and all the places in between. There is a wonderful crime-writing festival in Aberdeen called Granite Noir but there is no resemblance to the festival in this book. The Majestic Hotel is imaginary. I do have wonderful memories of the silver city, though, and my visit there on a book tour with Olivia Mead. Neither of us will ever forget Billy Bob the taxi driver who told us about 'education, salvation and damnation'.

There is also a lovely Catholic church in Shoreham but Benedict's church, and its parish priest, are imaginary.

I have tried to make my characters' backgrounds as believable as possible. In this respect, heartfelt thanks to Radhika Holmström, Harpreet Kaur, Balwinder Kaur Grewal and many others. Any mistakes or inaccuracies are mine alone. Thanks to John Rickards and Ed James for telling me about bitcoin. Again, any mistakes are mine.

This is also a book about publishing and I should acknowledge the incredible support I have received from all my friends in the industry. All the living publishers and authors in this book are entirely imaginary. In this light, I dedicate *The Postscript Murders* to my wonderful agent, Rebecca Carter, who has given me so much support, encouragement and friendship.

Love and thanks always to my husband Andrew and our children, Alex and Juliet. Thanks to Alex for telling me about plainsong and to Juliet for the information about rockpools. It's wonderful when your children know so much more than you do.

PS Thanks to Gus, who has just walked over my keyboard.

EG 2020